Immortals

Copyright

www.authorshawnmcdonie.com

ACKNOWLEGEMENTS

This book, and for that matter all my previous books, would not be possible but for one person. Tirelessly they put up with my many pleas for input. So many times, after my own confidence has left me and I was mired in self-doubt, they had my back. So many times, my wife would be asleep and I would ask one more question, one more ask of this or that. Endless revisions, and ideas on how to make my characters just a bit better. I often worry she will grow tired of me and despise my writing, yet she never seems to. In all of this my supportive and loving wife is always there to encourage me. Every time I was ready to pack this in; she would encourage me to write just a bit more. To see the good in what often feels to me, like drivel. And to appreciate that perhaps…. just perhaps… there is something to these stories after all. ALL these stories are alive because of her. It is with her support and sleepless nights that this work was possible. Eleanor you are the best…. I love you.

To Lizzie for taking the time out of her day to read such things and to be excited for an old man's fantasy of being a novelist. It does me such good to see how you enjoy my previous books. Your youthful eyes see things my old ones simply cannot anymore. I appreciate your insight and your encouragements. And as you requested…….. "Womp, Womp…."

To Daniel, one day I hope you can read this, and know just how much it means to me that you did.

Beta Readers do so much to help Novel creations. They give insight the author might not have and shine a light on your bias. Finding a GOOD Beta Reader however is a BLOODY CHORE. Thankfully I did and am thankful for Alicia@Writing_Away for all the help she has been on this series! Look her up on FIVERR if you need a good Beta Reader. You would be an idiot for not asking someone like Alicia for help!

Table of Contents

PREFACE

Carmes Prison, Paris France

July 28 1794

A lone woman stood in a prison cell awaiting the fickle hearts of the mob. The revolution which had devoured France was not done. The terror as some called it, was alive and well, and its reach was long and resolute. For this woman, it had found her not long before. She had been at home, awaiting her husband's return from Paris. When they had come for her, she was dressed to visit a friend. She was still in that same dress now, three months later. To look at her now her friends would be aghast, but she was not broken. The eyes betrayed what she really was. To most those eyes showed her strength of character and unwillingness to be bowed by the mob. But to a very select few, those eyes would reveal more. Yet, still she remained and still she waited, but for what exactly? Certainly, she no longer waited for her husband.

Like most things in life, the end, when it came, was anticlimactic. Her husband, Viscount Beauharnais was noble yes, but ahead of his peers in many things. He had embraced revolution when it had come. Young and intelligent he had seen firsthand in America how liberty would one day affect his people. He had served with Rochambeau in the American Revolution, seeing there a spark. The colonists had wrenched away from England and formed something new, even if few appreciated it. To many of the senior officers the American war was a side show. But to Alexandre, he knew better. He saw it as an end to things. To a way of life that was considered eternal, an end to the nobility itself. He wasn't alone, some of his fellows knew it too. Even if the others could not, or would not see reality forming in front of them.

When revolution had come to his homeland, Alexandre was ready. He sided with those who wished to depose the nobility. While this prevented his immediate arrest, it did not prevent his eventual fate. Many saw Alexandre as a traitor, either as a self-serving royal or a backstabbing fool. Josèphe knew better, Alexandre was no fool. Charming, warm, educated and a good match, he was many things but not a fool. The end, when it came, wasn't because of his noble birth, or because he had said the wrong words, to the wrong person. No, it was because he failed his masters in the Committee of Public Safety. He had been accused of performing poorly in battle. All the other excuses were given, but it was his failure alone, that doomed him.

Josèphe knew the moment they were arrested what their fate would be. Or so it had seemed anyway. Only five days after his death Josèphe fate began to shift when Robespierre himself followed her husband into death. The terror as it was called would go on, Josèphe was sure of that. It would take other forms, and live on in other ways. But it would live on. Even if these fools said otherwise. But not for Alexandre, or his cousin Augustin. They lay beheaded and forgotten to all of France. Symbols of traitorous action or perhaps just the incompetent past. Either way France, and those they left behind, would move on. Few would morn him, even Josèphe.

For Josèphe, it was difficult to mourn. She was imprisoned herself, awaiting her fate at the hands of the Committee. Alexandre was now gone. As were many of those who were loyal to him. There would be no rescue, no bribe paid to free her. It was only a matter of time before the "blunderbuss" estate came for her. She smirked at the jab at the mob's intelligence. Still Josèphe wasn't worried, nor was she frightened. For her there was still one card to play. One avenue of escape that she had been safeguarding until the time was right. Josèphe had been reluctant to play that card less it reveals to everyone her true nature. She hadn't stayed hidden this long just to announce herself to the world over these idiots. Josèphe was no girl, nor was she some worthless fop who did not know herself. None of these fools had any clue who she really was.

Josèphe closed her eyes and pushed away the grime and stink of the jail she was residing in. In her many years she had lived in ways that would make this horrible place seem palatable. In a moment she was transported back to a better place and time. One where life had been far easier. That time, now long lost to the winds of her curse, clung to her skirt like so many of her offspring before. It had been nearly 2200 years since that time, yet for Josèphe it lived still. Her first home and her first identity. Something precious to her, and it lived quietly inside herself. The land of her birth, a special place where so much of life had come into clarity for her. Sparta, its people, its ways all of which were written into her stone heart with a chisel. As a spartan woman she had relished the toughness of her people. Her first name, the one she was born with, was not Josèphe, but Cynisca. Josèphe was yet another name in a long line of them over the centuries. She smiled as she remembered hearing her name, her real one, spoken aloud. Archidamus her father was king when she was born. He had favored her among her sisters. Even now she could see the pride of her father in her achievements. She smiled relishing in the honor shown her by her fellow Spartans. She wasn't just some random daughter of a king; she had been an

Olympian. The memories flowed inside her and she gripped her sides and began to breathe slower. She had felt so alive, so in touch with that world. The smile that stretched across her face would have surprised anyone who would have seen. That age…. It had done more than mold her; it defined excellence to a young Josèphe. Some of that excellence, had been because of her. Perhaps only a bit… but she had brought honor and glory to her people through her own merit. There had been no limit to what she could achieve. It was her most beloved time of her long life, her youth. She cherished and adored that time like no other. But it was also a time of ignorance for her. Cynisca didn't realize just how wonderful she had it. Or just how difficult life could become.

That time and place was so close, yet so far. In all these years she had not returned to the place of her birth. Not once gone to see the ruins, or to see the Taygetus mountains in all their glory. She would not go to the real Sparta, that was just a ruin. But this… This was the old Sparta the one of her birth! Fully transported she relished in the sights and smells of her home. She could feel the warmth of the sun on her face and smell the Mediterranean on the wind. It was Josèphe's secret place where she went to in her mind when she was upset. There was much she could endure after spending a moment or two in this place. One day she would return to the real Sparta. Settle in the ruin that had once made the world shake in fear. Perhaps she could build up what the idiots in Thebes had torn down. That would be an accomplishment indeed. But after 2000 years the time of rebuilding the Spartan way of life was slipping further and further from her fingers. It would take centuries, and more than just her to do it. Yet it was a noble goal, one far more so than the nobility these fools had just overthrown. She hated the French, so capable with enormous potential. Yet squandered in such foolishness and ignorance. If only she had more time with Alexandre, she could have shaped this rebellion into something more. But she had run out of time, and the mob had ruined everything.

Her melancholy musings were interrupted when she heard the heavy doors of the jail open. Thankfully it wasn't the return of that pig who maintained this place. A man whose hands sought out her body if she did not watch them closely. The man who entered now she knew very well. It wasn't the jailor, but rather monsieur Tallien. Another butcher of Robespierre, come to taunt her. More than one had wished to bed her in exchange for her life. It wasn't uncommon for the wives of the accused to use their bodies to free their husbands this way. But for Josèphe there would be no such trade. Alexandre was gone, and no man in the Committee could possibly tempt her. Yet her irritation at her situation caused her to lose patience with the process. She had been waiting for someone far more interesting than Tallien to show themselves.

Still perhaps the time for waiting was over? She had far more to accomplish in this life than what she had done.

The fop came in pleased with himself and full of pride and arrogance. He spoke of Robespierre's death thinking her ignorant of events. Far from it, Josèphe had her ways, and she knew more than he did, she would wager. She had little stomach to listen to him preen on like the stuffed vegetable he was. So, she let him know she didn't care in the slightest about Robespierre's fate. Clearly from his reaction he assumed she would throw herself at him. He expected her to be terrified of her fate, willing to do anything. Hardly terrified, but terribly bored certainty. She smirked at him showing him that she wasn't a flower that could be trampled. She wasn't conquered, and never would be. Her indifference to her situation infuriated him, but clearly it also didn't dull his lust for her. She could read that plainly enough.

Josèphe was beautiful and desirable but there was more. Among those in the Committee it was rumored she was a witch. That she had an unusual pull on the desires of men. That story amused her, it hardly described what she was. Yet in a way it was true. In so much that she "could" have such a pull if she desired it. But she didn't, especially with the likes of monsieur Tallien. Yet living in this place, and having her head removed like her husband, wasn't what she desired either. When Tallien came in close to speak to her, he made a dreadful mistake. He allowed himself to get close enough for her to touch him. The decision, when she reached it, was simple and easy. Her last thrall had been killed and she needed another. It had been far too long since she last fed. Not from bread or water, but from what her kind needed to survive. She reached out to touch him and he thought she was warming to his charms. He was dreadfully wrong in this. Tallien froze not knowing the kind of creature that now held him in her grasp. Her physical strength was that of 10 such men. Josèphe easily held him against the bars as she began the timeless process that sustained her. She lustily fed from him and took what her body needed to fully rejuvenate her ability.

It felt divine to finally feed, the first in weeks. He was hopefully one who had the power to protect her and serve her. Tallien wasn't her first choice, but he would have to do. Eventually she would discard him and choose another. Preferably one who bathed more than he did. After taking his will, his eyes grew full and his mouth fell open. She smirked looking at the fool wondering just what he thought he was getting when he came in. It didn't matter; she would get what she wanted. It would take time, in that there was no doubt.

Once fed she commanded him to answer her questions. Josèphe spent nearly 20 minutes learning just what this worm was able to do for her. It was disappointing, he didn't have access to the kind of things she really desired. But the answers to her questions were useful. Tallien could indeed secure her freedom and more. He would of course, he had little choice otherwise. As an immortal, Josèphe knew how little Tallien could do to stop her. She had enslaved men to her ambition for centuries. Tallien would not be the last in that respect…. Not if Josèphe had anything to say about it. She explained his new reality to him, something he had difficulty coming to terms with. He was a strong-willed man, and because of this, he would buck against her power. But it was futile as she well knew. Josèphe was the daughter of a founder, and unlike the other countless Spartiate's who called themselves immortal. She was truly eternal, her power far exceeded those of the pitiful ones made by the orb. As Tallien departed to secure her release, she began to plot how she would re-invent herself again. She had done so numerous times over the centuries. But unlike other times where she would take a new name and change her age by killing some vagrant. Josèphe would stay as she was, using her reputation and name to go just a bit further.

If Tallien was right the Committee of Public Safety was in disarray and most of the pillars of the revolution were gone. It was a time for the bold and the strong, to take what they desired. And Josèphe was nothing if not those things. Standing in the squalor and reeking of odor, she still smirked and felt her heart rise. In a few hours she would be free of this cell and be in Tallien's home being properly looked after by servants again. A decent meal, another wonderful feeding from Tallien and then…. well then, her work would truly begin. Finding one she could use to make France… and by extension Josèphe, strong again. He would have to be more than this pitiful man she had enslaved. He would have to be a meteor, cunning and ruthless. And he would have to be young and attractive if he was to have her. But above all, he had to be ambitious and capable. Someone she could put all her immense skill and power into. A person worthy of her gifts and her time. He would not be easy to find, but she would do so. And then France would reach its potential, they would embrace their "liberty" but one governed by her. Saddled and bridled like the plow horses they were.

The masses were not fit to be called Spartinates only the chosen were. In Sparta's day, the mob had been called Helots and they were always a threat but a useful tool nonetheless. France unlike Sparta had not properly spent their soldiers keeping their Helots in line. That was the point of the Agoge, to spit out the sharp spears that would keep the Helots, and their neighbors in line. France had nothing like the Agoge, nor was its warriors of said quality. But the potential was there, there was much in the way of France and Josèphe's aspirations for it. Specifically, the English, their never-ending desire to meddle into French affairs seemed nearly as eternal as her. But for now, the first foe was the mob and their thoughtless and brainless governance of themselves. Their thoughts were only for base desires, to rape, to steal. That was hardly a way for a civilized society to function. Only the chosen could lead and govern with any real skill. A chosen few who had the education, and the knowledge to use the Helots the way they were intended.

Josèphe first had to find her meteor, then she could begin to build something with him. Perhaps in time…. France could be a new Sparta? If not well… it wasn't like she had any love for these people anyway.

Chapter 1: Doing the Right Thing

January 5th, 2058 – More than a year before Hope's
Choice

Ixtapa, Mexico

Not all jobs were difficult, some like this one required very little from Jacob. His team was deployed in Mexico. It wasn't a paying job; it was being done as a public service. The CEO of an American company was traveling to a resort town, not on business, but one of a personal nature. Jacob had little to do on this operation but what was, didn't please him much. As the most junior on the team, he was tasked with the dirty part.

His elders on the team had already done the more interesting parts. Doing so for Grey vampires wasn't difficult. They could walk unseen and be where others couldn't. It wasn't just a parlor trick it was far more. The call of being a Grey was something personal and not something shared with outsiders. That call was a drive and a curse at the same time. For Grey, it drove them to do things others would consider improper… deviant even. One of the reasons why they spent years in the Agoge was to hone that desire into disciplined action. Grey could not deny their call any more than Aqua could deny theirs to build families.   But Grey could hone that call into something constructive and honorable. Still, it required much from each Grey, a moral fiber and strength that was uncommon among humans.

Jacob paused in the hallway looking for the obvious. The CEO in question had another protection team, hired by his company. They were decent, and one of them was trying. Getting by the watchers was simple for a vampire who could disappear and walk beside someone unseen. It was revealing yourself when the real excitement began. Watching the movements and the eyes Jacob timed his movements well. When the careless man hired to the CEO's team left the door open, he moved quickly. Entering and pausing in an open space he watched to see if his movements had been detected. A moment later it was clear it hadn't been.   Like all Grey the excitement and pleasure he derived at this moment was intense. He was doing his job, but he was also feeding the Grey desire to hide and stalk their prey. He could taste their compliancy and it was delicious. Soon he would reach his target and he had no doubts what the outcome would be. The CEO would die, that had been ordered. But reaching him still had one last hurdle.

The CEO had come here to enjoy his desires, even now he could hear his latest conquest making sounds in the bedroom. From the sounds of it he was in to the rougher side of sex. Jacob wasn't a prude; he wasn't like his father or his older brother. If this guy wanted to get his rocks off by wearing leather and being rough, what did he care? What did bother Jacob was the age of this man's unwilling partner. That did piss him off, as it had one of the CEO's team. That guy had a family and a conscience that railed at him helping this dirt bag. The guy in question was assigned inside the room itself. He was the most senior and was most experienced. So, he was closest to the target than any of the other team. This man, new to the CEO's detail had his orders and they were not to his liking. That was apparent from the looks he shot the wall as the CEO caused the girl to scream. Only the discipline and patient nature of Jacob prevented him from doing likewise. He could not afford to allow an inch to his prey. His eyes were locked on the last guard, Jacob's real target of the day.

Still cloaked and unseeable Jacob calmed himself for what was to come. As soon as he spoke, he would be revealing his position and risking his own life. His target was angry, his face shown the emotion and his stance gave away what he wanted. This new hire of the CEO wanted to bust down that door and stop the fun.

Well, you are going to get your wish buddy. Question is, are you going to be a good boy and let me talk to you, or do I have to kill you too?

"Do you enjoy protecting monsters... Rick?"

A millisecond after saying the last word he was already on the move. Using all the skill and ability he could muster to move in silence. Shifting from where he was standing to another spot, still in Rick's blind spot and in a position to kill him if need be. Rick spun around too late seeing nothing and drawing his weapon. Now came the dance of life and death, and either Rick would listen, or he would die. Just so long as he didn't was all Jacob cared about.

"You can't you know... protect him."

Rick's eyes were wide, searching for the speaker. Unsure what to do Rick made a move to his protectee, and then thought better of it shifting back to this unseen threat. Jacob was still shifting moving in silence. His vampiric ability allowed him to be silent and unseen. But it had limits, if Rick started shooting where he was, it wouldn't matter how skilled he was. He would be a dead vampire, skills or no. Cursing only in his mind, he hated father for demanding this.

"Lay down your weapon Rick, it's the only way you will see Jeanie again."

Jacob froze, the weapon tracked faster this time and zeroed in on his chest. Even if he moved now Rick would likely see the shimmer and know he was there. This dance was too dangerous and he hated his father for making him dance it. But when Rick demanded to know whom spoke Jacob decided to oblige. He unshielded himself, allowing Rick to see him. His eyes were wide and he was breathing rapidly. The Glock now unsteady began to shift, causing him to bring his other hand up to steady it. As if his courage had returned, he asked how in hell he had done that.

"Does it matter, you have a choice to make Rick. The man you protect is going to die today. The only question is, are you?"

Rick was quick to point out that he had Jacob dead to rights. He did, but Jacob wasn't alone, he might die if Rick acted, but it would be the last thing he did.

"I am not alone Rick, if you so much as twitch your finger you will be dead before you can realize it. The only reason you aren't dead now, is that we want to ask you a question. Why serve such a man? Why pledge your sword to a monster?"

Rick smirked for a second before thinking differently. He was taking seriously what Jacob had told him about others. He should. Three of his brothers had him surrounded even now. After a moment or two of uncomfortable silence, Rick responded. Still holding the weapon directly at Jacob.

"It's a living, too old to learn anything else, I guess. Besides I didn't know the fuck was into this kind of thing. Look I don't like the man, but I can't let you kill him. I have a family to support and if I let the sick fuck die, then it's my head."

Mom's intelligence on Rick was spot on, everything she had said about him was accurate. Thank goodness because he was risking his life on it. Now came the sales pitch, and hopefully a happy ending.

"The only choice you have right this second Rick is to live or die. Your protectee is going to die today, no matter what. Don't sacrifice your life for that scumbag. I promise you we aren't here to kill you, just your boss."

Rick hesitated and asked again what in hell was going on. How did he just appear out of nowhere. Jacob just grinned and responded the only way he could.

"I would be happy to show you just who we really are Rick. But that means putting down that weapon and following my brothers outside."

At that moment two of his fellow Grey unmasked both on either side of him. Each had their weapons drawn and that finally put the fight out of Rick. He handed the weapon to the one closest to him. And with a look of anger at being defeated walked out of the room with the other Grey. With the final hurdle out of the way Rick was quickly escorted out of the hotel. The bodies of the rest of Rick's team were quietly placed in the room as Jacob's team leader and another vampire entered the bedroom. The young girl only 14 was quickly separated from the target and given to Jacob. With that Jacob using every smile and soft word he could tried to comfort the girl while simultaneously moving her to the transport. The trick was not to stop and keep your feet moving. She was too much in shock to prevent it even if she wanted that. She was frightened, in a foreign land and had the worst month of her life. The smiles and calm nature did more than anything to keep her feet moving towards the door.

Jacob helped her into the vehicle and made sure Rick was unarmed before they sped off. They had to get her and Rick out of here as quickly as possible. Killing the CEO and dealing with the aftermath would be the responsibility for the rest of the team. Their destination was a small airport where they had transport out of Mexico. Jacob's mind was split between watching Rick, the road and everything in between. That was why he was taken off guard when the girl began to shake violently. His soft words asking her if she was ok went unanswered as she continued to shiver and stare straight ahead.

"I need to go back; my phone he has my phone. My whole life is on that thing!"

Jacob dismissed that possibility without much thought. By this point the hotel was on fire, not much for them to go back to now. He just put a hand on her to explain the reality when she yanked her own hand away violently. Jacob was surprised but remembered the briefing from mom. He looked up in time to see the driver staring at him from the mirror. His fellow did so with nearly an accusing look.

Ok… ok, I will give her the drug. I didn't want to but…

One of the options given to them by their team medic, was a mild sedative. It looked like a small can of soda in shape, but in reality, it was a targeted dispersal device. There were no markings or labels, just black metal with a small nozzle at the top. Jacob quickly put it in front of her like the medic had trained him and pushed the small button on the back. It sprayed a thin amount of liquid onto her face. The shock of him doing that caused her to take in breath and open her eyes wide to the danger. Both accelerated the quick acting drug. Within a moment the small bit of fight in her ended and he helped settle the now unconscious girl back into the seat.

That didn't do much to help calm Rick, but even he saw now wasn't the time for questions.

"That just put her to sleep?"

Jacob nodded but the look from Rick held a lot more than that of the girl. Here was real danger, this man knew how to handle himself. And a few minutes ago, was standing between him and the girl. He switched sides once; he could do so again. That thought made Jacob return the stare with one of his own. He was thinking about the knife on his hip and pulling it and putting down this threat. He was authorized to do it, dad's wishes to the contrary be dammed. A moment after he had that thought however Rick smirked and relaxed back into the seat more. Turning his head to the front and seemingly ignoring Jacob for now. Jacob continued to watch him, unsure if that was just some sort of diversion. But when the girl moved again, he remembered he hadn't secured her. With that Jacob turned his attention back to her making sure she wasn't armed and putting away the sedative.

By the time they got to the airport the girl awake now, was a wreck but manageable. She asked a hundred questions, mostly not waiting on the answers to ask another. Jacob had been patient at first, even friendly. However, a few kicks and jabs to his ribs later and he wasn't interested in being kind anymore. A shove by Jacob sent her into the quickly acting hands of his fellow vampires. In a flash she was an unwilling passenger on the airplane they had waiting. Rick however wasn't going to get on an aircraft without some answers. And trying to grab him like he did the girl was a mistake, one Jacob didn't make. With the girl onboard he turned to Rick to give him the answers he sought.

"Rick, I have read your file, you were a good soldier in your youth. We aren't much different than some of the groups you worked with in Taiwan back in the day. The kind of work we do is black in nature. If you really want to know who and what we are, then you can board the plane and find out. Or you can stay and go your own way."

Rick huffed at that, he knew what would happen if he stayed. Having an American CEO die on Mexican soil was bad for business. Scapegoats would be sought, and Rick would be a damned easy one for everyone to pick on. If he stayed, he would either end up in a Mexican jail, or unemployable back home. Rick was blunt about the choice, and what he thought of it.

"Yeah, it sucks but I didn't ask you to watch the fuck, now did I? Look, my employer thinks you have what it takes to be a part of our organization. But it isn't for everyone. And to be blunt Rick staying here is probably a hell of a lot safter than working with us."

Rick cursed and took a few steps away from the plane thinking about the shit sandwich he had been offered. Once he calmed down a bit, he asked why staying was safer, just what kind of work did they do.

"It's not the work Rick, when you join my organization it's for life. You won't ever be able to go back to your old world. And not everyone who joins us survives the training. But its honest work, and you will have brothers you can trust, always beside you. As for your family, once you are done training they can join you. My company can deal with all the fallout and clear your name. But I won't shit you Rick, there is no going back once you get on this plane. No second thoughts, and no exit ramps if you change your mind. You walk on that plane and you will be one of us for life. No matter how long, or short that is."

Rick looked at him searchingly and laughed. Pointing out that Jacob was just a child. That upset Jacob but he knew old farts like Rick didn't respect men like him. But seeing the serious look on his face and considering his fate he asked about the girl.

"She is an American, her pimp had her trafficked out of the US for sex work. She is going back to Minneapolis where she has family."

Rick didn't respond to that just taking it in. Jacob narrowed his eyes wondering why he asked. Obviously, they weren't going to hurt her, Jacob wondered if Rick had just asked it to make conversation. In any case when he didn't say anything Jacob continued.

"Rick our mission today was to get her home, but not just that. My boss feels like you would be a good fit for our organization. I promise you the kind of work has far more honor than your current profession. You are going to be able to sleep at night, and if your record is to be believed, well you will find working with us to be an eye opener."

Rick then with a more serious face asked about the rest of his team. Jacob knew Rick had only joined the CEO on this trip, so he likely had zero ties to those guys. Still there was a danger here, but Jacob knew Rick would have to prove himself before the really told him the full truth behind what his company really was. By then Rick would either be one of them, or filling his grave.

"They're dead Rick, they weren't the kind of men we could trust and they also didn't have any problems with what their employer was up to. So, if you are looking for me to be sorry about it, don't expect it."

Jacob was watching Rick think and ponder his options. It was a big ask, trusting someone that threated to kill him moments before. But in life sometimes you had to make quick decisions. In truth Jacob had lied, Rick only had one real choice. To live and board the plane, or stay and die. The Mexicans would never let Rick leave after today. It was a crappy choice but Jacob knew what he would choose. Ten minutes later Rick was buckled into one the seats looking around the cabin at the men who were still on edge. But he had decided and Jacob was glad for it. Jacob had accomplished the mission and that would be another sign of his competence.

As the remainder of the team caught up and boarded the plane Jacob saw the team leader pause near the flight cabin talking to the pilot and the radioman. Whatever was going on caused his eyes to dart back to Jacob. That was never a good sign. A moment later he walked back into the main cabin to get the teams attention and stopped right in front of Jacob.

"We just got word; we are being recalled. We lost contact with your brothers' team. Your father wants us to muster for immediate deployment."

As the leader went about the cabin giving orders and prepping the rest of the team for a new operation, Jacob found himself focusing on thoughts of his brother and wondering what trouble he had gotten into. The look from the boss told Jacob whatever it was that his team would not let this stand. That more than anything gave him peace, if anyone could help it was his brothers. Both in blood and in service.

Chapter 2: Meridian Surprise

January 5th, 2058 – Sao Paulo, Meridia

Malcom was trying to look uninterested and just another poor slob having a meal. It wasn't hard, at the moment there wasn't a great deal happening. The city he was visiting was large, noisy and frankly smelly, especially in some of the areas he had been in. But others like that spot he was in now was more upscale. Malcom smiled as he looked at the foreign place he had been sent. His first real assignment as team leader. This was the life he wanted to have, traveling, learning, experiencing life far different than what he knew in Medford. Still, life wasn't that far different than what it was in San Antonio. Folks went to work, they ate, they lived short uninteresting lives for the most part, in the US or here in Meridia.

His task required good lines of sight, and as far as Malcom could tell this was the easiest one to obtain. Just because it also allowed him to feast his eyes on the sights, was just an added bonus. Thankfully it was just warm enough to eat outside, thus his excuse for lounging all day out here. Yet it was the rainy season, most wouldn't dare try to put tables out. His chosen roost was one of them. He had a keen eye for detail, critical in this kind of work. Still his eyes hadn't found anything to be alarmed about yet. His primary reason in being here was to watch the junction of two streets. He continued his scan of the area while working on his pastel. The pastel was yet another part of the message he wanted to send passersby. Pastels were street food, cheap and common, as was he. He needed to be ignored, that was the cloak of safety he was trained to embrace. Yet a part of him wanted a challenge, to be engaged by someone who found out what and who he was. It would be good to be able to prove his worth. He had done so up to this point, but he really hadn't been challenged yet.

Almost on cue a man in a business suit walking by took note of him. Malcom working his cover tried hard to appear as nothing, but his senses were alive and on fire. Desirous of a challenge, someone to show signs of challenge. Still, what his body desired was not exactly what his spirit or mind did. He was disciplined enough to keep that in check. At least for now, anyway.

Nothing to see here, I am just another slob eating a meal. That's it just bugger off and forget I exist. Or try me… give me an excuse.

The man much to Malcom's disappointment walked by. His momentary notice of the American bum only fleeting. Once he was clear and a full 10 minutes passed Malcom reset his expectations back to their normal one.

Pity, guy looked like he could handle himself. Why is it that this work is never like it is in the movies?

Malcom was young at only 23, young by anyone's measure. Yet it would surprise people to learn that at that age he was already experienced. He had traveled the world with his company; one he had joined at a very young age. It was that age that helped him with this mission. This part of Sao Paulo had a lot of 20 and 30 somethings walking around at all hours. Just like the man had done, most ignored him, even if he was a an American. In this part of Sao Paulo, it wasn't hard for him to blend in. To that end, his clothing was wrinkled and a couple days removed from a wash. It helped to sell the lie he was selling. The trick to be seen but forgettable, was to be someone folks WANTED to forget. The unwashed clothing, him being a foreigner helped to do that nicely. Making one person a ghost wasn't hard, but doing so with a whole team… well that wasn't so easy.

Malcom wasn't the only person working in the plaza. Including himself there were five out here now doing routine preliminary work. The kinds of work his team did when they were preparing for a larger visit by important people in the future. This work, boring and uninteresting in the best of times, was still necessary. You needed to know what was normal, so you could detect the abnormal. Later when they came back, Malcom and his team would be the eyes. Those eyes needed to know what they were looking at so they could tell their mouths the truth of what was in front of them. Malcom laughed at thinking about his mission.

Oh yes, I have developed such lovely eyes for this trash heap. It looks just like all the other trash heaps I have been before. Hell, if I know why this place is any different?

He finished his small meal and took his time cleaning up after himself, mostly to keep his vigil a bit longer. He was already well past the time he said ` they would break coverage. But Malcom didn't like going home, he liked being in the field. He so wanted something to be out of place, something to happen! But it didn't. A voice crackled in his ear piece. It only said one word, and that was to remind them to check in. The last member of his team was back at their flop of a safehouse monitoring things remotely. He was also their communication link to home. Malcom responded quietly that everything was fine. He only knew this because every 15 or so minutes, like he was trained, Malcom would make sure his team was where they should be. Each of them was all working to blend in, yet keep an eye out for anything out of the ordinary. He rechecked his last glance with another seeing each member exactly in place.

There wasn't anything more to do here, and staying too long on site was also a bad idea. They had gotten word it was time to pack it in after today. It was time to move on to another location, more days outside looking at nothing. Standing slowly, he made a show of himself to get his teams attention. He threw the cup in the trash and pulled his cap off his head. That was a signal to his people to break position, and work their way back to the safehouse. Each would take their time, some of which would take two full hours to travel only 20 minutes distance on foot. It was a lot of work to make sure they weren't followed. But for Malcom there was no such worry. Two simple attempts to clear a tail and then he was back at the safehouse. He should take his time, but Sao Paulo had zero going on. It was about as safe as it could be, considering it was Sao Paulo. As he walked in the new kid who was manning the communications for this op threw up his hand in a hello.

Malcom while young had been doing this for years now, and he was good. He had made a name for himself in this very team. When Jake was moved to intelligence, he was nominated to take over leadership. It was one of the greatest days of his life when he got the news. Even if he was the King's son, he had EARNED this promotion. Unlike his brothers who had gone into the Army or Marines for additional on the job training, Malcom had gone into the reconnaissance game. He hadn't wasted a moment of those years. Learning everything he could from Jake and the elders. Some whispered that he had only been handed leadership because of his father. But he knew better, this was HIS team, and it was his time.

His team's name was Epsilon. It was one of 4 recon teams that Moonstone employed. Moonstone was a PMC or a private military contractor. Based in Texas they only operated overseas. And over the last few years they had done a lot of operating. They were a thriving business, with 15 teams in the field.

"How are our birds?"

The boy was closely monitoring four other members of the team so he only looked back for a second and grinned. From the monitors Malcom could see each of his team running their evasion programs. Recon teams like his straddled the space between soldiers and spy's. They only had to be proficient in basic combat skills, but they had to be artists at observation. Their job was to blend into society and observe and report. Getting seen themselves was a sure-fire way to disappear in a foreign country. Moonstone relied on them to be the eyes anywhere it went. Recon teams came in weeks or even months in advance, learning the patterns of a place. That allowed Moonstone to avoid the messier kinds of fights they had fought in the beginning.

Malcom looked around the safehouse again seeing everything was as it should be. With that he went to shower off the grime and stink he had worked to accumulate. As soon as the door shut and the warm water flowed it was as if a gate opened in his heart. There was always a quiet enjoyment in this little slice of peace. The moment you knew you were safe, in a profession where safety was rare. His muscles relaxed; his eyes closed; he signed letting go of his obligations. Every professional has to learn when and where he can do that. You can't be 100% all of the time in anything. That only worked in books, real professionals had to know when and where they could unplug. There had to be balance, time when you were fully aware, and time when you weren't. Otherwise, you become numb to everything. Now was the time for him to unplug from his senses and put his mind into neutral. The warm water caused his mind to take over from his eyes and his ears. As he showered, he went over in his mind the purpose of all this watching. It was an odd feeling, part of him longed for this moment when he was away. Yet the moment he entered the shower a part of him felt vulnerable, as if danger lurked around the corner. It was youth and inexperience he told himself. He had seen his elders do this numerous times. They never seemed to have self-doubt at times like this. He smirked as he laughed at his doubts. There was plenty enough to worry about, and not some phantom stalking him.

In three days, this operations principal would arrive. The principal was the word given to the protectee, or in plain English the guy who had to keep breathing while he was here. Moonstone generally traveled with large protective teams for that kind of mission. The protection teams all trained hard to keep their principal alive. Protection detail was some of the most difficult work the company did. But it was also some of the most profitable, at least as far as Malcom could tell. In this case whoever the principal was he or she had to be important. Besides his team there were several others either here already or would arrive shortly. All told nearly 100 members of Moonstone were assigned. That had to be a record, generally they worked alone.

Moonstone used the Greek alphabet to name their teams. To Malcom it seemed natural, but he had grown up in the Agoge. Like most of his upbringing it was dripping in Greek culture. The Agoge where he honed his skills was a school modeled on Spartan culture and discipline. When speaking to a customer, who knew nothing of Moonstone's real origin or purpose, it was always confused them to hear all the Greek terminology. PMCs were a dime a dozen in the 21st century, but Moonstone was unusual. Every member of Moonstone belonged to a clan, a single one to be precise. Each were full-fledged vampires. All had graduated the Agoge back home and all had spent their lives training and working together. Many were family, and they would spend their lifetime working for the company. Malcom would have it no other way, he loved his clan and what they had built together. From the time he was 10 years old when mother had sent him to the Agoge. To age 16 when he had joined Moonstone, there was never any question what he wanted. He wanted to gain honor, become a respected, and valued man of his clan. That would lead to a good match, and the respect of his brothers. He craved that respect like a thirsty man sought water. He could and would sacrifice many things to obtain it, but honor wasn't one of them. The thought caused Malcom to smile in the shower. It was a conceit he had about his own nature. He was noble, something his mother often called him. But it wasn't just words, it was a way of life he embodied.

As the carefully prepared illusion of an American bum escaped with the water down the drain, so did his desire to ponder his own nature. Now wasn't the time for that, now was the time to work to achieve the things he desired. But something was off, the work was what he expected it to be. But not the pleasure he took from the work. Malcom expected to love every second of the job. But in truth there was something nagging him… even here.

I bet Jacob doesn't question himself like this, or dad or any of the others? Why can't I just relax and enjoy this?

Malcom though of his brothers, they more than anything guided his actions. Anything that fell in their eyes was something he wanted nothing to do with. Brothers, that was indeed what they were. Not all of Moonstone were physical brothers, although many were. Yet Malcom thought of them as full brothers anyway. Years in the Agoge, training every day, fighting, and learning. They had bonded tightly and looked after each other with an intensity. It also led to fierce rivalries amongst each other. When alone they could bicker and compete with the best of them. But when facing others, they were brothers. In the Agoge Malcom had learned what being a man was. He had discovered his strengths and his weaknesses. His brothers had pushed him to discover his limits. For any man just knowing these were critical. Most thought they knew them, but most didn't. A man could fight, love, suffer far longer than he believed. The Agoge taught him all these things and more. The Agoge didn't do what modern armies did in training. It wasn't about basic skills; it was about trust. Each warrior had to know the man beside him and behind him would not flinch, not flee. It did more than give him comfort, it emboldened him to stand as well.

Each child who entered the Agoge did so as individuals. They were called by their names, and treated with a mixture of scorn and sympathy. At first Malcom had thought they were comforting him. Eventually he learned it was not a tone of respect, but rather the opposite. It wasn't until the boy had suffered and shown real strength that this ceased. Then he was simply called "Paides", the equivalent in English might be trainee. It was both a rank, and a term of station of life. As a Paides he was no longer despised, but he wasn't honored either. Near the end of his time in the Agoge he was tested, it was never fully explained how this was done. But one night he was attacked by nearly all his fellow Paides. Bound and hooded he was taken away from the Agoge and left alone, without proper clothing or supplies alone in the woods.

It took Malcom three days to return to the camp. Just finding it proved difficult enough. But feeding himself, keeping himself safe in difficult terrain, and surviving the heat was difficult. When he entered the gate tried, hungry and ready for sleep he was confronted in combat. Two men, not boys attacked him. Malcom had used every inch of his skill and ounce of his strength not to be killed by them. Their blows were that of a man who wished to kill, not train. Pondering the memory Malcom felt both pride and awe at his reaction. He was a moment before ready to collapse but when he entered battle, he was a different beast. He managed to hit one of the attackers so hard he went back against the hut with force. The other man sliced a gash into his head but paid for it with a devastating blow to his knees that send him to the ground with a thud. Malcom was about ready to open his skull with his staff when father shouted for him to stop. He had passed his test and become a man that day. At that moment at age 16 he had passed from being a child to being a citizen, a Hoplite. That night standing next to his father and the other men of the camp he knew he belonged. Seeing their respect in their eyes, and being accepted into their ranks was the greatest moment of his childhood. He had never sat foot into the barracks again after that night. From that day onward he had been a man, and was given work like one. Moonstone was his home, and his life's calling.

Malcom turned off the water and paused before leaving. He thought of his brothers in the other teams, and those serving in the military. One day those brothers would return home and join them in Moonstone. All of those young Paides he had trained with were now men themselves. Few of those boys failed, yet some had. Those that did found other vocations, and purposes for their life. But they would never become Spartinates, or in other words they would never reach the highest level of spartan life. Malcom was well on the way to reaching it already. Perhaps in another 5-10 years he would and then he would be allowed to take a woman and create his house. In the Agoge the boys had all been taught to see this process as good and honorable. Not until they had achieved greatness would they become full members of their clan's social life. Malcom and his best friend in the Agoge had long talked about what honors they would gain, and which of their clan's women they would desire. Thinking of his friend he frowned; it had been far too long since he had last seen him.

Malcom worried about Darious. He knew Darious had been struggling with life apart from the clan. He had already completed his first 4-year enlistment in the Army. He hadn't left yet because he wanted to get into the Rangers. The training was useful and it would help him get something else Darious wanted. The hand of a grey woman he desired. Malcom thought that foolish, Darious's intended target was not someone Malcom thought worthy of such desire. Yet Darious wanted nothing but her. Malcom had no such weaknesses. He did his duty to the clan when it was requested. Wither that be serving in Moonstone or being asked to lay with a grey woman to help her create another. It was rare, but there had been times. That was enough for Malcom, he did not need a wife. He wasn't an old man with designs on a house yet. Malcom's ambition was for honor; the woman would come with that soon enough he reasoned. And honor would only come through the help of his other Hoplites.

As he dried off, he thought about his team, his new charges. All of them were chosen by him, as the old team had all been reassigned. This was his team, and most of them were straight out of the Agoge. So far, his little team had done well. Still, they hadn't been tested like some of the others. Team Gamma for instance had gotten into a full-fledged firefight down in Mexico. They had utterly slaughtered the hired guns, killed their main target and gotten out without causality. That was the kind of impact Malcom wanted to make. Even now Rene who led that team was being considered for elevation to full Spartiate rank. At only 30 it meant retirement from the field, a wife, and a comfortable living. If he was elevated it would mean his new mission would be to father children, rather than do battle with the enemy. Rene would be then and only then a full member of his clan. No longer considered property of his mother, and man of the house. Malcom craved that level of respect, but not the idle life. If he was Rene he would take the rank, but turn down the retirement. It was sometimes allowed, but rarely. Their king wished to grow the clan as it had stayed stagnate for too many years before his reign.

After dressing he was imagining himself returning home a hero, having done a great deed like Rene. He nearly missed it when he walked into the room. The chair where the boy had been sitting was empty. Turned over and on the floor. Malcom's senses came alive not because of a great noise was heard. Rather because the safehouse was deathly quiet. There was always noise from the neighbors and the street. But now….

Malcom only took a single step before powerful arms came from behind him yanking him backwards. At the same time a baton like object was shoved hard into his exposed underarm. The pain it caused was like nothing he had ever experienced before. While this was going on, the man, it had to be a man, had him off his feet. He could not find purchase to use his immense vampiric strength to break the hold of the intruder. A moment later he felt a needle pierce his side and he shot his head around to see whom had done this.

Malcom was astonished to find it was the boy, Jason, his new communications specialist who had stabbed him with the needle. He managed to get the boy's name out in an astonished question. But by the time he spoke the last syllable of his name, he felt his voice begin to slur. There were others now, strangers with hooded faces who moved to take him. In that moment Malcom was angry, astonished, and most of all dumfounded at his luck. He was going to die on his first major assignment and he didn't even know whom had done it? As his eyes began to grow dark, he wondered why the boy had turned against him, and just how he had managed to screw this up so badly.

January 6ᵗʰ, 2058 – San Paulo, Meridia

Malcom awoke to find himself lying on a couch. It was daytime and considering the looks of it before noon. That meant it had to be at the very least the next day. Before making a noise or trying to move he tried to gain his senses and see what he could see. There wasn't much other than some patio furniture. He was just starting to make out a vast fleet of vehicles when he heard his host speak. She was a young female; her voice was full of confidence and charm.

"Finally, I was wondering if you would return to us. Welcome, can I get you something to drink?"

Malcom heard the clanging of ice into a glass and turned his head slowly towards the sound. His first glimpse of her was these thin dainty hands filling a tumbler with a milky substance. The ice was going into another tumbler with what looked like something harder.

"It's called Vitamina, have you had that yet Malcom? Any visitor to my country should. I think it's wonderful, especially when the summer heat comes."

Malcom looked up at her, she was young perhaps his age. She barely had anything on, just an expensive looking bra and panty set showing from behind a silk semi-transparent robe of the same pattern. Her Brown hair fell down to her breasts, and she had a glorious smile and eyes that....Malcom stopped breathing when he saw her eyes. She grinned widely seeing his astonishment.

"Yes, I am like you, we are both immortal Malcom. You are among friends Hermano, be at ease. Take it, it's refreshing…"

She handed him the drink, he had heard about Vitamina before, it was some kind of fruit smoothie. Without thinking he took a drink and found it to be rather good. He pulled up to a sitting position as his host came near him sitting seductively in a chair opposite him. Once sitting she crossed her legs and smirked at him, knowing full well just what kind of show she was putting on. He took the moment not to stare at her beautiful legs but rather took quick looks for exits and means of defense.

"Malcom, I only want to talk. When we are done you will be free to return to your people if you wish. Although after you hear what I have to say, you may decide Sao Paulo has much to offer someone like you."

He smirked himself, shocked to be talking to another vampire, and a grey one at that. He said as much to her, but her reaction surprised him.

"Vampire! I am not a vampire! Don't try to compare what we are with some stupid American movie. We are nothing like those creatures. We are immortals Malcom; we do not bite necks or feast on blood! You know this Hermano, we are far more civilized and refined than that. Your mother let you watch too many movies. You would have been far better served reading Hermano."

He had never heard one of his people hate that word so much. Back home it was simply an accepted term. Moving quickly, he pretended to ignore the offense he had created, neither apologizing for it or acknowledging it. He asked her whom her family was and when she had left Medford.

"Malcom, not every Grey is from America. Centuries before your little group formed, ours was already well into its second Millennium. Meridia is our home, we have been in this land for almost as long as your nation has drawn breath."

Malcom heard the name of her country and again felt odd at hearing it. Meridia had only sprung into existence in the last 15 years. The rivalry between Brazil and Argentina had ended when both merged into one South American superpower. Since then, Chile, Bolivia, Peru, and Paraguay had all ceded their sovereignty to become one with Meridia. Meridia's strong man Carlos Silva had in a very short time rose to power and was dominating nearly all of Latin America. There was talk that Meridia had eyes on Columbia and Venezuela. Malcom had long thought America's next war would be in this region, one of the reasons why he had asked for any assignment that took him here. He asked her about Silva and if they controlled him.

"You ask questions, why? Is knowledge the only thing you seek here? Must you sit there staring when we could be communicating in the way we were intended? I wonder do your people not understand our ways?"

Malcom was confused for a bit, he was trying to figure out who this chick was, and what all of this meant. He was very slow to realize what she wanted. She rose to her full height looking at him with a searching look. She held out her hand, wishing him to stand with her. He took it and the moment he did he began to understand. She wished to dance the dance of their people. A very intimate experience and something Malcom had only heard about. Dad had only described it in small details. But as this woman moved around him, going in and out of sight she began to move faster and faster. Before long he could only catch the faintest glimpse of her as she passed from sight. As if his legs grew a mind of their own, he moved. Trying in vain to keep up with her, as he did, he began to see more of her and this pleased him. Without thinking he wanted to see more, so he moved faster, put more of his skill into his efforts.

He felt strange, was this just a simple game. He laughed as he had to use more of his abilities just to keep up. As a vampire he was faster and stronger than humans, but as a Grey he had special skills. He was thankful for them a second later when the dance became violent. He only saw the move to kick him a fraction of a second before she would have landed it square into his chest. He was too close to jump away, he simply angled himself slightly to one side allowing the bare foot to pass by him without connecting. The motion done more out of instinct rather than thought, felt good. As he pivoted his reaction to her provocation was natural too. As he sent a flat hand towards her face, he felt pleasure in unleashing his strength. To always be pent up like this, restrained it chaffed at his very soul. Letting this tiger out of his spirit and allowing his hands to crash down on something felt right, justified and more importantly a needed release. Yet he wished this lovely woman no harm, still his reaction was justified and already committed. But instead of connecting his hand found no soft surface to hit. It fell down on empty air as she too had pivoted at just the last second.

What struck Malcom just then wasn't the fact he has missed. But rather in how each of them had reacted and evaded. There wasn't any effort in doing so by either. It felt natural and smooth, unthinking… instinctual. He wanted to feel that again, to allow his instinct to act instead of his mind. Both were frozen looking at each other visible now. The grin on her face was matched with one of his own. When he lunged for her that grin became something more. The thought when it hit him did not last long, he stopped thinking a moment later and allowed his body full reign.

She wants this? But why?

It was a dance! Each tried to strike but neither could. As if they were of one mind and one purpose. It was violent, and any question that it was dangerous was unnecessary. If one of those blows landed the other would feel it. But neither could, no matter how hard they tried. Somehow, they moved about the room with precision and without disturbing an object. How such a thing was possible Malcom had no clue. But every act every counter was like music, and to feel this music was a special delight. Each effort was not in vain, neither was discouraged by the miss. Somehow it felt right, natural for them to duel like this. Malcom did not have time to complete these thoughts, only to half experience them. Animalistic in their nature, Malcom was living in a razors edge of time.

Once when he thought she was pinned against a wall he lunged for her only to grasp at air. She had used the wall as a spring board to bounce over him. Her counter was so close to hitting him he felt slightest bit of flesh graze his cheek. All his training and preparation was paying off. Sparing with father, with his siblings and then the Agoge. Every day hours on end honing his body. It was only this that allowed him to even have a chance at doing any of this. Clearly this woman had been trained as well, perhaps better than him! The dance seemed to last forever. Instead of being angry by it, Malcom desired it. To be tested, to show his skill and spar with this Grey woman. It was so similar to what he and his brothers and sisters had played at when they were children. A very Grey version of hide and seek. As Grey children it often ended in fist fights. One of the reasons why it was forbidden. They still played it anyway; it was too good a chance to get even when one of them ticked you off.

"Why do you hold back? I wish to know you Hermano, come dance with me, show me who you really are. All of your questions will be answered if you do."

Wasn't that what he was doing? And yet he wasn't trying to best her, only avoid her. Malcom indulged the Grey one, partially because he needed answers. And partially because he was aroused by her, a chance to continue this sounded divine. The fury of blows and kicks, and jabs began. Each trying to catch the other, each trying to avoid the other. Now there was a more dangerous edge to it. Each was putting ALL their weight and power into the moves. Since no blows landed only the sounds and grunts told Malcom of the change in tempo... and danger. His own limits were removed and he too took all regard for safety away from his actions. These were killing blows he was giving. Any human who was unfortunate to be in front of him now would be dead. As it was, only the air suffered. It went on like this far longer than what Malcom was used to as a child. This woman was skilled, and very powerful. He had to use all his might, all his skill just to stay in the fight. Finally, he began to see the patterns of her moves and anticipated her. Before he could even think it, he knew she was going for his left side. He acted before she could begin and lunged towards her exposed midsection. Finally, he connected with her, sending her off her feet. Once they ceased rolling, he found himself entangled with her on the floor. Each were breathing sharply pushed beyond measure. Each looked directly into the others eyes waiting on the next move. He was on top of her and felt her softness and could smell the scent of her. She smelled of lilacs and her smile was that of a predator. He asked her what her name was. Up till now she hadn't even given that.

"Does it matter? Why not take your prize?"

He felt her move and seductively pull at his loose-fitting clothing. He was tempted to make love to her, but he knew nothing about her, nothing about what she was trying to do. And something told Malcom if this woman was like the Grey women he knew. She was only testing him, most Grey women were like that. Devious, plotting, and always gaming you and everyone else to their own end. Malcom's body wanted to feast on her but his mind and intellect screamed at the stupidly of doing so.

"I would like to, but my purpose isn't to give in. And something tells me neither is yours."

Surprise and shock appeared for in instant on the woman's face. She seemed happily astonished to see that Malcom could not be so easily manipulated. Her sexual teasing with her hands ceased and she spoke with a different tone. Calmer and one without all the honey. This was the real person, not the image she wished to show. So carefully crafted to alure, to trap him he suspected.

"My name is Camila."

She seemed shocked and pleasantly surprised at him. Taking the hint, he rose up and helped her to her feet. A part of him rebelled against his judgement. He would have very much liked to make love to her lovely form.

Camila was a beauty, and he had never seen a woman look at him in such a way before. The dance as she called it made him desirous more than normal. Even now with his mind clear, his body stayed aroused, his body refused to allow him to relax. Thankfully he wasn't alone, Camila too was clearly affected.

"This is your first time, you haven't ever really danced our way before. I would wager you haven't. I can tell you want me, but still, you keep to yourself…. You are nothing like your friend."

He was inching closer to her and she was to him. He wasn't sure he could go another round of "dancing" without making love to her. When he put a hand on her she nearly melted into him. Yet she had compared him to his teammate, the one who had betrayed him. So that is why he bent, she had seduced him. That realization did much to calm his libido. Camila however was cooing softly at his touch and continued to grow closer.

"I should have guessed the son of a King would have more control than that boy. I wish you didn't, I would very much like to continue our dance."

Her confirmation about the boy made him ask in a hard tone about him. She was confused for a moment and then had to take a breath to re-center herself. Clearly the dance had Camila out of her comfort zone as well.

"Jason was offered what he desired, a few local thralls we have for his pleasure. He did not take much convincing Malcom."

After closing his eyes and forcing himself to calm down he asked his next question. Why was he here, and what did Camila have in mind?

"I could ask the same of you. You are in my country without permission. You lurk about, pretending to be nothing, when you are so much more. What is it you want Malcom, what is it you most desire in my country? I know your heart is of our people… that much is clear. But…what about you Malcom who are you?"

He smiled at her; it was hard to do much of anything else. She was radiant, lovely and she was working overtime on charming him. He wasn't buying it…. ok he was, but he knew better at least. Before he could answer she took ahold of him again and was the same alluring temptress she was earlier. Gone was the brief moment they had shared when he was sure he was talking to the real Camila. She had been astonished at his reserve. Saying her name and that tender look, he wagered that was said outside of her desires. She had reacted, rather than followed her plan. Now she was back on that plan and was working overtime on charming him. She wanted something, clearly she made it seem like it was him. Wither or not he was the real target of her affection he couldn't say. Jason didn't stand a chance against her. That thought didn't change his opinion of Jason, but he better understood why Jason had bent.   Thinking of Jason got his mind back on business at hand.

"Oh, I want all kinds of things, but right now I need to understand why Jason, why me?"

Now she wasn't so impressed, clearly, she thought less of him just by the way her expression changed. Her tone and words hammered that home seconds later.

"Isn't it obvious, you are both Grey. Inducing any Grey to join us is good is it not?"

Malcom raised his eyebrows in an unspoken word. Almost as if he had said to her… "AND"

"We struggle to sustain our numbers, especially with men. Bringing in two handsome, virile male immortals could do nothing but help, don't you think? Jason will be given many thralls and will live a very comfortable life here. Some of our Grey might even lay with him, the opportunity to have an immortal child is simply too tempting. Even with a man such as Jason. Just think what a man like you could have; you are nothing like him."

He quietly laughed at the obvious jibe. Clearly Camila had no respect for Jason. The boy wasn't horrible to look at so he suspected she looked down on him for the same reason why he did. The boy had betrayed his word for sex, and a chance at an easy life. He had walked away from his mother, his brothers even! Camila's comment was clearly insincere, if he stayed for sex, she wouldn't respect him anymore than she did Jason.

Is it really so difficult for them to produce another generation, it isn't for us? Why would it be for them?

Was such an issue real, or just something to disguise another need? He would have to ask mother when he got home… if he got home. He was locked on the image of her, desiring to look just a bit more, to see her just a bit longer. It felt right somehow, and then he better understood the nature of his kind. The dance was more than just knowing someone, it was a way for a grey to find a partner. The dance revealed directly how matched they were. On thinking this, his rate of breathing increased. He knew the answer to that question. This woman… was unlike any he had met before. She clearly saw his mind working. As she petted him and he drank in her beauty she tried to calm his concerns.

"You have to understand having an immortal child is rare. But if your lover is also immortal, well then, your chances are so much the better. We are few in number here, and adding you and Jason to our little group, would be a massive boon. I promise you if you stay your life will be pleasant. If you like…I could be the one to make it so?"

He allowed her to kiss him and he took her into his arms. The smell of lilacs and her soft skin was charming. But he wasn't going to sell his loyally and his honor for anyone. Yet he couldn't deny his body desired her, and there was more. She was his equal in skill. That such a thing was possible from a woman was eye opening. No Grey woman back home trained in the Agoge. How was such a thing possible, yet clearly it was. Seeing she was tempting him she placed a hand on him that searched him in a very intimate way. Instead of pushing him over the edge it had the opposite reaction. His internal voice said she was like all those Grey women at home. Testing, devious, and full of intrigue. This wasn't the real Camila, just her placing the strings on him. He removed her hand and took a step back from her lest he lose all composure and make love to her.

"And yet if I stay with you Camila, would I not be laying down my honor? Would I not be betraying my oath, my family and my brothers? What kind of man would I be? Is that the kind of man you desire… would you respect such a man?"

He paused to look at her and judge if he had correctly assessed whom she really was. Grey women were like this. In his father's time they even tried to seduce young men when they were accepted into the clan. It was their way of accessing just how far they would go. Those that chose the flesh and showed no code, no respect, would be treated without any. Those that denied their flesh, against their nature, displaying a higher code…. Those men were culled out for special treatment. Of course that was how things USED to be. But looking at Camila, he could imagine it was how things worked for her. She smiled at his words, confirming what he thought. Still, she continued her pace of temptation.

"Yes, but what does it matter? What does it matter if you can have our bodies but not our respect? Why does such a thing matter to you? You could be unburdened by responsibility. Jason will never have to work again. When he desires a new woman to make love to, they will be provided. Imagine it, a life full of pleasure, without responsibility."

His answer was something drilled into him from the time he was a child. Something father had taught him. On this there was no give, no quarter. As if the words had been chiseled into his flesh.

"A man without honor, isn't a man at all."

At the Agoge that way of life was taught in a way few could depart from. To go another way was to violate everything they knew. It was core to who he was, and to anyone he respected. He spoke the words, things felt rather than thought. Her response again confirmed he was right. The teaching as it had been driven into him by his elders played like music in his ears.

Life is duty, and duty is life. One cannot be a man without honor, any man who desires a life without it, who doesn't embrace it… crave it. Isn't a man at all.

"I wish you weren't American. I like you Malcom… more than I should. If you were syngéneia I would do much to have you."

He saw the sadness in her eyes and wondered what that Greek word meant. He started to ask her but she ceased trying to seduce him and took a few steps away. Now he would learn his real fate, and he wasn't confident that it would be anything as calm as Jason's. Yet Jason was a dog, and he suspected Jason would not live in comfort and sloth forever. At least he hoped not.

Chapter 3: Lost and Found

Travis looked out the window of the State Department aircraft, wondering again what awaited them in Sao Paulo. From time to time, he would turn on the small device imbedded in his glasses. It would project a heads up display directly into his vision. It sent a coded feed to Travis on the status of Moonstone's teams. The one that had his attention right now was Epsilon. Three days ago, they had been scheduled to leave Sao Paulo. They were the advance team for this trip. For weeks Epsilon had reported nothing that had been noteworthy. But as the team was leaving, something had gone wrong. One member of the team had witnessed hooded men caring one of their number, unconscious from the safehouse. That person was confirmed to be the team leader, which was Travis's eldest son from Yelina.

"Why are you so sure it's safe, if someone is missing don't you think that hints there is trouble? Even I know that it does! Come on, let's go back. It's not like this trip will yield anything productive anyway, even if they are serious this time!"

The scared weasel spoke nearly breathlessly. Travis tried to imagine how this dork would react to real danger.

Probably piss himself if someone so much as looked at him in anger. You make it too easy to despise you Tostig. You sure are a fucking little weasel, but you are my responsibility, one I can't ignore unfortunately. I am going to have to watch my attitude this whole damn trip. But it would be nice to see you face some real challenge. Not that it would do much for my contract with State. Still….

The weasel in question was the junior state department rep chosen for this meeting. He was from the west coast and the opposite political party of the one in charge. Which meant the administration wouldn't be too sad if something happened. In some ways it would be preferable than having him return. The US would have a weapon to use in the world's media against Meridia, and it would be an easy propaganda victory at that. All on the back of someone they didn't like, a surefire trade if Travis ever saw one. The weasel knew it too, which was why he was trying to get Travis to pull the plug and turn around.

"We lost contact with him, that doesn't mean he is missing. Mr. Tostig, I assure you that my team is ready, if it wasn't safe I wouldn't let you go. Not to mention, the man in question is my son. If I thought he was in real trouble, do you think I would risk your life?"

The sour expression on Tostig's face showed how little he trusted Travis or his PMC. Thankfully Moonstone had more than shown its ability over the last decade. Even if this drone died, Travis suspected it wouldn't affect his contract. Travis got up getting Tostig a drink and one for himself. The way Travis saw things, Tostig needed some liquid courage. So, the drink he gave him had very little water in it. But for Travis he needed his mind razor sharp. Unlike what he had just told this troll; San Paulo was not some place they should be going. Having not one but two of his people missing would normally cause him to pull the plug in a heartbeat. Thankfully Tostig didn't know about the second man. It wasn't a lie per say, they had found some evidence of premeditation in the bank accounts of Jason the new communication man. And it was clear in retrospect that his behavior was questionable. Right now, Jason's friends and family were being questioned, one of them had already hinted that Jason was acting strangely right before he left. If Travis had to guess his son was a hostage and Jason was a willing participant. At least he hoped he was a hostage. Jason could have just killed him and dumped the body.

But why, what caused this boy to betray us?

There would be hell to pay for someone, that was for sure. Six months before Jason had been excited for the opportunity. But the way he had handled communications it was clear Jason was not on the up and up. There were some signs that Jason was feeding the Meridians intel. Signs weren't proof however, and Travis reminded himself again to give the boy the benefit of the doubt. It was a losing battle if there ever was one but Travis tried anyway.

Once it was clear things had gone wrong, Travis had ordered both his aviation team and his assault team to Guarulhos. It was the International Airport inside Sao Paulo itself. They were given access to a military hanger just off the flight line. If things went badly Travis would lean on his best fighters. If need be, the aviation group could insert his fighters anywhere in the city. Giving them unfettered access seemed to indicate the Meridians were not a threat. For now, at least, but who knew if that was real. He told Tostig none of this, only assuring him he had good people ready to support him.

Along with those teams he had sent Eta, a protection team to the local American consulate. They would bolster the marines on duty there. Between the airport and their destination were three recon teams watching for signs of an ambush. On top of that, another assault team was in a safehouse in Sao Paulo, in case they got useful intel. If there had been time he would have assigned his infiltrator teams to go looking for him but that wasn't possible. Pulling the additional teams had been hard enough as it was. Right now, nearly all of Moonstone was in or heading to, Sao Paulo. That alone was enough cause for Travis to be here. Besides that, he wanted to know what had happened to his son. In a real tangible way Moonstone's real mission today was to retrieve his son.

The state department be damned! My focus here is the boy, besides… the moment the plane lands in Sao Paulo, Tostig would have done his job for his masters. No, we are here to bring Malcom back.

This weasel was only here to test the sincerity of the Meridian government. The real talks would happen later in the year and certainly not in Merdia. Someplace neutral and considered safe for both sides. Probably somewhere in Western Europe Travis guessed. This weasel was really only here to find out just how real these talks were to be. Meridia had hinted it would be in the US's interest. Thus, the Wilkenson's administration keen willingness to play ball. Merdia was a flash point for conflict, and seen as a possible future near peer. The US couldn't afford to have another power the size and strength of the US as an enemy in the same hemisphere. More importantly the US wanted to dissuade the Merdian's from going after more countries. It was already bad enough they had swallowed two major US allies in the region.

Travis was about to sit down when he heard a near inaudible beep. It was his glasses letting him know there was an update. As soon as he read it, he sighed, his son had called the consulate saying he was on his way. He hadn't left any codewords so it didn't completely reassure Travis, but it was a good sign. He let Tostig know that his missing person may have been found. In the meantime, he read the assessment Dolly had put on the feed. Dolly and Travis had a tight relationship and he trusted her implicitly. While no longer husband and wife they shared much. Dolly's short but encouraging notes on hearing the call, stated she believed it was authentic. Besides being his ex-wife Dolly also ran the most successful intelligence operation in the clan. She may have a small organization but they were capable. That was enough for Travis to allow himself to put aside his fatherly worries and again shift back to what State wanted. Thankfully he didn't have a responsibility here, his teams all were well led and didn't need Travis to tell them what to do. He would focus on keeping Tostig from bugging his teams and deflect his useless comments.

Two hours later they had landed safely and were in the vehicles without incident. They easily avoided one planned protest and were inside the consulate's secure perimeter. He was tempted to grandstand and tell Tostig "I told you so" but that tempted fate too much. For Travis he wouldn't feel good again until he had his son, and yes even Tostig back on the plane and over US territory. As it was, they entered the facility without incident. Once on the 5th floor Travis and Tostig met the US ambassador to Meridia and the local consul. They were here only to support and advise. In reality they were both senior to Tostig and far better equipped to handle the advisor to President Silva. Whoever it was, they were on their way and could be expected to arrive in a few minutes. Seeing the diplomats begin to prepare Tostig, Travis turned his attention back to his intel. There were several possibilities who this advisor was. Travis wanted to memorize as much as he could before the man arrived.

That was when Travis heard Tostig rant and rave over something said. Travis wasn't paying attention; he had his mind poring through the intelligence Dolly had gathered for this meeting. Hearing all the commotion he tuned back into the conversation, learning that Tostig was upset over pronouns of their expected guest. The ambassador didn't know them and Tostig was furious no one had bothered to discover them. What an idiot, they didn't have a clue who was coming in the first place. It could be any number of men or women close to the Meridian president. Probably a man, considering the nature of Meridia. The consul shot Travis a look of incredulity over what Tostig was upset about. The days of hyper focusing on pronouns was very 2020's. But Tostig was an academic and far left wing. Some in those circles still believed in all that. Travis just smiled and put a hand on Tostig. He put a tiny bit of strength on the arm and pulled him aside.

Using a tiny bit of force on a man like Tostig was a surefire way to either piss him off or cow him. It went about the way Travis expected.

"Our guest is almost here; I am afraid we don't have time to worry about that. I was just reviewing my intelligence for today and noticed that most of the major players we know about are all in Columbia for talks. So, whoever arrives is a new player. Do you have any intelligence on who is coming?"

Tostig was taken aback and Travis knew why. Tostig was too junior and too far out of the circle of trust to have been given any real intelligence briefing. But the question wasn't meant to be a real one, just something to get him away from pestering the ambassador.

"No… I wasn't told who we were meeting but I am sure it will be someone senior. Otherwise, it would be a diplomatic incident if they did."

The more he talked the more confident he sounded. This was a private unannounced meeting, so the typical diplomatic rules be damned. Tostig didn't really know what he was talking about Travis thought. After a smile at seeing the Ambassador escape the room, he turned his attentions back to the intel Dolly had sent. Her suggestion at who was coming was on a new power player known only to a few. It was a woman, lover to the president it was said by some. Her identity wasn't really known, but there were intelligent guesses on it. Dolly's money was on a woman named Rose. She was in the Meridian presidents inner circle and seemed to be at every major discussion. Yet she didn't have a title, or even a named role on his staff. Travis thought sending the lover of the president to talk business to be rather foolish at best. So, his money was on a junior defense analyst.

A few minutes later came word from his team downstairs. Travis now had the identity of the Meridian who was arriving. It was Luiz Montero, a military advisor to President Silva. Travis chuckled to himself; he should have bet real money with Dolly this time. He could hear the voice on coms describe Montero and then abruptly cease speaking. That made Travis freeze thinking something was wrong. It was confirmed a second later with everyone speaking at once over coms. It went against their training, only one voice on the channel at once was standard. It angered Travis and made his legs move towards the stairs. Either something was really bad, or his kids had violated their discipline. He used his master switch to cut in to everyone's mic and ordered everyone to be quiet. A second later Malcom's younger brother Jacob quickly spoke directly to his dad. Jacob was a part of the protection team he had assigned to the consulate.

"Dad… Malcom is with them, he looks ok. But dad that isn't what has all of us excited. There is a woman with them, and she has the most striking eyes you have ever seen."

Their coms were not exactly secure so Travis had to assume that meant there was a vampire among the Meridians. Travis acknowledged the transmission and then heard a description of the woman. Young, probably early 20's brown hair. He pulled up the small tablet he had with Dolly's intel. Dolly had identified what was known of Rose. Dolly had gone to a lot of trouble to find this intel out. She was convinced this was the person most likely to arrive, as Dolly felt she was the real power behind the Meridian President. It was rumored what this woman desired became reality. Foreign policy, local politics, spending… all of it seemed to go her way. Looking at the image Dolly provided she didn't look anything remarkable. Rose didn't look like she was in her 20's. This vampire was probably a ruby, someone working for the Meridians.

A few minutes later and the representative of the Meridian president arrived on the floor. The pretty girl was indeed walking behind him but she wasn't ruby… she was a Grey. And if that didn't blow him away, looking at Montero did. He too was a Grey vampire. Montero smirked at Travis as he walked by. He had to know he was here because there wasn't an ounce of shock on Montero's face. Travis quietly spoke into his mic for a status report. All stations reported fine, but Travis sure didn't feel it.

Introductions were given and Montero spoke quietly with Tostig. Security had been followed and everything was it as it should be, such as it was. The remainder of the Meridians were cooling their heels just outside the office as Tostig led Montero in and closed the door. There wasn't any seating for the staff Montero brought. As far as they knew the man was only brining security, not his full staff. A few minutes later and one of the consulate staff brought out some chairs. Travis tried not to stare but it was hard not to. *The girl was a vampire, a Grey no less.* He had expected it to be a Ruby; they were all over the globe. But NEVER had Travis seen a Grey not from Medford.

No wonder the kids lost their shit. Where in hell did you spawn from little girl? God… please tell me you aren't another of Finnan's children. That lying sack of shit. I bet you're one of his. The Agora is going to have a field day when they hear about this! First one of our boys betrays us, now this… Ok now his betrayal makes more sense. With legs like that I can see why he would.

He knew every member of his clan, and this woman wasn't one of them. Still, he couldn't just walk up to her and ask how long she had been a vampire and who her parents were. He was tempted to walk up but even Travis had to remind himself of his place. Finally, after what felt like an eternity a small group got off the elevator and escorted Malcom up to him.

It's about flipping time. Days and days without contact. What the hell happened to your team boy? Well…thank God the kid's ok.

As always Travis was careful not to allow his feeling for his son to hit his face. He had a lot of questions, but now wasn't the time to ask them. Malcom walked up and started talking, mostly apologizing for what happened. Travis cut him off, now wasn't the time to be dad. Travis had to be his boss first, and then later, much later, he could talk to him like a son again.

"What about your radioman? Where is he son?"

Travis could see how uncomfortable the boy was. This was a first class screw up that required the King himself to come down and clean it up.

"He set us up dad, he is working for our Meridian cousins now."

Travis smirked at his son's choice of cover. He was hinting that the local Grey vampires had co-opted him into working for them. He was about to start to apologize again when Travis cut him off.

"There will be time to talk about all that later. Right now, I need to know if there are any treats to our mission I don't know about? Do our cousins pose a threat to us?"

Malcom shook his head no but looked over at the grey vampire sitting not far from them. She was smiling and looking directly at Travis.

"I want you to go down to Vic and have him drive you back to the airport. Someone from team Mu will get you out of the country."

Malcom started to protest but he was here illegally. If the Meridians hadn't already protested his presence in the country they would soon.

"Dad what about my team, I want to lead them in retrieving the bastard if I can."

Travis smiled; Malcom clearly didn't want to leave with things a mess like this. Not to mention with so much unsaid. But there wasn't time, seeing his son frustrated and upset it caused him to break his cool façade. He put a hand on him and put more warmth into his face. No words were spoken but Malcom got the message. His father cared, but now wasn't the time. Before Malcom could leave however Travis smelled the scent of lilacs from behind him.

"Malcom, you really should introduce us. Is this who I think it is?"

Malcom took one step towards the incoming woman who looked radiant and beautiful. Travis had seen many Grey women who you could say that about in his time. And every single one of them were trouble. But it was a pleasing trouble to look at nonetheless.

"Father this is Camila Hernandez, she was my host the last few days. Camila, may I have the honor of introducing Travis Williams…."

Camila smiled like a cat and interrupted Malcom right after saying his name. She looked directly into Travis's eyes and gave that grin girls like her give when they wanted something. She finished the introduction for his son.

"Oh yes, the hero of the war with China. Leader of Moonstone, and father to a great, great many. Tell me Senior Williams, is it your title that makes you so popular or… do the women of Medford simply find you irresistible?"

Travis smiled back at the predator that stood in front of him. This Camila waited for his response but received none. Instead, Travis asked her why his son had been held captive and why Jason wasn't here.

"Captive? Oh no Senior Williams, your son and I have been spending quality time together. I have been introducing him to our culture and my fair city. As for Jason I am sure your son has already explained Jason has decided to stay with us. I can assure you Senior Williams, he will be well cared for. Even if he does not deserve such lavish treatment."

Before Travis could respond Camila was called into the office by the Meridian representative. Before she left however, she put a hand on Travis and whispered to him.

"Your son was an honorable man; you have trained him well my King."

She was slow to remove her hand and allowed her smile and stare to linger. Instead of a clean break she removed her fingers slowly from his chest. As she walked away both Travis and Malcom watched her slink into the office. He said out loud for Malcom to hear how much trouble she was.

"You have no idea dad, no idea…"

Chapter 4: Sisterhood of Judgement

San Antonio, Texas

Jan 9th 2058

Malcom had his bag and was making his way through the airport. There hadn't been time to talk to dad and explain himself.

It's not my fault that guy was a traitor! But the way the guys were looking at me… you would think it was.

In the back of his head, he knew the answer to the unspoken question. He had been the leader, he had chosen his people, and he had the responsibility. When things fail it was the leader's fault, always. For the first time in Moonstone's history someone had betrayed the brotherhood. Still, HE hadn't betrayed his team or the mission. He had resisted Camila, for three days he had taken everything from seduction to beatings. He told them nothing, not that he had to.

She knew way too damned much, did Jason tell her? Or did it go further than that? That fricking sack of shit! What the hell are the guys going to think now?

He was so brooding and angry he never noticed the woman who shadowed his every move. He was too focused on what was to come. He was going to have to face tough questions at the Agora. His own mother sat on that body. Men served and fought. Women did other things, one of them was to stand in judgement over the men. The Agora was made up of the most honored women of the clan. Each woman who sat there had reached the highest level of Grey life. Each having done something tremendous to achieve fame. And each had given birth to a powerful man who had found similar honor in his life. Thus, the women who sat on the Agora had even more reason to feel pride. Not just were they legends, they had given birth to, and raised legends themselves.

"Are you so blind brother that you do not see me?"

Malcom stopped dead in his tracks at the familiar voice. He smiled; it was a welcome voice to be sure. Still, she had gotten the better of him, something he had never allowed her to do once in her life.

"I have a great deal on my mind, Sis. Still, I am glad it's you they sent."

The young girl who appeared from nowhere in front of him was deeply concerned. This sister was a Grey, and like all Grey she could appear and disappear at will. She was what Camila would call an immortal. A powerful being having inherited all the same gifts from their mother and father. Jessie was his little sister, and like Jacob the three of them were Yelina's children from Travis. Malcom had many brothers and sisters, far more than he could count. But Jacob and Jessie were the only full brothers and sisters he had.

"I heard; they aren't very pleased with you. But you are going to be fine. It's not your fault Jason was bent. They will see truth; you did the best you could. Besides they already know who is at fault. They evicted his mother over it already."

Malcom wasn't surprised Jason's family would pay a steep price at his treachery, but not that fast. That told Malcom they were embarrassed and the Agora would look for scapegoats.   He just hoped he wouldn't be put in that group with them.

"And mom…. What does she think?"

Their mother Yelina sat on the Agora herself. If he faced the Agora there would be more than one familiar face.

"She's worried, mom is afraid they are going to exile you too."

Malcom closed his eyes for a moment, not once in all this time had he ever thought he would face such a test. He had done everything for his people and he believed that was enough to shield him from such a fate. Yet here he was, his judgement in choosing a traitor could cost him everything. For Malcom there was no life outside the clan. If he was exiled, they might as well take his life as well.

Jessie saw his brooding and wrapped her arms around his and started to lead him forward. He loved his little sister; she was eight years younger than him but they had been close since she could speak. Jacob and her were less friendly, far closer in age, her and Jacob had fought more than anything else. But eventually as they grew into adults, all three had bonded. In this clan, blood bonds were common. But their bond had to be stronger. Each of them needed close allies to survive. Jessie was still young, in her last year before she was to be proclaimed a woman. In the very near future, she would enter the competitive and dangerous life of Grey women. She would most likely go to work for mother in her organization. Hiding in the shadows learning all there was to know about enemies of the Grey. And then once she had found fame and honor would be allowed to choose among the Grey men a mate worthy of her station. It would be difficult, most Grey men shared her lineage. She would struggle to find a man worthy of her.

As she led him to the car, he noticed that in the time he had been away she had grown more. She was less a child now and more woman. A part of Malcom was sad to see it, her life up to this point had been one of merriment and challenge. But above all it had been safe. Soon she would risk her life as often as he did, and she would be put under the same sort of pressures he felt. A part of him wanted that for her, and another did not. When she turned to him, she teased him for all his brooding. Seeing her jokes did not land, she grew concerned.

"It's ok sis, I just need a good meal, a feeding and some sleep."

She winced at him saying that and lowered her head for a moment before responding.

"Bro, they want to see you the second you get to Medford. They are waiting in the chambers even now. Mom made me promise I wouldn't dally in getting you there. But you know what… to hell with them. Let's get something to eat first."

Malcom laughed and put his concerns, his worries, and his guilt over the operation aside. He would need to husband his strength for what was to come. The women of the Agora would be a worthy test. He needed all his skills to face them.

Medford, Texas – Cassia & Cyrus's Home

Jan 9th 2058

Cassia was dressed in the familiar attire of one who sat on the Agora. They had years before adopted the Greek peplos when they met in the gathering. It was simple in construction with slits on the sides for ease of movement. Most wore a simple leather belt or even rope that served as one. Spartan culture did not encourage adornment, so most eschewed bright colors. Still the peplos could be beautiful, and a sign of their power. Not all the women of the Agora liked the old ways. The peplos was a good example of that. More than one of their number had voiced hate for the classical garb. Not Cassia, she loved how it reminded of her life in ancient times. It lay against her young body highlighted by gold trim. A touch given to it by a master artesian from the Citrine clan. She loved how it blended what was and what would be. Only those in the Agora had such adornment, something tolerated because of their station. Cassia treasured each time she got to wear it. It wasn't some costume like it was to these children. For Cassia it was a real living part of her history. Sparta wasn't some fable; it was real to her. She had drawn breath hundreds of years before Sparta had even been born. That time, and this clan was special to her.

"You look lovely dear."

Cassia smiled for her partner. A man she had fallen for nearly 4000 years before. Her memories of that life were painful so she rarely touched on them. But standing there dressed as a woman of ancient Greece she remembered when they had lived like this. Nearly 1500 years after they met, they were living in Athens. That time had been far simpler for both. Neither had sought a bigger place in that life. They lived as simple common folk. Their children in those times had not risen like the others, and that had been fine. Their love and their happiness were nearly unmatched. Unlike now, when both were far too busy to love the other the way their partner needed. Cassia looked carefully at her love and took in his words. In that simple complement was regret and longing. It said more than the words conveyed. That she was ignoring her love far too much. She had her reasons, as did Cyrus. Things would have to change. Soon, she thought, soon.

"Thank you. Are you going to be home tonight on time? I was hoping we could have a meal together?"

Cyrus shook his head no as he finished tying his tie and running his hands along his suit coat. She knew he had a town meeting to run tonight, already knowing it was be unlikely for him to be home any time before midnight. He looked up and faked a smile for her, something both of them were doing a lot lately. Neither wanted to hurt the other but they were. For Cyrus his efforts with his other clans and the town were taking precedence. Neither of these beings were human, nor were they vampires. Once 4000 years ago, she had been human. A young girl taken with a visitor.

This Cyrus as he was called now, was no man, he was an alien. A being that had created the clans themselves. His kind had come to visit and decided to stay. Cassia liked to think it was all because of her. Her love, her charms that had induced him to make this place his home. He often said as much but now… well now she wasn't so sure. He was always so busy managing the town, or dealing with the clans he owned. He was the visitor for the Grey, the Aqua and the Amber clans. And she was not just his bride. It was with her that he had founded the Aqua house. From her womb had come Adad the first Aqua vampire. And nearly 4000 years later had come Travis and Jay. Generations of Kings and Queens had been created by her. Many of history's titans had called her mother, and Cyrus, father.

As she watched him leave, she remembered when he had decided to live openly among his children. Not hide away like he had done for century after century. He had changed her then, from the human to the hybrid being she now existed as. Part human, part visitor Cassia was now truly immortal. Far more powerful than any vampire and his chosen ambassador to his clans. She possessed all the powers of the three and appeared as such to their members. When an Aqua saw her, they saw the Aqua eyes of one of them. When she was with, they Grey they saw their own eyes reflected. This had endeared her to some of them, but to many of the Grey… well it was seen as a challenge.

Several Grey women had died after they attempted to test her ability. This Grey clan was her current obsession; she had to fix it. Thinking of her calling again she tightened her fist and her face exposed the emotions that coursed through her veins. Her son Travis was its king, and she would be damned if she allowed another to sit on the throne she had created for him. Yet, her son seemed unable to hold on to the crown she had placed on his head.

All he has to do is embrace what he is… but does he? Will he ever just stop being a child and be the man I KNOW he can be?

Cassia shook her head at nothing remembering her assessment of her son and his leadership. His failures had required her intervention and direct involvement. Even if she was SUPPOSED to be working with, and inside, all three clans… she didn't have time. The Grey took every second, every ounce of her energy to keep in line. Cassia closed her eyes and took in a long breath. Wondering just how much longer this would go on like this. Watching as Cyrus drove away, she was reminded of her own problems. Her relationship with Cyrus was not well. They were near eternal beings, but even lovers like them went thought difficulties. And clearly two decades trying to fix the Grey was taking its toll.

Making her way from her home to her office in the Agora. Cassia pondered many things, some more pressing than others. She considered ways to better her marriage, ways to encourage her grandchildren, and of course how to help her other clans. But as always all of that disappeared nearly as quickly as it was considered. For Cassia, the Grey and her son was her obsession. As she walked into the office she nodded to the others and smiled. Working as always to try to strengthen her relationship with the others. Of all those that sat on the Agora, Cassia held the most power. She had taken that power the same way all grey women do, by cunning, and at times, force. Many had attempted to stand in her way, and all had regretted doing so. Yet it wasn't for her own ambition that she worked so tirelessly. Of the three living sons she still had, Travis was the one she most worried about. Her other sons were well adjusted and living their best lives. Adad nearing the end of his days, had finally found peace. Jay was King of the Aqua and did not need her to save him. He would endure for 40 centuries or more without a breath from her. But Travis, he was on the precipice as he always was. This boy of hers never seemed to stray far from the edge.

A rotund older woman walked towards her, also dressed in a peplos. Hers did not flatter her form at all, yet Cassia would not say a word against her. This was her sons second consort, a woman that in a short time would again be his wife. She had given him several children, one of which was quickly becoming a renowned warrior. This child was fast becoming a force like Ares, and if Travis was not careful a rival for his throne. His mother had designs for him, and Susan was nothing if not ambitious.

"Mother, have they not arrived yet?"

Cassia smiled for her daughter-in-law and stated that no, they had not. They were overdue, Jessie had likely decided to defy the Agora again. Yelina's youngest was intelligent and capable, but undisciplined.

"I should have insisted we send Elena to fetch him; my daughter is not so willful as Yelina's."

For Cassia all of these children were her grandchildren. Unlike in times past, Cassia now was fully involved the lives of her Grey. She took a keen interest in all of them and marked well each and every one. She had to; it was those children that would eventually ensure the longevity of her beloved clan. Cassia had lived long enough to see so many generations rise and fall that she could not count them. And she knew she would be here to see all the ones to come. Long after Susan and Yelina were dust, she would still be here. That knowledge was unnerving to many, something Cassia used to its fullest.

Susan's girl, Elena was fast becoming a powerful woman in the clan. Just like her brothers she was a force to be reckoned with. Without a doubt that girl would join her mother on the Agora before she was 50. Cassia would have to watch her like she did all her grandchildren. But that watchful vision wasn't just a loving one, but one of caution. The sharpest knives were always those wielded by family. Answering Susan's clear jibe, she made it clear her position.

"Perhaps, but Jessie is only delaying the inevitable. Your Thomas and Elena do you so much honor. You have to be so excited. Are you looking forward to next year dear?"

Susan's eyes brightened; she was at the end of her separation from Travis. Next year Yelina would stand down as his wife and allow Susan the honor again. It was an agreement reached many years before. Three woman who loved a single man had fought for him, and argued over him. The end to that conflict saw Dolly going her own way, and the other two compromising. One woman would have him for four years. At the end of that time, she would return him to the other. This time however Susan would revert to her youth right before then. She would return to be a child bearing woman and begin again to build up her house. She already had two titans, she clearly hoped to add to that number. Susan like Yelina honored Cassia by calling her mother. It wasn't something Cassia required, or even asked for. Still when she said it, Cassia could not help but smile.

"Oh yes, it's been so long since I was young. Perhaps I should go see Isabe about getting a better looking peplos for then? Goodness knows I look terrible at this age; I simply can't keep the weight off now. I love what Isabe did with your peplos, you always look so elegant."

Cassia smiled at the complement and put a loving hand on her. Cassia still valued Susan and her loyalty, she had of course chosen all three women for her son years before. Each had done as she asked and been good wives for him. Yet each had failed him in their own ways. None of them had healed her son from the damage done by Aya and Tina. And most importantly they had not helped him become the kind of King he needed to be. Travis was still weak, and for a Grey that was deadly. As great as Susan and Yelina were, they had failed to push Travis to greatness. That was the primary reason why Cassia still spent all her time with the Grey when she had two other clans to care for.

Two decades before when Cyrus had inherited both the Grey and the Amber clans, he had awakened her. One day when Travis was finally ready to take up his crown without help, she would depart and begin to raise up the Amber. She would lay with her lover again and create another son, one worthy of wearing the Amber crown. But that was centuries from now from the looks of it. For now, she must stay here and watch over her Grey. She would not fail her Travis again; she had done so once and felt the pain of it even now. She had been selfish and stupid, and allowed her feelings to get in the way. It had cost her everything, nearly destroying both her modern boys.

"Mother you seem worried, is everything ok?"

Cassia smiled for her and assured Susan everything was well. But it wasn't, Travis was still in danger. He still had not taken up the burden she had asked him to. He was still not the man he needed to be. And Cassia wasn't sure how to help him. She pulled on her peplos and adjusted herself. Disquieted that she did not know how to save him. It was why she would stop at nothing. He was her child, and she had failed that boy once already. She could not fail this time; she had to save him… and his clan.

Medford, Texas – The Agora

Jan 9th 2058

Malcom stood alone in front of the Agora being pelted with question after question. He had already undergone three hours of questioning. Most of which was harsh and judgmental. At first, he had accepted it on its face, he had in fact failed. But the more these women judged him and found him unworthy the more he chaffed.

What did they know about combat, or work in the field?

He had NEVER seen any of them put their lives at risk for the clan. Never once seen any of these high and mighty ladies in anything other than luxury and comfort. A peace created by the strength of the men.

"Did you inquire to why Jason wanted to join you, ask about his purpose? Or did you just accept him without question on to your team?"

Malcom heard the words spoken with distaste from one of the new generation women on the Agora. Not one who had been Grey for centuries. This woman had only become Grey when he was a boy.

What in hell did she even know about being a Grey?

"Yes, I did, I questioned his mother and his friends and found him capable in his task. As you may not be aware, his skills are rare in the Agoge. He was more than qualified for the task."

Another woman far older and one of those like his mother had lived for centuries, spoke with shocked surprise. She wanted to know if he had only looked at his skill and not his loyalty.

"This was our first operation together and my task on this mission was also to assess that. Up until he stuck a fucking needle in my neck, he had performed his duties and given me no reason to question him, madam."

Another woman scolded him for his insolence towards the Agora. He started to nearly shout at her asking why they felt they had the right or experience to judge him? But caught himself when he realized the speaker was his mother.

"I apologize for my insolence ma'am, what happened to me and my team was unfortunate. Had I seen a sign of what he was to do, I would have acted. It is not the standard for a leader to run an investigation on his prospective recruits. That is what we ask your groups to do."

The dig was direct and not taken well. Several among them visibly reacted to his obvious attempt at throwing the blame back on them. The women of the clan ran groups that could best be described as mini-intelligence agencies. The men who failed in the Agoge and the women with the right skills, plundered the world for intelligence. Knowledge they could use or trade. Each person who joined a Moonstone team had an intelligence dossier written up by one of those groups. It was that dossier that leaders like him used to determine the fitness for service. So far none of them had questioned their own failure in this regard. As he suspected that landed like a lead balloon from the looks around the room.

"What exactly did you reveal to these other Grey? Hum… tell us child?"

What did I tell them… What do you think Nana; I told them what I was trained to? You sound like you think I betrayed my people?

His honor and his loyalty were things in stone. As it should be to any Man who bore his eyes. To have anyone question it was unthinkable. But to have NANA question it? When he spoke, he did so without thinking. Reacting rather than considering his words. Did they not know his heart bled for his clan? How on earth could he betray his brothers?

Jason may have, but not me, never, not in a million years.

His mother scolded him for addressing Cassia as "Nana". In this room he was to address her with the honors she deserved, not to try and remind everyone of his lineage.

Mom… THAT ISNT what I am doing! I just… ugh

"This grey woman, did you lay with her? Did you whisper into her ears all you know. Your report says you performed the dance of the Grey with her. You must have made love…. you are far too young to have denied your flesh. What did she ask of you as you bed her? Or did you only think of her body?"

The question, blunt and to the point, had come from his own mother. He stood in shock for a moment and then remembered he was a man and not a child anymore.

Fuck no.... I am not going to stand around and have you...EVEN YOU. say that to me.

Through clenched teeth he responded. Barley holding on to scraps of decorum that he still felt.

"I told them nothing my lady, I resisted and was beaten for my trouble. I asked questions and sought answers to what you would wish to know. I acted in honor, and spoke in honor! Not that I feel much of that here today."

The jibe he had told himself not to say, but he couldn't help it. He was pissed at being treated this way by his own mother and grandmother. He put steel into his eyes looking directly at her and saw the fire returned back in hers.

"A man receives the honor he has earned my son. And your actions are in question here. Do not test me or the others with your vain concerns for your ego. We have every right to come to the truth and judge you."

Now angry and tired of the questioning he moved from his place and approached the assembled Agora. Allowing his muscles to move after hours of being held at check, he felt his testosterone surge. At that moment he wanted nothing more than some man to challenge him physically so he could show them what he was really made of. Where once he had seen this august body with love and respect, now he only felt indigent rage.

"If you question my loyalty then act! I have never once given you question to doubt it! My honor and pride in my people is all I have. If that is nothing, then I am nothing. I told that woman no, and I resisted her even if I did want her. Yes, I wanted to have her.... I don't apologize for that. But I did as I was taught, and I honored you and you, and all of you."

He had pointed first to his mother, then to his grandmother and then to the others assembled. He was beyond pissed now; having felt they had thought him a traitor. Standing there with fists clinched and his teeth showing. His grandmother stood now and came to him without fear. The "Grey mother" as she was called. The others saw her with fear, and rightfully so. But for Malcom she was nana, and even in this place he refused to see her in any other way. When she was close enough to touch him, she looked deeply into his eyes and then put her hand on his face. Unlike his mother and all the other Grey, his nana possessed all the vampiric powers of her husband's clans. She could disappear in the wind like a Grey, stop time like an Amber, and she could enter the mind like an Aqua. He knew precisely what she was doing when she touched him. She took her time searching out his soul and reading all that was he.

Malcom had no fear, nor did he flinch at the rough way she tore through his memories. He had nothing to hide, no shame to bear in this. He had acted with professionalism and had been as he was taught to be. He stood and allowed the old woman to see what she wished to see. A few minutes later she reopened her eyes and put her arm down from him.

"This child is as he says he is. He did not dishonor us, nor did he lie in his report. He resisted this girl and learned many things, some of which I find useful. There are things however this boy has seen, he does not understand. Malcom you are dismissed, we will send for you when we have decided your fate."

Malcom looked at his grandmother searching for some sign of what that fate would be. It sounded like she was pleased yet not quite so. His senses told him this body did not approve of him, no matter what nana said. The looks of the others told him that much at least. But what could he say that he hadn't already, and what could he reveal that nana hadn't taken?

"I live to serve my clan, and my life is yours, as always."

As he walked out the doors he felt his heart sink. It was the first time he ever questioned his loyalty to his people. They had never questioned him in such a way, nor had anyone had cause to. It was an experience Malcom was not ready for, nor did he know how to handle.

Chapter 5: Consequences

Medford, Texas – Yelina's Home

Jan 10th 2058

Dolly was sitting in the home of her friend; someone she had known for nearly 80 years. Yesterday's meeting in the Agora had unsettled both of them. Dolly had come to comfort her friend but it wasn't just that. Both women had become Grey vampires long ago and both sat on the Agora. Long before Travis was born both had struggled to carve out a place for themselves in this clan. Yet Dolly was far older, 100 years before Yelina was born, Dolly had walked the earth as a vampire. She could well remember Yelina's mother and the day of Yelina's birth. She had held Yelina as a baby and comforted her. Such was their existence, immortals both. Each had seen much in service to the clan.

Dolly was sister to the founder of the American version of the Grey. Both her sister and Dolly had built up this clan from nothing in the 1860's. Dolly and her sister had been the greatest powers once, Tina had ruled without pause until her death. They had become the last standing Grey enclave on earth. Or at least until yesterday that was what they thought anyway.

"Has mother told you anything yet about these other Grey?"

The question finally put out there after an hour of small talk hung in the air like a mist. Dolly needed to know what Yelina knew. Treachery was in the air and the old cycles were repeating yet again. Others may not see it but Dolly could, she had lived and survived when so many of her peers had not.

"Nothing, but it doesn't matter. I am far more concerned about my own right now. I love my boy but he vexes me so."

Dolly looked at her friend with warmth and searched her mask to see just what was truth and what was a shield. Yelina had cause to be focused on her own troubles. Her eldest son was going to be censured for his actions, and her youngest daughter was ill-tempered. Her children were making enemies in the Agora, and if they weren't careful, it could be the end of their mother and her own organization.

"What about your people, do you have anyone in Meridia who knows anything about our cousins?"

Dolly was referring to the fact that each member of the Agora ran their own organization. The written intention of these groups was to further the needs and desires of the clan. But some of their number used it to enrich themselves. Dolly wouldn't dare accuse her clan-sister of that, but she knew Yelina had dipped her toe in that pond already.

"No dear, but I am sure you do. What does your people know about them?"

Dolly lied almost by second nature. Hiding the facts and what she knew had long since become part of her cloak. The tit for tat questions went on like this, neither really believing the other but both respecting the other. Both were rivals, each loved the same man and each had children from him. Dolly had chosen her path long ago, but she wondered if Yelina had changed hers recently.

"That is a shame, it would be nice knowing how this other group of Grey survived all this time. What do you think their showing themselves now means?"

Dolly saw the look, subtitle and coy but still very obvious to her. Yelina was no fool, and she had to be deadly careful with what she told her "friend." She took her time composing the lie and delivered it with the same accustom skill she had grown used to. Dolly was moving through a deadly field of truth and lies with so many now. But there was an ending in sight, all her efforts and all her sacrifices wouldn't be for nothing. Still one misstep could cost her everything. Yelina ingested the lies and the small truths with equal measure. What she really thought about it, Yelina kept to herself. It was time to steer the topic back to Yelina's troubles. Something Dolly didn't mind discussing.

"You shouldn't fear too much for your young ones. I am sure Malcom will recover dear, he is so young and he is a good man. He has plenty of time to find his way."

Yelina's mask dropped for a moment and for a time it felt like to Dolly that they really were friends again. Dolly's feelings for her were not fake, but it was complicated.

Sao Paulo – Meridia

Jan 10th 2058

"Stupid girl, who gave you the authority to play with the Americano's? Do you have any clue how much trouble you have caused? Hum, do you even think before you act?"

Camila listened to her clanmate speak with distaste over her actions. She wasn't worried in the slightest. Luis wasn't a power in the clan, just someone useful as far as Camila was concerned. It was mothers' opinion that really mattered, not this lap dog of hers. Luis wasn't her father, even if he tried to play that role from time to time. Her father had been British and had died when she was a little girl. Camila often wondered what he would think of them? Did he know his "little baya" as he called her would grow into an immortal? Did he know about mother, probably not. Ignoring Luis was not wise so Camila put on as humble a face as possible before opening her mouth.

"I served the clan, how did I do otherwise? I found a Hermano right in my backyard. What was I supposed to do, just watch him? Had he accepted me we would have another to strengthen our family. How is that not what mother would want?"

Camila knew better already. A hurried text from mother made that clear enough. It had wrecked the plan mother had agreed to, and because of this nana wasn't happy. But Camila would be dammed if she let this little man see anything from her. Luis went on explaining the why, and how she had destroyed the plans that had taken years to put together.

"You were supposed to take the technical one, not the son of the bloody King!"

Camila was dressed differently than she had been for her previous guest. There was hardly a patch of skin showing for Luis. He had wondering eyes, and she felt sick each time they did. She moved away from the little man and back towards the couch where she had entertained Malcom.

Now there was a real grey man. Young, strong, and far more in his head than this fool. All of that plus he was virtuous and good looking?

She used a well-worn method to get her way with Luis next. She insulted him and made it visibly clear she found him distasteful. Without letting him a moment to respond she changed the subject.

"I believe you have instructions for me Luis, something mother wants me to do. How about we use our time to discuss that instead?"

Luis shook his head in barely contained rage and tossed down a tablet as he stormed out. That was a well-timed use of insolence on her part. She knew exactly how to manipulate Luis when she wanted him to leave. As she picked up the tablet, she had to shake off the shivers of having to speak to the man again. When she was younger and not yet skilled, she feared him. Camila knew the troll wanted her, and he barely hid it when she was younger. But once she received her gifts, and learned to use them… well.

I wish he would try some days… then I could be done with him.

Trying hard to forget him she paged through the images and notes. Then she saw the updates and she closed her eyes. Malcom had lost his honor; he was being sidelined. She sighed not feeling guilty for her actions, but more pity for him.

He was such a delectable man, something about him and that look he kept giving me…. Oh my…. That, well that was unexpected.

Mother had given her a new task. Something that would be pleasing, if she was able to do as asked. The next page had additional information not shared before. Some of which she found stunning. Still a new thought crept into her mind. An idea, so bold it may work. What she had tried with Malcom was just silly and thoughtless, but it revealed so much to her. Trying to seduce Malcom had shown her that her training was not in vain. When the time came if she chose to do as asked, she would be able to do so.

I wonder Hermano what it must be like for you to have a will of your own? A life… a career, clearly you are living as you wish. I wonder what that must feel like.

Camila wondered what it would be like to select her own mate, to forge her own life? The very thought was treasonous, and if her mother knew there would be dire consequences. But Camila didn't care, she yearned to be her own woman. Even if it meant she wouldn't be all the things promised to her.

She returned again to what mother wanted and the specifics of her ask. Mother always allowed Camila flexibility to achieve a goal. Not telling her how to do such a thing, only what she required. From the tone it was clear mother was dead serious about this. Still there was opportunity here, opportunity mother might not see. Perhaps a risk could be taken here? Mother and Nana were getting what they wanted, and Camila had her own wishes and dreams. In the coming centuries mother's attention would be on other things.

Yes…. perhaps it's time for me. And you Hermano… You are the perfect one to help me.

Medford, Texas – The Agoge

Jan 10th 2058

Roger watched as the boys lined up for battle again. They had done this time and time again today. Some were going to be excellent warriors. They had the skills and talent they needed. But far too few of those had the heart. A couple of those without skill had lions' hearts. Such was the way of things, rare was the man who came along with both. Their King had only produced a couple such boys, one with Susan and another with Yelina. Each fitting successors to the throne one day. A day Roger hoped would not be soon in coming. Their clan was still nowhere near as strong as they had once been. War and conflict two decades ago had nearly destroyed the clan. It would be a lifetime before the Grey were what they once were.

Still, in these boys that Roger trained, he saw potential. Some would make excellent warriors serving in assault teams or protection teams. Others like the red headed boy was destined to hide in the shadows as either a spy or recon warrior. All Grey longed to hide in the shadows, watching and waiting for the right moment to strike. That was their nature, and both their gift and curse. To be a warrior however took more than just instinct, it required a team effort. Men working together for a cause, selflessly and thoughtlessly. The thinking came before battle, but in battle…. It had to be second nature. For a man to think during battle was a death sentence.

As Roger watched he saw out of the corner of his vision the eldest boy of Yelina's walked up. He had graduated the Agoge over six years before and had been exactly what he thought he would be. An excellent recon soldier, just like his father was. The boy however had not followed what Roger thought was his true calling. He was young and thought too highly of himself. Not surprising out of the son of a king, and the grandchild of the Grey mother herself. He was the child of legends, and as such, much was expected. This meeting Roger reflected would not be pleasant. It had fallen to Roger to give him the news. He would do it as it was required of him, but it gave him no joy.

It's a shame boy; you would have made a great King.

The moment Malcom came close to him he stopped the battles and had the boys show Malcom the respect the young ones were due for their elders. Malcom may have fallen in the sight of the Agora, but he was still a man of honor. He turned to his pupils and with a guttural voice announced the arrival of a Hoplite. The boys pounded their chest with their right fists and in unison shouted their reply. Their combined voices carried a long way.

"AAALA"

Roger turned to the Hoplite approaching and saluted him with the spear he was carrying. A sign of respect for another warrior. Malcom clearly not himself said nothing but returned the salute. Seeing this Roger dismissed the assembled boys and urged them to their next task. Less they stand around and see the destruction of a man. As soon as the boys were gone Malcom spoke quietly.

"Reporting as ordered…. It's good to see you again master."

Roger bit his lip for a moment, surprised at the obvious signs of emotion.

"Yes son, I won't make you wait for it. The Agora have found you failed in your leadership. You have been stripped of your command, and will not receive another. BUT…. they have not found you guilty of Jason's actions. For that… they have found another."

At giving him the sentence Malcom's eyes closed in pain. It was a dishonor and a severe blow towards his rise to spartainate rank. It also meant he would never be the man Malcom thought he would be. Few men of this clan would not face disappointment at their fate. All Grey men thought themselves as indestructible, invincible. Each thought they were the next great warrior. It made them strong, and made their fellows strong. But eventually every man found the weakness living deep inside. Many found that weakness only after the Grey women had sunk their claws deeply into them. For others… time was their enemy. Malcom's age and his temperament made him unprepared for this. Something the old warrior knew well. It would hurt Malcom deeply even if the emotion wasn't clear on his face when it did. Roger knew the man who lived inside that boy. He knew it because he saw himself so clearly in him.

"Your next task has been chosen by the Agora son. You will become master of this school, replacing me. They want to make sure we do not repeat my mistake. To weed out from our ranks any Jason's, less they disgrace our people again."

Malcom looked up in confusion, the Agora had found Roger responsible for Jason. He was being forced to retire from active life in the clan. He would keep his house, and possibly his wife. But his purpose, and his honor was gone. His only real hope was after a long time in the shadows they would let him die in battle somewhere. But he would have to wait decades for that honor and privilege, if the Agora had any say.

"Master, I don't understand, how on earth is it your fault? Why blame you? It was my choice; he was my pick?"

Roger handed the astonished boy his spear, the badge of office he had carried since it had been given to him by Malcom's father. He hoped Malcom didn't see the emotion he felt at seeing that go from his grip. With that badge of office also went the honor and pride he had in himself.

"Because they are angry, and frightened. The two of us must bear this even if we do not wish to. In their eyes, I should have seen Jason's treachery here in the Agoge. Perhaps they are right, perhaps I could have seen it had I only looked. I am not sure how, the boy I knew was weak yes, but not a traitor. Few of our boys have his skill in technology, it's not our way. Perhaps I overlooked his weakness because of ours. That is why they are giving you this task. It's a way to redeem yourself son, and prevent another Jason from hurting the honor of us all."

What he didn't say was that it was far easier to destroy Roger than the King's son. While true it also wasn't the boy's fault. He had read the report, there was no seeing this. Jason had done what he had done for things the clan could not, and would not give him. In no other clan could he expect such a payment. And until now, no one knew another Grey family existed. None of this really mattered, it was done. His life and his honor were shattered and nothing either man could say or do would put it back together.

Roger wanted to leave, not to stand around thinking about his disgrace any longer. But the boy was confused and he needed his guidance. Before he could show emotion, Roger put the steel back into the boy. It was their way, and now more than ever, the boy would need it.

"You're a Grey son. You have been given your duty and you will follow it. Duty is life, and life is duty..... Did I not teach this to you?"

Malcom's eyes watered and he took the spear and looked at it for a moment. He seemed torn on what to do next, even if it was clear to both of them. The salute when it came, was exactly the response prescribed by custom. The thunderous sound of it slamming into his chest echoed in Rogers ears. Seeing it held so by a young man gave Roger pleasure. There could have been far worse men he could have been told to hand it to. At least it would be in good hands. Roger responded in the only way he could.

"I honor thee, who honors me"

Medford, Texas – Nancy's Home

Jan 10th 2058

Nancy was at home when the doorbell rang. She wasn't expecting anyone so that twinged her senses at once. Art and the rest of the family were out so it was just her. At one time Nancy had been the greatest power in this town. The founder of the city and the leader of the Aqua clan. But that wasn't the reality of today. Now Nancy was mostly retired, others led both the town and her clan. And that clan was thriving under her son-in-law Jay. It was such a weight lifted from her to know whenever happened next, her beloved clan would go on. A lifetime of desperately trying to save her clan from the dustbin of history was finally at an end.

As she walked up to the door, she wondered just who this could be and hoped it was her granddaughter, Maya. She was worried about her marriage and Nancy had been thinking about going out to see them to try to help. Talking and advising was mostly what she did now. Both her clan and others saw her as someone worthy of seeking out. It was both an honor and a curse to her. At one point she had been at the cutting edge of her clan and had led it. Now she was often an afterthought, other than a vampire wanting confirmation of something they had already decided. Her importance was now greatly diminished. Yet Nancy wouldn't change a thing, all things have endings and Nancy was content with hers. As she opened the door she was pleased to see who it was.

"Hi Nancy, do you have time to talk?"

This was Travis, who led the Grey clan as their King. Jay and Travis had once been young boys who looked at her for guidance after the death of their human mother. They were young and vulnerable and they needed her then. Both were now pushing 50 and had their own grandchildren now. But that didn't matter, both boys still came to her when they needed to. Unlike the others when Travis came to her it was generally serious. He never just asked to confirm something, for Travis she was his "Brehon" an old word that meant advisor. It wasn't just an honorary title; she served a role in the Grey clan and had been allowed to see many private Grey matters. She was an honorary member of that clan now. She had been told she was highly respected by many among them…even if she doubted it.

He crossed two fingers and laid them on his hand. It was his way of telling her that this was private. A quiet sign between them less other hidden Grey know. So, she led him to the couch and when he was ready put him into the link. A skill her Aqua clan had and was known for. In this link only they could hear and see what was going on.

"Thank you, Nancy, I am considering ruling against the Agora. My heart wants to, but my mind says it's a bad decision. In any case I believe they are wrong in their judgement. I need to know your thoughts."

Nancy was surprised; in their clan the Agora was nearly an equal branch of their government to Travis's Kingship. The Agora could judge Grey members and render verdicts. They could ask the King to do things, and they held the keys to all funds among the clan. The men however served Travis, and nearly all of them worked directly for him in his PMC. The Grey had never really found the right balance of power between both, and at times it caused friction. But never in all this time had Nancy known him to consider violating their finding. It was a serious step in destabilizing their clan.

As Brehon she had access to anything she wished, thus Travis allowed her to search his mind and memories. The Agora had rendered a verdict against his son Malcom and several others over this traitor business. Travis felt it was too heavy handed and it was going to ruin his son's path to becoming his own man. But this Agora had both his wives, and Cassia behind it. Travis going against that will was nye impossible. Not without destroying his throne or their authority.

Nancy considered what he had been pondering the last couple days and saw the dangers. As a mother she had known the pangs of helplessness a parent feels when things go wrong for their children. But as a leader of both a town and a clan she had made very hard decisions. Going so far to choose her towns needs over her sons when she gauged her son too weak to help.

Thank God I was wrong on that... Poor Buck.

That decision had cost Nancy a great deal. The cold calculus of the moment however for Travis was that while the Agora's decision was not just, the blowback for confronting them was too high. Nancy didn't have to express her thoughts into words. In this place Travis could both feel and hear them as they occurred.

"I know I keep thinking that too. But if it's the right decision, shouldn't I do what's right? If I let the Agora run over Grey after Grey like this, then what use is a King?"

Nancy smiled and again marveled at their strong moral nature of both of these boys. Travis and Jay cared about their people; it wasn't just for show.

Their hearts bled for their people and you didn't have to be inside the link to know that. He was upset over Malcom but if it was just him, he wouldn't act. It was what they were doing to the former master of the Agoge and that poor woman they had evicted that was pushing him to consider unprecedented action. Nancy smiled for him and again was pleased with the man he had become. Cassia may be a strange woman but she had somehow raised two amazing boys. At thinking of Cassia, Travis grew upset.

"Cassia isn't my mother; she died long ago. I don't know this woman, Nancy. Honestly at times I feel like you are more a mother to me than she is."

That hurt Nancy, to have a son disown his own mother was harsh. It was a terrible reality for any woman who loved their children. But she understood why he would say that. Travis had been a child when Cynthia, his birth mother, had died. Time and the odd nature of this town had returned that being back to the land of the living, but in a twisted way. Cynthia was no mere human; she had been the consort to a visitor. This woman had many names and she had lived many times over the 4000 years vampires had walked this earth. Cassia was just the latest version of this woman and unlike all the other times had ALL her memories now. In all this however what was lost was the human woman who had raised those boys, and the immortal woman with strong aspirations for her adult sons. This new version of her had not connected with them. Travis wasn't alone in feeling this way. Jay had let slip in the link to Nancy how he no longer saw her as his mother either.

"I know she means well, I know she loves me. But I can't see my mom in all this? I hear her voice and I see her face but it's not really the same woman. It doesn't make any of this any easier. The things she and Yelina said to Malcom… I want to intervene and I think I should be based on the needs of my people. But if I destroy the only check on my power. Do I become a tyrant, that same one you feared I would become?"

Nancy smiled and sat next to him in her vision and put her arm around him. She had feared both boys becoming Kings because such things were outdated. Not to mention history had taught her just how power corrupted men. Nancy had over 1000 years of living history to know it to be so. But time had proven her wrong with both boys. Each had stout hearts and good women around them. Jay had her daughter Hanna to advise and love him. Travis had three such women around him and he leaned heavily on all three. But unlike Jay's situation, Travis was trying to somehow balance serial marriages between these women, and largely failing. If he challenged the Agora, he was really challenging his wives and his own mother.

"Travis your heart as always is right where it should be. But sometimes a leader has to sacrifice what one person needs for what the group needs. I agree the Agora is acting rashly, perhaps you can reverse this in time. But if you confront the Agora, you must do so with the knowledge you seek its death… and nothing short of that."

Travis was quiet listening now to the small bits and challenges that passed between them. In the end Travis came to his decision Nancy knew he would. In the link she felt his dissatisfaction, feeling worse rather than better. A good sign in a leader, he wanted better but had to settle for good. Next, he questioned himself and his rightness for leadership. Nancy knew that was coming and was ready.

"I willingly bent my knee to your brother years ago, and I haven't regretted it once. You are just like him son, both of you are rare and precious. I trust you, your children trust you…. Trust in yourself Travis."

Chapter 6: Rabbit Hole

Medford, Texas – Cassia's Office

Jan 11ᵗʰ 2058

Rick had been traveling with this band of warriors for days. In all that time however he still hadn't figured out if he had made the right decision. He had messaged his wife and let her know he was fine and even checked in with his old employer. His company informed him of his termination but oddly enough they did so with unusual care and concern for his welfare. Six months' salary plus the bonus that had been promised him when he signed on. The fact he wasn't fired for cause was a shock. But to get his bonus? His family would be living on that until he could figure out what in hell was going on. As of now he had no clue how to answer that question. Or what to tell his wife for the future. He didn't know these people, or understand exactly what they wanted from him. Nor had they explained anything about how they were able to do what they were able to clearly do. Disappear and reappear out of thin air, who does that?

The news had said nothing of his old boss. Other than a notice of his death due to a heart attack buried deep on the company website. What went down in Mexico was passing as quiet as a mouse. Rick knew better, his old boss and the whole team had been killed by these men. No way in hell he died of a heart attack.

Question is what in hell do they want from me? They know my age, its not like I am a young buck anymore. Why the interest, my back is broke, my knees are shot... Something doesn't add up here?

Rick had left the marines after only a year of service. Doing most of his time in uniform with the Army after he recovered from a bad injury in war. Past fifty Rick was winding down his life not ramping it up. Why did an elite force like these men, want of him?   One look at how they operated spoke volumes. All were young, in the prime of their lives and in peak physical form. They were disciplined like veterans, not like the children they actually were.

This Jacob fellow had proven to be every bit the child he suspected he was. He was only 22 and only a single year removed from his own military service. He had learned that much on the plane.

Dude is young, like baby young, yet so laser focused?

It astounded Rick, and a part of him wished he could be young again. In the 72 hours he had spent with them he had traveled to three countries and witnessed this "Moonstone" in operation. They had multiple teams including this "Theta Team" he had met in Mexico. Jacob and his team were good, and could run rings around him. The day they had returned to the States they had taken him out on a 14 mile "break in" as they called it. To see what kind of man he was.

Rick had thought them joking since this team had been deployed twice in the span of two weeks. But true to his word the 24 or so men of the team and Rick went on a run with full equipment. Thankfully he was allowed to run in comfortable clothing. All of the others however had over 150 pounds of equipment and gear strapped to them. He felt like he was cheating running with them in sweats and comfortable shoes. But 15 miles, at his age and against these kids? He was ready for them to shoot him after only five. Yet these boys had run without any sign of fatigue.

Whoever they were, these kids were on another level. He had worked with special forces before, but these kids….. something wasn't right with them. Later that night he had watched the team train on hand to hand. Some of the moves they made defied logic, some hands and feet moved faster than his ability to keep track. And yet… somehow these kids seemed untaxed, and ready for more. The one thing that he was used to and appreciated was the camaraderie. That he could identify with thanks to his own time in the service. It was clear these men all trusted each other. They teased and they taunted each other but the looks said a lot.

"Rick if you don't mind waiting here, someone will be with you shortly."

Rick nodded to the pretty young woman who had escorted him alone to a building in this small Texas town. He had heard of it before, an old acquaintance from the war had come from here.

Medford, Texas…. Sleepy… Old…and way too quiet for me.

It was smallish when compared to his home in Virginia. But that name, Medford. Now that brought back memories. Rick, Bobby, Jack, Hunter, Kip and Travis all had been in 2-man recon teams training together. All had deployed to war decades ago. As far as Rick knew he had been the only one to come home. Two of those guys had come from this place, Rick wondered if they still had family here. He had barely thought about them in the decades that had gone by. Mostly because of how Hunter died. Pushing that war back into the distant past, Rick stood looking at the small office he had been escorted into.

Whoever had this office it had to be a woman. Lots of pictures of kids, and then what looked like grandkids. Many of them were in uniform. Rick recognized that Jacob kid in several of the photos. Whoever this kid was he had to be family. Everything was ordered and neat, and then that symbol he had seen before. A grey circle with a Greek symbol at its center.

"It's not an A young man, its Greek for Lambda. That symbol has been used by armies for centuries."

The voice was female and odd in that it sounded young. When Rick turned, he was right, the speaker was indeed very young, but she spoke like she wasn't. It was all in the tone and the words she used. Spaced out, almost tired sounding like she was ready for a long nap. Then he noticed the way she carried herself and how she was dressed. They way she walked made him think of his grandmother not the young woman who walked in. She was confident, but not sexual. As if she knew herself completely and had nothing to prove to anyone. Her demeanor screamed intelligent, but full of herself. She wasn't that good looking, probably money Rick thought. She wore a simple piece of cloth with gold trim. But it was the eyes that most shook him. They were strong and piercing. Like she was looking past him to the image on the wall.

"What you see there is the logo for Moonstone. Welcome to Medford Rick, I hope my children have treated you well?"

She moved with ease past him towards her seat. Rick marveled at her, the cloth was not fully opaque and you could see all of her if you looked close enough.

"You must have many questions after spending days with my children. They are not what you are used to are they?"

Your children?....Lady you aren't more than 25, if those are your children I want to buy whatever your selling.

Again, she had called them her children. That seemed a bit creepy but some PMC's tried all sorts of stupid shit to keep people. Perhaps this chick had some sort of weird thing going calling all her employee's children, it didn't matter. Rick was ready to check out and go home. By this point he was pretty sure all those threats Jacob had given him were bogus.

"I have been treated well; I am afraid I didn't catch your name... you are?"

She smiled and asked him to sit which Rick did. He had never seen such a young woman act like she was 60 before. It was almost comical. Actually, it was if you considering what she was wearing. He had to stop himself from laughing at how weird these people truly were.

"Rick my son believes you are a good fit for us. Looking at your record I have to agree."

She had not answered his question, just went right into her sales pitch. She pulled a file from a filing cabinet. Something right out of an old movie, it was so strange he asked without thinking. She looked up, not expecting the question and explained that she didn't like computers. Rick didn't bother hiding his amusement this time. Talk about an old soul in a young body.

"Recon Marine 2033-2034, hurt in a helo crash off Taiwan. Fairly bad crash from the looks of it, the Marines gave you a medical discharge."

She looked up at him seeing his amusement and looked back down at the file.

"Somehow you managed to con the Army into thinking you were fully fit. I wonder how you did that?"

Rick remembered what it required, a favor from an old girlfriend who worked in MEPS. It was a time of war and most services were happy to take someone with his level of training. Most didn't ask too many questions when the Doc's signed off. Thankfully he never saw any before he joined the Army.

"Served with the 101st and did 2 combat jumps. Several commendations including a bronze star. Impressive career Rick, it's too bad your injuries caught up with you. You almost got your 20 in."

Rick frowned at that, after the war he had left the Airborne and became a trainer. He managed to keep that work for nearly a decade before medical figured out, he had a screwed up back. Only five years away from a pension he had to reinvent himself. Since then, not much had gone his way. As the woman spoke Rick could hear the doubt in her voice.

"Yes, I can see why my son likes you. But joining us is not for everyone Rick. Do you understand what kind of commitment it requires?"

He had long since decided to say thanks but no thanks to the offer and go home. He explained himself to her and thanked them for getting him out of a jam. Her face changed just a twitch, before she sent a cold feeling down his spine.

"We didn't threaten your old company, and bribe a foreign government just as a favor RICK. We spent those resources and took those risks because we believe you are worthy of joining us. I know Jacob explained the situation; you accepted his offer. Are you saying you don't want to join us now?"

It was creepy and there was something ominous in her stare. Lots of people try to be intimidating, that isn't anything new. But after you lived long enough you got the sense on who was faking it and who meant it. Just something about the way, she spoke, and how she looked at him. Serious as a heart attack, and without remorse or concern. This woman had killed before, and more than once if Rick had to guess. That realization and his own growing concern from whom this woman was, finally took hold of his judgement.

"Look I don't know who you people are. I get it you are serious. But I don't just pledge my soul to someone I just met. If you want me to sign up for your little cult, then you are going to have to convince me. You sure as shit aren't going to intimidate me into joining."

The smile on her face was immense and she stood and moved to sit next to him. As she sat, he could see all of her through that dress.

Just what did this freak want now?

"Take my hand"

Rick took it quickly and was going to quip some sort of rebuke when the room and everything in it disappeared. Rick wasn't sure what happened, he felt terror in the short moments he was still conscious.

Medford, Texas – Agoge

Jan 11th 2058

Jessie was focused she had some time before her own trials would begin, the least she could do was help her brother with his. Of her brothers she always liked Malcom more. He could be a pain sometimes, trying to be her dad more than her brother. But when it really mattered Malcom was always there for her. A few times he had taken the blame for things she had done. Jacob loved her and she liked him too, but it was different. She couldn't trust him like she could Malcom.

The sounds of combat were loud. Grunts and small shouts of anger. Malcom had them in hand to hand drills this morning. She was here to check up on him and find out why he had not come home last night. Malcom was home now, and as a Hoplite he was still mothers' property. His home and his place was under her roof. Mother was pissed at his insolence but she was also hurt. Mother was spartan in her heart and soul, but she was still a woman. She loved Malcom and it hurt her that he had not come to her.

"Woman you can't be here!"

Jessie was so happy the boy had called her that. He was around 14 and tried to use his newfound vampiric strength to put his hands on her. She responded like any good Grey woman would. She disarmed him in an instant and shoved him hard sending him off his feet. The next boy posted as a sentry was much older, at least 16 or 17 and he wasn't going down as easy as his friend. Or so he thought anyway...

It took three moves instead of one but the beast of a boy was cut down. She used his own size and girth to propel herself over his head, landing on her feet. As a woman she was dressed in the simple cloth peplos of her people. It was open and allowed her skin to easily breathe in a place like Texas. Even in January it could get warm sometimes. Her clothing wasn't restrictive like the boys was. Many of them wore armored leather bits to shield from blows from the staffs they were using.

Now seeing this for the test that it was, the boys closest to her entered the fray with an intensity. Jessie was far more ready than they. Most of them were pulling their punches, where she wasn't. One of the young boys managed to land a fierce strike to her face which enraged her. That boy nearly flew from the kick she landed. Another boy she kicked hard in the chest, he doubled over like a piece of paper. Avoiding another boy's punch, she rolled and used the one boys folded body as a weapon against the others. Using her motion and vampiric strength, Jessie took ahold of his hands and lept with all her might. It was enough that it sent the folded boy airborne and like a bowling ball collided with two boys moving in close. Then she saw a shape fly towards her in her peripheral vision. She reacted like the warrior she was at heart. She withdrew from the attack that was incoming and pivoted to deal whoever attempted it a fierce blow. But instead of landing on unprepared flesh it felt like it hit stone. Turning to see what had absorbed her strongest punch she found Malcom had simply grabbed it and had ahold of her arm now. Before her mind could warn her of what was to come, she felt herself be tossed into the air, far from where she had been before. She caught enough air that it gave her time to right herself to land. It wasn't graceful and most of her lower section was showing to the boys. But she was in a position to resist if anyone came to continue the fight.

Jessie smiled at the sight before her. In the few seconds since her attack, she saw at least five boys her age with bloody faces and egos that were wrecked. Malcom stood there dressed only in shorts and sandals with a long spear. When one of the boys started to move to attack her, he stopped him.

"Battle can come from any angle, any direction. Never underestimate your opponent. You saw a girl and held back your strength…. did she? She bested some of the strongest here, take that lesson to heart boys. Even the strongest among you can be beaten by the weakest. You must work as a team, not as individuals. Had you done so, she wouldn't have gotten past the gate."

Jessie stood tall, and moved her peplos so it covered her properly again. As a grey she was not afraid of her sexuality nor letting others take a peek at her. Jessie walked up to her brother and with an impudent look asked just who he was calling the weakest? She took pride in the looks she was getting. Both those angry at being bested by her, and those that desired her for other reasons. Malcom ordered the gate guards back to their posts and then ordered the assembled to go to their rest cycles. What that meant, Jessie had no clue, as a woman she wasn't allowed in the Agoge. Which was one of the reasons why she had decided to come.

"Nathan is going to want revenge for that slash on his face you gave him. I would watch your back for a few days if I was you."

Jessie looked back at the boy in question who was one that had been looking at her with anger and resentment. She just smiled for him, just to rub it in a bit.

"Sis what are you doing here, you know the Agoge is off limits."

Jessie had secretly wanted to train with the Agoge all her life. She had damn near twisted her other brothers arm off to get him to help train her. She knew she could fight, like a lioness she could. Today was about proving that and her worth to her family. But it was also to be here for Malcom. She knew what he had to be going through.

"Mom sent me, you know why don't you?"

A moment or two later she was in his office. A small room with a single window that looked out on the training field. Malcom put the spear in the corner and put back on the small cloth covering that served as the only clothing he was permitted other than his shorts and sandals. That she had heard about and like she had imagined, made him look rather silly. Malcom was fit and a true warrior yes, but he didn't look like those Spartans in the movies. He lacked the massive abbs and oiled physique.

"I needed to get things in order here first. If this is to be my duty then I must have it in order, do I not?"

Jessie knew sulking and this was clearly that. The Agoge had run with little change in 20 years. Or at least that was what father had said. What could possibly be keeping him here other than a hurt pride?

"What of your duty to us? Isn't attending our mother your first duty? I am to inform you that mother demands your presence today no later than 7pm. Father is adopting a new son tonight into the family and we are to be there to welcome our new brother. Even if he is as old as dad is."

That got his attention, father had never adopted a grown adult man before. This would mean a change in their station. Jessie desperately wanted to partake in that, a battle to see which son was better. The winner of that fight would be fathers' choice for prostatis, "protector of the house". It was a place of honor that Malcom held. A position he and Jacob had fought for two days over. That battle would now have to happen all over again. Jessie with her heart and soul consumed by her calling desired so much to take part. She knew she could take Jacob, and a part of her believed she could Malcom as well.

"Fine, tell mother I will be there."

He looked at her and a moment later started to laugh. He was amused at her antics, something else she had expected. Now was the right time to ask for what she wanted.

"So, since I am here and all, I would like to train some. I believe I have earned the right. Your defenses were a joke, was I your enemy I would have gotten into the heart of the Agoge with little effort. I think in honor of my achievement I should be allowed to train today."

Malcom roared in laughter and tossed the cloth back off of him and on to the small desk he had. Standing and taking the spear he was moving about animated now. Amused that she thought she could handle such a place.

"You caught them by surprise, next time they will curb stomp you. That pretty face of yours will be full of scars. Besides I can't have you making love behind the barracks with the first boy you take an interest in."

She was offended by his assertions but she knew he wasn't wrong. Part of the reason why she wanted to train was to see which of the boys her age would be one she would desire to have for herself. One day she would have her own house and it would be expected that she would pick among her peers which would father her children. Mother had done this with father, as did all Grey women. Men might think they were selecting or choosing, but they did nothing of the sort. The real power behind the clan were the women. It was they, not any of them, not even father, who really led the clan.

Malcom took a breath and now serious looked at her with something she had rarely seen, defeat. At seeing that her love for him made her want to rush to his side and comfort him. But that wasn't their kind of relationship.

"You know if you are going to wear that… you should get some actual muscle… like any."

They were siblings and they teased far more than they supported. At hearing that he brightened and taunted back a bit. He was sad, she could see that clear enough.

Fine…you want me to be your mother than I will.

"You know if you want to talk about it, I can listen."

She wanted to say more, encourage him to lay it out there. It's what she did when she hit the wall in this strange life they led. But Malcom was a man, and he could not. So, she changed her request just a bit to encourage it.

"It's not because I want to hear your problems or anything, God no. I just figure if you tell me what is going on then I will have more information I can use against you later."

He smirked and put both hands on the spear, his badge of office. He looked ridiculous standing there, like a dollar store version of Gerard Butler. But a moment later he began to open up to her. Like he always did after a bit of nudging. The reality of his fall was starting to sink in. He wasn't a child about it; he accepted that he had failed. Which Jessie knew he had from talking to mom. But the way they treated him in the Agora wasn't right. He deserved to be respected and they had treated him like something not worthy of it. Malcom went on for a bit explaining his new job, and how it suited him. He was trying to make this change something positive. But Jessie knew better, he was devastated that his own mother and grandmother had spoken to him without honor. In all the years she had known him she had never seen him take something this bad. Granted he hadn't faced something this serious before.

"As you can see, I am fine sis, I have my duty now and it's going to be fine.   No need to concern yourself on me."

She taunted him saying she never did in the first place.   But that was a lie both knew it to be.   Just like she knew what he had just said was all for show as well.   Malcom was hurting and crushed by what they had done.   No hug and smiles would fix this.   Everything Malcom had come to expect in life had been taken away, and she was worried how he would respond.

Medford, Texas – Cassia's Office

Jan 11ᵗʰ 2058

Travis saw him knocked out in Cassia's chair.   He closed the door and smiled to himself.   Long ago they had been friends, both going through the Recon course.   All of those guys had bonded over what they knew they were training for.   Their instructors had been brutal in how they trained them.   But for good cause, they had also been honest with how many of them they expected to return.   They had predicted half their number would die in the war that at that time, was just getting underway.   They weren't far wrong, by the end of the war only Rick and Travis were still breathing.   All the other guys were at the bottom of the South China Sea or buried in Taiwan or here in Medford.

His friend had never known what he really was.   Back then he was just a kid who wanted to serve.   For Rick it was visiting his recruiter, a far simpler one than Travis had taken.   For him it required his life to be forever altered, his will was taken away from him.   Travis laughed, while different their path wasn't really that much so.   Both had gone to war, both had their will subverted and both had faced terrible risk and carried the scars.   Only one of them was human and the other immortal.   Past that much of their experience back then was the same.   Grinning, he remembered how difficult Rick had made things for him in training and got a small bit of revenge now.

You have no idea my friend, none at all.   Well, its time to change that.   Hopefully you will see reason.   I need someone I can trust right now.

Travis kicked the chair Rick was sitting in hard, causing him to jerk awake.   There had been a time when he knew him before, that Rick would have reacted angrily to this.   Now Rick barely moved.   His youth was gone, and time had not been kind to him.   Rick only turned and looked with fear at who had disturbed his sleep. That nearly shocked Travis, in his mind Rick was this unstoppable warrior with a heart to match. What he saw now was someone else, not the marine he had known.

"Good morning sunshine, do you army types always like sleeping in the middle of the day?"

Rick was alert but he didn't recognize Travis at first. It had been two decades since they last saw each other. Travis had to remind him which made Rick's jaw drop.

"Didn't you die on some island...Isagaki or something? I thought you were dead man?"

Travis just grinned and Rick got up and took his outstretched hand. Since they were alone and the door was shut, he pulled Rick into a hug. Just like Rick, he had thought his friend long dead as well. When Yelina came to him with this job it had shook him to his core. He wasn't going to let his old friend die protecting a dirtbag. After the quick hug Rick commented on how ugly he was as an old man.

"I don't know if you know this Rick but you were fucking ugly when you were young. You haven't gotten any prettier..."

To the outside observer these two might be being course. Some who knew men better might think it was friendship. But for men like them it was something else. Both men had genuinely but quietly mourned the other. Seeing each other again brought out more emotions than they wished anyone to see. But as men, this only went so far. Travis moved to go behind the desk and talk business. Rick remembering where he was and what happened started to put two and two together.

"So, this is your thing, Trav? This isn't some sort of joke, is it?"

Travis smiled and told him honestly why things had gone down this way. Travis wanted to recruit him.

"What happened to the girl is she ok?"

Travis shook his head and filled in his friend what he had been doing the last couple of days. With the help of a few of Medford's best they had delivered the girl back home. Sophia an Emerald, had tagged along making sure the girl was physically healthy while getting a feel for her mental state. That damage would never be undone, but with help, and a lot of love she might build a life for herself one day.

"So, what was with that chick that was in here earlier. Did she give me something, because I don't normally pass out without drinking first."

Travis laughed and explained that the woman in question was his mother and that she had used her ability on him. Travis knew that would cause more questions; Cassia was physically less than half his age now. He could see the confusion grow so he cut to the chase.

"I know you spent time with my boy and his team. You have eyes, nothing is as it seems here, is it?"

That cut right to the bone and shut down the questions fast. For a human this place was a Disneyland of strange. A moment later Cassia came back into the room still dressed as before.

"We have a lot to cover here my friend and my mom has a very efficient way to get you up to speed. But it requires you to be still and open minded. Cassia is going to touch you again and link with you. She is going to show you visions and let you see just what we are and what we are offering you."

Rick was a quiet for a second looking between Cassia and Travis. Then he seemed to come to a decision and asked directly just what they were.

"We are vampires, my mother here has lived for over 4000 years, and will probably live for another 40,000 if she has her way. Those kids you have been running around with are all vampires. They can out run and out lift any marine you ever met. And if you agree to it, so will you."

Medford, Texas – Yelina's Home

Jan 11th 2058

Rick was still trying to process everything that he had been shown. It was a lot to take in, his friend was a fricking vampire. He had met his mother who looked like she was 20 but clearly wasn't. And through this link that Travis called it, he had seen so much. Abilities and skills Rick could only dream of. And all of these "Grey" had those abilities and more. He was being offered the chance to join them. Become a vampire like them, he would become young again and fit again.

Serious honest to God vampires… If I hadn't been in that link I wouldn't have believed it. I am still not sure I believe it. But damn, how do you explain those kids? Trav isn't wrong the way those kids were acting the other day… none of us could have done that. Whatever is going on, vampire or no its not normal.

Rick thought more about their offer. It was appealing, to be young healthy again. Not to mention steady employment with someone he knew. But there was a catch, a massive one. Like any vampire in the movies, he would have to prey on others. That he was both ok with, and not ok with. Thankfully he didn't have to choose today. But what of that boy's warnings? If he said no, would his friend take his life? If he had to guess the answer to that was yes. A part of Rick didn't blame him, if he was King of a group of vampires, he would want to keep it secret too. Just having that thought made Rick laugh out loud.

"What is so funny, I know my pasta isn't the best but…"

Rick quickly made his apology to his host, this Russian woman who was Travis's wife was looking at him with concern.

"No, I was just thinking about all the things I learned today. It's just a lot to take in, I guess. My friend is a King over a vampire clan. I don't think I had that on my bingo card."

Yelina smiled and passed down another beer. Something he was glad for.

"Every human says something like that at first. But our lives can be ordinary too. Most folks only see the things we gain. But they forget we still have to live. Our lives are more alike than you might suspect Rick. We still have to find someone to share our lives with, and a purpose for our abilities. My children here are finding this out now. Each is facing their own challenges, and being a vampire doesn't help does it children?"

Rick looked around the table and saw the mixed reaction to their mother's comment. One son, the eldest, was clearly upset at being here. Each time his mother spoke he saw that spark in his eyes. There was a serious beef between him and his mother. Meanwhile the other son, Jacob apparently was equally upset at attending. But his beef seemed to be with Rick. Why that was, he could only guess, perhaps he didn't like a black man sitting at his table who knows. The only one of her children to respond was the teenager. That one had trouble written all over her. Rick was afraid to even look in her general direction.

"I think all of us are more than ready for it. Jacob is proving himself in his team, and Malcom is doing wonders with his students. I know I was very impressed with their combat capabilities."

Travis cut in and asked just how she would know such a thing. A part of Rick knew where this was going, she had that look on her face, the one a cat has when they have the bird right where they want it.

"I tested them myself dad. The first time I attacked I easily got through. But after Malcom got them to work together, I had a much harder time defeating any of them. I still did, but it wasn't as easy the second time."

Rick smiled and tried to picture what hand to hand combat looked like for vampires. Meanwhile the teen was asked just how in hell she had gotten inside the Agoge. That was yet another Greek word that he was trying to figure out. From the way they talked it sounded like a basic training unit. Looking at how Travis's PMC operated and just who staffed it, he wouldn't be shocked.

"Jessie you're a woman, it's not proper for you to be there. What if Malcom wasn't there, can you imagine what could happen to you?"

Rick closed his eyes seeing before the others at the table just what the teen thought of that challenge. She made it clear in her response she would welcome the combat, but it wasn't just that. Rick could guess she wasn't exactly green when it came to sex either. That girl of Travis was more than a handful; she was a grenade with the pin pulled and the spool long gone.

After the back and forth of the dinner, and after the kids left it was time for some honest talk. Rick and Travis made their way to a side room where they could have a few beers and privacy. Rick liked Travis and his family, but he wasn't the same man he was two decades ago. That old version of him would have taken Travis up on the offer back then. But now… no way in hell. Life had changed him and he couldn't be that version of himself ever again. You can't go back in time, at least normal people couldn't. He didn't waste time in explaining that to Travis.

"Look Trav I appreciate everything you have done for me. You getting me that money and covering my butt means a lot to me. But a lot has changed man. I am not that punk kid that thought he could go anywhere and do anything. That little swim taught me that. I thought we were so invincible, and look at us now? You might be, with what you are, but me… Man even if you turn back the clock, I am still me. No way I would do half the things I did before…you follow me?"

Travis looked sad and it worried Rick, wondering if they would carry out the threat they had given him. To ease things a bit he asked about that kid that hung around him when they were training. Bobby had been from Medford too and looked up to Travis the whole time. He knew they deployed together, and like the others he had no idea what his fate was. Clearly, he was gone, but Rick wanted to know how. Travis smiled a bit on mention of his name.

"We were on Ishigaki together and it was hairy shit, but we made it out. After that we went our own ways and he joined up with another group of vampires. They died a few months later when the Red's overran their position. Every last one of them. I brought him home to his momma and his clan. I would wager you know a good number of the guys lying next to him up in Woodlawn. God knows I do."

Rick hearing that bit made it clear he had probably served with more than just them during his time over there. In a strange way it was a bit comforting to know that in the end, vampires were just as vulnerable as humans were. Rick shared a bit about some of his losses and then got back to letting down his friend gently.

"Look man I respect what you have going, but I am not that man anymore. I left all that behind a long time ago. Your boy told me there was no going back, but that is what I want brother. I got kids and a life, even if it isn't super amazing like yours. It's mine brother, and I want to live it you understand? The only reason I still do this crap is because it's the only thing I know. If I could teach, or fix cars, I would do that. God knows I never want to be what we were."

Travis looked at him hard and then took a long pull from his beer.

"Yeah, I dig it, Rick. What about us, can you keep a secret as big as this one?"

Rick didn't think anyone would believe him if he did, but he needed and wanted to leave.

"You know me man. Who am I going to tell. It's just my old lady and my boy. The only thing they care about is that the check doesn't bounce. They don't want to know what I do."

After a few moments Travis sighed and shook his head yes. It was quiet for a bit. Rick almost thought twice about it. But going back to that old life wasn't for him. Even if he could be …whatever they were. When Travis spoke, it worried him a little.

"I get it, after I got out, I didn't think I would ever be this again. But it's the call of my people, I can't seem to ignore it. You are free to go Rick. I will have my aviation guys get you back to Lynchburg. But before you go, I think there is one last thing I can do to help you, do you mind staying another day?"

Chapter 7: Mistakes were made

Medford, Texas – Agoge

Jan 12th 2058

Rick sent a text to his wife letting her know when he would be back. Things had not always been great between them but the bonus money was going to help with that. She could finally have a bit to spend on some things around the house she had complained about. Later tomorrow he would be driven out to a small airfield not far from Medford where one of those ancient Blackhawks would fly him home. Then he would have time to think about the future. Then and only then could he process all of…. this.

"When you and dad trained how physical did it get, you ever knock him on his ass?"

Rick laughed at Jacob's question as they walked down a small path. They were heading out to the Agoge which Rick now understood meant "school" in Greek. He thought about the question and the change in demeanor in Jacob. Ever since last night he had a beef with him. Yet before Jacob had been warm, accepting, and encouraging. On this walk from town this was the first thing out of his mouth. His bad knees and back were screaming but he kept his cool, it didn't look like they had much further to go. He considered the question and smiled at the memories. War wasn't what he thought of now, it was him and his friends and the bonds they formed.

"Sometimes, but your dad was tough. I never got one over on him more than once, he learns quick. Mostly it was our instructors grinding us. Your dad always seemed to have another gear. I guess now I know why. He could tap into being a vampire to push through. Would have been nice for the rest of us, that course was a cast iron bitch."

Rick paused only a moment and then asked what he wanted to ask. He was curious what had changed in the boy.

"How about you tell me what I did to piss you off."

Jacob didn't respond but got quiet again. Just as they rounded a bend on the road, he saw the Agoge, all of the kids were dressed like Jacob. And "dress" was about right on how to describe what he was wearing. Jacob was dressed in some sort of costume as far as Rick could tell. Travis and his people practiced Spartan cultural life. Something Travis's wife had explained at dinner. Rick shook his head at the stubborn nature of Jacob and turned his mind to what was before him.

As they passed by the sentinels one boy went running towards the larger group. Probably announcing their arrival. That was when he saw Malcom, Travis's other son. He was naked except for trunks and sandals. He carried a huge spear which Rick found comical. These kids were playing as ancient soldiers. If it wasn't for what he had seen earlier he wouldn't think highly of them. Still, he couldn't help but be amused.

Malcom shouted something, then he shifted his spear which he was holding parallel to himself to a diagonal across his chest. When Jacob and him were close enough he saw Jacob return what looked like a salute and then a huge chorus of shouts from the boys in unison. None of this impressed Rick, if they were filming some classical movie sure, but these kids were training for war.

"Welcome to the Agoge Rick, what do you think?"

Malcom seemed more welcoming than his brother so he put a small smile on his own face and looked around quickly stopping when he saw the looks on the faces of the boys. Some were bruised and battered, one had blood coming down his face. Rick asked if that one needed medical attention.

"No, we have rest cycles for them to clean themselves up and heal any major injuries. Trust me they are fine."

That was when Jacob cut in and informed Malcom that their dad wanted him to introduce him to Calvin. And with that the three of them started walking the dusty ground of the Agoge. All around them were young men of various ages. Some as young as 10 some as old as 17 or 18. Without asking Malcom started to explain the different training exercises they were running. That got Rick curious and he asked where all these boys came from, whey they all vampires? Malcom answered as Jacob continued to quietly stew in anger.

"Very few are actually. All Grey families submit their boys here when they turn 10. They stay until they fail or they meet their final test. By then they are vampires, the few vampires here are mostly trainers."

He was led to a hut where a young man was talking to a young boy who was trying to hide the tears.

"Calvin, what happened to the boy?"

Calvin whispered to the boy who ran away from the adults. That troubled Rick, it looked like these boys were being abused, certainly what they were doing wasn't kind. He was sure it made good warriors, but what about the men inside those calluses?

"Broken arm, but its right as rain now."

Rick nearly did a spit take at that remark, if his arm was broken, he needed to be taken to the ER not sent back to training. Instead, both of Travis's sons dismissed it immediately and left him to Calvin.

"So welcome to my body and fender shop Mr. Rick. Boss man says you need some tuning, sit here and let me give you a once over. Check your oil and make sure your spark plugs still work."

Rick nearly snarled at him until Calvin explained himself. The boy's arm was indeed healed; Rick still didn't like it or believe it.

"Come on man I heal people for a living, boss man says you are dinged up, and he wants me to see if we can help. Sit down and let me examine you. I promise I am better than any doc you have ever met before."

Rick shook his head and against his better judgement and sat down. Best doc he ever met was the one that gave him morphine and didn't ask any questions. The moment he sat Calvin started to do whatever it was he did.

"Wow that's impressive SCI; you try to French kiss a car going 80 or something?"

Rick laughed and felt his back tense and spasm again. It was old injury and something he felt all the time. He had grown to tolerate it, but not ignore it. He wondered if SCI was some sort of medical code word for what was wrong with his back.

"If you are looking at my back that is what happens when your Osprey hits the water. Not sure why I didn't get knocked out when we hit."

Calvin just kept hovering around him and circling like some sort of joke talking vulture. He no sooner came in front than he disappeared behind him again.

"Oh yeah, the rims are shot, and your fenders are cracked buddy. Oh, shit that's old! When did you get shot 2033 or 2034?"

Rick thought back and he had to answer both years. He took a round in the extract from his V22 crash from China's coast guard of all people. And then he took a round that trashed his left shoulder in 2034.

"Oh yeah you were infantry...no Airborne...yeah definitely Airborne. Those knees give it away; all you guys have that nice uniform lack of cartridge in your knees. My dad was in the 145th Airborne Brigade, in England. Never talks about it but even he doesn't have knees like this!"

Rick wanted to backslap the kid but he was semi-entertained at least. Calvin continued on for a bit and then settled looking at him directly. That was when Rick noticed he wasn't using any equipment, no stethoscope, no nothing.

"How in hell are examining me? What kind of doctor are you anyway?"

When Rick rose up, he found the boy had the strength of a truck when he pushed him back. That was his first sign the boy wasn't human. He must be like the others.

"I did not give you leave soldier; I am not done yet. Yeah, typical degradation of vision, probably not service related, just age. Oh, goodie no signs of TBI or mental illness, that's great for what you have been though. I would have figured you had TBI with that crash you talked about."

Rick decided to dish a bit back and asked if anyone had run a diagnostic on his head lately. Hopefully this little checkup would end soon.

"Probably should, goodness knows my mom and dad thinks I am nuts for joining this outfit."

Whatever he was doing he was intent on it. He was buzzing around him like a bee looking and looking, and looking? This guy was really different from all the other Grey. Curious now he decided to see if there was more to the Grey than he knew. Rick wasn't an idiot and with intelligence came curiosity.

"I bet your folks wish you were serving with the other vampires. Don't all of you Grey desire to be soldiers? They ok with you being a doc?"

The guttural laugh shocked him, that was when he realized in all these days he had been with Travis and his people there was hardly any laughing.

"Oh, hell no, mom and dad are Emerald's like me. Now my mother-in-law that is a different story. She is not thrilled her baby married me. But I think she is getting used to me. Her dad isn't a bad sort, and honestly its good work for an Emerald. I like to think I get a taste of what my dad did when he was in the service."

Rick asked him what in hell was an Emerald. That caused the boy to shift back to in front of him with wide eyes and a curious face.

"Oh wow, so no one told you yet. Ok…. So, like there are folks like you normies. Normies aren't cool and break really easy, and get old and shit. And then there are these like really awesome folks like me, and we have special powers. Cool powers, not the stupid shit you see in movies. And we don't have fangs ok… you humans always with movies and shit. Probably think I am going to drink your blood"

He air quoted when he said powers and looked all proud of himself.

"I am not a grey, my new airborne friend. Emerald vampires are sort of a cross between an environmentalist and a Mormon. With a bit of Doctor House tossed in for good measure…. And just like that I am done my man!"

He wrote down a few things on a sheet of paper. As he did his tongue stuck out of his mouth. He was a total weirdo, but Rick was starting to pick up that Medford had more than its share of that.

"Ok for a human your age, and with the fights you were in, your condition isn't that bad really. Have you noticed that your right arm tingles?"

Rick looked at the fool and knew full well he did. When he denied it, the boy just looked at him with a knowing face. So, he fessed up and admitted over the last year or so he had less strength in that arm and was having difficulty holding his right hand steady.

"It's your spinal injury; it's going to continue to get worse until you lose full mobility. Probably not just your arm, possibly your whole right side, although I don't think so. It's nothing that can't be fixed so don't fret."

Rick asked him how in hell did he know all this by just looking at him. Seriously hoping the kid was just nuts and Travis was doing this as a joke. But that wasn't like Travis, and this town seemed to be full of unexplained and strange things, they were vampires after all.

"I told you I am an Emerald; we are different than Grays. Greys can disappear, and Emeralds.... Well just think of it like Xray vision. We can see inside you Rick, and even better we can fix things too. I wouldn't be much use as a doc if I couldn't."

He consulted his notes again and seemed to be looking at Rick's knees again before making another note and continuing to review Rick's condition.

"I wish your back was the only problem. Your knees are mostly shot. As I am sure you know every time you try running. I can repair the cartilage but the bones themselves are rough from rubbing against each other. If they aren't fixed, they are just going to wear away the new cartilage I give you. I can't fix either long term, but I can help with the smaller items."

He expected to be let out so he got up again only to be pushed back down. Then strong hands held him as he began to do something different. Rick began to hurt as the boy began to work his skills.

Hey what the fuck are you doing!

"Healing you... what do you think?"

Over the next half-hour it felt more like an intense interrogation session than a visit with a doc. But when he finally finished Rick began to notice some changes. The biggest initial change was his eyes, he could see clearly now and read text without his glasses. His back still hurt, and his knees REALLY hurt now. But his vision was way better.

"I took care of the easy stuff for now, but you are going to need to see a better Emerald than me to get your back and knees fixed. I regenerated all your missing and damaged cartilage so it's going to hurt more now. I will call up to the hospital and get you an appointment to see my mom about those fixes. Mom can just about fix anything you got broke, except mental illness. Now for that I have a cousin...."

Rick now very unsure about walking, got up. This time without resistance from his new "friend" and told him not to bother. He would just see a doc when he got home.

"Yeah, I suppose you could, but human doctors can't regenerate your bone from the inside bub. They are just going to cut your knees out and give you brand new artificial ones. And don't get me started about your back, those quacks will paralyze you before they heal you. But if you like running around in a buggy that's your call I guess."

Medford, Texas – Agora

Jan 12ᵗʰ 2058

Yelina and the other members of the Agora were in a recess; all were tired from the latest debates. Like most days the topics were about funding and allocation of resources. Tit for tat trading, and politics that make the Grey world go round. When Yelina and the others had formed the Agora it was enjoyable. Now it was best described as the hemorrhoid of her existence. Everything that went on here was painful and slow. It was for that reason and not because of any hate for Susan that had started this latest argument.

Susan's favorite daughter was pregnant again, her third now with the Emerald. Among many in the Agora this was humorous. Having one or two children was fine, but at only 22 this daughter was already pregnant with her third. At this rate before she was a hundred, Elena would have her own neighborhood. Such was the ways of the Emeralds, they were breeders and taking one in to the Grey house was not something the others found desirable. Yelina wasn't like them, she had only meant to complement Susan on another grandchild. Instead because of her fatigue she had made the complement sound like a slight.

"Of all people I would have thought you would appreciate the blessings of life. You know Yelina you are so hypocritical; you have three babies with Travis, what's the difference? Are you just jealous that Elena is desired, and you aren't?"

That got Yelina hot and she asked her "friend" what she meant by that.

"Do I need to spell it out for you? How long has it been now for you 16 or 17 years since Jessie? You waisted the last four years with our love and produced nothing, I guarantee you when you get out of the way the Agora will be congratulating me again. Not for a child Elena creates, but one I create. I don't know why you still hold on to him. You should let him go; you only waste his time."

Cassia moved in to separate them with words that made it clear she would not tolerate further bickering. She called everyone back into the chamber to continue talking but Yelina only looked at her rival with hate. Between the Agora and the company neither Yelina or Travis had time for creating and raising children. That didn't mean they didn't love one another, nor did it mean Travis was done with her…. didn't it?

Medford, Texas – Travis's home

Jan 12ᵗʰ 2058

Travis was where he most wanted to be. At home working with his sons, and with all his teams at home resting or training. No one was in harm's way and everything was right in his world. Or at least as right as it could be. One son wasn't speaking to him because the Agora had demoted him. Another son was angry at him for even considering adopting another. And then there was his companions, the women who loved him or at least used to love him.

Travis paused on the task he was working on. He was focused on the three women in his life. One had left him years before, but not his clan or his side. A part of him wished to hold her again, but he dared not, less he angers the others. And then there was Yelina and Susan. It was a compromise no one liked, and worse was doing nothing for his individual relationships with them. And then there was the private bit of news he had been given a few days before. That bit of information troubled him greatly. He was still pondering that when he heard Pete and Elias get his attention. Someone new had arrived.

"Dad, do you want us to leave, it's not like we are working on anything critical?"

Travis smiled for his other sons, children he had from other women in the clan. Even if he had little to do with raising them, he was trying to form some sort of relationship with them as adults. Both served in his teams and both desired to know him. Thus, on days when they weren't busy or training, he invited his boys to work with him in his hobby. This latest son to arrive however wasn't here to work on guns. Jacob was angry and the others knew it.

"No Pete you two can stay. I like what you are doing with that stock by the way. I look forward to seeing your finished product. You have a real talent son."

Pete smiled before he caught himself. Travis wasn't giving false praise, the boy had talent. Elias far less so, but he didn't mind. For him it was about spending time and learning. As they worked, they often talked about life, women, and war. Travis had taught both of them more in the last six months than he had taught some of his other children in their whole lives. As he passed Elias, he put a hand on him and gave him a look. Travis hoped it got the message to him, that he was honored to have him as a son, because he was. Jacob stood there angry, ready to have it out with him. He had stopped short of entering the small building where they worked.

"Come on let's talk in here Jacob."

Travis led his son into the small trailer where Travis laid his head most nights. From the looks of it in the future he would be spending far more here than with Yelina in her home. Travis offered him a drink which he refused at first and then accepted after a moment. Travis didn't ask what was wrong, he already knew. He just sat and waited for what Jacob had to say. Jacob had never once confronted him in all his years. They had disagreed yes, but never had he come here like this. It was rare for his clan to question their leaders like this. Obedience was a moral for the Grey. Questioning your leadership was tantamount to rebellion. Yet here he was, angry and ready to unload. But his Grey nature prevented him from really doing so. But after a couple of false starts he began in earnest.

"I know you have the right father, but why this house? Do you not have enough sons to please you? Did me and Malcom not shed enough blood for you the last time? Why not ask Susan or Dolly to be his sponsor? Why must you throw him into ours? How will it help your friend if me or Malcom cut him down?"

Travis looked at his son, he was a mixture of anger and fear. He didn't say it but Jacob feared Malcom in battle. Malcom was his brother and had always bested him. But the last time they had fought for the honor of the house, Jacob had come within a hairs breath of killing him. Neither Travis or Yelina desired the battle, but it was necessary. And Travis knew for Jacob it was a major obstacle in his growth as a man. He was allowing his fear and envy to rule him.

"I nominated him for yours because your mother desired it. And I agree with her logic. Susan will be young again soon and desires a child to raise, not a full-grown man. And Dolly is no longer my wife, one day soon she will take another husband as is her right and duty. Asking her to sponsor my friend would be wrong. It has to be your house son."

Jacob was holding the cold beer and then sat it down gently but his blood was up now. He repeated again the same questions about blood, and how Travis risked his friend's life and that of his sons.

"Jacob, a man cannot ask for more or less sons. I can only try to do the best, with the sons I have, and thank God for each of you. But this man is not a stranger, and I owe him more than you can know. Asking him to join our clan only strengthens our people, and repays a debt. I don't wish to shame you or Malcom. I know your hearts beat for this clan, and you honor your mother with what you do."

He watched Jacob try to deal with his fears. To confront Jacob on them was not wise. Jacob had to come to grips with his fears on his own. But it didn't hurt to explain a bit why Travis wanted this man to join them. Even if it wasn't the real reason, or even the primary reason.

"Son when I went to the Marines I was… different. I was concerned I would miss out on the war, and I didn't know myself then. When I got to the recon school I was in over my head and… well I guess I was freighted."

Jacob looked at him with a puzzled look. To Travis being afraid was normal, and he was well acquainted with how it felt. But in the clan, he was King, and showing fear as a Grey was a surefire way to get yourself killed. This boy had never seen him visibly afraid before. Jacob asked him in an unbelieving voice what he was scared of.

"Failure, dishonor, I guess. But it didn't take long to get scared of something else. They pit each of us against the other, weeding out the weaker amongst us. This one guy had it out for me from the start. Every time the instructors weren't looking, he would mess with me or my equipment. Said I wasn't strong enough or good enough to be recon. I lived I fear of that guy, dude had my number and for the longest time I couldn't do anything but fail around him."

Travis remembered the utter fear he had of Rick then. Rick was strong and tough and had this ominous look about him. He could drive fear into Travis with just that look and it felt like all his vampiric ability just fled when he did. He hated being a coward around him, but the guy was just better at everything. And the instructors just loved to pit them against each other.

"It got pretty bad for me; I was sure I was going to get sent back and reassigned. I had accepted that pretty much too. Felt sorry for myself, and gave myself a ton of pity. And then one day they set us up against each other in hand to hand. And I didn't fall for the same stupid things, and I won. Then I won at something else, and then something else. Pretty soon I wasn't the weakling anymore. That guy… he didn't think I was any different so he challenged me that night to "the show.""

Jacob looked at him not knowing what that meant. Back in those days trainees would fight each other at night to settle grievances. Friday night or Saturday night was generally when it happened. Right after lights out and in the showers where the others couldn't hear. Travis explained a bit about "the show" and how it worked. Jacob had already guessed the guy in question was Rick.

"Yeah, it was him. Even after I started to win the battles in training, I was still scared shitless of him. I damn near wet my pants when he hit me that night. Dude hit me so hard I saw stars. Rick has this look when he wants to hurt you. I swear that look is way scarier than anything I saw on Ishigaki. If I had just been plain human Travis, and not a vampire, no way in hell would I been able to stand up to him. But I did, he still never let me get a clean shot in, vampire or no. But I grazed him and I showed him I wasn't going to lay down for him anymore. We never did finish that fight; instructors broke it up before we could. But it didn't matter. We had settled our beef with each other."

Jacob opened his beer and looked at the floor for a bit. Before Travis continued, he wanted that lesson to sink in to his son. Jacob didn't need to fear his older brother, even if Malcom was better. He also couldn't be afraid to lose; he had to put his fears and worries aside and just make the best of what he could.

"After that he saw me differently. I didn't win though son, had it been even, Rick would have beaten me into next Tuesday. I earned his respect that night, not because I won. I earned his respect that night because I didn't quit. I stopped fearing him and started to see him for who he really was son."

Jacob was quiet and thoughtful. Travis wanted to say more, explain more. But that wasn't their way, and Jacob wouldn't accept it anyway. Jacob had to come to terms with this on his own. The small nudge from dad was as far as it could go. Travis just wished Rick was actually staying. A man like Rick with his years and experience would do wonders for his people. Not to mention he would start day one as a vampire with few equals. He waited to gauge his reaction to the story before he would dare tell him that Rick had rejected his offer and would go home. He needed Jacob to accept this and not discard what he had learned. He knew his son and guessed by looking at him it had hit home. Sure, enough a moment later his face changed.

"I think I understand what you are trying to say dad. Do you mind if I stick around a bit? I would kind of like to hear more stories about those times."

Travis stood up and told him to grab a couple beers for his brothers and led Jacob out to the shop. No more was said about Rick or Jacob's fears. Travis focused on making each son feel a part of his world. Something his own father had done many times when he was a boy, at least before vampirism had taken hold on his family. In so many ways Travis missed those days, before Medford, and before he was King. It was far simpler, and back then his mother and father were happy. Now one of them was dead, and the other... might as well be. Travis didn't know this woman anymore; Cynthia was gone and in her place was this Cassia woman.

Such thoughts were pity for oneself and not worthy of Travis's mind. He had sons to mold and shape, and he clearly wasn't done with them yet. Perhaps that was the fate of all lovers and parents? You build up something and then watch it be torn down. But in the process, you plant a seed that grows into something wonderful. Travis just hoped he did a better job than his parents did. God knows he had enough seeds planted, he just hoped he had enough water for the task.

Medford, Texas – Susan's house

Jan 17th 2058

"You weren't there Travis; she mocked my daughter! Do I mock hers when Jessie runs around doing stupid things, or when she defies the Agora? No, I keep my mouth shut because she is my beloved's daughter. But what about our daughter Travis? What about our Elena, or Helen, or Silas? Do they not deserve the same respect that hers does? Does she really think her babies are perfect, because I can tell you they aren't!"

Travis rubbed his forehead and hated to be in this position. He had hoped this blow-up last weekend would be over by now but it wasn't. Susan and Yelina's war with each other was escalating. All week in the Agora they had been fighting and it was getting out of hand. ALL of these children Susan was talking about, were his. Just as all of Dolly's were and many other grey women, he had been forced to be with over the early years. It was bad enough when he had to referee with women he barely knew. It was quite another when he had to keep Susan and Yelina from killing each other. He was growing tired of the rivalry, so much so he had quietly stopped having children with them years before. Susan had only managed to have her last child because he had lost track of her cycle at the time.

"You are right our children deserve her respect, every bit as much as you respect hers. I will speak with her, but please my love, no more open conflict in the Agora with her."

Susan was not satisfied with that at all. Susan wanted more than just a promise of words; she wanted more. She was smart enough NOT to suggest any course of action however. She knew better than to do that. From what Yelina had said Susan had crossed a major line herself. She had insulted her, so much so Dolly had called him warning him that his wives were creating a vendetta against one another. Those weren't soft threats in the Grey world. It was common for Grey women to die because of disputes over children and power. After letting her rant, he was ready to stick his head into a blender. But Travis knew Susan could only go on like this a bit longer. Especially when they were apart like this.

The rub of it was, Susan loved him. Being separated from him was part of the cause of the issues. Yelina was equally guilty when she was separated, although she expressed herself differently. Susan was hotblooded and her issues required more effort on his part to fix. But when issues arose with Yelina, they were nearly impossible to fix.

Both women are more trouble than they were worth.

Travis frowned at the thought, it wasn't accurate or true. He needed and loved them both, they were the mothers to a good portion of his children. And they had stood beside him when he needed them most. But now….

"I will do more than speak to her, but Susan. She is my wife and the mother of some of my children. If you push too far with her, what am I supposed to do? How can I love a woman who murders another I love? The things you said to her in anger… I fear you have created something I can't stop."

Susan quiet now looked at him with hurt, then her shoulders dropped. She knew he was right, her words were more than enough to push them to violence.

"I don't mean her harm, it's just Travis… It hurt me that she didn't support my girl."

"I know, but we both know what this is really about."

Travis explained it but he doubted if Susan was listening. It wasn't about Susan.. it was about the Agora.

"She is just tired of the endless battles there. I know her dear; she doesn't wish harm on your babies. She is just tired and needs a break, perhaps just as much as you do."

Susan was quiet for a moment looking very defeated and looked up putting a hand on him.

"I don't need a rest… what I need is you."

He could see that need in her, it was something he was sworn to provide. Something he wished very much to provide. But he couldn't, he had sworn his body and his loyalty to Yelina and Susan's time was still a year off. He quietly pulled her hand from himself and tried his best to comfort her with words. Knowing full well that was impossible.

Travis's phone went off, he was going to ignore it, but against his better judgement looked at the screen. Seeing the area code, he knew it was Washington.

"Go on.. check it."

It was his State Department contact; they wanted him in DC in the morning. He turned to Susan and against the rules opened his arms and she quickly and wolfishly entered them. This kind of affection was against the rules but the rules be damned. His wife, and she was his wife, needed him. But this agreement could not stand much longer. Something had to give and Travis had no idea what that could be. Whatever the solution was, it would take much from him.

"That was Tyler from the State Department. They asked me to attend a briefing about Meridia tomorrow morning."

Susan pulled back from the hug but not from his arms. Looking at him in disbelief that something had happened so quickly. Everyone expected Meridia to take months to decide.

Why ask you back so soon? Do they want Moonstone for the big meeting?

That didn't sound right to Travis. Surely a high-level meeting like this they would want their own. He wondered what on earth had made them want him there?

"Susan, I need your people to look into this before I go up there. Something is going on and I need to know what it is. And I beg you please bury this thing with Yelina for my sake."

Susan shook her head yes and then returned to his chest. There was much he wanted to say, much he wished he could do but couldn't. The day was fast approaching when he would have to say goodbye to one or perhaps both of these women. A part of him wished for it, he was tired of living like this. But to choose one… it was something he could not do.

Lynchburg, Virginia – Rick's Apartment

Jan 17ᵗʰ 2058

A week after Rick had returned home and very little had changed. He was still without work; he had begged every friend up the east coast but there wasn't anything. His age, and his physical condition didn't help matters. Whatever that Emerald kid had done had fixed his eyes and killed the arthritis in his hands. But his back and knees were still a mess. He would go see a doc but with what? He had no money and no health plan coverage. But that wasn't really what was on his mind. He only had to look at the sad eyes of his young son to know what was.

He had come home on Monday to find the apartment cleared out of nearly everything. His savings, and all the money from that job was gone. His wife who had never been happy with his situation, had decided to take advantage and clear out all the money he had earned and returned to Atlanta. She had left their son in the care of their adult daughter, explaining she would only be gone a couple of days. Rick knew better after a call to his mother-in-law. His wife was already shacked up with someone she had been seeing on the side. She wasn't in Atlanta anymore, and even her mom had no clue where she was. Her mom was a godly woman and hated what her daughter did, but there wasn't much she could do. Other than to offer to put him and his son up in her home.

Rick thought seriously about taking them up on the offer. His daughter was wonderful in helping, but she was trying to finish her college degree and had her own life now. Rick had tried getting a loan and even called some old friends about money. But lots of folks were suffering and no one could help him the way he needed. Normally he would have a good gig lined up by this point and just need a bit of cash to tide him over until the next job paid. But those days of constant employment were over. He was just too old now, and when you are desperate folks hear it.

He knew he couldn't stay here. His landlord didn't like him to start with. But Atlanta wasn't much of a landing spot for them either. It was kind of her mother to help out, but what work would he have there? There was one place that had offered him work. But it wasn't a job but a life they were offering. A life Rick had put behind him. He knew there wasn't much he wasn't willing to do for his son, but this was asking a lot. Even as he cast about for ANY other solution he knew he would sacrifice for him if need be. But what about his son, would they want to change him too? Seeing that Agoge, Rick knew what would happen to his son. He didn't want that, but he was desperate. It only took another look at his crestfallen son before he conceded his pride and his better judgement. He dialed a number in Texas and hoped for the best.

Chapter 8: Trials of the Concubines

Medford, Texas – Agora

Jan 18th 2058

Dolly was watching everyone enter and waiting for Susan. The moment she walked in she took her arm and led her aside to an empty corridor.

"Please tell me you and Yelina are not going to repeat what happened the last time?"

Susan and Dolly at times had butted heads, especially when she was still with Travis. But after Dolly left, their friendship had resumed. Part of that was because Dolly and Susan both had younger sons of Travis in the Agoge. And those boys had become fast friends in that space. Susan heard her concerns and brushed it off with reckless abandon.

"Susan, I mean it, what you said to her… I don't think she is going to let that go unless you do something."

Susan's face locked on to hers like it was a hawk tracking its prey. Equally Dolly knew she had hit a nerve.

"It's that bitch that owes me an apology. And I have you know Travis agrees with me. Now sister, please let go of me we have an important meeting today."

Dolly let her loose and shut her eyes as she moved past. What she was afraid of, was happening and there was precious little to stop it. A part of Dolly however considered the ramifications of such a war. As a loyal and loving servant of both the clan and the Agora, she had the King's ear. She knew from how he looked at her, his heart as well. Perhaps this was the moment she should do as she planned? Dolly shut her eyes and hid her own feelings, and her deep-seated anger at what she had been forced to sacrifice.

Medford, Texas – Cassia's Office

Jan 18th 2058

Cassia was angry and yet again disappointed in her chosen. Dolly had come to her before the meeting telling her what she already suspected. A full-fledged vendetta had formed between Yelina and Susan. She was going to deal with this and put an end to this stupid rivalry.

All they have to do is make love to him, give him children, that's it! They have all the power and money they could want. Little princesses with their own kingdoms to rule. As if they would be anything without MY son. Fine…they want to act tough… lets act tough.

Once both were in her office, she wasted little time to get her point across. She pulled the 7-inch blade from its sheath and threw it down on the floor before both women. It stuck hard into the wood and its landing made a sound that echoed through the room. Neither woman was surprised, instead both looked at the other looking for a sign of action. They did not flinch at the audacity of her action.

Oh shit…their minds are set. This isn't some little tiff.

Seeing their reaction, she swallowed and hoped neither saw the fear she felt. It confirmed to Cassia what she feared, it had gone too far. Both were looking to kill the other. She quickly put on the mask of a calm, in charge, Queen Mother.

"So, this is how the two of you honor my son? I see where the two of you are. I thought I made myself clear before, I asked you to love my son and serve him. NOT tear each other apart to have him for yourself!"

Neither responded, and neither backed down. Cassia was enraged, she had hoped Dolly was only being reactionary and that things were salvageable. There was one last card to play to pull them back from war.

"When I heard the two of you had a vendetta I didn't believe it. I know you resent each other and I don't blame you. A Grey woman shouldn't have to do what the two of you do. Any Grey man would be fortunate to have such a wife. But my son isn't just any man, he is our King! He needs all the support he can get to build this clan up. He needs more children, and more sons to build this clan!"

The more she spoke the more confidence Cassia actually felt. She remembered why she had done this in the first place and the sorry state the clan was in when she arrived.

"Each of you swore to me, SWORE to me, on your honor that you would do as I asked. Is this what I asked? You call me mother, is this how you honor your mother?"

Cassia had nearly screamed at them and each was breathing quickly, angry and resentful at this conversation and at each other.

"I have half a mind to have both of you killed. It would not be the first time we have removed someone unworthy from his bed. Do I make myself clear?"

Cassia had never actually done this, but her husband had. Travis had never forgiven him for doing it. But something had to stop. She doubted even this would be enough to really end this. Now was the time to put love back in her tone. She did so with as much sincerity as she dared.

"Yelena, Susan, both of you call me mother and I am honored by each of you. The children you created I cherish and adore. Please daughters...I beg you... Please do not make me choose between my fondness for you, and my loyalty to my son. Because if you do, I will kill you both, and neither of you will have him. I swear this on the graves of my children."

It was very quiet for a time as each woman eyed the other. Susan and then Yelina began to argue over the slights and Cassia with a loud and angry voice announced the ending of this discussion.

"Let me be clear, I am not here to decide which of you is virtuous. I don't care, I only care that my son has the love and support he needs. If one of you so much as lays a finger on the other, or if one of you has an accident? I will not hesitate, both of you will die and I will find him new women to comfort him. Far more worthy women. END this vendetta now before me, and swear to me you will faithfully love and support him."

The two women looked at each other and finally it was Yelina who spoke.

"Susan, I know I hurt you, but I didn't intend it. I know what I sounded like when I spoke, but I am so fricking tired of politics. I let my frustrations over the Agora come out in my words. I truly am happy for your daughter. She is a fine Grey woman who will be someone to fear in the centuries to come."

Susan quietly accepted it, which Cassia hoped she would. If anything, Susan was not Cassia's worry it was Yelina. Susan was hot tempered and could fly off at the handle. But when Yelina wanted her dead? Well, there was no way on earth anything Cassia could say or do that would stop her. Thankfully that tone and that voice made it sound like she was sincere, for Susan's sake and Yelina's, she hoped so.

Susan pulled the blade from the floor and handed it back to Cassia. She kicked both women out a moment later and crashed back into her chair. Cassia wasn't really a Grey in every respect. Her heart couldn't be, she was many women rolled up into one. At times like this she had to channel one experience into herself. But it always felt fake, and she feared the others would see it. Like right now, a part of her felt guilty for her own actions. She had wanted to secure a strong powerbase for her son. She had taken three strong women and built around them a following. Creating three powerful bullworks that would insulate Travis from those that wished his throne. It would also give him three wombs to create more warriors for his needs. At the time it had served the clan and been the solution to the battle for power. But at best, these women were concubines not wives. Time was proving her choice to be the wrong one, Travis had found love with them but not happiness. Worse he had stopped growing as a man. Something he could ill afford. The weight of this was crushing Cassia, it took everything she had to keep the Grey wolves at bay.

Travis needed stability and a real partner instead of this hen house of problems. Cassia wanted and needed to finally lay down this Grey burden. But it would take a century or two by her estimation. That was why she had fully immersed herself into this life and this clan. Giving up relationships with her other grandchildren and her other living children. She had lost out on knowing Jay or Adad's children like she should have. Now one of those girls was already in the ground. With the door closed and no one to see Cassia, she wept at her desk. She was no warrior, no baston of strength. She was just a mother trying to save her son, and his birthright. Yet a voice inside told her that she wasn't innocent, she had her own wrong doings that weighted on her. There was a soft knock on the door, Cassia knew at once who it was. She told Dolly to enter and didn't bother to hide her tears.

"Mother what happened, did they settle with each other?"

Cassia saw the concern but also saw past it as well. This woman as lovely and nice as she was… well she wasn't any better.

"Yes, dear I believe so."

Cassia motioned her into the room deciding now was as good a time as any. Her heart was already a wreck, might as well deal with Dolly as well. It was time for Dolly; she hated it but it just was. Nothing in the Grey world could last eternally. Each man and woman eventually had to move on.

"Dolly, I care a great deal for you and love you. But don't think I am blind to your heart either. I know you desire my son back in your life. But you made your decision and now you need to live with it. I want you to select a new husband. Child, I have given you plenty of time to mourn what you lost. You know as well as any Grey your duty. Our clan is still in danger, any great battle that comes our way and we will be right back to where we were 20 years ago. Please child, its time."

Cassia saw the face knowing the battle behind the eyes. She just hopped she wasn't going to try something. If she did then Cassia would not give her the warnings like she had done the others. Dolly had made her bed, any violation of that would mean her life. No matter how much she cared for her, or wished Dolly had stayed with him. If anything, it would have been far better if Travis had chosen just her and discarded the others. Even if Yelina loved him with all her heart, which Cassia knew she did. It wasn't what a King needed. He needed a strong woman with skills and talents to keep her King alive. Dolly had that, but Dolly had also chosen to step down. It wouldn't have been Cassia's choice but it was done. Cassia watched the emotions change and the mask return.

"Yes mother, I will do as you ask."

Ken the eldest child of Dolly's entered the room. Apologizing for his not announcing himself first. Before Cassia could respond he whispered into his mothers' ears. The look on her face and the quick snap of her head said something had shocked her. She wasn't long in explaining.

"That girl from Sao Paulo, are you sure son?"

Ken was young and not Cassia's favorite grandchild. He had failed in the Agoge at age 15 during his final trial. Kicked out of that school he had still become Dolly's right hand in her organization. His sharp mind and attention to detail were one of the reasons Dolly's organization was the best intelligence gatherers in the clan. So, if he said it was her, it was probably her. Cassia cut off further discussion and checked any more emotion she had left the best she could. Things were moving fast now, and it was time to continue with the Grey theater.

Chapter 9: Politics of life

Washington DC – State Department

Jan 18th 2058

They were nearly at "foggy bottom" as this area of Washington was known. Travis didn't know enough history to know why it was called that, but it was a pseudonym for the State Department. He had flown in this morning at 4am with a small team. When he went to see clients, he generally took one of his wives, his business manager and two body guards. With the recent battles between his wives, he felt it was best to leave them at home. Instead, his oldest child Jackie was with him. She was his only child from Tina, the first leader of the American Grey clan. Jackie had been raised by Dolly her aunt and joined her organization only a few years ago.

Jackie was bright and at one time had a good human career ahead of her. She was majoring in business and attending Stanford when she turned into a vampire at age 20. That had changed a great deal for Jackie, she dropped out of Stanford and took up the job as business manager for Moonstone. She was bright and had taken to the roll with gusto.

"Susan just sent another update dad."

Travis was in the back with her and had been listening to her report on the current status of the teams. The Agora handled funding for the clan but Travis was pleased with how Jackie was managing their assets for the company. Two years into her management they had a far better handle on operating expenses and cost. Their operating income had risen as had their margins. This allowed Travis to consider new teams and a small expansion of the operation. It wasn't because of new work; it was because Jackie made them more efficient. He hit the small button on his glasses and read the update.

"Damn it… Susan didn't find anything."

Jackie asked him if he was worried, already knowing he was. Travis just smiled for her and explained that he didn't like going into a meeting blind.

"Well hopefully we don't have to deploy the whole company again like we had to in Sao Paulo. That operation ended up costing us a lot dad. Pulling all those teams wasn't in the estimate we gave the State Department. And from talking to our contact, it was pretty clear they aren't pleased with our performance there. They already denied my initial request for additional funds."

That was to be expected especially with what that little weasel wrote up about him. He had expected it, all things considered. But now he was wondering if he shouldn't have just left the dork in the US and done the rescue mission on his own. But that was water under the bridge now. They had a few minutes before they arrived so he decided to ask his daughter how her life was going. She looked confused for a minute and then shut the laptop she had open.

"Dad, I don't have time for that. Staying on top of things for us is a full-time job. Besides, it's not like I have a clock ticking, I am a vampire it can wait a century."

Travis looked at her closely and saw she was nervous. He knew why, Dolly had told him privately that she was quietly seeing a human in town. He raised the partition in the car that separated the driving area from the passenger area. One benefit of that was it prevented his two bodyguards from hearing what they said.

"Why are you so shy about that boy? Do you think I won't approve of him or something? Dolly already told me about him; he seems like a nice guy. I went to school with his mom; she was a sweetheart."

Jackie looked torn and put the laptop back in her bag and looked out the window for a minute before speaking.

"I like him dad, a lot. But I don't think he likes me. Mom says I should just enthrall him, but I don't want to do that. I want him to like me for me, I don't know why I bother?"

Travis felt for her, it was hard when you loved someone and they didn't return it. For a vampire there were other options, but it said something about Jackie that she knew better.

"I think your wise in that. If he isn't interested then you should move on. But you might recommend he go see an Emerald to have his eyes checked. Clearly, he doesn't have vision worth a damn."

Jackie laughed and smiled. Travis had said it honestly; his daughter was beautiful and intelligent. What that boy was thinking he had no clue. Dolly had done an excellent job in raising her. And thankfully she was nothing like her mother. A subject the two of them never spoke of.

If she ever asked about Tina, he would tell what he knew. But Travis would rather she didn't. He had no love for Tina, never had. He had been thankful when Aya took her life. Tina's death had made many things possible, just not his freedom, at least not for long anyway. That dream of being normal, and having a simple life seemed so far away now. The mountain where he had found peace and purpose, those short years had been bliss. But like many things in his life it was a distant tempting thing, just out of reach.

Freedom is such a pipedream, if only my children knew how little power I really have. How little choice I have in this life. Would they be surprised… would they care?

Travis shook his head at that as he pondered his own lot. Jackie was a good daughter and in time she would find her man to go along with her newly found purpose. She was content in that purpose, that was obvious to Travis. But for him, this was a duty and nothing more. The image of him as a plow horse was one, he often saw as the perfect representation of himself. Chained to a clan and a people he both loved, and resented. They had taken his will long ago, harnessed him for his ability and name. Tricked him with the appearance of choice, all the while creating unbreakable bonds that shackled him to the clan. They were sweet and wonderful bonds, ones he cherished. But they kept him from being both the man he wished to be.

The day Tina had died had at least given him a level of freedom. From that day onward he was no longer the whore of the clan. Open to any one Tina agreed to give him to. Just letting that memory cross his mind caused him to wince. He quickly recovered and asked Jackie what she thought of this meeting, especially what she believed it was about.

"I tried asking but they wouldn't talk. I don't think we are being fired; we clear too many contracts. Besides we are still charging them less than our three biggest competitors."

The partition started to go down and his main escort told them they would be arriving at the location in a minute.

Washington DC – State Department

Jan 18ᵗʰ 2058

Once inside the building Jackie was left with the two escorts cooling their heels. She was left texting back and forth with Dolly and thinking about Dad, the job and everything in between. But above all she was thinking about

Malcom. Her half-brother and one of her best friends. What the Agora did to him was just wrong. It pissed Jackie off the moment mom had come home talking about it. His own mother had sat up there acting like he was some sex starved halfwit. Didn't she know her own son? Anyone who knew him knew what kind of man he was. The only thing that really drove Malcom was his calling, not any woman or frivolous thing. He wanted to be the first of the children to make Spartinate. It was all he could think about growing up, and what his heart was set on as an adult.

Jackie sighed and closed her eyes, she liked him. He was a friend and her brother. He deserved far better from his mother and their grandmother. That was why she had told him what she knew. He deserved to know, that much didn't bother her. What did was the lie she told in the process. Tapping her shoe on the tile made a hollow sound. It was cheap material, government standard issue for buildings. She continued to tap hearing the sound echo off the empty corridor. It represented how she felt right now, hollow. She shouldn't have told him the secret, much less lie about it. Jackie stood and walked over to the door where the meeting was underway. Wondering what dad would find out. Hopefully State was going to pay them and perhaps offer another lucrative job. They could use the money; well, they could use the "official money" anyway. Dad didn't know about that, and never would. There were lots of things dad didn't know about.

It wasn't right, not just her lie, but all of their lies. All the crap about honor and morality was just for show. Behind closed doors the women of the clan did as they pleased. And lately their behavior was reprehensible. Jackie didn't want to be like the other Grey women. Jackie had fought all the "little" suggestions from mom or Susan. They wanted her to be like them, like all Grey ladies. What Jackie wanted was far simpler, and far more honorable in her eyes. But lying to get it…. Was she any better than Dolly or Susan, or even Yelina? A ding from her phone announced another text from mom.

"Your father is a good person to talk to about your relationships dear. Heaven knows you won't ask me. Your father is a good judge of character; you should keep talking to him about it."

Jackie smirked and shook her head. Mom wanted her to talk about her life. Whom she loved and how she loved was only her business. But it did feel good, at least a bit, to talk to dad about it. At least with him she knew he was real. He was honorable and would never betray the ones he loved. Jackie closed her eyes and let out another breath. That wasn't fair to her mom. It wasn't like mom was whoring around on him. They weren't together anymore. But they belonged together, anyone could see that. It would kill dad to know mom had other partners. And then there was the bit she had told Malcom, the real reason he was put aside. It wasn't fair....

Medford, Texas – Agora

Jan 18th 2058

Dolly got a short text from Jackie; she wasn't pleased at her mom telling her father about her crush. Dolly smiled at it, Jackie was very private and didn't even want her father knowing she dated. She responded back reminding her that her father loved her and it was perfectly normal for him to know. The two of them had a difficult relationship. When Jackie was 16 both Travis and Dolly had sat her down and told her the FULL story of how her real mother had died. Up till that day Jackie had adored her father and took every opportunity to catch his attention. But after that she had blamed him for her mother's death.

Both of them knew it would hurt her, but she was going to learn one day, and it was best if it came from them. In the long run what had managed to soothe over Jackie was the fact that she had been her mother as long as Jackie had memories. And she knew both her and Travis loved her. But to hear that your father's mistress killed your birth mother was a hard pill to swallow. Dolly knew she had been key in helping with that. As much as she loved her sister, her death was necessary. Tina had allowed her experiences to twist her and the clan was poorer for it. The Grey needed change, and they needed the kind of person Travis was to lead it.

It didn't hurt that Dolly was in love with him by the time Tina had taken her last breath. Tina had long made life in the clan difficult and unlike Jackie, Dolly knew her sister would never change. Jackie didn't know her mother, and had no clue what kind of woman she was. It was natural for the girl to think Tina wasn't as bad as what her father had claimed. It had fallen to Dolly to share the worst parts, and reveal just how horrible Tina really was. Those had been difficult conversations.

By the time Jackie was ready for college she had come to terms with her father. He hadn't killed her mother, and it wasn't like her mother had kept Travis for himself. Hardly, Tina had farmed Travis out to any Grey woman who was willing to pay for his services. Forcing him to be a whore, and enjoying every moment of his displeasure. Aya had wanted to free Travis from his bonds, and she had succeeded.   Had her heart been only for Travis then perhaps her fate would have been better.   Instead Aya had taken the crown for herself and betrayed the entire town nearly killing the clan in the process.   Dolly shifted in her seat hating any time she thought of Aya.   She quickly stuffed all memories of the woman away as always.   Still, Aya had cleared the way for Dolly and her own designs quite nicely.

At least the bitch had done that much.

As horrible as would seem to anyone else, Dolly was relieved when her sister died.   Not just because it freed a man she loved.   But also, because it set her beloved clan back on a path to growth.   For Jackie once she realized the hell Travis had been put through, she began to understand.   It didn't make it easy, but it was easier.

They had known the likelihood of her changing was very high, but even in ones like her it wasn't a guarantee.   Jackie had also asked for them not to force matters.   But once she turned, she realized her place and her future was in Medford.   The call of their clan was strong, like it was for any vampire.

You go through all that little one and you still have a good head on your shoulders.   Says a lot about you dear....

The girl often reminded her of her sister when she would smile.   Tina had been a lot like Jackie when she was young.   That life she had been forced into changed Tina and turned her heart so black that nothing could make her smile like that again.   Seeing Jackie like this made Dolly think this would have been her sister's fate had things gone differently.

"You have a lot of nerve coming here, please child, explain to us why we should bother to speak to the likes of you?"

Dolly looked up; it was starting already.   The young grey woman that had tried to seduce Malcom was standing in front of the Agora.   Dolly put her cell away, and thoughts of her daughter.   Jackie was not her concern now; it was this mess that had just walked in.   Camila was pretty like Malcom had described and very confident in herself.   She stood there in something that looked like a peplos but wasn't.   Lots of silk and modern style and expensive adornments were in show.   Never in the history of the Agora had a woman come here looking as elegant and stunningly beautiful as she did now.   There was no fear in her face.   On the surface it seemed as if she was an angel, pretty, calm, demure... but Dolly knew that kind of woman well.   She was dangerous, sly, cunning, all in all, a classical Grey woman.   A part of Dolly wished her Jackie was more like her.   But she loved that Jackie had taken in the best parts of Travis's character. The women of her clan needed far more Jackie's than they did Camila's.

"I thank you for allowing me to address you today. I believe my people may have offended you in some way. I am here today to clear up any misunderstanding that may exist between us. The Grey of Meridia are so pleased to discover we are not alone in this world. Please dear ladies, let me place your minds at ease. Our people want nothing but peace and harmony amongst our families. I am not here to ask for anything or to demand, rather simply to learn. The Grey of Meridia wish to know our kin and create a bond between our peoples."

Several of the assembled openly mocked that, one asked her directly if they were so interested in harmony why did they kidnap one of their own, and seduce another? The harsh way it was said bounced off her regal and beautiful frame as if it had been said in love. Clearly Camila was no wilting flower, she was strong and someone not to underestimate.

"When we discovered your people spying on us did, we kill them as was our right? I submit to you that I would expect this body would be well within their rights to do so to another vampire who entered Medford without permission. Malcom was questioned so we could understand your people. It was my honor that I was allowed to do so. I found Malcom to be an amazing man, strong, confident, and noble. If half of your men are as glorious as he, then truly you are a blessed people."

Dolly noted the face and the expression, it wasn't fake. The girl was clearly impressed with Malcom, the way she said it and her face as she did, gave it away. She was flushed and her one hand seemed to move about more than usual. If Dolly had to guess her heartrate was a twitch higher when she talked about Malcom. Dolly decided to enter this conversation by asking her about Jason. She asked her to explain Jason to the Agora. That caused a few around the room to nod in appreciation for the question.

"Jason contacted us a few days before he came to Meridia. We were intrigued by the possibility of another Grey so we decided to accept his request to join us. He is our clan-brother and if he wishes to know us, and be one of us, who are we to deny our brother? Even if his actions show him to be, less than trustworthy. We are a poor family without the great and bountiful blessings of Medford. His blood will help us grow in the centuries to come."

Dolly cut in to this crafted response by asking her to explain why she tried to seduce Malcom. At the accusation she looked appalled and shocked. Dolly had to smile at the well-crafted response and prepared emotions.

"SEDUCE! My lady I did no such thing. We danced as all Greys do, to know one another, to learn. I did not take him to my bed, nor did he ask me. We danced and I very pleased to know the man that he is. Have you not done so with a man you wish to know? Did you not dance with your husband before he became so, my lady?"

Dolly could feel the emotions stirring to life next to her. Yelina was a fixture next to her on the Agora and she knew when her friend was building up for an explosion. Dolly understood why, Malcom was Yelina's property, her son. For Camila to toy with him like this, away from her influence or approval was a direct challenge to her authority. Something no Medford woman would allow. On cue Yelina nearly spat out the words as she spoke. She asked if Camila wasn't seducing him, why was she dressed in next to nothing. Did she not offer her body after the dance? Camila smiled and slowly approached the place where Yelina sat.

"You are his mother are you not, he looks a great deal like you, my lady."

Yelina nodded her head and stared to say something but stopped when Camila responded.

"When we danced dear lady, we did so in such grace! He and I moved about effortlessly; we were as one! OH, I have never seen a man like him, truly you have an amazing son. Each move he anticipated, every move, every step he was in tune. We danced as one, it was... well it was nothing like I have felt before my lady. Once we danced and I knew he was such a man, I tested him. Not once did I land any blow, not once did he on me. It was perfect the dance he danced. When he defeated me, how could I not offer what he had won rightly? Do not the women of Medford act this way, how else do you select your men?"

There were grumbles among the ladies as some on the Agora were in favor of returning to the old ways. Much of what she described was what their clan had done at the beginning. It had been much altered by Tina, and then Travis, but there were some around the table that wanted to go back to this way, thus they liked what they heard. Dolly decided to ask what Yelina was unable to, Yelina was flustered at the implication. Which was Malcom was already mated to this woman by ancient right.

"But he did not take your body, is this not so? His report to us was clear that he rejected you and your advance. You claim that this was an honest misunderstanding. Yet your very first words to Malcom were to warn him that he may wish to stay. Long before you danced, you were trying to seduce this boy. I may not be as in tune with the ancient ways, but I am no fool Camila."

She took a step back but was unable to answer as two of the Agora accused Malcom of being untrue in his report. He had not said a word about how they had danced. Cassia however jumped in shutting down any further discussion about it.

"I have seen my grandsons mind and memories. He did not hide a word from me. Dolly speaks true young lady; you are speaking from both sides of your mouth. Admit it, you did try to seduce our boy."

Taken aback by the rebuke she looked shaken for a bit and looked down. When she looked up Dolly had to give it to her. She was a pro at manipulation; her response was near perfect.

"Yes, I admit when I laid my eyes on him, I desired him. Any Grey woman of worth would desire the son of the King. To have him is to touch power itself. If that be for my people or just as his wife. I was taken by him, yes. Would any other Grey woman do any differently than I, if you saw such a man before you? I have no husband. It is my time to do my duty, either for my people or for yours. I allowed him to see my body, so what? It is mine to give and to show, is that not our way as well? I see many lovely women here, are you hiding your loveliness… should you? If I have offended you, I can only say I am sad that I have. But my actions were only in line with what our clan teaches. I saw a powerful, worthy man and I wished to know him. It is the right of any Grey woman to know a worthy man. So long as she is equally worthy, it is her right. Do men not exist for the pleasure of the women?"

The meeting went on like this for the next hour. Each question answered in a way that made it clear she was just an innocent woman of the ancient Grey ways. By the time Cassia adjourned the meeting there were many on the Agora eating out of her hand. Even Cassia seemed to cut her slack, which was troubling. Yet it was hardly surprising, the only members of the Agora who were not convinced seemed to be Dolly and Yelina. The last act of the day was Cassia granting her permission to stay and visit with their people. An exchange of knowledge and culture. At hearing that Dolly smiled, it was a tacit approval of what would come next. As the others congratulated Camila and welcomed her, three other ladies stayed behind. As they approached Susan went up to Yelina and asked for permission to go first. Yelina was surprised at this but stepped aside for her. Susan smiling walked up to Camila, she was holding her hands in front of herself as she spoke.

"Camila, you have said much of the ways of the Grey, and if I may speak for my sisters here, I am happy you have come.   I believe an exchange of knowledge would be very beneficial to you. For instance, when you speak of the dance and the Grey ways, there is something you should know."

At saying this Susan without warning used the back of her hand to send Camila on to the floor. In all of Dolly's time in the Agora she had never heard someone hit that hard before. Camila shot her face up at Susans smiling face. Camila's expression unhidden and unhinged showed she was every bit the Grey women Dolly suspected she was. The wolf behind that pretty face was vicious and cunning. And one worthy of putting down.

"Here in Medford, Hoplites are property of their mothers. A grey woman who does not want to be called a whore, must ask his mother for permission to court. You did not do so young lady, and have wronged my sister here. You will ask her forgiveness and if she does not give it, then perhaps we will see how you and I dance."

Dolly was amused on many levels. For one seeing that little trollop put in her place was worth much to her. But it made Dolly's heart beat in happiness that Susan was standing up for Yelina and her honor. There had been a time when the three of them were united in both love for Travis and their clan. They had grown close as they had worked so desperately to hold on to the clan with their fingernails. Fighting others who wanted power, other clans who wished to see them fail, and of course all the normal challenges to life in general. The three of them had stood tall together and it had been a long time since the three of them had been as one. Yelina spoke with amusement.

"I will forgive her insult, although my son would probably prefer I not. I am sure you think yourself irresistible but you aren't Camila. You cost my son his place, and I will not forgive that little girl."

Dolly spoke now, speaking for all three. As she did, she felt taller somehow. Perhaps it was because the insolent girl was on the ground where she belonged.

"I think you should bugger off, learn what you come to learn and go. I would suggest you stay away from Malcom if you know what's good for you."

Dolly watched in satisfaction as she picked herself off the floor and left. Dolly felt a part of things was back where it belonged. But when she turned back to her friends, she hoped to find them in good spirits. Instead, she watched as both walked away without words. Sighing, she felt her phone buzz with another text from Jackie.

Chapter 10: We Are From the Government and We Are Here to Help

Washington DC – State Department

Jan 18th 2058

Travis's alarm bells were going off from the moment he saw the attitude in those he was being introduced to. Previously when he had come here, they were cordial and professional. Now it was what it looked like when you got caught stealing. Lots of cold short stares and emotionless statements. But he rolled with it as he was led into a SKIF. That was government parlance for a room that was secure. Jackie and his guards had to wait outside but Travis was offered a seat at the center of the table. His contact had come in briefly but not made eye contact with him and left just as rapidly. After a bit three men entered the room and sat across from him, sealing the clear-cut message. One of the three men who entered was important; Travis had seen him on TV many times.

If the fricking National Security Advisor is here then I am in for it. What the fuck have I gotten myself into now?

"Mr. Williams I am undersecretary Cartright I specialize in South American affairs here at State. To my left is Admiral Jackson, and this is Mr. Grayson he is the President's National Security Advisor. We wanted to talk to you about Meridia and your contact with their government."

Travis saw the looks and paused not really knowing what to say. The guy from state reminded him of his old High School principal with the way he carried himself. Official, emotionless, coy, but not a dummy. The National Security guy looked a bit bored and detached, the last guy, the Admiral was different. The Admiral was the first to go after him.

"If you don't mind us saying son, you haven't been fully honest with us."

Overweight, with a belly that seemed to flow like rain over his belt he would appear on first glance harmless. The fact he was in a suit and not a uniform told him he was not working for the Navy, but another agency… one with a nefarious history. But what grabbed Travis now was that look. Clearly the old Admiral knew how to get attention and focus young men. One look at his face and you knew he was the most dangerous man in the room. Intelligent, with eyes always searching, looking. When he spoke, he did so with a deep bass voice, and an Alabama draw. Travis imagined if God was black and southern, he would sound very much like this man. He was honest when he said he had no clue what they were talking about. After a pause and quiet staring contest, the man from the White House handed him a photo.

"I think you remember her, Camila Hernandez. She attended the gathering at Sao Paulo with the delegation?"

Travis shook his head yes and looked up seeing the man from the White House looking at him with interest now.

"That image was taken in Medford today. I believe the building she is going into is frequented by yourself, and members of your organization."

Travis was handed several more showing her entering the Agora and his heart nearly stopped. These were taken from a camera on street level. They had someone in Medford watching them.

My God, not this again… I thought we were clear of these people! I can't live through that again. I won't see my children live like that again.

The last thing the town needed was the Government in their lives again. Travis calmed himself. The last time the Government knew of them it had been murderous. Many human and vampire lives had been lost to free them from that tyranny. Only the actions of his father and his people had freed them for good. That in of itself had been superhuman… or inhuman in nature.

"Gentlemen I can't give you an explanation for it. The first time I met her was in Sao Paulo with your man. From the way it looked to me she was part of his staff. Other than that interaction, and one she had with my son we haven't spoken to her, ever."

Next questions were around the kidnapping and the man who had went over to Meridia. They made sure to remind him they knew that Jason's mother had also boarded a flight to the country recently and not returned. Cleaning out her bank accounts and taking the maximum number of bags on her flight. Clearly, she wasn't coming back from the way it looked.

"Yes, a member of our team seems to have decided to quit in a rather unorthodox manner. We are not sure if this was a planned thing or if it was done on a whim. I know he wired money to his mother so she could join him. As for my son, he was taken by several armed men who entered his flat. They drugged him and when he awoke, he met Ms. Hernandez. She offered him work, but he refused. I am not sure if she is recruiting for their own PMC or just looking for intel on us specifically. We are investigating, but we are not sure if the two things are related. It could be a coincidence or it might not be."

The looks from the three made it clear none of them thought that. He was asked again for every contact he had made to Meridia. His answers didn't please them in the least. Then he was shown every single communication he had made or his company had made in the last year.

"Mr. Williams the NSA was tasked with reviewing your communications, and while they were not able to find evidence of contact, we believe it is still there. The NSA says you are running five separate intelligence programs on three continents at the moment. You have as many as 100 individuals loyal to you gathering human intelligence all over the world. Um… none of that is in your contract with us, nor have you advertised that. Care to explain?"

Travis was kind of impressed they had missed the other four programs they were running. The number of people they had overseas was low too. Even Travis didn't have the full number. Each high-level member of the Agora had their own organization, and each of them ran it to gather intelligence. Travis wouldn't be surprised to learn they had other things on the side they didn't tell him about.

"Moonstone is like any PMC; we need actionable intelligence to do our jobs. While we rely on our clients to help with that, we do not solely rely on them. We have limited assets that we deploy when necessary. Does that have a global footprint, yes. But I would hardly say we are giving the CIA or any other 3 letter agency a run for their money. It's just good business, it helps us to keep our people alive, and yours."

No sooner had he said it and the guy from State accused him of trading intelligence for cash, possibly US secrets even. Next, he threatened him that a forensic accountant had been hired to look over their documents and to determine the scope of their operation. Before Travis could comment the White House guy interrupted him and turned on a screen behind them. Audio popped and the screen showed a familiar site to anyone who watched TV dramas. The president, and a few others were sitting in the oval office staring at him. President Wilkenson spoke next with his very familiar slow cadence.

"I hope the three of you have gotten to the bottom of this by now. Son, I don't care what you have going on the side. The only thing I want to know is why the Meridians are asking for you by name? I can't run foreign policy if I have some no name merc playing diplomat!"

The Admiral looked amused at the interruption while the other two were far less so. Once they got the president up to speed on where they were they explained that the Meridians had agreed to talks but only with Travis. When it got quiet again, he realized they were waiting on him to explain.

"Gentlemen your guess is as good as mine. Other than this woman trying to recruit my son, and the work we did for State, I haven't had any dealings with them. I don't know anyone in their government, nor have we had anyone approach my family."

The Admiral then spoke loudly and reminded Travis that Ms. Hernandez was in his home town right now meeting with members of his company. At hearing the Admirals voice the president immediately seized on it.

"James, I didn't know you were there. Look, I don't have time to deal with petty things like this. Why don't you take charge of this and deal with it. Do what you have to, but I want that meeting kept, but with a real diplomat instead of this amateur. Bobby get your ass back here, we have more important items to cover. Cartright we will get this sorted, coordinate with James once he gets to the bottom of this…whatever it is."

The line from the White House died and everyone stood. When Travis did the Admiral spoke with authority and told him to sit his ass back down. With a smirk the National Security Advisor left in a hurry. The man from State spoke quickly to the Admiral and before leaving looked smugly at Travis.

"I think it's safe to say you violated your contract with us. And I wouldn't expect payment for that last job if I were you."

With a small smile he left the room, leaving it quiet and isolated. The Admiral put his glasses back on and opened a lap top he had hidden beneath the table before.

"I hate these SKIF's at State, they haven't updated them since you were in the Marines. I bet a 12-year-old could hack into here with his Xbox. There, now we are more secure and you and me can have our talk."

Next the black man opened a small satchel and removed several items. Travis knew a setup when he saw one and this was obviously one of those. The

Admiral was putting on a show, he was in charge and had all the power. He was flexing on Travis and wanted him to know it. Travis was about as sure as he could be, the man was agency.

"Your military record son, it seems a bit incomplete."

The black man slid over a slim file with a printout of his military record. Much of it was gibberish to the un-initiated. What caught Travis's eye, and probably that of the deep voiced CIA man, was the section that detailed duty stations. It was all blank, not blacked out or restricted…. Just blank.

First, they say the Meridians will only talk to me, then accuse me of stealing… and now my military record? What the fuck is going on?

Travis let it slide and did the best he could to remain calm. He needed to focus on what was at hand and not panic. Looking at the blank section on duty station he had flashes of memories of serving in the war. A lot of that time had been spent on Guam with the other vampires.

"Appears to be, you know how it is sir. Records get lost, people forget, doesn't change anything though. I remember very well where I was, and what I did."

For a long time, the black man looked down his long nose at him through thick glasses. Finally, he smiled a bit and shook his head in agreement. Then the look changed and Travis had his worst nightmare realized.

"Yes, well it's the same with us. Back around the time you were climbing hills in Taiwan I had the displeasure to work for an ingrate named Talbot, ever hear of him? Doubt you have, I suppose you being wherever you were, you never heard of him. Well back then son, our company had me working a project named Viper. I can talk about it since as far as the agency is concerned it never existed. Kinda like that section on your DD-214."

Viper had been a codename for the Governments containment of vampires. The Government didn't just want to control the vampires; they wanted to reproduce their powers. Or at the very least subdue them. They had spent years doing this after they had moved and taken over Medford. Everyone, Vampire and human alike, had been forced into a pseudo prison. All of this was rolled up in the Viper project, a project that had come to an abrupt and violent end. One that Travis didn't want to talk about. If this man knew about the existence of Viper he knew way too much. As far as Travis and the vampire council knew, any human with knowledge of Viper was either dead… or a friend. Still, it wouldn't help his cause showing fear. Travis took a breath and asked him what the problem was. He wasn't admitting anything, just going with the flow.

The CIA man took off his glasses and fished for a wipe to clean them. As he did, he spoke without looking at him.

"My concern is that international diplomacy requires a diplomat, not a howitzer. I see what Moonstone has been up to and I agree your company is useful. But I remember what happened at the end of project Viper. A lot of messes got cleaned up, and a lot of messes got created. I don't want to see that kind of result occur again. The problem we are facing isn't one that can be solved with a fist. It requires a thinking man, a considerate man, a loyal man. I am not convinced you can be any of those things son."

With his glasses neatly put back on his face he gave him an intense stare. Travis didn't like this but it wasn't like he had any control here, or over this man. No point in playing, Travis went in without looking. If this man had worked on Viper than he might be holding a grudge. Lots of folks who worked with Viper died the night it came to an end.

"So, you know what I am, and what my people are. What happened after Viper wasn't our fault. A few wanted to be like us, for some humans that doesn't work out. We explained that to them, but they didn't care. No one wanted their deaths, but it wasn't murder."

The black man rose from his chair and walked around the table sitting on the edge of it near Travis. His smile was wide now and he didn't hold back. He spoke quieter now, just for Travis's ears. But in that quiet tone was one of victory.

"We both know that isn't how it went down. But it's a good story, I will grant you that. Travis, I don't give a tinkers toss about some congresswoman who wanted immortality and wound-up dead. It was all the humans working around the project that disappeared, that is what I take issue with. I want to know why they disappeared and how."

Travis looked at him wondering if he knew already. Probably did, if he was plugged in enough to know about this, then he probably had everything. He closed his eyes and hoped for the best.

"Your buddy Talbot ordered most of his team out, the ones he wanted to live anyway. He had orders to liquidate the town, men, women, children. Humans and vampires alike he was going to kill everyone to cover their tracks. He figured a few of his own people dying was a good cover, I guess. Had my people not acted there wouldn't have been a town left."

Travis paused not wanting to directly admit to the mass murder, but it was what it was. He could lie, but to what point?

"So, we acted, those that resisted died. Those that lived chose to join us, a few agreed to stay quiet and were left human. I know it sounds like a pile of shit, but it's how it went. I don't regret a moment of it though. Talbot had it coming. The congresswoman and the General got caught up in politics afterwards. That wasn't my clan's doing, and I wasn't there to see it anyway."

The CIA man nodded through most of that and when Travis got to the part about the congresswoman, he blurted out the word "Amethyst", which was the name of the clan both the general and the congresswoman had joined and been killed by. Travis was shocked when he said it. In a way it was entertaining, in other ways it wasn't. Travis tried to continue like it was nothing.

"Yeah, power struggle in the clan. I think the congresswoman thought she could take over. Don't know when they died, but it had to happen before 2041. After that, all of them were gone."

The black man still smiling shook his head and mentioned that he knew about the night of the fangs. That was the night the Amethyst clan ceased to be. That name for the night was something only used in Medford. That caused Travis to look up in shock. He was well informed, too damned well in fact.

"Did you think the CIA was just going to completely forget about all of you? Yes, we know, and yes, we are aware of the other clan's connections in the Government. For now, your kind are well plugged in, so what. You can say the same thing about PETA and the Boy Scouts. So long as you don't try to take over our government, or society in general, we will look past it. But we have been watching son, trust me."

Looking closer at his adversary he seemed entertained by all of this. Travis sure as hell wasn't. The man pulled away from the table and went back behind the desk. Pulling up some files and then pulling down the glasses.

"Says here your Grey clan was founded by a man named Finnian. That each of you possess the ability to cloak yourself in darkness. Hide in plain sight and all that. I am sure you find that useful in your line of work. Ah… here is what I was looking for. Finnan, your founder you call him, wasn't just a founder of a clan, was he? Sometime around 900 BC he founded the city state Sparta. The same fellows who stood at Thermopylae correct? So, all those 300 were vampires then?"

Travis nodded and explained that in ancient times they called themselves Immortals. He waited for the next set of questions. The black man made a joke about Immortals fighting Immortals. Whatever it meant it went over Travis's head. The Admiral saw his confusion and smirked.

"The Greeks fought the Persians at Thermopylae, the greatest warriors among the Persians were called the Immortals. A group of 10,000 men, the best Xerxes had. So, it was a battle between Immortals then."

Travis was a bit irked that this man knew more about his clan's history than he did. But he wasn't the best in school when it came to history. He had seen the old movie on the battle but it wasn't like he was paying that close attention. Mentally he was keeping a log of things he was going to have to tell the other clans. This news was not going to go down well. After making a few more notes the Admiral smirked and pushed back in his chair.

"I never liked those stories about your people. Throwing babies from the hills and the like. But your people are good warriors, no doubt about that. Do you still like killing baby's son?"

Travis found himself responding like he was a Marine again. He was rough when he said no, to the CIA man's question. It went against his faith and his judgement to do so. Suddenly as quickly as his meeting had gone sour, it shifted again. The man seemed to almost come to some sort of moment.

"Who are you really Travis?"

For a long point he wasn't sure how to respond. Then he realized that he must think he was much older. So, he quickly explained that he really was the age he looked.

"No, I know all about your origin and your age. I want to know who you are. Why do you get out of bed in the morning Travis? Why are you here now, offering your services, to the very same government that tried to wipe your people off the map?"

He had to stop from rolling his eyes. What a stupid question. Still Travis was sitting there with his dick in his hands. Might as well entertain the question. He hated the answer but it was the truth. It sounded naïve and in a way it was. It harkened back to a time when he saw his country in a very different light. When things made a hell of a lot more sense and when his life wasn't that complicated.

"When I was a kid, I just wanted to be respected. I wanted to serve, and do what everyone else was doing. Then I went to war and I saw what that really was. It's not a movie or some stupid game. Countries use their sons and daughters as pawns. Pawns get used and thrown away. My concern now is my family and my clan. Yes, I saw what nearly happened to us. All due to your agency and people like Talbot. The ass got what was coming to him. But I love my country, and I want to help when I can. But I am not a fool, I don't trust you people, and I won't hesitate to protect mine if you make me... sir"

The man rocked back in his seat and looked at Travis coldly. He was quiet for a bit before the continued.

"I think that is the first fully honest thing you have told me so far. I wouldn't expect you to feel any other way, Travis. The position of this agency is that your people are American citizens and not a threat to our government. So, relax, I think we can work together."

Travis heard the statement and knew from the moment this meeting went tits up this was where it was heading. This man wanted to own them again. Control them into doing his bidding, doing God knows what.

"For the record I know all about your military actions and those of your fellows. Those files weren't purged by your associates and they can never be. I don't fear your people Travis, I know what kind of warriors you are. Your people fought bravely and it's clear where their loyalties are. Now about this Meridian mess, now that we better understand each other do you want to take another stab at why they contacted you? I seriously doubt it was by accident."

Travis smirked but somewhere in that face of his Travis saw a tiny bit of respect. Perhaps it was for his service, or perhaps it was for his strength he wasn't sure. But he clung to that tiny hope and tried to act as if nothing was wrong, and that the world hadn't just fell on all vampires again. He had to take a long breath so he had oxygen in his lungs again. He felt like he hadn't taken a breath in 10 minutes.

"Camila and the Meridian rep were both Grey's. Shocked the hell out of me when I saw them! I have never seen a Grey outside of Medford before. We assumed we were all that was left. I get Camila wanting Jason and Malcom. Getting two male Grey's helps them with procreation. The more you breed one of us with you humans, the weaker the bloodline. Eventually you stop having little vampires. I am going to guess that is why Camila was so interested in them. But if both of them are plugged into the Meridian government, it might be one of their kind has control over the government itself. Asking for me directly, sort of makes me think one of them does. Otherwise, it doesn't make sense."

The admiral agreed with his assessment and handed him another photo to look at. He seemed happy with himself which didn't please Travis too much. The picture was of a middle-aged woman he had seen before. It took him a bit to recognize her as Rose, one of the persons he had suspected might show at the meeting in Sao Paulo. Dolly had suspected Rose was a lover of the president of Meridia, Rose served on his staff of the Meridian President.

"Her name is Rosa Hernandez; she may be Camila's mother we aren't sure. The intel you shared before about her is correct, at least as far as we can tell. She is his lover and she's a Grey."

Travis was afraid to ask but he couldn't help himself. If he knew Rose was a vampire before, just how did he discover it? Seeing his face the Admiral took clear pleasure in his discomfort.

"After Viper ended a few of us kept tabs on you people. It's been almost a hobby these last few years. All that tech we came up with in Medford... we still have it son. Comes in handy from time to time. Like today for instance. Thanks to these I can see your eyes, and that of your daughter. By my estimation you clan is doing rather well. You nearly doubled it since you took over."

The admiral had shown him a pair of sunglasses; Travis had seen them before decades ago. Still, none of that explained Rose, and how he knew about her. It could be other intel he was getting from traditional channels but there had to be more. Asking him made the Admiral laugh.

"The Meridians have asked for you to show in Paris for talks in five days. The place they chose in Paris is Chateau De Malmaison. Fancy 18th century Chateau, restored by the French government and currently a museum of the Napoleonic era. That's how I knew."

Travis was confused and it showed. The Admiral laughed and smiled a bit more.

"I take it you didn't get a lot of European History at Medford High then? Son, that woman is the spitting image of Josephe, as in Napoleon and Josephe. That place was their home until the end of his reign. My people ran a background check on her, we checked her DNA against that of their descendants. Rose and her, are the same woman son. It seems as if Napoleon's wife wants a word with you alone. Care to guess what she is going to ask of you?"

Travis blurted out the only answer he could, which was he didn't have a clue.

"Your King of the Grey son, she wants something and she is going to use the power of a nation state to get it. Best you be figuring it out quickly."

Travis looked at him and sighed, now came the question. What did he want and what was going to happen next for his people.

"That all depends on you, son. You heard the president he wants the talks with Meridia. But no one is going to tell him Meridia only will talk to vampires. That kind of honestly doesn't bode well for one's career."

Travis laughed at that and then heard the Admirals solution. One that required something from him… shocker.

"I can get the President on board with you going to this little meeting. State will be pissed, and want to stop you. But I can make it clear that you are doing something for me. If I stick my neck out for you, I think I can get this to go away. Perhaps even get Cartright to pull that pole out of his ass about you. I know you need that contract with State, and if you fix a problem for me, I think I can fix your problem."

Travis wasn't thrilled with what he heard next and what the CIA man wanted. It was big, and it was certainly not legal or safe. But if he was on the up and up then Travis wasn't against it morally…. For the most part. But he needed to know just what trump cards he held and if possible, how many in Government knew about them. He could do all of this for the CIA and then watch them still do what they wanted.

"Long and short of it is son that I don't work like that. I could have used my knowledge of Viper against you decades ago. I saved this little gem in case I really needed a solution to a hard problem the agency can't solve. Neither of us have a great history working together but we both need each other."

Travis then asked the obvious, what happened when they didn't need each other?

"Let's just see how things play out and give each other a pass for now. I am aware how powerful you and your friends are son. If you want to come for me, I know you can get me. It's not one-sided, I am taking a big risk too. And your little meet and greet goes down in five days. I have to help you long before you are helping me. My little request isn't something you can do tomorrow. It takes planning and preparation, and time. If anything, I am the one trusting you. But that's the great thing about deterrence, it works both ways. Bottom line son is if you love your family and your country as much as you say, then you win both ways."

Travis had only heard the outline of what he was asking for, and what he was asking wasn't coming cheap. It was going to require nearly all of his organization operating full time and for weeks. With State stiffing him on the contract he was going to need cash fast. They had made a lot of purchases based on that money coming soon. The Admiral passed another folder with documents for an account and a number with an amount.

"Will that do son?"

Travis had never seen that many zeros before and was convinced this was a bad idea. This much money, and this much risk spelled disaster. But what choice did he have? After making the agreement the Admiral told him that he would send a plane to San Antonio to pick him and his team up when it was time to go see the Meridians. He already had in mind the team he would bring. As he walked out, he grabbed his daughter and his guards and got back in the car for the airport. Surprised that he could still breathe after that.

"Dad, you look white as a sheet, what in hell happened in there?"

Travis's mind was going fast now, considering all the ins and outs. Mostly he was boxed in but he sure as shit wasn't going to swallow this whole. He started by handing her the info on the money and the account.

"Holy shit dad! Did state give us this much?"

Travis explained that it was the agency and that they would speak more when they got home. By the time they were half way to the airport he had a new set of orders for his daughter.

"Jackie, pull the amount from the account that State owes us but not a penny more. Then do what you have to on our finances. Who do we know in Europe who deals in arms?"

Jackie ran down the short list, all of which Travis knew already. None of those were up to this task.

"When we get home, go see the Rubies about moving large sums of money into Euros. Whatever you have going on at home put it on hold. I want you on a flight to Italy as soon as you can get it."

Jackie had only gone abroad a couple of times and never for Moonstone. Travis outlined the rest of the ask on the way. When he was done, he put a hand on her.

"I am going to be putting you in harm's way. If you can't handle that say so now?"

That changed her excitement to resentment in a flash. Just how a Grey should respond. He didn't have to say another word, Travis knew she was ready.

Chapter 11: Grey Dancers

Medford, Texas – 5th Street

Jan 19th 2058

Dressed in blue jeans a baggy shirt and a ballcap, Jessie was making her way across the street. Her objective was to walk down the street unobserved and to place a small mark on a post in front of a specific store. This was child's play, something she had been doing since she was 10. The objective was to mark a contact signal. They could be used to tell an asset, you want to meet, warn them, or just order them to their dead drop. Most marks were in chalk, something easy to place, wore off easily, and went unnoticed.

What made this test difficult was she had to leave the mark without stopping or being observed by the three persons watching the store. First step in this was to change her appearance and her look. This was accomplished with what she carried in a small bag. It changed up her clothing and her hair just enough. No one said anything so she had to have gone unnoticed. Pushing her luck, she was still lucky and went un-noticed when she walked by the place a 2nd time. On the 3rd pass she was to leave a specific shape on the post. Again, she had to do this without breaking her stride. That was the pass fail, not be observed at all, now that was the grand prize.

With her third pass she had a new shirt and had gone from a pony tail to short choppy hair. She accomplished this with a wig, and not a great one. What sold the whole package was the change in her walk. The first time she had went by, in a hurry and as if she was looking for something. The second time she was slow, and paused numerous times as if she was window shopping. The third time she walked with attitude, short powerful steps that told everyone to get out of the way. It was too showy but this very thing had worked for her in the past. She sold it with confidence and a change in her makeup.

Jessie crossed the street making sure she didn't fixate on her target. That post was not in her sight except for just when it needed to be. Otherwise, she was following her training, searching for tails, and doing assessments. Most folks she knew who walked by. It always pleased her when a friend didn't notice her, it meant she was really pulling this off. She almost lost her focus when a very pretty girl walked out of a store in front of her and walked past. Girls that good looking in Medford were not rare by any means. But ones that good looking AND who she hadn't seen before? It almost made her blow her cover, but she laser focused back on the mission and right on cue made the mark. She covered the small move she made by snarling at a fat guy who was coming out of the store. The move of her head and his reaction did a great job she thought.

Her heart was racing as she turned into the alley and met with her instructor. Without a doubt Moonstone's best person at running ops like this. Susan only taught the best and it said something about Jessie that she had selected her.

"Not bad, that little thing with Grover was cute. Good thing you look like you do or he might be upset with you. You get top marks, good job."

Before Jessie could leap for joy a cell phone went off in her pocket. That was strange because she wasn't allowed one in training. Susan frowned immediately and told her to answer it. Jessie was confused it wasn't her phone and she had no idea how it got there. She found the volume turned it up on high and answered the call.

"Hi Jessie, that was a nice change you made. If you ever want to learn a good brush pass you know where to find me."

Susan pointed up the street and Jessie turned to see the woman at the end. It was that same pretty girl she had seen earlier. She asked directly who she was but the girl just waved and walked away.

"That's Camila, you didn't see her put that in your pocket…. Well, you lose a point for that."

Jessie was pissed, not just because she had screwed up her eval, but because if that was who she thought she was. This was the girl who had messed up her brother's life. Susan confirmed it after she asked.

"Susan, do you mind if I introduce myself. I would like to give her a piece of my mind."

Susan smiled and encouraged it; the only advice she gave was not to kill her.

"I was thinking of just breaking the skanks arms, that should be enough."

Medford, Texas — 5th street

Jan 19th 2058

Malcom had been called by father to a meeting along with many others in town. He wouldn't say what it was but clearly it was important. Every single team commander, and several clan leaders were already in Dolly's house to attend. Malcom was glad he was invited, even if it was only because he was head of the Agoge. As he walked down the street towards the location where Jessie's phone pinged, he thought about his work.

Since becoming head of the Agoge he had been restless and irritated. He was no longer in line for fast promotion and with that mark against him it might be a generation before he had another chance. Still the surprise in returning to the Agoge was how much he was starting to enjoy it. Teaching young people was hard but it was easy to see how he could get used to it. Unlike that silly outfit he had to wear. Thankfully he was able to change when going into town.

As he walked up close to the Dojo, Malcom wondered how his sisters evaluation was going. Today was her last major field test before she was certified. Other than finishing her studies and getting her diploma she was nearly ready to enter adult Grey life. If she had been born a man Jessie would have given him and his brother a run for their money. Jessie had the heart of a lion and was a natural fighter. But her judgement wasn't the best. Time, and a tiny bit of experience was all she needed though.

As he got close to the Dojo's door that thought pierced him. He hadn't faired very well when this latest challenge had hit him. It had only been a couple of weeks but reality was starting to settle in. His old mentor had checked up on him a day or so ago and made some observations. One of those was to ask him to break down his mistakes in Meridia. It had been enough time that Malcom had come to realize he had let his guard down there. He SHOULD have taken more care in breaking cover and returning to the safehouse. And once inside he shouldn't have been so quick to allow himself to relax. Had he been aware and alert they wouldn't have gotten the drop on him. He was still sore about the demotion but he was starting to see that perhaps he wasn't so blameless after all. If he ever got another opportunity, he wouldn't let it be lost like that again. The only thing still left unresolved was his mother. They still hadn't talked since that day. As he got close to the Dojo he returned to the present.

The sounds of combat where loud in the Dojo but that wasn't unusual. From the sounds of it, Jessie was fighting another woman. Jessie was good, and she had the heart to fight with the best of them. Her judgement in battle was sound, and it generally didn't let her down. It was all the judgement she used leading up to that moment that generally got her in trouble. He was still smiling as he entered and saw who Jessie's opponent really was. Jessie and Camila were in a serious battle and Camila was showing her that she wasn't a slouch. Malcom was so astounded he didn't react at first. He just stood there like an idiot while the woman who had ruined his life attacked his sister. It took a solid 5 seconds before a voice screamed inside him to act.

Malcom watched as Jessie now unsteady after a blow to her face backpaddled. With an opening Camila was in a move to land a solid roundhouse kick to her midsection. With the speed of a cheetah and the skill of a warrior, Malcom moved silently towards his prey. He was no longer thinking, only reacting. In his mind was two moves he would make nothing more, and nothing less. He was focused on the planted leg of Camila. That was his target, to swing his own leg connecting with hers thus destroying her balance. All of Camila's weight was balanced on that leg right now. He could see the move in his mind as he pivoted and moved his own self to land the blow.

His leg was moving and his eyes were locked onto the spot where it would connect. But at the last moment as if in slow motion Camila seemed to fold into herself and roll away. Malcom had processed that and changed his next move on the now alerted foe. As a vampiric woman Camila was beyond strong. As evidenced by the broken wooden beam that was part of the structure. Camila had destroyed it with a single blow. But any Grey woman had limits, and the closer he got to her, the closer he could use his superior strength to his advantage. He lunged towards her with a fist.

Medford, Texas – Medford Dojo

Jan 19th 2058

Jessie had not seen her brother enter. She had been locked in a "friendly" sparing match with Camila for the last five minutes. Both of them were tired, having gone at it with everything they had. By now she was no longer lividly angry at her. She didn't like the bitch, but she had to admit that Camila was the most skilled female fighter she had ever seen. Her moves were uncanny and she seemed to be able to anticipate everything Jessie threw at her. She was toying with Jessie, that much she knew. It wasn't just anticipating her, she almost seemed bored waiting on what she "knew" was coming. It was clear to Jessie that Camila could land any blow on her she wished. Camila made everything look easy, which upset Jessie. Still, she had to respect the bitch's skill.

The fight had settled down towards the end as they spoke. At first Jessie had been needling her. But Camila took all that in stride and simply and calmly discussed things as they took shots at each other. Even Jessie could see she was not at Camila's level, but that didn't stop Jessie from trying to learn all she could. That had come to an abrupt halt when her brother jumped in.

Malcom had come out from nowhere and nearly landed a devastating blow. She had watched her brother use his skill before, had been on the receiving end of more than one lesson from him. But this was something different, he was pissed. He wasn't holding back, he was using all his force and trying to hurt Camila. At first Jessie smiled, her brother was surely going to put Camila in her place. If anyone deserved a bloody nose over their actions it was Camila. Yet as Jessie watched she was astounded to see that the two were nearly evenly matched. Camila avoided each blow, sometimes with only inches to spare. Likewise, Camila's vain attempt at hurting him was batted away like feathers by the raging Malcom. It was the look on their faces that shocked Jessie the most. Each was giving their all and it was taking every drop of their ability to stay in the fight.

Jessie wasn't sure who started it but the pitch of the fight changed. No longer were each trying to land devastating blows now. Instead, they had reverted to using speed and stealth to win. Both began to move with such speed that Jessie struggled to keep up. Each would disappear mid move only to reappear a millisecond before their punch or kick would land. Yet neither could land a single blow. Each had the number of the other, and anticipated the others move. It was about this moment that Jessie's mouth fell open. The rhythm of their movements were perfectly in time. It was almost musical, as if the fight had been choreographed for the cameras. Now the faces didn't show anger or hate, rather they showed…..

Jessie watched in fascination as what had been anger and resentment before was now something else. Both were still trying hard to win but instead of anger, now each seemed unnerved by the others skill. Their moves seemed effortless and the noises they made were less in pain or discomfort but in something else. Jessie's hand came up to her face as she watched what had been a violent display start to become one of desire. It was a dance between two, effortless and beautiful. It went on like this for what seemed an eternity. Jessie watched in stunned fascination. She had never seen two matched so evenly before. Each wanted to win, but neither could. Towards the end of the fight the anger was long drained out of the faces of each. There was longing in those faces, and it dawned on Jessie that these two were attracted to each other. That thought made her scoff, Camila had zero chance with him.

Then out of nowhere Camila stopped and knelt in front of Malcom. Both were breathing hard and Malcom towered over her, angry again. Jessie was curious if Malcom would send her down with a massive punch, but instead he froze at the sight. Each looked at the other and neither moved. It dawned on Jessie at that moment that Camila was giving herself to him. That pushed Jessie into action. She needed to save her brother from such a fate.

Jessie now appalled came forward to get them to snap out of this stupid dance. Her first words were ignored as Malcom continued to stare directly at Camila. She had to hit him on the back of the head to get him to snap out of it. But even then, he was still locked on Camila. Finaly Jessie had to pull him away by force. As she did, she looked back at Camila who was staring at him. She paid Jessie no attention whatsoever. For Camila the only thing she was interested in was Malcom.

What on earth is going on? What magic does this witch have? Malcom isn't the type to just fall for some skank! Especially not one who had cost him everything!

As she led him away from Camila, she asked him what the hell he was thinking. Malcom didn't respond, he just looked back at the still kneeling Camila and paused again.

Chapter 12: Domino's

Medford, Texas – Dolly's Home

Jan 19th 2058

The second Travis arrived back he had been secretive and quiet. Jackie had pretty much disappeared from view as well, which worried Dolly. She was concerned there had been a blow up between father and daughter on the trip. But when Travis called this meeting, she knew better. Along with Yelina and Susan was each of his team leads. This meant a serious meeting amongst leadership. Then came the surprises in who was invited and who wasn't. Cassia was not invited, as was none of the other members of the Agora. Attending this odd event were non-Grey vampires. Nancy, Art, and Ashley were here for the Aqua, and Marcus and Alessia for the Rubies.

Every time someone asked a question Travis would just tell them to wait a bit longer. The last two guests to show was Mark from the Emeralds and Ed from the Cobalt. Now things were getting interesting indeed. Four clan leaders in one house, and not on either clan or council business. Yelina snuck up close and asked her what was going on.

"Hell, if I know, he has one of the teams surrounding and sweeping the house. Whatever it is it has to be big."

Travis had asked her to remove the furniture in the living room and now she knew why. Everyone was gathered in a tight circle skin close to each other. That was when she noticed the Aqua were all spaced out evenly among them. Her guess was confirmed a moment later when Travis told the Aqua among them to open the link. The place the Aqua took them to was the same field where Jay and Travis had been crowned. Travis entered the center of the circle and began to speak.

"Please forgive this violation of our code, but I assure you it's necessary. As you know I just came back from Washington, where I was meeting with the State department. The meeting did not go as I thought it would. I was confronted by a man there named Jackson…"

On cue one of the Aqua summoned the image of the man from Travis's mind showing all of them this man.

"He claims he is from the agency, and he claims to know about Viper. Here in a bit, I will show you the conversation we had and what he wants. What we do about it and how we respond I want you to table until you hear everything. Please try and keep your thoughts and your memories quiet as our Aqua friends do this. In this place everyone can hear and feel your thoughts and emotions. We don't want this meeting to devolve into a fight over trivial things. What does matter is the humans still know about us, and we are being watched right now by the agency."

Dolly could feel the emotions and thoughts of the group. That was about the worst thing the clans could hear right now. Over the next ten minutes the Aqua replayed both the conversation Travis had, and his thoughts. Dolly paid more attention to the others than what was being projected to them. She could feel Yelina's worries, Susans pride in her husband for his boldness, and the fear in the young vampires. From Mark she felt the anger and resentment at the specter of the past coming for them yet again. In Travis she felt his calm heart and strength of character. Without thinking she allowed herself a thoughtless moment to love him, truly he was their King. She stowed it away as quickly as she could, but all here would have felt it and known it, including Susan and Yelina. By this point the projection ended and the muttering began.

"I know, these people can't be trusted. I doubt anyone here would argue with that. I respect every soul here; I would trust my life with any of you. I called you all here tonight to seek your council. What is being asked is just of my clan, but what happens next will affect us all. Once I know how I will respond I will brief the council, but for now I need each of you and your wisdom tonight. You have heard the Admirals offer, and you have heard my heart on the matter. What say you?"

The Aqua struggled to keep this many in the link so they could not talk all night. The debate was spirted and fierce. But it was clear from Travis he was not going to back down or run. Once it was clear where their King was headed the rest of the clan supported him. The last questions of the night were how to respond, and how to execute what Travis wanted to do. That was when Travis turned to Dolly and looked at her. She could feel both the love and respect pouring out of him towards her. She had been in the link before but having Travis be open like this and blatant caused her to blush.

"Dolly, I need you to task your people, every asset you can move into the region. And I want you out there leading our effort. Until I can arrive every Grey there will follow Dolly, her word is my word."

Dolly looked at him and knew she would anger the others who loved him. In this moment that was fleeting she didn't care. She couldn't be more in love with him or prouder of the man he had become. And her heart soared at seeing his love for her in the open.

Medford, Texas – Yelina's Home

Jan 19th 2058

Yelina was not pleased, not in the slightest. This was her time, not Susan's and especially not Dolly's. Dolly had given him up, had agreed, what did she think she doing? How dare she stand there in front of everyone and act like that. Yelina thought back to the link, and the brazen way Dolly had acted. Clearly, she still loved and desired him. It was such a slap in Yelina's face.

Lately it feels like I don't have a husband. Why aren't you here Travis?

Every waking second Travis had, seemed poured into the business or the clan. He had promised more than once that this cycle, would be different. But it had only gotten worse. She couldn't say anything, this latest challenge was going to take every bit of their effort to deal with. But what about them? Her relationship with Travis was dying right in front of her. She resented this latest problem, and she resented Travis for not being there. This was his home, and yet where was he? Was he with Dolly or Susan right now? More likely he was working or dealing with some other need. But when was he going to be here?

Yelina was cleaning her kitchen and doing so in anger. The agreement reached years before was intolerable. It dishonored her and Susan both, but because he was King, they were to let it go. Yelina paused from scrubbing a stain on the counter to remember the words from mother. It was clear Cassia was growing just as irritated at the situation as she was. But for her, the only thing that mattered was children and the clan. At one time Cassia and her had been close. But that had been a long time ago. Just like it had been a long time since she had really been his wife. That thought caused more resentment from Yelina. After Travis's return he had lain with her, far too little. In over two decades they had only one child together. It wasn't like Yelina didn't want more; Jessie was nearly grown now. In another year she would be living on her own. Yelina was lonely, and felt unwanted by the man she loved. She resented all she had given him. All she had sacrificed for the man. She had given up her freedom, her home, everything.

He wants me to be loyal, well how much more loyal can I be? He doesn't know the half of what I put up with because of him!

Yelina stopped and took a breath. That wasn't fair, he did love her. She only had to speak to him to know. It was this arrangement, that and his duty that stood between them. Susan she could deal with. If Cassia hadn't intervened, she was going to challenge and kill her. The Grey way was clear and Yelina had been building up to this for years. She had long come to terms with the fact that she might have to kill Susan to have happiness.

Yelina looked over at the fireplace in the far room and saw the place where a picture had once stood. She had taken it down in anger years before. It was of Travis and those that love him all together. It was taken the day of his coronation; the day each had sworn their loyalty and oaths to him. Yelina had removed the image because it had Susan and Dolly in it. She was resentful of having them looking at her all the time. It had been years since it stood there but still Yelina looked at the empty space where it hung. Almost as if the ghost of the image taunted her. As much as her Grey nature yearned to do as it will, she had denied it. Doing as she wished would destroy the man she loved. And that fact was eating at her and poisoning the love she had for him. If something didn't change soon, she would go mad.

There was only one way to settle this and that was for them to act as Grey women did. By denying their nature it was destroying all four of them. She knew her love would not act, he could not and would not choose among them. It fell to them to act and Yelina had been very close to acting when mother threw down her challenge. Now she risked both hers and Susans life by just thinking about this. Dolly might be hoping for exactly that to occur. Clearly, she still loved him, and it would be so easy for Dolly to push them just a tiny bit further into acting rashly. Especially Susan, she often acted without thinking. Mother was many things but she wasn't afraid.

If she said she would kill them then she would. She had acted without warning before with others she valued less. With a warning given…. no, mother would not hesitate to kill us both if she had cause.

Perhaps that was what Dolly was planning, and why she was so brazen in the link. The fact Travis yearned for her still didn't help matters any. Yelina slammed her hand back down on the counter trying to get the stain out that refused to yield.

"Mom, are you ok?"

Yelina looked up to see a concerned Jessie. That was when she remembered that Jessie and Malcom had been no shows at the meeting tonight. She vented some of her anger and frustration at her daughter for this. She felt horribly guilty for doing so, but nonetheless her body needed the release. Holding back this anger and resentment was like holding acid in your mouth. Jessie was hurt for a moment but recovered quickly explaining that they had arrived late but after Yelina had left. That was when she explained what Camila had done. With that knowledge Yelina's temper flared and boiled over.

"She did what exactly!"

As Jessie explained again Yelina stewed in anger and decided that if she could not deal with the likes of Dolly or Susan then perhaps…just perhaps she could deal with the likes of Camila.

"Mom, I don't understand, why would Malcom act like that. That woman took his honor. Why would he want her, does she have some sort of power? I mean she is pretty sure, and he is a man and all. But that isn't like Malcom."

Yelina looked over at her daughter. Jessie wasn't a child, and Yelina knew full well Jessie had long since made love to others at this point. She wasn't a fool, but she was young.

If Jessie can see this then mother is right about what she told me. Malcom loves the girl but doesn't realize it yet. It's only a matter of time before she owns him. Unless…

Yelina turned around away from her daughter lost in thought. Malcom was a good son, but he was man. Few Grey men could resist one as powerful as this child was. Even his father had bent to the combined will of the Agora before. A process that had never really stopped. But this dance, no that was no joke. Even if many young Grey scoffed at it. But others old enough to know better didn't. Yelina wasn't quite that old, but she still knew. Even if they didn't practice this anymore, they had for centuries before. Grey women it was said could only do this with one person in their lifetime. No matter how many centuries it lasted it would only ever happen once. Camila believed Malcom was this to her, and from hearing Jessie it sounded as if it might be for Malcom as well.

Fine, it's on your own head little one. If I can't deal with Susan, might as well deal with Camila. So be it….

"Dear where is Camila right now?"

Yelina heard the tone she used without thinking. She could feel the blood lust and desire ripple though that tone. Even if her child, inexperienced and innocent of such things didn't. As Jessie's pace she wouldn't have any innocent areas of her nature left soon.

"I think she said she was going to Duff's. Mom, are you ok? You are acting weird."

Yelina just smiled for her and put on her best loving nature. Inside she allowed herself to savor what was coming to Camila.

San Antonio, Texas – Style Hotel

Jan 20th 2058

Travis unknown to Dolly had traveled to where she was staying. He couldn't let her go without seeing her, and he couldn't wait another day without knowing the truth of things. In preparation for this he had asked his brother for a favor. One that was a major ask. He wasn't sure what he would find but he needed to know. After knocking he only had to wait a moment for the astonished Dolly to open the door and gasp at seeing him.

"We need to talk before you leave, can I come in?"

She gathered herself and only nodded. As he expected she was alone with only the minimal she needed. It would take another day or so to arrange international travel but as soon as she got the go-ahead she would board the next flight. Thus, she had wanted to be close when State approved it. Dolly allowed the quiet to go on a bit before asking what he wanted to say. Instead of responding to her he put his hands on her and used Jay's ability to create a link. This was temporary and it wasn't nice of him to force a link without telling her. But after his last guest had explained reality to him, he needed to shock her. Less Dolly control her mind and keep from him the truth. It took a couple of minutes to get what he needed and then he closed the link. Dolly was not exactly pleased with the mental intrusion.

"What the hell? Why Travis, why violate me like that?"

Travis went over uninvited to the seat next to the table and sighed heavily. In a way he was disappointed to be wrong. This wasn't what he was looking for.

"I am sorry Dolly… truly. But I had to know something, I needed to know if you were…. still loyal."

Dolly threw down the purse she had in her hand and roughly grabbed a chair and moved it to face him and sat in it with force.

"What in hell made you think I wasn't? Travis… I love you, you asked me to lead this mission and I didn't question it. I acted and did exactly as you asked? Why would you question me?"

Travis looked at her and knew now all he needed to know about her. She wasn't whom he was looking for, Dolly did love him and serve him. He took one last look around the room to make sure there were no hidden grey watching. Any Grey could hide, but not from him.

"An old friend of mine came to see me a few days ago. They warned me that one of my family has turned against me. The way she described it, well I believed it was one of my beloveds. I had to know Dolly, I always trusted you and… I love you too. But this mission can't afford having you be bent. I need you Dolly, more than ever, I do."

Dolly looked at him softly. Once, before Dolly had become a lover, she had been a mentor. In this painful world of the Grey, it had been Dolly and her wisdom that had seen him through hard times. Seeing that look now, reminded him of that time.

"And I am here for you, I don't know what this person said, or who they are. but why would you believe them over me? Who could possibly have that kind of influence?"

Travis smiled in her move, it was done softly and with love. But depending on who he revealed it to be, could have a serious consequence. Dolly was not above murdering someone who slighted her. Seeing he needed her loyalty he decided to share.

"It's Mae… Bobby's old thrall. She came to warn me that a conspiracy was underway that threatens my power. She was rather convincing."

Travis saw the look on her face at mentioning an old wound. Mae had been the once human thrall of her deceased son, Bobby. Travis knew Bobby well, having grown up with him. Both had gone off to war with stupid thoughts of glory and honor. They had been friends and seen much together. And it was Travis who had brought his body home to Dolly when he had died in that very war. He could see her reliving it again now. For Travis the loss of Bobby had more than one barb to it. Before Bobby's death had come more than one fight between them. He had died with a grudge against Travis, one he deserved.

And what did I do after offending my best friend? Why sleep with his mother of course! Not that I had a choice in the matter, still… God forgive me but I am glad I did.

"Mae has been gone a long time Travis, what does she know of our life. She is human, she probably just resents what my son did to her. Tell me truly do you believe her… why?"

What Dolly didn't know was that Mae wasn't human anymore, and she was involved deeply. Mae was now leader of her own clan. Something that had happened without the knowledge of those in Medford. Her clan was far away back on Ishigaki. But those who had an interest against his clan had contracted Mae to help. Apparently, they had no clue Mae had links to Travis. Without telling her about Mae's clan he tried to explain.

"Mae is close to vampires in her new home. Mae knows about all our organizations and she knows all about the work we did in Taegu last year. She is well informed, some of what is leaking out of our group could only come from a wife. That is why I suspect it's one of you."

Dolly cocked her head to one side and playfully responded. Travis smiled at seeing her like this, she was lightly teasing him and there was a dance to her eyes right now. She was alive, and they were alone together. It felt intimate and comfortable, a place he had longed to feel with her again, even if he shouldn't.

"And your first thought was me… charming. Well, I hope you believe me now, I am loyal to you Travis, I always have been."

Travis took her warm hands and remembered the time she had taken his to explain she was pregnant with their son. Things had been simpler then, no less dangerous but with them in lock step behind him it seemed easy. That time would never come again, to that there was no doubt. Travis moved off what he wanted to talk about, and back to the subject at hand. He explained the need for secrecy and the risk both were taking. Dolly put her hand up to him and sighed a hurt thing that told him she was disappointed. The playfulness was gone now, something that surprised Travis. It shouldn't have but it still did.

"Everything I love in this world is associated with you. My children, my clan… everything. And you accuse me; can you not see me?"

Travis looked at her and felt something inside him shift. He owed her much; she might not be his wife anymore but he still loved and valued her. Holding hands he spoke about their son, now a man. How proud of him he was and of their other children.

"Its all because of you, they are rocks for my clan because of you. I would like to think I had a hand in how Jackie turned out but again it was you. You have been a good mother to my children, and a good friend to me. Truly I am sorry, I don't think our clan could have survived it, if it had been you. You mean so much to all of us."

Folding her legs she placed his hands on her knee and held them there. The smirk on her face was plain and told Travis everything he needed to know. She wasn't angry at him, and the flattery, while true, had done its job.

"Charmer… you always were good at getting me all warm inside. I felt you inside, at the meeting… I felt your love for me. I was afraid you didn't anymore."

They smiled together for a bit as he used his thumb to rub her hand. It was intimate but only just, something Travis was willing to do to show he did indeed still care. Then she looked down at their hands and sighed. When she spoke again it was with sadness.

"Mother asked me to move on, choose another husband."

Travis heard what was something he knew was coming. He had been shocked mother had allowed her to go this long but still, it angered him nonetheless. He didn't want Dolly with another, even if it had to be that way. When she paused, he was still ruminating with his thoughts when she pressed his hands to get his attention. He looked up to see something new in her tone and face. A seriousness that spoke volumes to him.

"I don't want another; I don't require another. I have the one I want… here."

Travis wanted her as well, wanted her beside him like before. It was selfish, and it didn't consider Yelina or Susan and their needs and hearts in the slightest. But right now, Travis was worried. If it wasn't Dolly then it was likely one of them. The only reason why he had the courage to check Dolly was because of the mission and the need to trust Dolly with it. The whole clan was relying on her and she couldn't afford to fail. He responded the only way he knew how.

"I miss you more than you can know."

She smiled and reminded him again that he was in the link with her. She knew exactly what he wanted and how he felt. He suspected what would come next, and wasn't disappointed.

"Lay with me love, I don't care what mother says or what the others want. I want you."

Travis felt her advance and kiss him and logically knew he should reject it. But his heart and his body only wanted one thing. To have someone that he loved again, someone he had not felt in several years again be with him. He reached a decision that went against his beliefs and his better judgement. He lay with her and enjoyed every moment of it. Making sure that if this was the last time they made love that she would remember it.

It wasn't hurried or insane, the two had known each other a long time. It wasn't said but Travis suspected she knew the chances of this ever happening again were nil. Neither wanted to rush, neither wanted to hurry. Travis took his time, pausing just to look at her. From the sounds she made, he knew this meant something to her. It surely did to him.

Denying yourself from someone you share so much was painful and, in that moment, Travis allowed himself to forget his word and his reality. All that mattered was her, and to be with her. But like all things, even this moment passed. In a way Travis thought making love to her anticlimactic. He had dreamed of doing this for years, yet in this place it was lacking in some way. Quietly and in a place deep inside himself longed for it, desired it. Yet it was hollow for some reason, he wasn't sure why. For a long time neither spoke. If the others knew he had lay with her, it might destroy everything. He was going to have to say goodbye but neither of them wanted to. Each was beside the other, at rest having completed their love making. They spoke about various things couples do. Most of it was small and common. But eventually the topic came back to them, and what had to be. Dolly was clear she wasn't for being a good girl.

"Mother made me swear I would take a new husband. I suppose I could, marry my thrall in name. But my children, they wouldn't have to be his. When the time is right, I could come to you, or you to me. It's not like we are cheating; I am your wife and you swore you would protect and love me for all my days. If we keep it quiet enough, no one needs to know."

Travis knew that was just wishful thinking. She was not his wife; they had given each other up as part of the agreement. And as Grey, secrets never stayed so very long. Besides, how could he look Yelina or Susan in the eye, even after this? What she suggested was for them to carry on like this forever. That he could not do.

"Nothing would please me more than to have you. But I swore an oath my love, I can't."

She reminded him that he broke that oath already, by loving her and taking her now. She didn't mean to be crass but it still felt that way.

"This has to be the last time my love, after today…. We can only be friends."

She spoke for a long time trying to convince him. The thought of being with her more and seeing that look in her eye for him often, was a temptation. Then she mentioned his suspicions and asked what he would do if it was Yelina or Susan, would that change things for them.

"Perhaps, I don't know. At some point soon I am going to have to search them like I have done you. It might be another member of the family but I doubt it. The evidence I saw, well it had to be someone close."

Dolly was still offended that she was the first suspect but after a time in his arms with kisses and teases she relented again. Neither of them wanted to part, he was tempted to say yes to her ask. To lay with her in secret, that would be in line with his desires. The thought of that thrall having her, and fathering her new young, sent resentment down his spine. This was his place, but yet it wasn't.

"Travis I can never just be your friend. I desire you, and you desire me. What we did was going to happen. Travis, this can't be stopped, we just are. I knew it that day when my sister selected you. Saw what kind of man you were. I denied myself, said you belonged to Tina and I should honor her. Then I agreed to this stupid arrangement, I shouldn't have. I should have challenged my sister for you that first day you joined us. Made you my property then and there. Never should have let the others get in my way…"

She rose up in bed and towered over him, alluring, teasing. She sat on him making sure her body was tempting him and her bare breasts were inches from his face.

"I will wait and when you are ready, I will be there to have you again. As your wife, as your mistress I don't care. You can't get rid of me Travis, we are immortals. I am not leaving your bed forever. When I get back from Europe, I expect to be back in your bed again soon. I want you to remember these, they are your property, not some thralls."

Travis laughed at her but did so in love. She knew exactly what he was thinking and used it against him.

"Hopefully tonight bears us fruit. I know you Travis, surely you aren't going to let my thrall do your work for you?"

In saying that she smiled, as did Travis. The thought of them creating yet another life together was pleasing. He did the only thing he could do; he took ahold of her and enjoyed her. Even if it was wrong, he was still here now. And he was going to enjoy every second with Dolly he could. She moaned with pleasure at his touch which always excited him. Of the three of them Dolly wasn't the most erotic, or even the loudest of them. But what Dolly was that the other two was not, was she was the most diabolical. She knew him in every way possible. And she knew how to motivate and drive him. In this he allowed her to do as she pleased. And what pleased Dolly right now was him. It felt right and good, even if every fiber of his mind screamed this was a mistake. It was bad enough trying to balance relationships with mortal women, but immortal ones?

Chapter 13: Fathers Fall Short

Medford, Texas – Rick's Home

Jan 21st 2058

Rick and his young son had showed up with all he owned, which fit into 4x8 trailer. The house Yelina had given him to live in was a two-bedroom 1200 sq foot home. As she gave them the tour Rick felt the unease in his body. He knew there wasn't any other course of action. To take care of his boy, this was the price. But he had a condition, and that condition was going to be a problem.

"I know it's a mess Rick but most of the furniture isn't bad and with a little work it will be right as rain in a couple of days."

He shook his head and couldn't hide his concerns. She read it with ease and mistook his worries for being unhappy with the place. How on earth could he be, they weren't going to charge him rent. No utilities, a place for him and his son to live. The price however wasn't free; he would pay for this place with his soul. After asking his son to watch the TV quietly he led Yelina back outside to the front porch.

"Yelina the place is fine, that isn't what has me upset. It's my son, it's one thing for you people to change me. But my son is off-limits, he gets a normal life out of this. No Agoge, no vampirism for him."

Yelina started to respond but he opened his eyes more and showed more of his rougher side in his countenance. Considering she was a vampire it didn't intimidate her any.

"Rick when you become a Grey its required of you. Your son will learn in the Agoge our ways and be the better for it. If he passes the test we will offer the life to him. But it will be his choice, not ours or yours. I can't make an exception for you, if I do, I would have to for any other Grey woman who wishes her son to be spared."

Rick paced about; he remembered that boy with the broken bone going back to training the same day. He was just a kid, not an adult. It wasn't like it was for him and Travis. In their training, they were learning skills to use in combat. The Agoge was intended to do the same thing. Rick didn't want that for him, he wanted his son to go to college and do anything other than to be a warrior. And he wanted his son to have a normal childhood.

"You are going to become my adopted son Rick. Until you rise in rank you must accept my orders and live under my rules. Your son will attend the Agoge."

Rick made it clear he was joining not his son. Instead of replying she motioned him to sit which he refused. Yelina put her hands in front of her and put warmth in her tone. She was trying he could see that, but she wasn't a weak woman either.

"I realize this is difficult for you, but I am not going to offer you something I can't give. Being a Grey comes with responsibilities. Your child as the son of a Grey will be required to live as we do. Your daughter will not, as a woman she has her own life now. I am sorry Rick but if you accept our life, then your son must as well."

Rick slammed his palm down on the railings and started to lose his temper. But he saw the look on her face, she wasn't worried in the slightest at this. And he knew why, she could break his neck in a heartbeat. Even the women of this clan had more strength than any man could possibly have. A part of her wanted him to try, he could see that in her eyes. It was time to reason with her, not threaten. But Yelina beat him to it.

"If the two of you are not prepared to live as Grey, then don't. You can stay here as long as you need to, years if necessary. This is my home, I say who lives here. As my guest you are free to live and raise your son as you see fit. But if you wish to be a Grey warrior, and you wish to do what you have asked…then both of you must accept."

Rick was a proud man and the thought of living on Yelina's kindness for years without him lifting a finger to earn it, was not something he wanted to contemplate. He reviewed his other options, there really weren't any. He was too old to start over, and he was dead broke. He bent the only way he knew how, he begged her to allow her son to be free and not be one of them.

"Rick I am not heartless; I won't force you to do anything. I know it hurts your pride, but just accept our help. You can stay here, find something in Medford you can do, and raise your son. You don't have to be a vampire; you don't have to join Moonstone. Travis isn't trying to force you to do anything, even if he should have, considering the secrets you know."

She put the keys in his hand and then clutched his hand which surprised him.

"You mean a lot to my Travis, and that is good enough for me to help you. Just accept my help."

Rick was tempted to accept but he decided to peek across the abyss and see what lay on the other side. What if he and his son accepted their offer.

"What if he fails this Agoge, first day say he goes in and tells Malcom he refuses to participate?"

Yelina explained the rules and what would occur if he went and failed. He still wouldn't be free of Moonstone, hardly so.

"If he does, then he will work for me in my organization. He will be trained by me and my people. He might face the same dangers you do one day. The Agoge will help prepare him, even if he cannot be like you. Either in the Agoge or through me he will be given the chance to earn the right to be a vampire. It will be his choice to undergo the right. So long as he is found worthy, then he will become like us."

Rick didn't like this but he knew he couldn't just sit there doing nothing, and he couldn't go home.

You sure know how to twist a man don't ya? Ok, fair enough your house your rules. But my boy… he can't be us, not now not ever. Why can't you just accept that?

He felt trapped between his need and his desires. He wanted to hate Yelina for it. But what she was doing was to protect her people. If he wanted to be part of them, then he had to accept their ways too. At least on paper anyway.

"Travis will drop by when he can. Moonstone has him busy right now so don't be surprised if it's a few days. There is a box in the kitchen cabinet with cash. It's enough to get you by for a while, and that's from Travis. If you try to return it both of us will take it as an insult Rick. We are here for you, if you need us simply call."

Rick liked her, she was tough and unflappable. He respected her even if he didn't like being pushed. His curiosity however was peaked about the adoption and wondered just what that meant, and if there was more hidden crap he needed to know. Asking her about that caused her eyebrows to go up a bit.

"It means exactly what it sounds like. In Grey society children belong to their mothers. To join the clan, you must belong to a family. If you take up the life you will be tied to me so long as you breathe. You will answer to me, if I give you an order you will follow it, Rick. And since you are looking for things to worry about, let me give you another one. As my newest son you will have to undergo the right all boys do when they become a man. If they have siblings, they must fight to determine who among them is the strongest.   Only the strongest can be protector of the family. Malcom has that honor now. If you join us, you will fight both Malcom and Jacob for that honor."

Rick smiled and laughed, now this was just plain stupid. But these Grey liked to do things to honor the past. He asked the obvious question, why on earth would he fight her sons for such a title.

"Because it's our way, holding the title is a stepping stone for advancement. You will join us as a Hoplite, but only because you have already achieved fame as a human. Otherwise, you would have to attend the Agoge like any other boy."

Rick smiled at the thought of him going through that ordeal as an old man. He started to laugh until he realized it was 10-year-old boys in that camp suffering right now.

"Achieving spartainate rank is the pinnacle of male life. All Hoplites work to achieve this honor. As a Spartainate you are eligible to obtain a mate, and become part of a new house under your wife. Hoplite men compete fiercely in all things as they should. That is why only the best men in a family can be considered for promotion. Only those with the rank of protector can even be considered. If you defeat my sons, you will become protector of my house. You do this to rise in the ranks, but also so you can know the worthiness of your brothers. In this life Rick you fight with and for them. Another family may wish to cause me and your brother's harm. It will be up to the strongest among us to defend us. If you are the strongest then I must know it. It will be you if you are the strongest, I must rely on the strongest to protect all I own."

Rick asked about Travis and why it wouldn't be him defending his family?

"It's not his place Rick; I am of the Agora. Higher in rank than any Spartainate can be. I have the most to lose, and as such my protector must be the best. As King he has more than just my house to consider. Only the protector can defend us if need be. Rick, take my advice. I have lived as a Grey my whole life and I wouldn't live any other way. But it's not for everyone, if you aren't committed, then it's not for you. Accept our help and swallow your pride. Even if for a year you can stay here and get back on your feet. Surely by then you will find something. There is no shame in this, what your wife did is not your fault."

Nothing else was said. The vampire gave him a knowing look and turned to leave. Rick watched her depart, what she said burned in him and he knew why. He didn't like taking handouts from anyone. But what choice did he really have? Rick went inside looking to make sure his son was not into trouble. Thankfully he was doing as he was told for the moment. That would only last a few minutes at best, he would get bored of the TV soon enough. Rick went into the kitchen and found the box. Next to it was a note from Yelina with a couple of menus to places that delivered. He read the note and was upset at what it said. She had predicted the conversation pretty well.

"A wolf can only live as a sheep so long. Eventually a wolf must be a wolf. When you are ready to be one again, call."

Rick crumbled the note and threw it onto the counter, cursing at her. The anger didn't last, there was no point to it. Letting out his held breath Rick put his hands on the counter quietly and with gentleness. He watched himself do it and smirked at the change in his nature. Once when he was young and foolish he had been a hothead, prone to anger and violence. Something he had learned that was necessary in his young life. But in truth, came natural to him and his heart. Time had changed him; in ways he was still discovering. The wrinkles and bad back were what most people thought of about aging. But for Rick it was his own spirit that was night and day. He had grown soft in time, peaceful and thoughtful. Something he had treasured, and he thought others had as well. Like always what was didn't last, he feared his old life coming for him again but… not like this.

He looked at the cash, the home, and felt the pull of what this place was. He allowed his mind to ponder it, considering her words as carefully as he could but it didn't help. Instead of calling for pizza he called all his friends again. Hoping one of them had a new lead on something. To give in to these people, meant more than just his soul. Looking in the living room again he saw the naïve child who knew nothing of what dangers were close by. For him he wished he never would.

"Yeah, hey Mike, its Rick. You remember the other day when you said you had a line on an opening in PM Arms? Did you find anything else out, cause I am still looking man and I really need a break.... Yeah, though not, hey man, thanks."

Medford, Texas – Agoge, Malcom's office

Jan 21st 2058

Malcom looked at the boy standing in front of him. Jonathan was 13 and in his 3rd year at the Agoge. He was the youngest child of Susan and was also Malcom's half-brother. There were many half brothers and sisters Malcom had in Medford. His father had produced many children from his early times in the clan. It wasn't something talked about in front of the King. But among Malcom and his siblings it was. Their father had been forced into these relationships against his will. That much was known. But it was something none of them really understood. They tried to, but at least for Malcom he didn't want to think on it too much. Mostly they tried to pretend it never happened. The main result was that any sibling who didn't come from Dolly, Susan or his mother Yelina, were considered less in the eyes of those who were. It wasn't anything personal but yet it was.

This boy was not like them. He was what Malcom would consider a real brother. He wasn't the youngest of his father's sons, but close. He had been fighting and his emotions were up. But now, after his feelings had cooled had come the shakes. Good, Malcom thought, he needed to be on edge. The last person he had standing here had not been so intimidated. He hadn't spoken a word the whole time he had been here. Jonathan on the other hand would break given a push. Malcom was sure of it. He didn't know Jonathan that well, but he knew he could lean on his relationship if he needed it.

Jonathan's best friend Clint, was like him, another son of Travis. Both boys were the same age and had been close their whole lives. Coming to the Agoge together they had bonded even closer. But Clint was Dolly's son, not Susans. This didn't stop the two boys from becoming tighter than any full brothers could be. Yet this morning the two had been found fighting. He had already spoken to Clint who refused to explain what happened. Thus, he was now staring down a bloodied Jonathan to discover the truth.

"Come now, you didn't just fall down and hurt yourself. You were seen punching Clint. From your comrades account, the two of you were out for blood. What happened?"

The boy shifted uncomfortably but still didn't speak. Malcom quickly channeled his mentor and how he would speak to him when he was this age.

"You two are brothers, and I know what that means. We are brothers, even if we have different mothers. No different than you or Clint. Tell me, no more games, what is going on between you? That isn't a question it's an order."

Still the boy didn't speak, he looked hurt at the reminder and looked away. When he spoke, he did so quietly and with great reserve. Clearly, he didn't think Malcom would like what he had to say. Malcom had to strain to hear the words. It sounded like the boy said he wasn't his brother. Waiting a moment Malcom reminded the boy that he was the son of Travis and Yelina. They shared a father and a legacy, something Malcom had always been proud of. Even if him and his father didn't see eye to eye a lot. The boy didn't look impressed.

"Mother says it isn't the same. Says the day is coming when we won't be anymore. Says I should only see Thomas and Elena that way."

Malcom looked at him and pulled up a chair and thought more about the words. He knew there was rumbles that the mothers in their lives were at odds again. That had been true as long as Malcom could remember. But in the end, they would always rally around their father. Especially when things got hard, and unknown to this child, things were getting hard. Their mothers would rally around Travis and fight as they always did for their clan and their King.

"I know I hear things like that from my sister too. But that doesn't explain why you and Clint are fighting. I haven't been here that long, but until today the two of you fought the world together. I saw how he helped you on the course the other day. I don't think Jacob would have done that for me back when we were here. We are brothers, no matter what our mothers say. Unlike them we have to live and fight together. We have to depend on each other and trust one another. I just want to understand is all. I know you son; your moms' words didn't just start this today."

He was young and still wasn't that mature yet. He struggled to contain his emotions and the tears fought hard to depart his eyes. He only managed to keep them at bay while he was silent. The moment he told his story they couldn't be held back any longer. He explained that Clint had returned from seeing his mother and had been worried about what was to come. He had shared a secret with him, something he was worried would destroy everything. By this point the boy was fully in tears and near sobbing. But it wasn't fear, but anger that tinged his words.

"He said the Grey mother is going to kill my mother. That my mother and your mother would die because they were fools."

Malcom laughed at that, Nana was a hard woman yes, but she wouldn't harm Yelina and Susan. Then the boy shared more, that Clint's mother had lain with Father the day before. That caused Malcom's heart to stop. If Dolly had made love to Father, then the accord that kept the peace was dead. That explained why Clint was so upset, and why Jonathan was so angry at him. He asked the boy if Clint was mean about it, but it was clear in his response that he wasn't. Clint was scared, not just for his mother but for his friend. Next, he asked why Clint would tell him that? It sounded like a dumb question the moment he said it.

"I made him tell me. He came back last night so upset, I knew something bad happened. We always tell each other everything and I told him I would understand. But I didn't expect dad would…. Do that! At first, I just said he was lying; I knew he wasn't but I felt like he was saying dad was bad."

Malcom summoned Clint back into his office and a few minutes later was at the bottom of it. Both boys cared about the other, that was why they fought. Clint was hurt because he had trusted his best friend would tell him what he needed to know. He was genuinely scared for his brother. Jonathan was upset because he felt like all the things his mother had said about the others was just crap. But when Clint shared what he knew, then he saw his mother had a point. In a flash Jonathan was faced with losing his best friend AND knowing his mother's life was in danger. Malcom was angry at the adults in the room. And not for the first time felt resentful at the frailty of grey women. Looking at the boys he couldn't just leave things like this. It was time to be the grownup, that their mothers couldn't be.

"Before today the two of you fought together and endured together did you not?"

Both boys looked at each other and gave nods to the statement.

"What our mothers do, or not do, is not on us. Jonathan, you didn't pay any attention to your mom when it came to Clint. And that's because you trust him. As far as I can see he hasn't done anything to break that trust."

Malcom could see the disagreement in Jonathan on that. But it wasn't because Clint had broken trust. It was because of the message and what it meant.

"It's my job to teach you and to prepare you for what is to come. You need brothers behind you in everything. Being brothers is more than just blood, its trust. You need to know you have each other's back. I think Clint showed you a lot of trust in telling you what he knew. But Clint don't be shocked if that message isn't well received. Jonathan has every right to be pissed. None of us can let what our mothers feel to get in the way of our duty. We have a duty to each other, and that duty is life. You two might not be Grey yet, but you will be. When the time comes, you are going to need each other. Don't let your fear of change cloud your judgement. When you are out there, there isn't time for feeling. You have to know you can trust the person next to you without question."

Malcom paused to let that wisdom soak in. He knew both boys were tight and if they decided to, could overcome this. But it was asking a lot, and it couldn't be solved with just words. Malcom knew this situation required his intervention. Seeing he was winning them to his way of seeing things he continued.

"I may not have earned your trust yet, but I am still blood. Trust in me to deal with this. Say nothing to your mothers or your other siblings. Let this rest with me and I promise you I will do all I can."

It took more convincing but the boys mended things the best they could. In the end their respect and trust for each other amounted to more than anything. For now, things were made right, but only because someone who knew better was there. They respected and trusted him because he was an adult, and he had achieved status in the clan. As both boys went off to combat training, they were again tentative friends. One day they would be comrades. That wasn't a platitude, the boys would serve on the same team together. They were already slated to serve on Beta team with Jonathan's older brother once they were ready. In that future the brothers would have to rely on each other to survive. And for the moment their trust was restored. But Jonathan was right to be upset. If father had really lain with Dolly again then there will would hell to pay. Malcom was considering his situation and how to deal with it when he got a call to come to town.

Medford, Texas – Cassia's Home

Jan 21st 2058

Yelina sat at the table looking at the others and wishing like mad she wasn't here. One had once been someone she dearly loved. Someone she had pledged to protect and serve for all time. Yelina had lived up to that oath, even if the years had taken from her the enjoyment of doing so.

"My dear you haven't touched a thing; please try the chicken it's an old family recipe. I guarantee you haven't had anything like this in Meridia before."

Not for the first time Yelina noticed how Cassia worked people. Camila seemed to be her latest target. The girl had managed to illude Yelina since she violated her orders to stay away from Malcom. Some way or another Cassia had gotten wind of her looking for the woman and had interceded. Camila's life was justifiably hers at this point. And Yelina aimed to collect on that life. She was furious and wanted to tie all her anger and worries around the neck of this troublesome child. Camila responded by taking a bite, and complementing Cassia on her cooking. Yelina had to stop her eyes from rolling at all the fakery. By all rights this girl's life was forfeit and Cassia knew it. By preventing this, she was again pushing Yelina in ways no other Grey woman would tolerate.

Decades before Yelina had come to trust and love Cassia. She was the mother of her love, and it was Cassia who seemingly pulled him from the abyss back into her arms. But it wasn't enough, not for Yelina, not anymore. Irritated and disrespected she looked at Camila and did nothing to hide her hate. This went on for a time as Cassia entertained her guests. Sitting uncomfortably beside her was Travis. A part of Yelina wondered what he was thinking but she was too angry at Camila to ponder on it too long.

"You know dear I am glad you came to visit us. It's so nice to know our family has another branch. Do you like it here, are you making friends?"

Cassia spoke like the grandmother she was but it was so disingenuous. Cassia was every bit as pissed at this girl as she was. The private conversation she had with her and the rest of the Agora made that clear enough. But they had to be careful, this girl was not on some holiday. She was here to do something;

it was up to them to discover what it was before she did it. Sending her back home while a lovely thought, wouldn't prevent the Meridians from doing it behind their back in secret. At least in this way they had an eye on her and could learn something. At much as Yelina looked forward to the day, she could kill her, even Yelina had to agree that patience was warranted.

Camila spoke about the town, and spouted all kinds of nonsense about Medford's charms. Then she spoke about Yelina's family and how she adored both Malcom and Jessie. That caused Yelina's hands to form fists and it took all her self-control to prevent Yelina from using them. A part of her didn't understand from where this anger originated. But it didn't take long to remember. This tart had stolen her sons honor, possibly his future. And she was a plotting, devious little shit. But even Yelina had to acknowledge her hatred of Camila was just an outlet. The people she really had a bone to pick with, were untouchable.

"You know I was thinking we should return the favor my dear. Do you think your Meridian family would welcome one of ours to visit you?"

Yelina looked over at Cassia who said it without a sign of humor. Cassia and Camila continued speaking and considering it before Cassia out of nowhere suggested that her other son be the one in this unique "exchange program." Before Yelina could respond Travis put his foot down.

"Mother I get it you want to build a bridge, but this woman tried to recruit my son. Tortured him when he wouldn't talk, AND she seduced Jason to join them. To be honest I don't understand why we don't send her ass home."

Yelina thought Travis was being too crass, but she agreed completely. Cassia however continued to explore the idea as she then revealed her plan for Camila. That bit of knowledge caused Yelina's jaw to drop.

Medford, Texas – Cassia's Home

Jan 21ˢᵗ 2058

Malcom approached the house of his nana, a place he had once enjoyed going to. Hearing stories of his father and of the long distant past was a treat. But it hadn't taken long for Malcom to understand why others feared the Grey Mother. He had seen several glimpses into whom his nana really was. The first time was when a classmate had revealed how his nana had been the one to torture and kill her father. They had been friends for most of his life until they were in the 5th grade. She had stopped talking to him and looked at him in fear. He had eventually gotten her to admit why, something she did in a bare whisper. He had thought it so unbelievable he had asked nana about it the same day. When she revealed that she had indeed drained the life from the girl's father for failing in his task, it changed his view of her forever.

His nana was a person you couldn't cross. That message had been received loud and clear. Even now that memory of the look on her face, sent chills down his spine. If she had threatened to kill his mother and Susan, then it was something to take seriously. As he walked up, he was surprised to see his father exit the house and approach him.

"Glad you are here son; we need to talk."

Malcom looked right at him and felt his distaste for his father grow. He hadn't lifted a finger to help him at the Agora, and he hadn't even bothered to speak to him since. Then of course there was the news he had lain with Dolly again. It was possible it was a false, but Malcom doubted it. Over the years it was obvious to anyone with eyes that father cared for Dolly. How hard was it to believe he had lain again with a woman he had once called his wife? Once he was close enough to his father, he felt his own anger rise up. But he held it in check the best he could.

"Son I am sorry about what happened. I promise you I will make it right, but I need you to be patient."

Malcom knew he was referring to his career and to what had happened back in Sao Paulo. But all Malcom could think about was him and Dolly. All the speeches about morality and honor, they were just words. Malcom had spent his entire life looking up to his father and his elders wanting to be just like them. But since he had returned, he was very disappointed to learn just how fallible they really were. Malcom was coming to understand just how naïve he really was. Did that mean everything he held dear was just some construct dad created to control them?

"Dad, it doesn't matter anymore."

Malcom stopped himself from saying another word. If he did, he would speak with his fists rather than his words. His dad saw his anger and looked sad to see it. Malcom wanted to scream at him but what would he say?

"Son, I know you are angry and you have a right to be. But this new duty they gave you will be good for you. You can shape this generation and make a massive impact on the clan. I think it can make you a better man for it. Eventually what happened at Sao Paulo will pass. I promise you in time, you will be back on the path you wanted. From what I hear you are a good teacher son."

Malcom hated that a part of him agreed with that. In the short time he had been working in the Agoge he had found the work to be rewarding. But the trouble was coming home had revealed the lies. The honor they claimed was so important to them, was for only when it was convenient. They were lying to their children and to each other. How was he supposed to instill these lies into the young men he was responsible for? Especially when he was starting very much to not believe them himself. He saw his father for the weak man he really was and it crushed him. A small voice said he should challenge the old man and take his throne. As King, he could make things right. But that was as silly a thought as believing in the lies his parents had told him. This was a corrupt system, that much was becoming evident. Unknown to either his mother or his father he was now fully aware of just how corrupt the Grey women were too.

His sister Jackie had told him in confidence of the secret the woman of the Agora was keeping. Apparently, the point of the agencies the women ran was to make money, not to support Moonstone. They were enriching themselves, in violation of the covenant the Grey kept at being communal with their wealth. They then used this wealth to violate their oaths. The Agora members took trips to New York once a year. They went there to let down their hair. From the way Jackie described it each member of the Agora was worth millions of dollars' now. With that money each woman on the Agora had built for themselves a luxurious second home in New York where they could party however, they saw fit.

Jackie had been invited by her mother to one of these events. Swearing on her life never to reveal it to any man of the clan. She was as disgusted by their behavior as Malcom was. When he had been blackballed Jackie had explained the reason for it. Jason's mother knew personally of the Agora's degradations. She had helped organize the trips and helped to obtain the sex workers for the lady's pleasure. Jason's mother could have revealed everything about them. She was paid a great deal of money to leave Medford and join her son. They were desperate to destroy both that woman's credibility and her ability to strike back. Malcom was just friendly fire in their plot to cover up their own crimes.

Malcom closed his eyes as his father went on trying to comfort him. Instead of listening to him he kept thinking of Jackie and how she described the trips. While on this trip no behavior was off-limits. Her mother had participated, as had Susan, Cassia and all the others. Jackie even claimed that his mother Yelina was in attendance. Something he didn't believe until he checked and found her travel plans matched the dates Jackie gave. Malcom had promised to deal with things but right now he didn't even know how to process it, much less solve it. His brothers didn't deserve this, they were loyal. Those two boys were like him and Jacob, they were giving their lifeblood for this clan and believed in what mom and dad had sold them. The life was more important to them than anything else. Not to mention the brothers that had already given their lives and slept in Woodlawn now.

"Son, you seem…. Distant, is something else wrong?"

Malcom wanted to scream at him, tell him hell yes! But if his father didn't know about the dishonorable way the Agora acted, then he wasn't strong enough to do something. Besides, father wasn't any better. He had taken Dolly, when he had no right to dishonor his mother that way. But he couldn't confront him, not now. So, he lied and felt the burning distaste for doing so in his belly. He hated himself for doing it, but he needed to know what to do before he acted. His father didn't seem to believe the lie he told. He knew he was pissed, but thanks to what happened to him in Sao Paulo dad accepted it was just that. That was when the door opened again, to reveal another surprise.

"Malcom! I didn't know you would be here."

At hearing Camila's voice his mouth dropped open. He turned his face towards his father who explained that Nana had invited Camila to be dad's new adjutant. A position held by his sister Jackie. Before he could even ask his dad interrupted.

"I have Jackie doing something for me son, and…. I suppose I do need another adjutant for the moment, But…."

At hearing this Malcom turned away and started walking back to the Agoge. His father, then his mother and nana all called out for him to stop. He did nothing of the sort. When his nana who had asked him to come yelled at him to stop, he simply gave her the bird and continued walking.

Chapter 14: Revelations

Medford, Texas – Agoge

2 days later

Jan 23rd 2058

Cyrus was walking down the small path to the Agoge. It was early morning before dawn. But the boys were out, still up from the evening before if he had to guess. Cyrus knew this from the sounds of battle just over the ridge. They were training hard, even at this hour. Cyrus shook his head not approving of either this school or this way of life. It was pitch black and the last thing he wanted to do was be out here. Yet here he was walking in the dark. The reason as basic as it sounded was something was horribly wrong with his grandson. He had refused to return to his home the night before, and he was refusing any orders from his mother or from Cassia. He had flipped all of them the bird the day before. Cyrus's wife Cassia was offended and was ready to have him removed from his post if he didn't apologize. Someone needed to speak to the boy. This should be his father doing this, but Travis was on a flight to France a few hours after it happened. From talking to his wife, and the boy's mother, it was clear no one wanted to punish the boy. But he had been rather vulgar and insubordinate, things Grey generally weren't to their superiors. The longer this went on the more severe the consequences, for everyone.

Cyrus shook his head at trying to understand this clan. While he was the Grey visitor, he had not in fact created the clan. Another of his race had done this, Cyrus had only inherited the Grey when that visitor returned to their home world. The grey were nothing like the Aqua, his beloved clan. The one he had created and lovingly watched over the centuries. With the Aqua he understood each of them, taken great pains to do so. It was Cassia who knew these people not him. Yet here he was, before dawn walking out to deal with a Grey issue. He grumped and complained as he found uncertain footing in the dark. He should be home right now! It wasn't like he was retired and had nothing to do today. As mayor of Medford, Cyrus had enough responsibilities and tasks to fill all his hours. He didn't need this and he let out an angry sound as his left foot twisted from stepping in a small hole.

Cyrus stopped and allowed himself a moment to heal and to get himself in the right state of mind before going on.

I hate this form so much sometimes, two feet with two legs preening about all day long! When I could just float from here to there without a care in the world.

Cyrus thought of his real nature and longed to be that again, at least for a few hours. He was no human, he only pretended to be so he could enjoy the parts of being human that he enjoyed. On thinking of that, the smile returned to his face. Cassia had proven far more interesting a study than the other humans. Cyrus wanted to learn all he could, about these humans, and Cassia was his teacher. Learning was key to any visitor, but learning from Cassia? It was the most satisfying thing he had ever done. He laughed in the darkness at the memory.

Cassia had met him while he was in this form and unknown to him decided she desired him. The girl had no clue what he was, only that he was attractive and interesting. A way out of the life she was leading. He was such a naïve being, not realizing this woman wished to have him or what that even entailed. When men say that a woman had opened their eyes, they had nothing on Cyrus. Taking a long breath, he felt his lungs and remembered that as a human he could enjoy moments like this. It wasn't like sex, or love, or joy, but it was… pleasurable in its own way. He wanted to change his love, to make her entirely like him. Then they could be as one in his way, not just in hers. But that was not to be, it was risky and he dare not take a chance at losing his love.

As his anger of his twisted ankle subsided, he reminded himself why he was out this late. This wayward child, was the same grandson he had taken time to know. When he had graduated this very school, Cyrus had taken the new "man" out for drinks. Cyrus wasn't a warrior nor did he find those that were, to be beings to emulate. Yet so many of his children and grandchildren had been such. Both of his recent sons had fought in the last major war. Each had been horribly changed by the experience. Wishing for these new children to take up that life seemed madness. But for his son Travis and their people, it was core to their being. Even if Cyrus wished to change this, he could not out of respect for Travis.

As he stood there his body healed itself. Something that was handy in times like this. They had modified the early humans they had met when they came to this world using their ability. That act had been in accordance with their ways. They were travelers and explorers, but above all they were seekers of knowledge. Testing, experimenting, questioning everything they found, everyone they met. But this place, this earth was different. Here in this strange place Cyrus had found a different calling. He wasn't alone, several of his fellows had followed his example. Those visitors that still remained had all gone native. Taking human spouses, and living among them as members of their families. They would never go home now, that was certain.

It had been a rewarding decision on their part. But the price of it was far more than any knew, especially for Cyrus. That decision and the price he paid to be like this, would shorten his life considerably. That remembrance took away the pleasant feeling he had and reminded him that his time here was short. Even his race died, but to humans it seemed as if his kind were eternal. Cassia was strong, stubborn, and fully capable of taking care of herself.

As Cyrus took steps closer to the Agoge he thought back to when Travis was a young man, around the age his son was now. Cyrus frowned in the darkness remembering. The young son he had been absent for, had been broken by the life. When Cyrus had gone to him with his mother, the boy was wishing for death. Abandoned by his lover, and broken by what the Grey clan had done to him. The boy had gone to the mountain and embraced what could only be described as self-destructive behavior. Since they had come home to Medford his wife had been obsessed with Travis, and securing his future. At first Cyrus had encouraged it, still guilty himself over not taking an active role in raising the boys. But as time had gone on, Cyrus began to suspect his bride was not up to the challenge he had given her. Cassia was to be his voice to his three clans, helping him forge each of them for the future.

As he passed several squads in combat training, he shielded himself from their view. He didn't want them to question his presence or to interrupt their efforts. He shook his head at the sight. All of the boys were exhausted and many were on the brink of collapse. It was one thing to push men in training, but children? Still other than raising his son Adad, he had little experience in it. There had to be a better way, a way to harness the strength of the Grey and edifying nature of the Aqua. Some middle ground for each to strengthen the root of both. Perhaps that was possible but as of yet Cyrus had no answers. The only thing Cyrus was sure of was he hated taking human form on a permanent basis.

He walked up behind Malcom and began to read his thoughts. Then he quietly searched his memories and found what was bothering him. He wasn't ready for the facts he was exposed to. Cyrus had been very slow to learn how relationships work. Cassia had basically been the one to teach him everything on the subject. To learn that someone he had been partnered with for so long had violated his trust was unthinkable. At first, he just dismissed it as rumor.

But then he thought back to that look she gave him the other day. It was distant and weak, and a false mask she wore for him. As if he was punched in the chest, he took a step back and shut his eyes. He wasn't ready for that fact, and he wasn't ready to learn that his wife had betrayed him that way. Malcom had been careful, searching for the truth of things. Cyrus decided not to speak to the boy. Rather he put a suggestion in his mind for him to let the children rest. Cyrus had that ability and only a moment or two later he watched as Malcom sent the boys back to the barracks to rest. The looks on the kids' faces was all he needed to know. They were exhausted and ready to collapse, that was the right call for sure.

Next Cyrus put another suggestion in his grandson's mind. Something he might not follow, but as tired as he was he may. He hoped so, the boy himself wasn't far from breaking. A moment later he watched with satisfaction as Malcom let out a long breath and then walked back to his quarters. As Cyrus watched the field grow quiet, he took the opportunity to ponder what he should do. Normally he would have sat with Cassia and asked her thoughts. But the days for that were gone. Now they hardly ever spoke, and from what Malcom had discovered she had begun to move on from him. At least with what entertained her in bed anyway. Angry, hurt and unsure what to do, he laughed and started back to town. He considered as he did how to respond. It would take hours before he had any clue how he would.

Chapter 15: Travis's Waterloo

Paris, France – Château de Malmaison

Jan 23rd 2058

Travis was dressed according to how State requested him to be. He was trying to forget how much he had spent on this custom suit. But it was a requirement, he had to fit into the larger group attending from State. Normally Travis eschewed any overspending. As sovereign of his clan, he had every right to tax his people for his own welfare, but he didn't. Everything he had was something he had paid for. But this suit was the first exception to that rule. It was simply more than he could afford. But like the helicopters his company owned or the high-tech communications gear they used, it was needed. Moonstone had paid for the suit and he had to accept it. Still, he could get used to wearing something like this. With him at this reception was Art and Nancy. Travis looked over and nearly laughed at seeing Art tug at his dinner jacket for the fifth time. Art had been a soldier, a cop and a laborer. None of those things suited him to one of these functions. Nancy on the other hand was stunning wearing a low-cut red dress. He walked over to Art and decided to tease.

"Art if you fidget any more people will think you have lice. Just look at your lovely wife and be like her. Well perhaps not quite like her, I don't think red is your color."

The smirk he had on sold it; Art still irritated at his coat narrowed his eyes but playfully. Nancy hearing it, was playful in her response. But she liked the complement just fine. Art however was too focused on being uncomfortable.

"I wish you had asked me to shoot something rather that dress up for this…whatever it is."

Nancy put a hand on Art, clearly, she was having a blast. Travis was pretty sure she didn't get to go to receptions like this. In this case it was being thrown by the French government. Only members of the delegations were permitted but Travis had managed to squeeze in Art and Nancy. Nancy sipped at her drink and looked around the room.

"I don't see your Rose anywhere or anyone else with our eyes."

Travis nodded agreeing, as far as he could tell the three of them were the only vampires. There was no sign of Rose or anyone who worked for them. The Meridian President was in attendance, flanked by bodyguards at all times. When Travis had walked in both a man from State and a member of the Meridian team asked Travis NOT to approach the Meridian president. He wasn't given a reason but he could guess.

"How long do you think they are going to make you wait?"

Travis took a sip from his drink and wondered that himself. He saw the US Secretary of State give him a hard look as the man made his way back to the table. Most of the US delegation was giving him the cold treatment. So clearly the Admiral hadn't done anything to fix things for him yet. Travis seriously doubted he ever would. Travis felt a warm feminine hand on him and saw that it was Nancy who was looking at something behind him. Her demeanor seemed to indicate that Rose had finally made her appearance. When he turned, he saw a middle-aged woman highly made up in a lavish white dress. She was pretty but not terribly so. But it was the eyes that made Travis nearly lose his breath. Bright Grey, brighter than any he had seen before.

"Mr. Williams, I am so glad you were able to attend. Were you so frightened of me that you needed to bring a Marine to protect you?"

She acted as if they were dear friends in gripping his hand. She quickly pivoted to Art looking at him and Nancy.

"I should have known he would bring the two of you. Arthur and Nancy welcome to Malmaison, my home is your home."

Not surprising to Travis, she knew all about who they were. Grey women were hardly ever surprised by anything. Nancy asked her about the comment and she smiled sipping at a drink saying that this chateau had been her creation.

"Come we can talk in the study; we won't be disturbed there."

The three of them were allowed out of the reception room and down a long hallway, after a few twists and turns they were in a private room. There was a large man with a Meridian flag pin on his lapel. Cleary he was a body guard for Rose. Once they were past him, she closed the door and offered both of them a drink, which no one took. The seating was far more comfortable and the noise wasn't deafening, something Travis was thankful for. Rose started by talking to Nancy.

"If you don't mind me being so direct, how is it to be back home in France? It's been a long time, no?"

Nancy smiled and agreed but she stopped short of giving her any information. Rose picked up on that and grinned.

"There is no need my dear, I am well aware of your past. We Grey can be annoying like that. We like our knowledge and we never make a move without it. Here try this dear, it's from your home region, I don't know how often you get bottles of it in Texas."

Rose handled the glass over to Nancy. The moment she sniffed what was inside her face changed, clearly Nancy was impressed.

"As I said, it's something you should appreciate. I have a taste for it myself; I am sure you can imagine when I acquired it. Arthur, feel free to take off that jacket and relax. We are all friends here, no need to be formal. I am so happy to finally meet all of you. It means a great deal to me and my family."

Travis watched as Art gladfully took off the jacket much to Nancy's disappointment. Rose was all lovely and welcoming but it was a nice segway for Travis to ask why they were here. Rose however was not interested in getting down to it.

"I will be happy to talk of such things later. Tonight, we are strangers. Until we are not, we cannot discuss business."

Nancy made a comment on the wine saying it was some of the best she had in years. That made Rose brighten up and she poured another two glasses one for Art and one for Travis. But Travis was more than just a bit unnerved by all this. She forced it into his hands anyway.

"Please, it truly is divine Travis. I wish you could have tasted the wine the Athenians made; I can still remember it vividly. Now that Nancy, that was the only thing that compares to what is in your hands. I would give a great deal to drink a cup of Athenian wine again."

Nancy asked her if she really was Josephine from the 19th century. Reminding Rose of what she had previously said about the chateau.

"Yes, I was indeed that woman once. Just like you I have had many names. My time in your homeland wasn't long, but it left its mark on me. From this very office me and my love led France. I could lie and say I long again for that time, but I do not. I only miss him; the power and the fame are things for the young.

I only wish to watch my little ones grow and see them push our people further. Is it not the same with you Nancy? I know you led Medford and your clan for centuries. Now you have turned that over to others, no?"

Nancy smiled and described how Jay was leading their clan and that another was mayor. Travis appreciated the fact that Nancy cut out the whole part that the new mayor was a visitor. Nancy wasn't a fool; she was being careful on what she revealed.

"My clan and my town, are in good hands, it's been lovely to have them lift that burden. It allowed me to spend more time with the ones I love. Do you have a new love, Rose? Is there another that could compete with Napoleon?"

Rose smiled and put a hand over her heart and shook her head no. Something about the way she held herself and looked at Nancy said so many things. This was not a stupid woman, nor was she a child. In a look and in a single word she had relayed how she loved her husband, and how likely that would change in the future.

"I have had many loves and lovers, but none like him. Alas I am not as fortunate as you with your Arthur. From what I have gathered he is proving to be your own Napoleon is he not? I have heard it said you were willing to give up your clan and your gifts for him. I am so happy to see you didn't have to, and that he shares your eyes now. I am envious my dear, if I could have turned my love…. well like so many things we can't hold on to what's gone now, can we?"

Travis asked Rose about herself, and about her origin. She had already hinted that she was from Greece. At mentioning it she glowed. Travis wasn't sure if she was a great actress or if she loved merely the word that much.

"My home, was Sparta. I was born there and spent my first years as an immortal, as a Spartan. I am so pleased to see you have embraced our culture, Travis. To know that our people are living as we once did. It fills me with such pride for what you have accomplished. Finally, after all these centuries to know the Agoge lives again! It pleases me very much, far more than you can possibly imagine. But I am ignoring our other guest with all this talk of ancient times. Look at poor Arthur, he is dreadfully bored. Arthur what do you think of this France? Does the snow and cold make you long for your home in Texas? I know the last few days here I spent it under many blankets."

Art laughed and said an unequivocal yes. Both Travis and Nancy laughed with him. He had been bitching about the cold the whole time they had been there.

"This part of Europe is nothing like your home or my old one. Sparta is a warm climate. Nothing like this, I never got used to your home Nancy. The culture and the wine yes, but the weather not as much. Is it hard for you to be away from the place of your birth? Do you think you will ever return?"

Nancy said no, confidently at first. She loved her home as Travis well knew. Then she paused while she was looking at the glass she held. When she spoke next it was still Nancy, but as emotional as she allowed herself to be in public.

"At times I suppose. I will wake up and I am back here, human again. Father or mother is calling me. A part of you never really leaves I suppose. One day perhaps I will drag Art here but no, America is our home now."

Rose smiled and agreed with a soft and loving tone. She seemed to be cheery at speaking of home.

"Arthur you are so fortunate, all your years in your homeland. Cherish them, truly. One day you may find the need to leave it. Believe me when I say you will never be the same."

It sounded somber but with Rose's enthusiasm still intact, it still somehow felt not so. But the pause in her voice signaled something new, her first real surprise of the evening.

"I, like you Nancy, miss my home. I am Spartan at heart and will always be. You spoke of your family; one must keep them close. Otherwise, you will lose them. I learned this painfully long ago. My father was King Archidamus, he was a good King. Not a great father but I still respected and adored him. Family is precious and we as children take it for granted. But alas, family can be a short-lived thing. Like any of us who live that long my father's name changed with the seasons. I believe each of you knew him better, as Finnan."

Art put the glass down on the side table losing his smile and pleasant demeanor. Travis had suspected it being how old she was. And if he did then, so did Nancy. Very little escaped her keen mind. Art however was young like him, and said what he thought. Finnan and the town didn't have a great history, so Art was on guard the moment he heard the name. He asked if Rose had a grudge with them over his death. Travis thought that was the wrong time to ask it. But Rose took it in stride.

"No Art, my father and I have been estranged for many centuries. He left me and my people long before our fall. I was angry a long time after he abandoned us. But I have lived long enough to understand that is our way. Not just my clan but yours as well. I have heard told your story Nancy, I believe you too have had to do so many times. An Immortal has to be flexible; you have to dance on the winds like the sails on a ship. Otherwise, if we try to never change, never grow, then we stand still. To be calmed like that is to invite death. It's a hard lesson for us to learn but we all must learn it."

Travis was enjoying the theater. He still wasn't sure if this was a performance or someone sharing their heart. He suspected the former rather than the latter.

"My father and I were not close. But I respected him and he taught me a great deal about life. I was glad he came to me before he died, it is from him I had heard much of your people. But the man who came to me at the end was not the man who raised me. That man wanted to die; he was tired of living as an immortal. From what I understand he caused great harm to many in the end. It's why I have stayed away Art, I deeply wished to know my kin but what my father did well…"

She put her own glass down and approached them and smiled.

"There are so few of us immortals left, I hold no grudge against you or my own. Travis to answer some of your question before, I asked you here because it's time we knew of each other. With fathers passing the old ways are dying. And they should pass; I believe all Grey should know of each other and help one another. Father believed each grey community should stand on its own, and for its own. But I see the value in relations, I believe in time those of us who lead Grey communities can help one another. I know there is much that must be done to earn your trust. And for the two of you I know my clan has wronged your town. But I am glad to see Travis and his leadership is doing much to bridge that gap. I can only assure you I do not wish to do anything to risk that."

Nancy took a long pull from the glass and with a tone then asked her why send spies to Medford and why take one of their clan? Travis loved it when Nancy spoke as if she was a Grey, she didn't very often. But as his Brehon, she had that right. If it came down to it, he knew the Agora wouldn't back her, but he would. Having Nancy be his closest advisor had paid many dividends over the years.

"Your clan, did I miss something?"

Nancy sat the glass down and took a step closer to Rose. Her demeanor was that of a woman who was tired of playing. She was confident and sure of herself and her wisdom. It was a state Travis had seen her in many times over the decades.

"I am the grey Brehon, I council the King. My King may be young but he isn't a fool, Rose. He knows you are speaking from both sides of your mouth. You say you want peace but your actions say otherwise. You have one of your Grey snooping in Medford right now. The very one that offended the Kings wife, damaged his sons honor. These aren't the actions of a friend."

Travis watched closely how Rose responded. The look on her face was one of amusement, then one of contemplation. Rose smiled thinly and then began to explain herself.

"I had wanted to keep tonight festive and light. You are my guests and the last thing I wanted to do was start with the mistakes we have made. But I see I was in error in that. I forget I am not dealing with Europeans; you Americans always do business first. Since I am the one in the wrong, I should have started there."

Rose had a certain charm Travis thought as she continued to explain her thoughts and her motives. Most of it was hogwash as far as Travis believed. Nancy had already shared her thoughts on these other Grey. But in reality, no one really knew for sure. Rose turned to speak directly to Nancy now and with that opportunity, Travis examined her closely. She was pretty, but it was her mind that was biggest asset. This vampire was no fool, whatever she was planning she wouldn't reveal it here.

"I am not that familiar with how the Aqua live. But for us Grey some things are taken for granted. We search for knowledge; it's in our blood… our call if you will. Just like you build strong families we seek knowledge, and we build strong warrior houses. My young one is ambitious, she saw Malcom and desired him to stay with her. I can't blame her; without the orb we struggle to grow our numbers. But let me assure you, she wasn't acting under my guidance. She was acting as a woman looking for a mate. As for Jason my family did lure him to us. Recently I dispatched a team to discover the truth of your people. I had hoped enough time had elapsed since father's death that we could begin to speak in a civil manner.

That team uncovered, rather by accident, that Jason was untrustworthy. He was selling information to another group we know of. When I was made aware of this, I decided to use him. As is our way, to betray one's brothers is the highest act of dishonor. Luring him to Meridia was intended to be a gift to you. Knowing a man is capable of evil is one thing, proving it is another. By proving his dishonor, we have given you the gift of truth. A man who was betraying you has been removed. Amongst us that is considered a great kindness."

Travis saw the look Rose was giving him. He smiled back and shot a look back at Nancy who just looked back at him. He didn't need to link to know what Nancy was thinking. He took over the conversation at that point.

"Asking my government to have me assigned to this meeting was dangerous. Many questions were asked of me, our secrets could have been revealed. Why not just come to us, or reach out to me? Bringing us here seems reckless and dangerous to my clan's safety. You say you want to build a relationship but yet lured one man and interrogated the other. You ask for a relationship.... But relationships are built on trust. I fear we will struggle to have any?"

Rose was very much like Nancy in another way. She was confident, bold. Someone not to underestimate or take for granted. She could be a powerful enemy, or a powerful friend. But Travis was unsure how to navigate things towards the second. Thankfully Rose seemed to know how to.

"Well said brother. I can assure you our intentions were the best. But if I was you, I would hesitate to believe me. Trust is not a thing to be given; it has to be earned. I believe in time you will see my people and yours are destined to be close. But those bonds have to be formed in time. I give you my word that Meridia desires nothing but a close relationship with Medford. For now, you only have my word on this. But I promise you brother, you will see the truth in this."

Rose shifted from a posture that relayed strength but firmness back to one of comfort and ease. As if just saying the words meant they were all fine now. Travis liked how her body and her smile conveyed so much. Travis could only marvel at how this woman communicated. He wondered if one day he would be like them. Old, wise and miles ahead of the young vampires around him. For now, he put away his self-doubt and continued to listen. Rose offered more explanations and reasons why Meridia was not his enemy.

"Sending her to you was not meant to offend. I asked her to clarify our position with your people and to mend things. I see she still has much to learn on how to speak to others. If you desire Jason's return, I will order him returned. Truly I had wanted to honor you by revealing your traitor. As for Malcom... Well, my young one is just that, young. Please understand few of my people know of you. To see another Grey is... exciting. For Camila she has only heard stories of your people, to meet the son of a King was a thrill for her."

Rose walked over and refilled her glass offering more to the others. No one else took her up on it so she settled back a moment later leaning against the table closest to them. She seemed lightly guilty in her demeanor, but only just.

"Perhaps we were too eager with Jason. Without the Orb of our clan, our numbers stagnate. I admit our motivations are rather selfish, Jason will hopefully father more of our kind for us. But yes, Travis this is not the way to begin a trusting relationship. Please accept my apology for our actions. Each of us are excited at the possibility of brothers and sisters being so close. To know our clan will live on, and that it's thriving again. Believe me when I say we in Meridia are very happy for our family in Medford."

Nancy and Rose went on discussing Jason. Watching her closely Travis saw she really believed that outing Jason would be seen as a "gift." Travis didn't see it as one and wondered why she could possibly think anyone would see it as such. Not to mention if she really believed that how could they trust him. Almost as if they were linked Nancy asked something similar to Rose.

"He and his mother will never be trusted, only used. We will make sure their offspring are taught the difference… and they will be watched. But as I said, an opportunity to save our clan is precious and rare. It must be lovely having the orb of our clan at your disposal. You can create as many Grey as you desire, and you can see much inside the vampires who follow you."

Everyone in the room nodded at the comments about the Orb. Each had long lost any wonder with such things. They were key yes, but hardly new and exciting. Besides, there were other ways to create Grey vampires than just children and the orb.

I don't think she knows about the visitors, she doesn't know about dad yet I wager.

She went on explaining why historically how the Grey viewed those in their ranks when they violated their oaths. Then she circled back to Malcom.

"What we did not expect was to find Malcom there when we arrived to collect Jason. He was supposed to be out of that building for another 20 minutes. Malcom walked in just as our team was preparing to leave. Again, I forget whom I deal with, I should have just told you. Instead, I thought to honor our ways. My people warned me against it, they said Tina did not honor our ways and that you would not understand. I see in your countenance that they were correct. Travis, I can only assure you my desire was to help you…. not hurt. I had been intending on using Jason to lure you into a meeting in Sao Paulo. There I would reveal myself and my people. And share with you all we knew."

Travis wondered if this was just a convenient lie or something his people had missed. He made a note to inquire with his mother on it when he returned. Was Jason working with more than just their Meridian cousins? Mom had run that investigation, perhaps she knew more? If Jason could betray them for sex with thralls, he could be believed to sell secrets. That unnerved Travis but he put it aside to deal with his host.

"I was the one who decided we could use the traitor as a peace offering. Bringing him to Sao Paulo so we could then meet. I gave the order to have him used as a "

."

Travis stopped breathing and curled his toes in his tight-fitting shoes to beat back the harsh feelings. His breathing increased just a touch and he nearly gasped at the phrase Rose just used. It was the Greek word for "whore" something that made Travis uncomfortable at once. Cold, efficient, and very much the fate of someone who brought dishonor to his house. In the Grey clan of Tina's day it was the opposite. The best a Grey man could hope for was to be made a "pórni." Travis had been that way for years, serving as the sexual plaything for Grey woman after Grey woman.

"My people made a mess of things. By taking your son, we caused serious offense. I wanted to speak to you directly one ruler to another. That is why I told your State Department that you must attend. I had not anticipated how you would feel vulnerable to your government's attention. Considering you have been working for them for years now, I believed you would not be troubled. Travis on behalf of my clan, and myself, I have offended you. I have no excuse other than my own gain and incompetence. I do not ask for forgiveness, only that you allow me the opportunity to show you my regret."

Travis listened to her statement and carefully heard her tone and her words. His judgement said it was sincere, but even if it wasn't it didn't pay to be rude now. He wanted to know more about them. Even if they were his enemy he wanted to know more.

"Ok, I accept that your people might feel that way. And normally I would not pursue any relationship. But as you said you are family. I believe ignoring this opportunity is a poor reward for either of us. For now, let us consider this closed. Jason may stay with you, but should I find him in Medford again, I will kill him and his mother."

He saw Art and Nancy shift uncomfortably over that statement. They were Aqua and were far nicer to their enemies than Travis. For him he couldn't afford it, Jason had made his bed and he knew it. Besides Travis had little love for a Grey who betrayed his fellows. At thinking it a small voice reminded him that he had just betrayed his wife not days before. He shoved that voice away as fast as it arrived. Not wanting to re-examine his actions with Dolly yet again.

"I am curious about your people Rose? What can you tell me about them?"

Rose thanked him for understanding and said a tiny bit about her family and how they had come to the area before she had married Napoleon. She still didn't reveal much other than a vague understanding of when they arrived. Nothing on how many there were, and more importantly what they were doing or what they wanted from Travis. They went back and forth and after a bit Nancy and Travis reengaged in the conversation. Rose was intensely curious about them. Travis was happy for the time to himself as Rose focused in on Art and Nancy. He wasn't getting anywhere with finding out what he needed to know.

"I find it so amazing that an Aqua is the grey Brehon. I must admit I am fascinated by your clan. In all my years I have never met an Aqua. I have met Obsidians, Emeralds, Rubies, but never Aqua. Is it true you can link by touching? The intimacy such a power must create, it's fascinating."

Twenty minutes later Art had been talking nearly all of it about living as an Aqua. Rose did nothing but encourage it and was utterly charming. As Art was talking about how merging worked, a man entered the room and whispered into Rose's ear. After the man departed Rose stood, obviously this evening was coming to a close.

"Apparently your Secretary of State has said something to anger our President. I am afraid I am going to have to see if I can settle his temper. Please, I know we have just met but I demand you stay in my home. There are plenty of beautiful rooms you can choose from, and the staff here are excellent. I insist, I simply must have you stay. I can send our people for your things at the hotel. And Nancy, I promise you another bottle of this divine vintage for you and Art to explore together. Not to mention the staff here are well versed with Norman cooking. I seriously doubt Texas has much of that."

Nancy laughed and looked at Travis. While they were here, they were working for him. His first thought was to decline, but he wanted to know more. Nancy and her Aqua talked endlessly about the amazing thrill of seeing others in their clan and getting lost in their eyes. Grey liked seeing other Grey... but not that much. Still, this Rose her eyes were brighter, stronger than any other Grey he had seen before. Even her father's wasn't so bright. Looking at them he wanted to know more, understand this ancient woman who he might have to face in battle one day. Or, if she was to be trusted, have as a friend. What better way to find out than to stay and discover it today, rather than some year in the future. Travis accepted the offer which visually made Rose very happy.

"Good I am glad we have that settled. I know we got off on the wrong foot, but I hope we have begun to put us back on a different path."

A moment after she departed, Nancy and Art walked up and without warning put him into the link. Art was the first to speak inside it.

"Charming, she knows how to get what she wants I will say that."

Travis could feel both Nancy's agreement and irritation at Art's feelings for their host. In the link it was difficult to have private thoughts or secrets. Which was why linking was highly frowned on by the Grey. For Travis however he trusted both these Aqua with everything. Each had shown him over the decades just who they were. Nancy asked why he had said yes to staying the night, and what the State Department would say.

"Honestly, I don't care what they think at this point. Staying here might help us understand what it is she is doing. Do either of you believe her? She seems genuine but I have a hard time believing she went to all this effort to just be friends."

Travis felt both speak in the link as one. Neither of them believed her explanation on Jason. Nancy especially found her words to be very carefully crafted. It could be because she wished to hide her true intent, or that she was a skilled diplomat. Travis pondered much of what they were thinking, and allowed them to peer into him as they wished. His trust in these two was absolute. It didn't take long for Nancy to find the warnings from Mae. He hadn't shared that yet with Nancy who was upset at him holding that back. Mae had warned Travis not long before of a threat against the Aqua, along with the one on his own clan.

"I don't know what it means Nancy, you can see I was going to tell you soon. I wanted to see what this woman was doing before I spoke. If there is some vast conspiracy, we need to know who is involved. And keep in mind it's not just your clan, one of my own wives is involved."

Where Mae had been a little vague on the details about the threat to him, she wasn't on the one to the Aqua. This group wanted to see them pay for what Eleanor had done in the past, and for the Aqua in harboring and accepting her. But was it real, and how far did this conspiracy go? So far it was only talk, but Travis suspected Mae was being truthful. After the three of them conversed in the link some more, Travis could feel both of them calm down.

"Travis this game you are playing is dangerous. You should have come to me and Art the moment you found out. We can help you, if one of your wives has betrayed you then we can uncover it. What you are doing with Dolly is dangerous."

He felt the worry Nancy, and even Art had for him. In the link Travis could feel their emotions. It was very similar to how parents worry for their child. It was the Aqua way to love and foster familiar relationships. They couldn't help but love, and build up what other clans desired to destroy. This call of theirs went afoul of how the Grey operated, but Travis didn't care. The one caveat he had kept from his human days was his desire for a loving family. The one he had grown up in had been destroyed by vampirism, and he often resented the clans for it. With Nancy he had found more than an advisor, he saw her as a more realistic mother. One he could trust, and one he could recognize. He smiled at her in the link and allowed both of them to see his admiration for her openly.

"I know, but I am a Grey and I must approach this in our way. Even if I grow so dreadfully tired of it. Let me deal with this our way. I would much rather I endanger myself in this, than you. But I promise you if I learn more about this group, I will tell you. In the morning, I suggest you linger in your room. Try to stay away from me and Rose. Find out what you can from the servants about our host. Meanwhile I will see just how forthcoming our host is."

Chapter 16: Grey Fealty

Medford, Texas – Agora

Jan 23rd 2058

Jessie was tired but still excited. Today was the day, both mom and Susan had let her know to be here that she would be inducted as a woman of the clan. Her last test passed Jessie would be recognized as a full member. It was a quiet time and a special one. Once today was complete she could begin her life. It may just be a ceremony in name but it wasn't to Jessie. Soon she would have her own home, her own path, everything. Her poor brothers still had to live with mom, and answer her orders even after years of being made Hoplites. But for Jessie after today that would be a thing of the past.

"The Agora is ready for callers, step forward if you wish."

Jessie sighed and looked down at herself to make sure she was presentable. She was of course, but she did this in case something was amiss with her clothing. She wore something basic for today. Just sweats and a t-shirt, no underwear. In a moment she would be given clothing as a woman. Her mother had taken great pains to have Isabe create a peplos for her. That was waiting on her inside, as was her mother and grandmother. Jessie took a breath and stepped forward as two guards opened the large doors to the chamber. Once inside, the doors shut again revealing the large room she had never been inside before. Only those of the Agora, or those who had business were allowed inside. Jessie saw two of her older half-sisters waiting on her smiling. Carrie and Siri were both several years older than her. Each had sponsored her for today. Right on cue her grandmother rose and asked a question. She did so in a tone of fake surprise. It was all theater, but it was honored tradition. The point was to highlight that only a recognized woman of the clan had the right to petition this body.

"What is the meaning of this child entering? Whom do you think you are girl?"

Instead of Jessie answering her half-sister Siri did. Meanwhile her other half-sister Carrie smiled brightly and excitedly for her, clutching her hands in anticipation for what came next.

"A child ready to be a woman. She has proven herself worthy in my eye and I submit her for your approval."

The moment that was said, the stoic faces changed around the table. Jessie couldn't help but smile back, she saw the pride and excitement in her mother's face as well as her grandmothers. She tried to hide it but Jessie knew her well enough that she was well pleased. Others sitting in judgement however were less excited. They didn't like children of Travis and resented the power his children had.

It's good being the daughter of the king... .... Screw them.

"Yelina what say you, this girl is of your flesh. Do you think she is ready? Has she met with approval in your eye?"

Jessie saw the love in her mother's face and she only answered with a smile and a nod. Her grandmother nodded as well and then turned to Susan.

"And you, her teacher is she ready to be a woman? Will she serve this clan, will she be of service?"

Susan stood and walked up to her with a frown. As much as Susan made a show of distaste, she knew Susan liked her deep down.

"She is rough around the edges still. She has much to learn, and I fear she is too confident in herself.... But yes, my student is ready."

It was quiet for a moment as the others in the Agora were allowed to speak but none did. Dolly would have said something if she was here but she was in Europe. Once it was clear no one would object, or would speak against her, then things proceeded.

"Jessie what you seek is not for the timid, a Grey woman is not a sheep. A grey woman is a wolf. She rules, she takes, she lives as she sees fit. Are you truly ready to be a woman? Once you are there is no going back, your childish mistakes will not be forgiven once you are. You will be a woman, responsible for your actions and judged on them. Do you still seek to be one of us?"

Jessie responded the only way she could. With strength and confidence that she was ready. Her words were still echoing in the room. Both of her half-sisters were looking at their grandmother, waiting for the word.

"Then as the Grey Mother, I welcome the newest wolf in our den. May your life be blessed with strength and victory. May your sons be strong and lead the way. May your house be known and feared."

At that Siri and Carrie pulled sharp knives from sheaths, their blades were polished and the light in the room bounced off their surface like from a mirror. With care and precision Jessie's clothes were cut from her body.

"As a child you dressed as a child, you thought as a child. You were loved and nurtured as a child. But no more.... You are a woman of the clan now. A wolf in the fold, one to be feared, one to be trusted. From this day onward you may bear the honors of a woman. You may live as a woman, love as a woman, and rule as a woman."

By this point Jessie was down to only her shoes. The old shirt and sweats were in pieces on the floor. It was demeaning to some, but not Jessie. She was LONG since ready for this day to arrive. To live as she desired, to be respected as she deserved. This day for Jessie couldn't have come soon enough.

"Place the orb in her hands."

Jessie held out her hands for the grey orb that was cold to the touch at first. But a moment after she held it the gem grew warm. It left her grip a second later hovering a few inches from her still outstretched hands. Jessie had always pictured this moment and in her mind, she had seen herself proud but strong. Not closing her eyes to the changes, the Orb would give her. But the moment she felt the electric charge hit her, all of that went out the window. Her eyes flew shut and her mouth flew open. Jessie could feel the pain and struggled to keep her shock at its fury from her lips. It was another test of her resolve; those that shouted out in terror or pain were looked down on. The moment was thankfully brief and she felt the orbs changes at once. Once the crackle of the lightening faded, she could hear things around her again.

"You look amazing, well-done sister!"

Jessie's eyes opened and she saw Siri smiling at her with her new Peplos in her hands. Jessie could feel the most important change already. Her hair was now that of a woman, it was long and lush and it wrapped around her like a blanket. As a child she had to cut her hair lest she offend a woman. No more....

"With this peplos you are one of us Jessie. Long may you be so."

The orb which had floated above her now moved out to the outstretched hand of her grandmother. Once there Jessie witnessed it stop spinning and return to its former shape. Her sisters placed her new peplos over her tying a silk knot around her waist. It was temporary and only given to new women. After today she would use other items to secure her peplos, but for now it was symbolic. Of her new place, and value to the clan. She was no longer a child; she was a woman.

Without warning the doors to the chamber opened and a male voice called out.

"There is another who wishes to speak, may I enter ladies?"

Without approval the man walked in causing all in the room to begin speaking at once. NO man was allowed entry without permission, especially not in a time like this. Jessie knew the man the moment she heard him speak. It was grandfather. Once he got close enough to her, he smiled and nodded to her.

"Congratulations kid, I am proud of you. It's a big day, sorry for crashing it."

Nearly all the Agora began to speak at once, which caused the Grey Mother to silence all of them with a harsh tone. Then with the room silent again, the Grey Gother addressed the intruder.

"Husband, this is not the time for this. This is Jessie's moment NO man may enter at a time like this. I must insist you wait outside!"

Jessie watched as her grandfather looked back at her and smiled before he began.

"I am not a man remember; I am a visitor. It was my kind that created this clan and all the rest. I am not bound to your rules, to your ways. I am above them, and I will address this body…. Now."

Jessie and her sisters were quickly ushered out of the room. As the doors shut behind them, she could hear harsh words spoken to grandfather.

"What the hell was that about?"

Jessie just shook her head as the three of them started to guess what was going on aloud. But they had barely begun to speculate when another voice from behind them spoke.

"Heck if I know, the old coot made me come up here and didn't say a word what was going on."

Jessie turned to see Camila standing there in her own extravagant peplos. She looked bored and irritated at being summoned so late in the evening for this. Jessie started to say something but stopped when she heard the shouting breach the door. They were supposed to block nearly any sounds from the chamber, but apparently not this time.

"Are they all shouting at grandfather?"

Siri looked worried for him; it wasn't a shock. Grandfather wasn't hard to like; he was funny and nothing like other Grey. Where Grey liked to pretend to be immortal, he truly was. He could live for millions of years. Carrie was worried they would hurt grandfather's feelings being so rough with him. Jessie wasn't too worried, the old coot as Camila called him was tougher than he looked.

"I thought the Agora was for women only, why does your grandfather get a pass?"

Jessie smirked and laughed a bit. That was when she realized Camila had no clue who Cyrus really was.

"Didn't you hear him; he is a visitor. He has the power to create a clan from scratch. There isn't much he can't do honey."

Jessie felt so pleased with herself, getting one over on that smug bitch. Smiling she turned back to the door and wondered what was going on. Whatever was being said no one sounded pleased.

Paris, France – Château de Malmaison

Jan 24th 2058

Travis had been escorted through the long hallways to a room smaller than he had been in yesterday. Inside he found Rose by herself sitting at a small table. She was dressed comfortably in what looked like riding breeches. Perhaps it was just how someone like her dressed in the morning. As soon as he was close enough, she rose and met him half way between the table and the doorway. Her face had a huge smile and like before you could see the wisdom and experience show in her countenance.

"Good morning brother how did you sleep last night? I wager you haven't spent a night in such a bed as that before."

Her charm oozed and the smile could light up a block. But she wasn't wrong, his room was a sight.

"You can say that, I don't want to even guess how much that cost to furnish. Are all the rooms like that?"

Rose smiled and escorted him to another table, one that stretched along the far wall. On the table were what looked like fancy containers. What they were made from Travis couldn't tell but they looked like silver. A moment later a lid was removed showing different types of typical American breakfast items. Sausage, eggs, bacon, pancakes. The choices seemed to go on forever.

"If Nancy was with us, I am sure she would be telling you this is not how her people eat. But thankfully neither of us are French. I acquired my love for your breakfasts before you were born. The Europeans stick their noses up at your people but I have to say Americans know how to eat."

After making a healthy plate for himself he was satisfied to see that Rose wasn't going light either. The table they sat at was small and intimate. Clearly it was not intended for more than four to sit at.

"Where is Nancy and Art, have you seen them yet?"

Rose smiled and crossed her legs. She summoned someone from behind him and a moment later a man dressed in what Travis could only assume was a period costume began to speak.

"Sir, your friends are still in bed. I believe they took Madam's advice to heart last night and heavily indulged."

A moment later Rose described all the things her chef had created for them last night. Travis had eschewed eating, but apparently Art and Nancy sampled many Norman specialties. Unlike his Brehon, Travis had spent the night reading about his host. In a way Travis marveled at talking to history this way. His host if the world knew of her would be story number one. Historians would be knocking down her door asking for insights into her husband and her own life. Movies had been made about her, and many books written. Travis wondered if one day something like that would be said of him. He seriously doubted it.

"Imagine Travis if you were visiting America for the first time in 1000 years. This breakfast spread would be enticing, no? I am sure Nancy had a wonderful evening introducing Art to her culture."

Travis laughed and admitted after that long he would indulge as well. Besides, Travis also knew they were doing exactly as he asked. The food was excellent and frankly so was the company. Rose was easy on the eyes after a while. She was the kind of woman that the more you got to know the more you were attracted to. Something about how elegant and refined she was. It heightened her physical looks and pulled you in.

"I have to admit I am curious, clearly your former home still considers you, its owner. How is that possible, from what I was reading last night Josèphe, at least the historical one died here in 1814."

Instead of answering she got up quickly and retrieved another two slices of Bacon for her plate. Offering more to Travis who declined.

"Yes, it was time, my love was exiled by then. His health was poor and we had gone our separate ways. Even to people who love each other as much as we did, love can still end. I knew it was time to revert and move on. But I have always kept an eye on this place. Its dear to me, not just because I oversaw its renovation. It reminds me of my love, and I am not ready to see it fall into dust. You see I have an understanding with the French government. They of course do not know whom I really am, but they like the access I can provide them. They believe by granting me this favor in using this home from time to time, that they will get better access to our president. Perhaps a trade deal thrown their way, the odd military contract. To be here again and to call this lovely place home it's well worth it."

That astounded Travis, was she living here full time? Astonished he asked precisely that.

"For the last couple of years yes, I still travel back to Meridia from time to time but yes, I am happy to say it's my full time home again. At least for now. Like all things its only temporary. No matter how well built, we will outlive these places. You will need to get used to that Travis. You will outlive even your country eventually. I have outlived several of my adopted ones since I became immortal."

That thought hit him like a truck. America to Travis was powerful and home. The thought that one day it would be like Sparta, Rome, or any other former power was troubling. Looking back at Rose he saw a supportive glance. Art was right, it must be easy for her to get her way.

"Thank you for your hospitality, Rose, I must say that I didn't expect this. I had rather thought our meeting was to be somehow darker."

Travis took a sip of juice from a crystal goblet. Odd having a common meal with uncommon people, yet here he was.

"I am sure you didn't know what to expect. I am not sure what Camila did to your son, but I am sure she came on strong. She is young and full of her own loveliness. It's hard for a young Grey woman not to want to push Grey men that way. You have several Grey wives; how do you find us? Are we as difficult as some of the other clans say we are?"

Travis started to smile but chuckled without thinking. The three women in his life were often difficult on him and his world. There had been times he wanted to be single again just to have a moments peace.

"I think I can appreciate what Malcom went though."

Rose smiled and took a sip of whatever she was drinking. She was deliberate and controlled in most things but in speech she seemed common and comforting today. Perhaps it was intended just for him?

"Well, I am not young like you or Camila, I am even older than your Brehon. Time changes us Travis, it smooths our edges and softens the stone that we stand on. There was a time when I was Camila's age, I would be asking you to dance right now. Just to see what kind of Grey you were. But the days for such extravagant feeling is over, I am afraid. I long for peace now Travis. Oh, I know we are supposed to be warriors, and have heart for battle. But after many battles, both mental and physical I no longer crave battle. When it comes, I meet it like a Grey, but I no longer desire it. I have seen my fill of death, and the smells of war. Looking at you now…. I believe you feel the same."

Travis looked down for a moment. The truth was the war in China had removed any desire for battle in his heart. He had seen his friends die, and watched as others suffered. War never translated well in any media. You can't hear the cries in books, and you can't smell the burnt flesh in movies. And unlike in film you can't just go home and pretend it never happened. Those sounds and smells never left you. As a Grey yes, he would face battle when it came. But desire it…. never again.

"Yes, that is true for me. When did you see battle?"

The glass in her hands came down and she looked out the window for a moment before she responded. The story she told was ancient, but with the change of setting could be believed to have occurred in any century. When she was done it left a quiet between them that went for far longer than either of them had planned. Neither wanted to be weak in front of the other Travis suspected, but truth was truth. Seeing the opportunity Travis made his move.

"Rose I love my people; I would do anything for them. We aren't a wealthy people, and we aren't a powerful one. I know there is more you aren't telling me. Please, as one Grey to another, be honest with me and tell me what it is you want."

The quiet lasted for only a moment this time. And Rose put down the napkin she had just used to wipe away the last vestiges of the meal. She took a breath and looked with apprehension towards his reaction.

"Oh Travis, I wish I could link with you like the Aqua do. There is so much I wish you could see in my memory. I admire you, truly I do. I have heard the stories from my spies. Your people love you, and they serve you willingly. The Agoge is creating a new Sparta, not just some poor copy. A real home for warriors, one worthy of the name. Travis it's clear to me that in time you will be as strong as Sparta once was. Nations will quake with fear at the power you will wield Travis. Your people grow stronger by the day, eventually you will be able to outclass my people. You, Travis, are our greatest threat. In time our two people will come to blows to decide who will lead. Right now, I believe my people would win such a fight. We are fewer in number, but we are powerful and we have the advantage. We know all about you, and you know little about us."

The way she said it made it clear she didn't fear him now. But something in the way she said it he could hear the tired refrain in seeing what would be. Travis felt the same every time he knew he had to send others into battle or enter it himself. Knowing he would win, knowing he would be victorious but tired of the wages of war. It was never really the Grey who paid them, at least not since he had led. It was the weak and the innocent who paid the wages. In war it generally always was.

"I could resist you, wage war on your people. Try to cut down your power before it outstrips my own. But I believe that would be in error. I believe the future of our people is to be one. That is why I asked you here, I want to prepare the two of us for that day. The day when my people will kneel before you, the day they will see you as their king."

Travis processed that but couldn't quite wrap his head around it. What about her, in that arrangement if he was their king would she be his Queen? On asking Rose smiled and laughed.

"Even for a vampire I am far too old for you. No, even I would bend my knee to you Travis. But I have to admit I did consider what you suggest. I am sure I could open your eyes in the bedroom to all kinds of new realities. If only I was a few centuries younger, the things I could show you."

The smile on her face was electric and the man in him wondered just what kind of realities she had in mind. But he was outclassed here, Travis knew it. Grey women were seducers and users. They manipulated and controlled the men in their lives.

"What about you, if you aren't going to be my wife, what role would you have?"

Rose looked at him and asked if he would like to take a walk. Curious he said yes without thinking. They walked without speaking at first. Exiting the room where they ate, to walk down one corridor and then another. He was wondering if this was her way of avoiding his question but a few minutes later when they were back in the formal dining room from last night she turned and spoke.

"Travis when I say I am too old what I mean to say is I believe my time is coming to an end. Even children of founders eventually die. I have outlived nearly all the ones I know. There comes a time in the life of a Grey when you just know. We only can be leader so long as we are the strongest. My power is ebbing Travis, soon either I will be gone or I will be usurped by another. It's our way, and I do not curse at it. By this path we both have walked, I have always been triumphant. But in another century or two…"

She put a hand on him. It was warm and thin and he was captivated by her charm. This wasn't just any woman, this being had held the adoration of many who had lived some of the most amazing lives. Napoleon was not the first historical figure who had been enraptured by her charm. Nor was he the first to obtain power and fame with her help. Seeing some of the portraits made it clear Rose had many times before.

"I could wage war with you, but to what end? More death and destruction. But most importantly it would kill the best hope for my beloved Sparta. Travis, you have reignited the fire that has been out now 2000 years! If I thought I could stand beside you for another 2000 I would demand to be your wife. I would help you craft the strongest power the world has ever seen. But I know in my bones my time is short. I just do Travis… Besides what does a young bull want with and old thing like me. You have wives enough."

There was a knowing smile that intrigued Travis. To have such a person as your wife. If only his others could allow her a place beside him. With her knowledge and wisdom, who could stand against them? The humans she had put her strength behind had nearly conquered the world, more than once. What would happen if he was her champion, instead of just a human? Travis felt the temptation and put it aside just as quick. One Grey woman was difficult enough, but three or four? They would eat him alive in a month. She was still grinning over her insinuation at how love making would be between them. She could clearly motivate men, that was for sure.

"Travis in time your clan could relight what father let burn out years before. You could save my Sparta. For that there is nothing I would not do. As for me and what to do with me, you needn't worry. Time will see to my place soon enough. I will be sleeping soon, hopefully back in my beloved Sparta. But you, Travis you are my greatest wish come true. I want to try to help bridge my people to yours. None of my people can do what you already have. Build something that will last. You have the Agoge, a thriving Agora, and numbers that never stop going up."

Travis saw the passion Rose had, and couldn't help but believe her in some way. You couldn't act in such a way if not some of what you were saying was deeply held. She smiled sweetly when he put his hand on hers. It felt a bit unbidden to take her hand, and it had to be all he would do. Still, it felt exciting. Travis felt his heart move with feeling. He had never dreamed this would be what they would be talking about. When he started speaking, he did so quickly, too excited for his own good.

"Let's say for a moment that I would wish for such a thing. How would we build such a bridge?"

Rose led him by the hand to another room, this one with oil paintings. There were many old canvas paintings here done by what Travis assumed were the old masters. Rose stopped him on front of huge one. It depicted a family; from what time Travis couldn't guess.

"The best way to build a bridge is with time and trust. I believe if we encourage our young to get to know one another, then we will find it to be elementary."

Travis looked up and saw what she meant. Rose wanted them to marry off their children to one another. He asked and she shook her head yes.

"That is really why I sent Camila to Medford. She is a powerful Grey woman; she is our brightest and best. She will make a wonderful mate for one of you. In time perhaps a few centuries there will be no need for deception, no need to tread lightly. We will be one family then. Also, by then your Medford Grey will be so powerful that the nations of the world will not be able to ignore you. It will be time for our kind to be known to the world again. We will take our place where we should be."

Travis didn't like the sound of that. In ancient times when their kind had been far more widespread, Kings, and rulers were all vampires. The net result hadn't been more peace, hardly so. The clans had fought bitterly amongst themselves.

"Look the thought of our clans coming together is lovely. But to rule the nations again. Rose our kind didn't exactly win awards the last time. You remember what it cost humanity for it to be stopped? Fifty million dead, all of Europe devastated. To be honest I don't want our clan or any clan to rule nations again."

Rose squeezed his hand and took it and interlocked her fingers into his. They walked a few more steps until they came to another portrait. This one of a king and a queen.

"Travis it can't be helped. Medford can't contain the clans any longer. The Emerald number in the thousands already, the Aqua are in the hundreds. How long will it be before our clan numbers in the hundreds of thousands? We are superior Travis, when we are that large, we will rule. It is as predictable as the rising and falling of the sun. With the wrong King yes, you are right it will be terrible. But with a good king, one we trust and believe in. Just think what can be done. You will rule your America one day, a new Sparta, one of your creation. My daughters and sons will serve you; they will sire many more for your army. My Meridia will be yours as well. Think of the power of an entire hemisphere at your command."

Travis heard the wisdom of it. He hadn't thought much about his people past the next decade much less century. But at their growth rate, it wouldn't be long before even his clan was the size of a small city like Medford. By then the Emerald might be in the millions. It wasn't like Travis didn't know this, but he had never heard it described like this before. Travis's gut which he had long since learned to trust, told him she wasn't wrong. She put a warm hand on his chest as she spoke with warmth and excitement.

"I don't want our clan swallowed up by the others. The time is now to build a bridge to our future. One for our king, and the clan I love and have served for all my life. I know it's difficult for you to accept. And that is precisely why I offer it to you. Only someone unworthy would desire this. Travis, you don't, your heart and mind was made to be a King. And a good one."

She turned to face him and knelt before him. Travis couldn't help but feel powerful and wonton seeing her do so. The look in her eyes and look on her face spoke volumes. He had seen such a look on his lovers a few times before. Submissive, desirous… it sent shivers down his back.

"I submit to you now, and for always. You Travis are my King and I will follow your lead. My people, as long as they are loyal to me will follow you. I swear this now and before you. For all time my house is yours."

Chapter 17: Fall from Grace

Medford, Texas – Cassia's home

Jan 24th 2058

Cassia watched as her husband got dressed. He had said nothing to her the entire time. He had not come home last night, and was only here now to get a few things.

"Cyrus please talk to me."

He didn't stop nor did he respond. She was fully cowed by this point. The tears she begun to shed last night hadn't really ever stopped. She knew he was angry, that was obvious. But it was this silence that was killing her. Her love knew about her sins, stupid things done thoughtlessly. Hundreds of years of loyalty and love thrown out the window. She called out to him with a voice that screamed her emotions. Begging him to stop and speak to her, to love her again. That caused him to pause, he didn't turn but he finally relented and spoke.

"What do you want me to say. I thought the two of us were… well I thought wrong I guess."

Cassia closed her eyes remembering the shame of what he had said in the Agora. He had outed her and all of them for what they had done. Explaining that their children had begun to learn the truth, that was how he knew. He exposed their secrets both of hording money but also the trips in New York. Some in the Agora had challenged him accusing him and saying it wasn't any of his business. But Cyrus had shut them up quickly with a quiet threat. Cyrus could remove their vampirism at will; he could kill them at will. He was the Grey Visitor, and he could end the clan if he desired it. That had finally cowed the others. But for Cassia it was seeing the hurt in his eyes that destroyed her instantly.

"I was an idiot, Cyrus! What I did with those men meant nothing to me…nothing! I love you; you're my husband… the…the father of my children! I don't want to lose you!"

It was quiet for a very long time and she saw his shoulders slacken and his head lower. Still, it took another full minute for him to speak.

"I know… I don't want to lose you either my love. But what you did, and what the others did, I can't forgive. You will resign from the Agora today. Your done with this clan, now and forever."

Cassia was quiet again and heard what she didn't dare think would occur. She couldn't tell him yes, if she did then Travis was doomed.

"Cyrus I can't do that. Travis will fall apart in a year or less. You can't want that. Please I swear to you this will never happen again. I could NEVER do this again to you, I love you too much for that."

The shoulders regained their posture and this time the pause was shorter. She didn't need to hear the words to know what it meant.

"No, you will not set foot in the Agora again as my representative. If you do, I will take what I gave you away. Do you hear me woman?"

Cassia nodded but realized he couldn't see her. So, she replied the best she could. Her voice was broken by feeling, it was if she could burst with shame. When he turned however, she saw there was some love for her in his face. A fact that made her rush to him without an invitation. She worried that he would reject her but he didn't. He took ahold of her and wrapped his arms around her. Something that caused Cassia to sob uncontrollably. After a moment being held, he began to speak again.

"I hate what you have done, truly I do. But I can't live without you. But you broke my heart… you really did. I need time … time to figure out what I do next with my clan."

Cassia asked again about Travis and the Agora. She was his will in the Grey; she was meant to be his representative to each of his clans. A role that was as much a part of her as her hands or her feet. She said so and was shocked by his response.

"Not anymore, Cassia after today you are my wife… nothing more. I love you but the fact is you aren't cut out for what I asked of you. I should have…"

Cassia was infuriated at what he was saying. That she wasn't cut out to be what she was born to do?

"Should have what… Cyrus this is MY CALLING. HE is my son and I am going to save him! Look I messed up, but no matter what you think of me, my son is all that matters now. No… I am not leaving the Agora; this clan is mine. You gave it to me to rule over and to craft. Well, I am doing that, and then when

Travis has things in hand… THEN I will leave. Honey this is what you need me for, to make this clan right.

Cassia instantly knew she had errored again. Things she tried to take back but it was too late. When she paused again, she saw a look she hadn't seen before.

"It's over Cassia, resign today or I will make you. As for being my wife… I think we both need a bit of time to consider if that is what is really best for either of us."

Without another word he disappeared, as a visitor he could do so by leaving his human form. Something he never did anymore. She shouted for him to return but he didn't. Angry, resentful and embarrassed she cursed at his memory and threw the nearest object she could lay hands on.

Medford, Texas – Cassia's Office

Jan 24th 2058

Susan stood in shock watching the woman who had been known as the Grey Mother pack up her things. Cassia's fall was so complete and so sudden. Everyone had assumed she would outlast every living soul in the clan. The thought that she could be taken down by this was… just stunning. But Susan didn't linger long on her mother-in-law's fate. Cyrus knew about all of their secrets and if he was willing to walk into the Agoge and take down Cassia, then there was no telling what he was willing to do.

Susan awkwardly hugged Cassia who was still in tears and told her she would check up on her later today. But Susan wasn't really thinking on that, that was just something to say in the moment. What was really on Susan's mind was her future, and that of her children. And of course, had he told his son about their cheating? A couple of the young girls helped Cassia out with her things. Standing silently in the corner was Cyrus. Brooding, angry and imposing like a statue. He loomed over everything, and no one was comfortable in his presence. Once Cassia had left the room, he shut the door leaving him alone with Susan. She took a breath and decided to ask what her fate would be.

"I take it you are going to tell Travis about all this? Have you…. already?"

Cyrus looked at her with anger, his arms crossed across his chest. He was no longer fully in human form. Only his upper body was. Below that was a mist that seemed to be dark, and never stopped swirling. Almost like a mini thunderstorm Susan thought. That informed Susan of what she wished to know,

Cyrus was not pleased and there would be hell to pay. However, when Cyrus spoke, he did so with a great deal of sorrow. As he did the cloud below him changed from near black to light grey.

"I am disappointed in you, in all of you. I know you love my son, I can feel that in you, even now. Why Susan, why betray him like this....why betray the things you say you believe in?"

Susan thought about her answer, something she had been thinking about all night. Why had she really? The honest answer was she was tired of being alone, tired of being patient on a woman who wasted every moment with her love. She wanted to live, to experience what it was to be powerful. New York was just a way to blow off steam, to have fun and forget about the rules for a moment. A way to let go of all the strain of trying to lead this clan. Something that wasn't said much but was known by all. Travis didn't lead the Grey, the Agora did. That fight to govern this nearly un-governable people was a strain on all of them. Susan didn't have to put this response into words, Cyrus simply read it from her mind.

"I have watched humans live for over 4000 years and still I can't understand them. Why are so many of you hell bent to destroy the things you love? You love my son, desire him, but you still betray him."

She looked down trying to look and feel sorry for something that in truth she didn't feel sorry for. She needed that release, they all did. But clearly Cyrus did not approve and clearly never would.

"My wife as you can see will not be back. The Grey is my clan, not hers. From this day forward she will concern herself with my home, not this clan. So, I am forced to make a decision. One I frankly would rather not make. As you say, my son does not really lead this clan, the Agora does. I have eyes, and I see that clearly enough. Since Cassia will not return, the Agora needs another leader. I suppose that should be you. If I give you the Agora, what will you do with it?"

Susan stood there with her mouth open and her mind blown. The last thing she thought she would be hearing was this offer? She figured he would be denouncing her actions and telling her how his son was devastated at the news. But he hadn't said a word about Travis.

"What about Travis, haven't you told him about us?"

Cyrus moved about the room, his lower section that of a visitor a vapor now greyish white instead of the black it had been before. His upper body remained human but his eyes were gone. Blank and terrifying at the voids that filled their spaces. It made Susan uneasy and she feared what he was planning.

"No, I don't have the heart to do that. As a visitor it's my duty to help my clans, not control them. I watch and learn as you live your lives. Eventually I intercede when I believe it's time for the clan to evolve. This clan just went through that process, and frankly is still not done evolving from the last change. I need to let that process complete. No, I am not going to tell your husband of your actions. But you should…. Eventually he is going to find out. Some of the children already know, eventually all of them will. If you want my advice, you should tell him as soon as you possibly can. Otherwise, if he hears it from his children, he may not forgive you. Just as I cannot…"

Susan swallowed at that, and the change in the cloud's color again. It was growing darker again….

"I know… I will Cyrus, I promise you. But now isn't the time, the clan is facing this thing with the Agency. His mind is all on that right now. If I told him about me and the others it would crush him at the worst possible time. I won't do that, when things quiet down I promise you, I will."

She watched hoping that was enough, she wanted to ask him which children knew. She could guess it had to be that damned Jackie. Dolly had brought her to the last gathering, and she wasn't at all pleased with what she saw there.

"Don't concern yourself with the children, I will take care of that. What do you plan on doing with the Agora, that is the only thing you need to concern yourself with."

Susan was relieved, then she had a thought. If Cyrus was going to let her be leader, she might be able to…

"NO! If you touch a hair on Yelina or Dolly's heads I will strip your memories, and leave you old and human by the side of the road in some foreign land. I won't kill you, like Cassia threatened. I won't do that to my grandchildren or to my son. But they will never know what happened to you, and you will never see them again nor will you even remember them."

Now that storm was all black and the eyes were no longer empty. They were filled with the same black storm that was below him. It filled Susan with fear, but it also made her feel something else. If she couldn't kill her rival, she could possibly do something else.

Medford, Texas – Aqua Hall

Jan 24th 2058

"Lizzie something big is going on I know it!"

Jessie was sitting with her best friend. They had become vampires at the same time and gone to the new vampire orientation together. While not a Grey she was dear to her. Both girls liked each other but for reasons that would surprise their parents. Each admired the others more extreme sides, wishing they could be just a bit like the other. Jessie for her part admired Lizzie's hard lines and seemingly endless faith she had in her family, her clan, and her way of life. While not believing like she did, she liked the ease and confidence Lizzy had. For her friend Jessies suspected deep down she wanted to be a bit freer from her call and the strict guidelines she followed. To be able to let her hair down from time to time and not feel bad for it. Something Jessie had no problems with, at least none that Lizzie saw.

Lizzie was on the bed looking at her friend as she put away another item in her suitcase. As usual Lizzie was sure nothing was amiss.

"I mean I know you are worried but it's not like you know what they said. It might just be about money or some small disagreement. I bet it will be just fine. Did you hear anyone say they were angry with you?"

Jessie huffed again saying no that she hadn't. Jessie had just relayed what happened last night at her imitation ceremony. At first for Jessie, it had been everything she ever dreamed it would be, then grandfather arrived. She still wasn't sure what happened.

"Well then it might be nothing about you at all. So…… how does it feel to be a quote un-quote a woman now? Do you feel all that and a bag of chips?"

Lizzie giggled and her smile spread from ear to ear. Jessie couldn't help but smile back.

"What do you think of my hair, it's almost as long as yours?"

Lizzie sat up in the bed she was sitting on, and gave her a critical eye. Then she pulled Jessie up and forced her to turn around. Lizzie with some giggles stood behind her so the two of them could look in the full-length mirror at their hair. Jessie's eyes narrowed and she sighed when she saw her friend still had her beat by several inches.

"Womp, womp…. you lose."

Both girls giggled and she hugged her friend for the boost in her mood.

"Seriously Jess, it's beautiful and I am so happy for you. Do you get to choose a man now, or have you already?"

Jessie smiled at her friend who had just claimed her own mate the week before. As an Aqua, Lizzie could speak the words and have any Aqua male she desired. With her however she had selected what Jessie thought was the strangest of choices. Cletus wasn't the brightest, and he certainly wasn't the bravest. But he was a good man, if just a human. But Lizzie loved him and that was all that really mattered to her.

"No, I…well I suppose I could if I wanted to."

Lizzie's face pulled back in shock and then she turned her face in mock puzzlement.

"This coming from the girl who had everything planned out, like to a tee? Spill it, who is he?"

Jessie laughed and giggled again, something she found easy to do with Lizzie. Her friend had that ability, to peel back her melancholy with ease.

"Well don't laugh but it's my thrall…. I think I want him to be my one."

Lizzie looked at her with puzzlement and then smiled. She put her hands on Jessie's and spoke in a soft voice.

"There isn't anything wrong with that. If that is who you love, then he is perfect for you. Why are you so shy about it, I mean come on… you aren't ever shy with guys?"

Jessie looked down and questioned it herself. Why was she so reticent about it? Jessie wasn't sure, but she loved that her friend didn't care. So long as she was happy was all that mattered to Lizzie. There was a buzz on her phone and she looked down at it. It was grandfather asking her to come downstairs. Each of them went to the window and saw he was waiting outside. That made Jessie worried and Lizzie saw it.

"It might be nothing; I am sure you are fine. Hey I am going to miss you. You text me and keep me up to date, ok? I don't want to lose my best friend."

Lizzie was going home to Idaho in a few hours with Cletus, taking him home to meet her family. And she was going back to her home to live. It might be years before they saw each other again.

"I know, I will, I promise Lizzie."

The two hugged tightly as vampires dared to do. There was one thing Jessie was sure about, this friendship wouldn't die on her account. But her clan had to come first, and hopefully an assignment to go with it. Hopefully that was what grandfather wanted, to give her a real assignment. After hugging her dear friend one last time they parted. Jessie was torn between being sad to see her friend go, and what was possibly to come. When she got downstairs, she saw grandfather wasn't alone. With him was both Camila and Malcom. Before she could ask what in hell was going on grandfather spoke.

"Now that you are officially grown its time you get your first real challenge. All of us are going on a little adventure. Its Grey business so you can't say no or ask what it's about. Just follow my orders and try to keep up."

Jessie had never known grandfather to give orders before but the idea of a real mission, that changed her mood in a flash. Looking at Malcom and Camila however neither of them were anywhere near as eager as she was. A minute later they all climbed into the minivan with grandfather at the wheel. She was desperate wanting to know where they were going and how long they would be gone but he had made it clear that wasn't allowed.

Medford, Texas – Cassia's office

Jan 24th 2058

Yelina was walking quickly into the Agora. Last night had been a nightmare come true. All the little dirty secrets the Grey ladies had been holding were outed. In all her years she had never seen Cassia so devastated or so quiet. Yelina was walking with purpose. Everything was coming apart for the clan. She quickly made her way inside the office to Cassia's desk. She had to be a mess with what happened last night. As she walked in, she was shocked to see Susan sitting at the desk, rather than Cassia.

"What in hell do you think you are doing?"

Susan was smug and pleased with herself and she stood up with too much authority. Something had happened this morning and I put Yelina on guard immediately.

"My job. As of this morning I am acting Grey mother. Cassia resigned first thing. It's a shame you weren't on time for our session. If you are curious no one nominated you, just me. So, no vote was required."

Yelina's mind quickly processed this bit of news. Cassia had resigned, that in retrospect wasn't a surprise. Having your visitor husband expose your lies and deceit and threaten the Agora was too much to overcome. Not to mention he had demanded it in the session. Still Yelina was a bit surprised Cassia hadn't put up more of a fight.

"Oh, one other tidbit for you to digest this morning dear."

Susan emphasized the word dear with a poisonous tone. Susan had clearly made her move and now Yelina was paying for it.

"Catlin moved to have your voting privilege revoked. Since you are still considered dishonored, it doesn't make any sense to allow you a vote. I tried to argue for you, but that was impossible after what happened with Malcom."

Yelina balled her fists and listened to excuse, and the tone. Her words were dripping with sarcasm. The dishonor that was at the center of this wasn't Malcom's, but hers. When the clan had thought Travis dead nearly 30 years ago, they had asked all those with claims to his bed to move on. In other words, for women like Yelina to take another man. Yelina had refused to bed another man ever again. For Yelina at the time, she just knew she couldn't. She loved Travis and wanted and needed no other. Even if he was gone, it didn't matter. It was something that cost Yelina her beloved honor. But with his return it was all semantics. She was his wife, and her honor should have been restored.

"You can imagine my horror when I went into the archive and discovered the finding of your dishonor was never lifted. I would like to argue on your behalf sister but alas with poor Cassia's removal I feel we have no grounds."

Yelina burned in rage at her smug and happiness over her fall. By removing her vote, it took away all Yelina's power. Yelina looked directly in Susan's eyes and was blunt.

"Perhaps we should finish what we started the other day."

Yelina felt in her spirit she could take Susan, especially now. She was overweight and never spent an hour outside of her chair.

"I don't accept challenges from lesser women. I…"

Both women were interrupted by text messages that hit both Yelina's phone and Susan's. Without pause Susan was the first to look down at her phone and then exclaimed in shock. That made Yelina look at hers.

"Mom, going on an assignment with Malcom and Grandfather. He says we won't be back for a while. Don't worry about us we will be fine. Love Jessie."

Yelina was still processing the message when she heard Susan curse Cyrus's name. The tension between the two faded as quickly as it had risen. Yelina knew that look on her former friend. She was not pleased with something texted to her. A second later Susan asked Yelina what Cyrus thought he was doing. Without having to ask, Susan showed her the text.

"Mom, grandfather wants me to tell you that we are on assignment for him. Says don't worry, that we will be back in a few weeks."

Susan upset and unglued by the news was openly asking what in hell Cyrus was up to.

"Was that Johnathan who texted you?"

Johnathan was Susan's youngest, still in the Agoge under Malcom's charge. Susan was very protective of him. She never said so, but Johnathan had a big heart like his father. She was always concerned about him, worried that he would get hurt. Worried the pressures and stress of life would crush him. Yelina shared her own message now.

"He took Malcom and Jessie as well, I don't know what he is up to but weeks? You don't think it's a threat, do you?"

Susan looked like all of the fight was taken out of her. Yelina on the other hand wasn't moved at all. Her children could take care of themselves. The only thing she had on her mind was how many moves it would take to separate Susan's head from her torso. Susan sat back down and looked very concerned, almost in a panic.

"He was pissed last night, and God knows he has the ability to do anything. Why our children Yelina, he can't mean to harm them?"

Yelina closed her eyes for a moment and sent another text. But it failed to be delivered. Susan tried next asking where they were going. But hers too failed to deliver. The two women looked at each other and without further word it was clear neither would act. At least for now, they would stay at peace. But it was only a stay, the accord that had lived for decades was over. One of them would stand, and one of them would fall. That was now a fact, no matter what Cyrus or Cassia desired.

Medford, Texas – Cassia's Home

Jan 25th 2058

Hanna took a long breath and looked at her reflection in the glass. She was waiting on Cassia to open the door and she was taking one last look at herself to make sure she was presentable. Hanna's relationship with her mother-in-law was always strained. When Cassia was Cynthia, the human mother of Jay, they had clashed massively. Going so far to order Hanna to stay away from her son, less she reveal what kind of monsters she and her mother were. That woman, long gone now in fact had hated all vampires. Despising all that they stood for and desperate to keep her Jay away from her. Hanna sighed remembering the painful way Cynthia had spoken to her back then.

Why anyone listens to you is beyond me, every single judgement call you have ever rendered has been a disaster. Clearly the boys take after Cyrus.

Hanna pressed the button again and patiently waited. She was as presentable as she could be, but it wouldn't be enough. After waiting another minute, she knelt down which was difficult in her skirt. Under the welcome mat was a key, something she used to unlock the door. Stepping inside she called out to her but heard no response. It took a bit but she found her sitting alone in a small room used as a library. She had a book in her hands. She clearly had been drinking from the sight of the table beside Cassia. When she looked up Hanna took a breath.

"Can we talk, I want to help if I can."

Cassia closed the book slowly and tried to sit it on the table which was full of things. After a millisecond of delay, she shoved hard sending all the empty bottles crashing in to the floor. The house was mostly empty so the sounds echoed off the walls making it sound frightfully ominous. Clearly Cassia was tipsy from the slurred way she spoke. Some words she held on too longer, others were normal. She probably wasn't drunk, hard to do when you were part visitor.

"You want to help me…. With what, I am perfectly fine…. Can't you see that?

Hanna took the footstool which had been kicked over at some point and right sided it so she had a place to sit. It was awkward with her choice of outfit. Seeing her struggle to place herself on the little stool, while not falling down, made Cassia smile for an instant.

"Cyrus came by to talk to me and Jay before he left. He told me about New York."

Cassia's eyes seemed to glaze over and the confidence and amusement she had earlier, disappeared. A part of Hanna didn't want to hurt her, but another part did. Cassia when she was Cynthia had taken great pains to prevent Hanna from coming together with her love. Just like she had tried to destroy Adad's relationship with Eleanor. Both times her mother-in-law had been wrong, and both times many had paid a price for her judgement. Recovered, Cassia just told her to get out.

"I will if you want, but you're my mother too, I want to help if I can."

Cassia laughed and took the bottle that still had something in it and poured some into a shot glass she rescued from the floor.

"Why, so you can hold it over me forever? What in the world could you possibly say to me that will make any of this better?"

Hanna looked at her and saw the truth in something her own mother had warned her about once. Hanna and Jay's marriage had not always been wonderful, there had been others who had tried to get in-between them. Hanna had been hurtful and bit back at her love over it. And in so doing nearly lost Jay. Seeing Cassia like this told Hanna how she would have fared if she had sent Jay packing over Allison.

"I can't fix anything and I can't tell you anything you don't already know…. But I can be here for you."

Cassia blew her off but stopped short of telling her to leave again. At first, she was just quiet and resigned. But a minute of two of silence ended when she began to become emotional.

"It was nothing, just a stupid, thoughtless moment. He has to know…. those men meant nothing to me. I was lonely and tired and…. I needed to let go for a moment. If I didn't, I would look weak in the other's eyes, I can't do that

Hanna. I know you can't understand that, but I can't be weak as a Grey. Not if I want Travis to be successful."

Hanna highly doubted Cassia had violated her marriage for her son's benefit. But yet in a twisted way Hanna knew the Grey were very different.

"No, I suppose I don't understand. It has to be so hard though, being Grey, yet Aqua too at the same time. I know you will do anything for your boys, that I don't have to question at all."

The words about her boys hit with the impact Hanna wanted. For Cassia her world circled around those boys. That also included her oldest Adad.

"What were they like when they were little? Jay and Travis had to be a handful?"

As an Aqua, Hanna had linked and merged with Jay many times. She knew every story and every moment inside his memories. Hanna didn't need to ask Cassia about those memories. But she did, because doing so would take Cassia to a place she most wanted to be. In a better time when she was in a better place. After a delay Cassia smiled and put the glass down and decided to engage with her.

"Jay was always the quiet one with a sensitive heart. I worried he would struggle to find a woman who could understand it. I never dreamed a woman like you could find him... well. Travis was my handsome one, I figured I would have real problems with him when he got old enough. I never got to find out..."

Hanna had thought she would take that moment to enjoy it and talk about good things. Instead, Cassia was doing this....

"It has to be hard being all those different women. Being Velena, Cynthia, Crispinia, Electra... and now Cassia."

She rolled her eyes at Hanna and turned to look at something on the far wall.

"Not really.... I remember all of who I have been now. it's all under control. I......I remember being Adad's mother... Being human every time Cyrus returns me to the world. But Cynthia... now that life... that one...."

Cynthia as she was known for Jay and Travis's human days, had been dead for a good portion of their adult life. Her life had come to an end one night when her human husband had discovered that Jay was not his biological son. That had ended their marriage on the spot and Cynthia as she was known as then, had gone drinking. Completely in the bag she had taken a walk into oncoming traffic and been hit. Cynthia hadn't been suicidal; she felt sorry for herself. Jay was only 19 and Travis still a boy. Her death had nearly killed Jay, as Hanna's thrall that shock of losing his mother had sent him over the edge. Thralls were like that, if they got upset enough it would break the connection between vampire and thrall. The result was nearly always death. Some just went to sleep and never woke up again. Others became violent and self-destructive. Hanna had found Jay unresponsive days after his mother's death.

I barely saved him, all because you gave up… just like now. You will never know how close I came to losing my Jay. You stupid selfish thing, you brought Ite into this family. You nearly killed both Jay and Travis by walking into traffic… and now! I have half a mind to walk out of here and tell Cyrus to forget about you.

Hanna calmed herself by remembering that moment when her daughter had given up her heritage just so Jay could live. That sacrifice had done so much, not just for her but her people. It was humbling to watch her daughter do that. Focusing on saving rather than cursing, Hanna calmed herself.

Why can't you be more like Amy, or mom? Your Art is a wonderful man, clearly, he doesn't get those things from you. How on earth do I honor you..?

"My Travis… now I knew he would be something. Jay was always weak, always so mousy. I thought he took after his father… I had no clue he was Cyrus's. Now I am not sure who he takes after."

Hanna looked away angry at her mother-in-law, hating how the woman saw her husband. She gritted her teeth and remembered that this thing was the mother of three beloved men in this community. Watching her slip back into the void while satisfying, would hurt a lot of people she cared for.

"You know I hated you…thought you and that mother of yours were such perverts. Why would any 50-year-old woman want to date an 18-year-old boy. You weren't dating Hanna; you were grooming him for later… sicko."

Hanna stood and opened her mouth in hurt anger and disgust.

"I did no such thing…. I loved… I do love your son you…"

Hanna had to take a breath, otherwise she would tell her what she REALLY thought. In a lot of ways Medford would be better off if Cynthia went back into the void and never returned. But as hurtful as her words where…. she had groomed Jay in a way. Teaching the boy what kind of man she desired. Showing him in the link all she had learned so he would be ready for her when the time came. That wasn't why she fell for him, and it wasn't her intentions.

But she had fallen for him, so perhaps she was right she did. But it wasn't fair… especially coming from the likes of her.

"I needed a thrall; I didn't expect Jay to want more than just to feed me. And I definitely didn't expect to find the love of my life that way. But he is Cassia. I promise you if I live for as long as you, I will still be beside him. He is my husband, my love… I cherish him Cassia… I do!"

Cassia who had not been looking at her turned her head now to face her from the chair.

"I ain't talking about loving him…. I am talking about something else. It isn't natural for a girl like you, to be with …. him. I mean I love my son but…Do I have to spell it out for youuu. He may be a good man now but he looked like an elephant with those ears…. And that stupid expression he always carried around. I wouldn't find him attractive, a boy like that in my day…no self-respecting woman would have him."

Cassia laughed as she again unleashed on her son. This was Cynthia talking now not Cassia. The part of her that had looked down on her own son, and found him distasteful. She thought so much of herself and her beauty.

Yet inside you bitch, you are nothing but an ugly mess….

"And you! Hanna, you never understood me…never. I know you because we are alike. Both of us are lovely, strong, its ok it's just us. Either of us could have any man we want. Especially with that chest of yours… you know that. Yet you chose Jay….. my ugly little duckling. No woman like us chooses a boy like that out of love. You selected him because you wanted to mold him… make him your perfect little boy. One day you are going to grow tired of him. Now a man like Art, I bet a day is going to come and you will spread your legs wide for him. Mommie Nancy can't live forever, then you can slide right in and take Art all for yourself."

Hanna closed her eyes and all warm feeling she felt for Cassia dried up. She had put up with her for decades now. Tried her best to encourage Jay to spend time with her. All for Cassia's benefit. It was what her mother had taught her to do, to respect her loves mother.

Well not anymore….

"You know ever since you stumbled out of the portal I have put up with your shit. Jay wanted to cut you loose years ago, said you do nothing but hurt him. Which is true… you pushed him into becoming King, just like you pushed Travis into it. FOR WHAT! So, you can get your kicks by having POWER! You know what you son said about you...what both of them said? They said their mother is dead... that's what. And honestly lady I agree. If you want to lay around here and drink your way into the grave again... then fine by me. Goodness knows your boys would be better off. You nearly got us all killed before with Ite, how many millions of people are dead now because of your choices... huh? You kept Eleanor from Adad and look what happened. The last time you got drunk and partied, Jay tried to join you. Well not this time honey... this time if you die, he won't fucking notice.... I will. I..."

Hanna felt tired, so tired after yelling at her mother-in-law like that. She thought she would feel better, telling the witch the truth. Instead, she felt hollow and broken. She only wanted to help, and this was her response. This wasn't the kind of woman Hanna wanted to be. Not the kind of loving soul she worked hard to be. Not to mention what her poor husband would think if he saw this conversation in the link later. That was when Hanna noticed Cassia's expression. Instead of being hurt by all of this... Cassia was all smiles.

"Nice being honest with each other for once isn't it. Now take your skinny ass out of my home and don't come back."

Chapter 18: Admirals and Aliens

Paris, France – US Embassy

Jan 25th 2058

Travis sat alone in a small room inside the Embassy. He was waiting on the Admiral who had flown over the night before. Travis was reviewing all he had been told both by his host and his own team. Nancy and Art had managed to question her staff and found nearly all of them loved and respected Rose deeply. Only her assistant which turned out to be her thrall knew more about her goals. He confirmed what Rose had told him privately. That she wished to pledge herself and her people to his future. It was tentative, they would go slow over the years but the intention was set. Rose had sworn her allegiance privately, and Camila was the first olive branch. Rose gave Travis the right to give her in marriage to whomever he saw fit. Camila didn't know this yet, not that it bothered Travis much. The way Camila was acting no man in Medford would want her. Travis had thought about arranging her to be with Jacob, or save her for Rick if he ever took the plunge. But that wasn't important, what was salient was that a major power base had pledged their loyalty to him. As odd and strange as that sounded.

Yet the more Travis thought about it, Rose made a lot of sense. It was inevitable for vampires to rule again. No matter his own desires to the contrary. In that world his Grey would have to have power and a place, just to survive. Otherwise, they would end up like the Aqua did. Hunted and exploited wherever they went. Nancy had admitted this reality had already crossed her mind as well. Clearly her and Cassia had thought about this one long ago. For the Aqua they would rely on his brother to lead them. And Travis was confident in Jay. His brother had the heart of an Aqua long before he ever was one. If anyone could lead them to a peaceful and productive future it was him. But his older brother would need a powerful friend. One who had the miliary might to protect him and his people. One day the Aqua and the Grey would be more than just a band of exotic people, more than nation states. They would in fact be their own races. Most of the Earth had at one time been vampiric or thralls to them. That time would come again, no matter what any of the leaders said they wanted. Travis and Jay would live to see that as fact, not fiction. It would occur in their lifetime, and they would have to be ready. It was time to plan on that and prepare while he still could. Incorporating Rose's group into his would only strengthen both the Grey and the Aqua.

"So young man what did Rose want of you?"

Travis looked at the Admiral closely. He didn't trust the man at all. Something Rose had also told him to be careful about. But oddly she endorsed using the man. She had been direct in saying that eventually some humans would leverage their positions and power for places in the clans. Travis held the keys to some pretty powerful incentives. In Rose's opinion this was what the end game was for the Admiral. In accordance with her fealty to her king, Rose had given him Meridian intelligence on the situation that the Admiral wanted delt with. But more importantly, details on the Admiral himself. The operation the Admiral had enlisted him to perform was in Greece. He claimed the CIA wanted their man to win the latest battle for power. Travis took a breath and went in head first.

"She wants to bend the knee, not at first but over time."

The Admiral sat down with a thunderous thud and took a moment to recover.

"Do you really believe that boy? First time she sees you and she offers to serve you? I know she is legendary at manipulation but it generally takes more than one visit to make men jump to her orders. You must be weaker than I imagined."

The smile and then laughter unnerved Travis a touch. It matched his own concerns and that of Nancy. Nancy advised a great deal of caution with Rose. That was fine but what about this devious shit? Only Rose had been confident on that front.

"Possibly not, but either way it serves both our purposes does it not? We continue to have dialog, and exposure. Hopefully we get more insight to what she is thinking and doing."

The admiral still laughing at Travis finally opened his laptop and started clicking away for a bit. After a moment he asked without looking at Travis what he had learned, just how much influence Rose had over Meridia.

"The president isn't her lover; he is one of her offspring. He isn't a vampire yet but she would like me to make him one. Rose is Meridia, at least from what she claims."

On saying that the smile disappeared, Rose had been the one to suggest this ploy. When he looked up Travis knew he had him.

"She also said our meeting wasn't by chance. And that you approached her first before you roped me into this. She claims you work for her, have for a long time."

With that the Admiral sat unmoving without reacting. After a second, he simply allowed the chair to fall back to its furthest point. If it hadn't a stop position it would have spilled his enormous frame into the floor.

"She told you that? She really did bend the knee then."

Travis could see what Rose had claimed was accurate. The Admiral coming to the end of his life, and in ill health, wasn't ready to go into that good night just yet. He liked power, and he felt like his influence was good for the country. Experience and power and all that. In reality he was just selfish, and unwilling to die and hand over power to someone younger.

"This arrangement of ours is over Admiral. Not that you were going to help me anyway. Rose can't turn you; she lied to you. Only I can, and if you want that help you have to prove to me your value. You can start by fixing my relationship with State. Then we will see."

It took about a half a minute for the blood pressure of the Admiral to hit boiling.

"Just who in hell do you think you are talking to me like that, I could break you and that whole town of yours with one call."

Travis knew that wasn't an idol threat. Once long ago the government had come within a whisker from killing everyone in Medford. The council had been blunt on this score; they were reliant on him to do WHATEVER was necessary to keep the government from taking over again. If it meant taking over the US government and going to war with the likes of this fat man…. Then so be it.

"Let's put all our cards on the table. I can make a call too; the Ruby have powerful friends in the government. I checked there are some enemies you have been accumulating in your career. Some of them are up on the hill, just waiting for a chance to force retirement of your ass. With the right amount of money, I could make that happen. Or I could just kill you, and anyone you hold dear. Not that you do, from what my wives say, you are the only person you care about. Perhaps you care some for your mistress. I have to say, you like them young Admiral."

The room got still and Travis for once wondered if he had gone too far.

"You just threatened to kill a senior government official. Forgetting it's a federal crime, do you really think I don't have my own claws? I could have a Delta team come kill some of those young kids of yours in the Agoge. Or hell, just have the Navy drop a bomb on your compound. You sure want to play in this arena boy, cause if you do, I can play. You can stalk around in the dark, but I am damn sure going to end it if you pull something."

Travis took a breath; he wanted to just reach across the table and heart attack the guy. He was closing in on the need to revert himself and the more this stupid game got played, the more he wanted to end it. But that was him acting rashly, without thought. If the Admiral wished him harm he would have just done it. He wanted something, and Travis could deliver. Now that both sides knew what each other was prepared to do, and more importantly actually wanted, they could trade fairly. The Admiral had probably wanted to keep his actual desires secret until he had Travis hooked. Then he wouldn't have to give anything to get what he wanted. Travis would belong to him. Well Travis had no intention of belonging to anyone. So, he smiled and began again, negotiating with his real advisory.

"Or we could just be civil, I can make you a Grey, and you go on living for centuries. We will help you recycle yourself, find you what you need to revert. In exchange you do what you already promised to do. Fix my relationship with State. Pay for this op using CIA money, and take the fall if things go south. Which we both know would, with that much money going missing. You were going to wrap it around either my neck or Rose's depending on who was weaker when it was over. This way only your name and memory take the blame."

The Admiral was confused, Travis still wanted to carry out the op. The answer to that was less in his interest and more in what Rose desired. Rose had asked for the privilege of living her last days in what was left of Sparta. With her in command of that city, and Meridia. Travis as King, and in control over all of it. Rose wanted one last chance to reform the Greek people in her father's image. On this Nancy was more than worried, she felt the chances it was all TOO GOOD to be true was a serious concern. But Rose was playing all her cards right so far. Travis would see how all of this played out. Either way Rose was showing Travis her cards. She was manipulating everything, that much was clear.

The key question was, did Rose have any real intention of serving Travis. So far, all things pointed to yes, but did they really?

"You realize what will happen if our man becomes president? She will worm her way into his cabinet. She will have full control over a NATO ally? You think she works for you, but Travis as far as I can tell that isn't who this woman is. Are you sure you want to play in to her hands like that?"

Travis smirked and made a contemptible sound with his mouth. He asked the Admiral why he played along then, already knowing the answer.

"I don't have a choice son, she has me by the short hairs. If I so much as twitch she can do all the things you just threated me with. The way I see it, it's not my call. But you, why play her game like this. You know full well she is just going to betray you. Why give you the keys to her kingdom, when she can just keep them?"

Travis didn't answer, the honest reason was because he didn't have one. He was trusting someone he had just met. But his gut screamed at him that he should. And in his estimation, it would be best for his people.

"You worry about your end of the deal, and I will worry about mine. This fellow will be Greece's next president and then Rose can shape him how she desires. If anything, NATO will get a more powerful Greece out of it. Wont that helps our allies? Aren't they always complaining about baling out Greece and it holding down the alliance?"

The Admiral grumbled and then handed over another fob. Travis looked at it with a questioning look.

"It's so you can get the money you need. The other account I gave you is tracked. I hope you didn't empty it yet because if you do it will trigger and investigation. This one wont, its clean and is plenty big enough for you to carry out the op."

Travis shook his head and saw the look on the Admiral's face. He wasn't happy, which told Travis he could probably trust him to use the money. It didn't matter; the Ruby would launder the money in ways even the CIA couldn't find.

"You just happen to have this on you?"

Jackson just smirked and grew comfortable again. Clearly the man felt at ease knowing he had a long future ahead of him.

"It was my retirement fund… just in case. Try not to use it all, when I am Grey I might have need for that."

Travis pocked the fob and looked at him with different eyes. This part was still theater but necessary.

"When you do become Grey you will serve me Admiral. Betray me and I won't hesitate to kill you. Keep that in mind… ok?"

Henderson, West Virginia – 34 Flemming Street

Jan 26th 2058

After two days of travel the party had arrived in some backwater in the mountains. There were a few inches of snow on the ground and it went without saying it was cold. In point of fact the onboard navigation said it was 22F outside. In Texas it was 55F, Malcom had traveled before so in a way he was prepared. The others… not so much. The drive up here had been something else. More than once, Cyrus had nearly turned around. The state route they were on was all curves and with the snow nearly impassable. But this morning they had finally gotten here. But why they were here or what they were supposed to be doing was a mystery to him.

Standing around Malcom looked at the others with him. Jessie his sister and Johanthan and Clint his half-brothers. Nearly frozen and shivering in the cold was the elegantly dressed Camila. Malcom was freezing too, but he was too amused at Camila shivering openly in the cold. She had selected the nicest looking coat at the store they had stopped at in Huntington. Thankfully Malcom had forced all the others to buy actual coats for this kind of weather. So, while cold, him and siblings were only uncomfortable. Camila on the other hand wasn't getting any benefit out of that stupid fur topped thing she had picked out.

"God what is taking that old coot so long!"

Clint said something harsh to Camila not to speak of his grandfather that way. Camila looked sharply at the boy but a word from Malcom caused her to back off. Just then a foot or two of snow came loose from the overhead and fell on the street below them. It caused Camila to shout in terror and jump towards Malcom. Unimpressed, and annoyed at being this close he pushed her away.

"It's just snow melting off the awning silly. Look, here he comes now."

Camila wasn't the only one to make a noise of happiness that grandfather was finally returning. They had been standing outside this closed up store waiting on him for 15 minutes. With him was a middle-aged woman with blonde hair. She was nicely dressed but with snow boots on. A moment later she walked up the steps to the store and with a large set of keys began to work on unlocking the door. Malcom looked again at the now closed store. It had "Henderson Consignment" in gold letters stenciled on the glass. Behind the glass was what looked like the remnants of an old country store. Everything from the glass in the large window to the old wooden planks in the deck to the aged door screamed this place was from the 19th or 20th centuries. It was the kind of thing you would see on period tv shows. Mom especially loved those shows and made all of her kids watch with her. His mother had grown up in the 19th century, and lived in the 20th. Those times were not fiction to her, why mom loved those times, it always escaped Malcom. Finally, the door which refused to budge for the first few pushes finally yielded. There were lots of satisfied voices at seeing that door open but they were very disappointed a moment later to find the store didn't have working heat. It was as cold as it was outside.

"Don't worry the heat won't take long to start. A brand-new heating system was installed last year, and the store still has power so I can have it all toasty in a few minutes."

The woman was clearly the person in charge, probably the real estate agent if Malcom had to guess. She might be the owner but he doubted it. Malcom pictured the owner of this place having a massive beard and no front teeth. This blonde woman was far too well dressed to own a dump like this.

"You can look around if you like but please don't touch anything. I have no idea what the previous owner left. They closed the shop up a few decades ago but they were living on the 2nd floor. There… just give it a few minutes and we will be warm…. So, Mr. Douglas I have to ask why come all this way to Henderson?"

Malcom looked at his grandfather who was all smiles. He had changed himself to look the grandfatherly age. He looked like he was 70-80 now. That would take Malcom and especially the boys, time to get used to. They were used to grandfather being in his 30's-40's all the time.

"Oh, me and my family are looking for investment possibilities. We were in Huntington yesterday looking at some properties, and we were planning on looking at some in Logan tomorrow. But my grandson and his wife over there saw this online and claimed it was something to see… so here we are."

Malcom was confused for a bit and then realized that Camila was standing next to him. He frowned a bit at pops making him play the role of husband to her but he rolled with it.

"Yeah, I saw the price and thought…. Why not?"

The woman's eyebrows narrowed but her smile never left her face. She wasn't buying his lame attempt at acting, neither was Camila. She had nearly laughed at his stupid remark and decided to help.

"Oh dear, you know it was my idea. Honestly, I just looked at the scenery and just had to visit it. Me and Malcom want to settle down in a cozy place and start a family. Have a nice little store to keep us busy as we have all those babies he wants. You know I am not sure I am all for that many babies, but it's the only thing Malcom can talk about! And if we are going to have that many, we need a nice big place to raise them in, right? Malcom comes from a big family and to him it doesn't seem right unless he has four or five little ones running around. Can't you picture it dear, you behind the register and all our young helping in the store?"

Malcom saw even Jessie was smiling at the joke and the woman was just nodding pretending to agree when she clearly neither cared or thought it a good idea. Seeing her chance at an easy sale the agent stepped in to save Malcom from having to respond.

"Well, this store is certainly big enough. It has a massive 2nd and 3rd floor. They used to keep inventory on the 2nd floor but the last owner turned both floors into living spaces. I think they were thinking about turning the store into a hotel. Our last hotel burned down a long time ago you see. But yes, if you want a big family Malcom this will certainly fit. Isn't another property like it in all of Henderson."

Pops then took over the conversation and introduced the others. Using their real names, he said that Jessie and the boys were also his grandchildren. He explained that Malcom and Camila had been helping him raise them since his son had died a few years before.

"I am so sorry Mr. Douglas, but I have to say that is so honorable of you to take on that burden at your age. Are you planning on joining them if you buy?"

Malcom turned away just then to move about and warm up. As he did, he felt a slender arm of a woman slip into his. Camila walked in lock step with him staying skin close. Malcom had wanted to look around the store, if it had been abandoned for two decades there was no telling what they would see. It didn't smell all that good that was for sure. Once they were out of earshot of pops and the real estate agent, Camila purred.

"So, what do you think husband, is this the home for us?"

Malcom wanted to snarl but he was too cold. Looking down into her face she was no longer shivering and looked highly amused. He decided to be crass to turn off that huge smile she was giving him.

"Yeah, I was thinking I would start by knocking you up. Why don't you drop those pants of yours and I can have you right here in front of everyone."

Camila's eyes narrowed and her mouth opened slightly showing teeth. But she wasn't offended or thought him improper. She was entertained, something he really didn't want. After a very slight pause Camila smiled and put a gloved hand on him.

"Don't tempt me, if that heater doesn't start working soon we will. Why are we here Malcom? What possible Grey business could we have here?"

Malcom blew a raspberry from his mouth, the hell if he knew what pops was up to. He looked around the room at objects that hadn't been moved in a very long time. At one time this was a neat little store, if not for all the cobwebs. As he looked back towards the hall where the others stood Malcom felt strange. He began to recognize parts and pieces of the store. It wasn't the first time since they had walked in, he felt this way. The long wooden counter of the store especially seemed... well familiar.

"Something about this place, ever since we got here, I feel like...."

Camila squeezed his hand when he didn't reply with an answer at once to his statement. She was deeply curious why he had dragged them all the way east at the drop of a hat.

"I don't know, I feel like I have been here before. Not that I have, but something about this store brings back a memory."

The agent came into the back room that Malcom and Camila had stepped into. She looked hopeful on a big sale, no doubt.

Well, she is in for a shock, we neither have money nor do we have any intention on buying property in the middle of bumfuck land.

"So, what do you love birds think? Do you want to see the living spaces upstairs?"

Camila said yes at once and started to ask some more questions about the store and its history. As they spoke the woman was a bit embarrassed that she hadn't introduced herself. Her name was Paula and she was working with Heart reality in town. Camila barely let her get the words out before her question.

"Paula I am curious about the previous owners were they from Texas by chance?"

Paula smiled and shook her head with a negative. She looked down on a sheet. Paula reshuffled the sheets on her clipboard looking for something. She stopped after consulting nearly all of them.

"No, they were locals but I can't really remember their names. Two women owned the store when I was young, it was such a nice place then. Oh, here it is, a Mr. Timmson owned it, he just died a couple of years ago. He used to own a lot of property in town. He ran a small auto repair shop at one point, but that was long before my time. His daughter was the one who hired us. She lives in another state now and isn't interested in it. Which is a shame, it's honestly the best property in town if you ask me. So much potential, all it needs is a good cleaning and a hard worker and it will practically pay for itself."

An hour later they had taken a tour of the entire building. It took far more than 15 minutes for the place to get warm but it eventually did. The place was massive; the rooms weren't huge but there were a lot of them. It looked like everything had been neat and tidy for some time. Malcom thought it odd that the 2nd and 3rd floors were so neat and clean, while the main floor looked like no human had sat foot in it for decades. Pops was in another room talking to the real estate agent and Malcom was still in one of the bedrooms with Camila. That was when she saw her opening and took it.

"You still want to tangle; this place looks comfy enough."

He was going to tease her back but instead she without warning landed a kiss on his mouth. In that moment something overtook him. It was as if a switch was flipped and suddenly, he was desirous. The kiss became passionate and he found both her hands and his exploring the other. As quickly as it started his reason returned and both separated at the same moment. Camila smiled like a cat about to play with its food.

"Sorry I wasn't thinking… I just wanted to."

Camila seemed confused, aroused, excited. Malcom felt the same. The second she had touched him he had desired nothing but her. As soon as she let go, it was gone. She started to dart her eyes looking from spot to spot on his face. Confused and unsure of himself, he just stood there.

"Malcom what are you doing to me, I had no intention of kissing you. That wasn't me, I just felt compelled and I…"

Camila's hand came up on its own like it was not her in control. Malcom was going to respond but like her, his own hand came up without his control to meet hers. When they touched both let out a little noise of pleasure and shock. He felt flushed and began to breathe in quicker and quicker.

"Malcom… why…. are you doing this…how are you?"

Both began to caress each other's hands and as they did Camila's eyes opened wide. When she turned back to Malcom, they locked on each other and her eyes glowed brighter than Malcom had ever seen before. It was daytime yet the glow was clearly visible.

"This ….isn't me….. Camila…. Is it…. this….. place?"

Malcom struggled with words; his other hand was now locked with hers. Both were breathing heavily and he felt himself drawn into her. Both were being sucked into a kiss, yet as far as Malcom could tell it was not either of their idea. Time seemed to move in slow motion, much to his annoyance. He wanted this slow ponderous process to end so his lips could touch hers. Once they did, neither held back and Malcom felt a surge of desire and satisfaction. As if being separate from her body was painful and touching it brought only pleasure. Breaking from a kiss was only possible for seconds. No sooner than they took a breath, they would begin again. Each time it was without his control, but it wasn't unpleasant now. This went on until both were aroused so much that all other thoughts departed. The room disappeared and to Malcom the only thing in the world was her.

He wanted her, now, no more foreplay. He tried to see if he could control his body, to move himself into position. To guide both of them to the small bed, but he couldn't. Then as quickly as it started, it ceased. Leaving both breathing heavy and locked in a stare standing skin close.

"Malcom your eyes are so bright!….I can't look away"

Malcom knew just how she felt. Malcom was transfixed looking at hers. It was almost like she had ahold of him and he couldn't shift an inch.

"This isn't me Camila, what is going on?"

Suddenly Malcom noticed that the buzzing sound in his ears was lessening. Odd in a way because before that moment he hadn't noticed any sound before. As he did, he felt control return to his hands and then his body. Camila now free immediately left the room without another word. He followed her as she made her way back to the others. She walked up to the boys who were looking at another room. Her eyes however were still glued on him. As he grew close her mouth flew open and she shook her head no as if she was scared of him. But then she took a step towards him and their hands found each other again. The boys ignored them as yet again the room seemed to disappear and the two began to kiss and whine for each other. The more they interacted with each other, the less control either had. He was becoming less a man with an intellect, than one with a raging desire to make love. The only thing he could think about was having her.

Camila shoved him hard and nearly off his feet. She drove him to the wall and began to madly kiss him. The force in which she drove him was enough to make a huge noise. This finally got the attention of the boys.

"Bro… what in hell are you two doing? Oh, your mom is going to be so pissed dude."

Again, like a switch was thrown the two of them separated and looked at each other like the other was the aggressor.

"What in hell are you doing Malcom?"

Malcom looked back at the boys who were grinning and laughing a bit.

"Me, I didn't do anything you were the one that nearly bit my lip just now!"

Jessie peaked in the room and with a stern voice said that grandfather and the relator were already downstairs. Malcom and Camila were still looking at each other and he could feel it. Almost magnetic like he could feel something pushing him closer to her. He wanted her, to tear her clothes off and to make love to her. But the thing that made him nearly mad with lust was how she was looking at him. She clearly wanted him every bit as much, more perhaps. He so wanted to give in and show her all of who he was.

"Malcom NOW, we are going downstairs!"

It took another shout from Jessie to break whatever spell she had over him. The whole time walking back to grandfather the only thing Malcom could think about was her. They got there just as they witnessed pops ask a question that seemed to upset the realtor.

"I am sorry sir that isn't how this works. The owner lives in another state and I don't feel comfortable calling her asking for that."

Cyrus pulled a roll of hundreds from where Malcom had no clue. He pulled away a thick stack of them and said something soft that Malcom still a bit away couldn't make out. The realtor's eyes bugged out of her head and she stammered a response Malcom didn't hear. But a moment later she pocked the cash and hurried out of the building. Once it was clear she was out of earshot and across the street grandfather turned and faced them.

"Finally, she won't be back anytime soon. This is our home for now. Go upstairs and find a room you want and relax. In the morning, we will go out and pick up some food and supplies for the long haul. Jessie I am putting you in charge of that, take a peek at the kitchen and see if we need anything."

Camila stepped from behind him as she did, she had her hands on his ass, the feeling was electric and it caused Malcom to shut his eyes.

"Why are we staying? For that matter why in hell are we here in the first place?"

Malcom heard everyone gasp in fear, Camila's hand which had been exploring his backside disappeared in an instant. Malcom opened his eyes to witness his grandfather transform into something that clearly frightened everyone. It didn't bother Malcom in the slightest, he was one of the few who had seen pops in his real form before. The old man before them was steaming. As if he was ice melting in a hot skillet, with the vapor coming off what had been a solid person. It took a few seconds but the solid form of Cyrus disappeared revealing a gas like substance that was semi-transparent in places. When he spoke next the others took a step back.

"Don't be alarmed, this is the real me. You have no idea how irritating it can be to take human shape. Compressing yourself into such a small biped for hours on end, humans have no idea what irritation really feels like…. Trust me."

Malcom laughed but the boys were frightened and Camila was gob smacked. Malcom didn't try to say anything, Pops was more than capable of settling them down. Both him and Jacob had been introduced to the real Pops many years before. It was an honor, one few Grey had been given.

"It's ok, you have nothing to fear. I just have different abilities is all. You can relax, all of you. As long as I am here, you are safe. I may look different to you but I am still your grandfather"

The boys both shook their heads yes, just a bit more reassured. Jessie was quick to say how cool it was. Malcom didn't disagree; Cyrus was someone he really wished he could have gotten to know more. But being days away from home wasn't good for any of them. It was time to take the lead as the eldest among them.

"Pops don't get me wrong I am honored to be with you. And I am glad the others finally get to see you. But why are we here? This place is the middle of nowhere."

The mist that was his grandfather shifted and billowed. He was using his abilities, causing shades to shut and lights to come on. At the sounds it caused the boys to take another step back. This time Malcom said something, Pops was just making sure they were alone and their discussion was private.

"It's ok guys, it's just pops he will never harm us, ok?"

Malcom could hear pops voice in his mind. It was cool because hearing him there you got more than just words. You got emotions with it too. He could feel the pride his grandfather had in him, something that always made Malcom feel just a bit taller. Then the voice shifted, pops wanted all of them to hear this.

"Your brother is right; I know seeing the real me is unsettling but it is necessary. Keeping a human's shape taxes my ability and reverting to the true me for a time is, I am sorry to say necessary."

Malcom could detect what sounded like pain or sorrow in his voice. It worried Malcom to hear it but he filed that fact away for later. He would have to watch pops closer to see if was something to be concerned about. The second he thought that he felt a private bit directed at him. Malcom wasn't sure what emotion his Pops was sending him. Whatever it was it was gentle. A second later Pops began to speak to them all again.

"Malcom to answer your question I brought all of you here because I need your help. This town may seem backward and odd, but its far more important than any of you can know. A very long time ago something was lost here. Something very valuable and very powerful. At the time me and the others felt it would be safe. But something has changed, and it's time we secured what was lost. I selected each of you because of your wisdom and abilities. You are my Grey, and each of you bring something special with you. Talents and skills no other grey possess. I want you to use your abilities to learn all you can about this town and its people. Find this power before it hurts someone. It will not be easy, nothing you have trained for has prepared you for what you will find in Henderson. Each of you will have to be at your best, there are dangers here, besides yourselves."

Malcom thought that interesting, what dangers in this place could be concerning to them?   Malcom nearly laughed this stupid little town couldn't possibly have anything that could touch the likes of him or Camila, much less Jessie. Malcom watched as Jessie asked for more details. This would be Jessie's first real challenge outside of a class. But before Pops answered her, the mist turned nearly white and Malcom heard his pops ask in a sweet loving voice what was wrong. He was asking it of Clint, Dolly's youngest son. Clint didn't respond right away, which made pops respond for him.

"I feel what you are feeling Clint. I hear the doubts you have and your worries. Your wrong, you aren't useless. Just because you are human doesn't mean you have nothing to contribute. I promise you before our task is complete, you will see that clearly enough. Both of you boys are special, you don't know it yet, but you are. Each of you is special to me, and special to this clan."

Malcom unwilling to let Jessie ask her question again, interrupted the soft emotion flowing towards Clint. As a grey it showed his weakness and that was something no Grey male could let stand long. Best get them off this topic and on to important questions… that were still unanswered.

"Come on pops, you have to give us more than that. Is it a person, a thing? Throw us a bone."

Cyrus moved through them and beside them, Jessie gasped at feeling him move past. The air became warm and Malcom's felt a reassuring presence. It was one of the coolest things he had ever seen or felt as a vampire. He was glad his sister could witness it too. The boys were scared but when they felt that presence, Malcom knew they were feeling what he felt. It disarmed them immediately. You just knew he loved you and you were with someone who cared. How his grandfather conveyed that he had no clue, and he didn't care, it was just cool.

"Two decades ago, I came here in search of your father Malcom. He was lost to his people, and to me and his mother. Someone had freed him from the clan and made him human again. Travis came here, to Henderson to live out his days. And here he remained for years. His mother was desperate to bring him home. Your father had much left undone in Medford. He needed to return, and she wanted to see him become the man he would become. She wasn't the only one, I wanted him home too. Your father was needed there to love and raise you Malcom, and your brother. Eventually he created you Jessie, and you boys. He came back to Medford for all of you, he returned for his children. But he left something precious here, something all of us need to find."

Malcom had been hating his father of late. Hating the lies he had told, and hating how he had cheated on his mother. Yet he couldn't help but love him, and desire to be respected by him. That duality circled inside him causing Malcom to try desperately to push all thoughts of his father from his mind and heart. To both love and hate something is to invite madness. But feeling the words of his grandfather, it was impossible. Cyrus didn't just convey words as he spoke but feelings. Was this feeling now coursing through him, Cyrus's feeling for him? Or did it represent something else?

"Do you remember when you were a boy, and all of us came here together. Your grandmother and me, Yelina, and Jacob. You had breakfast in that diner across the street Malcom."

Malcom thought back and remembered being a little boy. He was young, 6 or 7 at the time. But yes, he was here. The memories flowed now and finally Malcom could remember. It had felt like days and days driving. Mom had been so excited to go, but Malcom and Jacob were bored. Malcom realized why mom had been so excited.

She was getting dad back, no wonder she was so happy.

For Malcom and his brother however at least back then, dad was someone they didn't know. Those years after that day, he had spent a great deal of time with him. His father was a fountain of knowledge; he had never stopped teaching. He wasn't a loving father per se, but he knew a great many things and that was why Malcom respected him. Seeing everyone looking at him, Malcom realized they were waiting on him to speak. A little embarrassed Malcom took a breath and tried to share a little. The one powerful memory he had of this store.

"I stood right here, father was saying goodbye to someone and she was crying. I remember I asked mom why she was crying and she looked upset. I don't remember who that woman was, but that was the day we left to go back to Medford. That was right before the fight with the amethyst, with you…."

Cyrus changed color again and the mist seemed to bunch up around him. Touching him and going through him. The next words he heard were only in his mind and not for the others to hear.

"Yes, son I know, you saw my human body lain out. You thought I died that day. I am sorry you saw that, but this life is not always what we want Malcom.

What you saw that day was necessary, it was something I had to do for all of my children. Say nothing of that day to the others. It's in the past, and not why we are here. I know you are angry at your father; you feel betrayed by him and the others. I came to you the other night and looked inside you. I saw this war you are having with yourself."

Malcom hadn't noticed it, but that wasn't a huge shock. Pops could do whatever he pleased. That was when Malcom felt his own heart soften just a bit.

Pops I hope you know how to fix things; those boys are looking for me to solve what to do about dad… and I don't have a clue. I tried talking to him but, Camila was there. Pops… I.

"I know…. I refuse to let you be this way. I refuse to stand by while you rip your heart to shreds over this life. It's one of the reasons why I brough you son. I sat by once, watching it destroys your father, and I let it happen. I won't let that happen again, not to you. Please trust me a bit longer, give me time to do right by you. I need you to lead the others, encourage them, protect them. Will you do that for me, and without question? I promise when the time comes you will understand why."

Malcom felt the intense emotions flowing from his grandfather. He was beginning to understand something he didn't before. Cyrus regretted deeply his role as father to Travis. He was shocked to see how emotional and guilty Cyrus was. This was a side to a father he had never seen before. His dad was many things but he never showed any weakness. At least not visibly, he never cried in front of them, he never was emotional. He had to have those emotions but you never saw them. Feeling this wave of emotion from Cyrus, It shocked him to his core. Cyrus was desperate to help him, and to connect with his son. There was a longing there, guilt and fear. Malcom had no idea what to make of any of it.

"Yes of course I will. You have my word pops."

Chapter 19: Obsidian Night

Henderson, West Virginia – 34 Flemming Street

Jan 27th 2058

Malcom woke up at 6:30 thanks to his phone. Which was now only good for being an alarm clock. Apparently, Henderson had no cell coverage at all. He reached across the dark shape in front of him and turned the alarm off. He was going to let it snooze for 15 minutes when the dark shape in front of him finally registered. It wasn't a thing; it was a person. As his eyes adjusted, he saw Camila naked in his bed. He knew at once he had been with her. The flashes of memory that hit him told him he had lain with her more than once last night.

Almost on cue he felt sore and torn, the grunt and finding just how much, caused Camila to wake. The moment she was awake both of them began to lose control, almost as if they reverted to a more intuitive form of humanity. Where only procreation and the pleasing of their flesh mattered. Camila now more aware moved first. Pinning him on his back and moving to mount him. Malcom didn't stop her nor did he mind in the slightest. He began to react and anticipate her moves before she was even ready. The moment they connected however the pain was enough to break the power over them.

"Ouch…how many times did we do it last night? I am flipping raw!"

Malcom had to agree, not that he was some great lover and had experience with such things. At most his experience with sex was fleeting and brief. Camila gave out a small feminine sound of need that motivated Malcom. But again, on meeting the pain was intense.

"What is wrong with us, I barely remember last night. We didn't drink last night, but all I can think of…"

Camila agreed by sticking her tongue in his mouth and kissing him with force. But again, the pain got in the way. That was when Camila noticed something on the headboard shelf above them. Malcom angled his head to see what she was locked on to. It was an open case, with some sort of pendant inside it. The moment she reached out and touched it, the light from her eyes nearly doubled.

"Ok that isn't normal, you think this is what pops is looking for? What caused us to...."

Camila put the neckless back in the case. She laughed for a moment and looked down on Malcom. Still naked and laying on him she slithered over him and off, so she was in a sitting place next to him.

"Fuck like rabbits... I don't know. I don't even remember a lot of it. But what I do..."

A kiss, then another, Malcom wrapped himself around her. The feeling of control, the feeling of dominance in that position felt wonderful.

"Yeah, what I remember was good for me too."

Camila reached out and took ahold of the box. Closing the box seemed to have an effect, minutes later Malcom's mind began to clear and he was no longer part animal. The two of them looked at each other but said nothing. Malcom tried to understand the feeling she was trying to convey but, in the end, she just took ahold of her clothes and left the room with the box. She didn't say a single word to him once she had her will again. Did that mean something? Malcom was left sitting on the edge of the bed in the room alone. Wondering what in hell came next. Along with the burning pain on his member, he felt hollow inside. What he had done wasn't his will, no matter how pleasurable it was. He had done exactly what his mother claimed he was incapable of stopping. That thought caused him to lower his head in a small amount of shame.

Yet hadn't mother done the same, and not because of some device? Hadn't mother gone to New York and fucked some random dude for fun? Hadn't father taken Dolly when he needed it? It would be so easy to just accept this and move on. He suspected Camila felt no shame over what they did. Yet he very much did, perhaps none of them were worthy of honor? Malcom shook his head and let out a breath. He thought he was far better than this, and to his disappointment he wasn't. He got dressed and made his way towards the sounds of someone moving. The sounds were light, which he suspected was the sounds of a woman.

On reaching the 1st floor he was rewarded with seeing Camila dressed quickly and searching for something.

"Where is Cyrus? He isn't in any of the rooms?"

Malcom smirked; he didn't need a room when he was like this. Ignoring the frustrated expression on Camila's face he turned to go to the center of the room and began to try to see if he could sense him. Once it was quiet again from him moving, he quietly called for him, once and then twice.

"Good morning kid, you sleep, ok?"

Malcom turned and saw that his grandfather was back to his human shape again. He had a smirk on his face which told Malcom he probably already knew what the two of them had been up to.

"Pops I think we found what you were looking for. A neckless that drives folks mad? That ring a bell?"

Cyrus's face shifted with a questioning look while Camila approached with the box. When she opened it, Cyrus quickly snaped it back closed.

"Yeah, kid you don't want to let that thing out of that box. Where did you find it?"

Camila explained that it was in the room Malcom had selected.

"Hope you didn't put it on; this thing has a terrible reputation. It started out part of the Obsidian clan's orb. It has a tendency to cause vampires, especially young ones, to be highly motivated. You get me? Um, you two didn't keep this open for long, did you?"

Malcom smiled and shook his head no, saying they had closed it the moment they found it. Which was true, but not really completely accurate either.

"Well good, glad we found this thing. But this isn't what we are here to find. You see Henderson is sort of a nexus for things like this. Over the years objects and people are drawn to this place. As interesting as this little bobble is, it doesn't hold a candle to the power we are looking for."

Malcom's mouth fell open as Cyrus proceeded to walk away with a smile. When Malcom looked over at Camila he was surprised at her expression. It wasn't one of amusement, she was upset. The moment she saw him looking at her she left quickly heading back upstairs. That left Malcom alone in the room again. He wasn't sure what to make of that. He had expected her to be as she always was. Didn't she want to bed him? She had been all over him since the moment she met him. Why be so coy now?

Malcom hated this, everything he believed in and everything he knew to be rock solid wasn't anymore. Just who the hell was he, and what was he doing here? He was trusting his grandfather, perhaps the last time he would give anyone that level of trust. What if grandfather proved just as fallible and dishonorable as the others, what would he do then? For the first time in Malcom's life, he didn't know what he wanted to do next. His whole life had been a plan, one stone to the next. But now, as he stood alone feeling disconnected from...everything. He wondered if perhaps life would have been better had he been born human. He didn't regret the wonders he felt and saw, those were amazing. But his north star was dim now, it didn't light the way and he was getting lost.

Henderson, West Virginia – 34 Flemming Street

Jan 27th 2058

"What is going on with you?"

Camila had retreated back into her room feeling something she never did, vulnerable. Yet she wanted Malcom to follow, needed something from him. The object they had found still had a pull over her, but not her body. She could resist him and what charms he had. But what Camila needed was something far more important, something far more elusive. Something no man had ever given her or shown her. But it was something no man could. It was just a myth, a phantom, a bit of either not unlike the form she had just seen. There but yet not there.

"Hey, speak to me. Tell me what you are thinking."

The arms when they took her were leaches that stole her resolve. All the armor she had fashioned in her spirit, the brave and noble mask she wore. All of it melt from her leaving the woman that she despised. The fallible and weak being that became emotional on his touch. Seeing her weakness he stopped speaking. She wanted him to hold her but instead he spun her around to see her face, the worst thing he could do. It revealed to him the being Camila didn't want others to ever see. The real woman behind the mask. Malcom seemed to have that ability, as if he had liberty to see through her.

"Look what happened between us, I know it wasn't really us. Is that why you are upset?"

Camila took a step closer to him seeing his hand not far from hers. When they had been under the power of that thing, they had interlocked their hands together, trying to overpower the other. It felt comforting to her, as she struggled to regain control over her emotions, she used his touch to do so.

"I know, it's just I haven't felt like this before. Not having control, I know you probably think me weak… don't worry I will be fine."

Malcom looked at her oddly and then put a hand on her face. Something that she didn't prevent, yet she wished he hadn't done. When he kissed her, it was welcome. It felt sweet but Camila took no pleasure from it. Like everything else in her life, it wasn't natural, it was just a vestige of strings unseen.

"You have been after me from the second we met. Why hesitate now? I would like to see if, I don't know if we are something to each other?"

Camila thought about many things, but none of them seemed to last very long with Malcom so close.

"I need time, what that thing had us do. I need time Malcom."

His face changed, clearly disappointed. But it only lasted a moment. Perhaps then it wasn't something he wanted that badly? Malcom with nothing else to say, nodded and quietly left the room. She was glad for it. A relationship with him now, was not something she could explore. That thing had stripped away her strength, and gotten in the way of everything. Camila had two paths in her life; one she had been made to be. Another was failure at being that thing. Success or failure, there was nothing else. She had said those words aloud every night since she was six years old.

Having Malcom in her bed had been the very thing she had desired not long before. She had been twisting him to obtain it since they met, he wasn't wrong on that. But the reason why, he wouldn't and couldn't understand. Being here and playing her part was what she trained for. But it wasn't what she wanted, not really. Setting on the bed she thought back to how this mission made her feel. On one hand it was everything, her mother's love, her nana's love all hinged around this mission. They had showered her with money and time to prepare her for it. But outside that mission there was nothing, and nothing but this mission could be allowed to exist.

What would happen if she returned home having failed? She had a good idea what would be said and done to her. No, there was no point in going home without complete success. Yet if she did succeed, she would likely as not, never go home either. She would be with these American's the rest of her days. Was that what she wanted? Would that make her happy? Would such a thing be so bad? Looking at how Malcom was turning to her charm, it was clear she had his heart right where she wanted it. It confirmed her training was spot on. She could do with him as she pleased, but it didn't.

All her life she had been so glued to this duty, and it had felt right once. There had been a time not that long ago she was fully dedicated to being right here. But now that she was, and within sight of her goal she had second thoughts. Yes, she could win, and give her people the victory they sought. But what about her after that? Once she had that victory, she would live on for centuries. Her mission would go on, yes but to what end?

If this was Malcom instead of her, he could at least have a real ending. Unlike her, Malcom with his people could win a victory and return home. Receive the honor and love of his people and the prizes promised to those who won. He would go on, create a family and live in the warm knowledge he was fulfilling his purpose and his own will. Camila had thought the same way for her mission, but not anymore. She saw the selfish lies in all of them. She would give everything so her mother and grandmother could have what they wanted. After that…. She would be an afterthought. Where was the honor in that? To live her whole life coupled to someone she didn't love, and couldn't love. Yet it was her duty, and one she had sworn to uphold. Looking out the window she felt as if the building she was staying in was just yet another jail to keep her locked away for all time.

Chapter 20: To Thy Own Self Be True

6 weeks later

Medford, Texas – Rick's Home - Mar 1st 2058

It had been weeks after he had moved to Medford, and Rick's life wasn't getting any easier. He had been given a few nibbles for jobs, even going as far as working five days for one person. But without someone to watch his son full time it was difficult. He just wasn't making any money. The only reason he had been able to do that one job had been thanks to one of Travis's girls watching his son. That was something he wasn't overly comfortable with, but what choice did he have. He was back home now and listening to his son talk to her about everything from Medford to video games. Something the female vampire clearly never had any experience with.

Rick heard and knew why, that girl had been preparing to be what she was all her life. From the time she was 10 years old she had been learning the skills someone like her would need. She was going into a dangerous game and she had no time for childish things. That wasn't what his son needed, his boy wasn't like him or Travis. He would never be a wolf as Yelina called it. And that wasn't a bad thing, in fact, Rick was happy for it.

Rick had already made his decision, something he had been fighting since he met this family. If it was just him, he would walk. But he had a son, and to a lesser degree a daughter that still needed him. Both of them needed money to help get them started in life. And his boy needed a real home, one where he knew his caretaker wasn't likely to die in some battle halfway around the world. He needed stability, love, and most of all hope for something better. If he stayed here, he would be forcing his son to the same fate he had. For Rick his fate had been sealed a long time ago. When he had taken the Marines as a ticket out of a life with no choices. Back then it seemed like the right call. Now if he had it to do over again Rick would have taken his chances in Lynchburg. His boy needed another option, and there was only one way to give it to him.

Yesterday he had spoken to Travis and made peace with what was to come next. The boy's grandmother would take him in and finish raising him. He didn't know yet, he would find out slowly over the coming months. For now, he was just going to his Mamaw to spend some time. In small bits he would learn the truth of it and hate him. Rick didn't ponder much or be introspective on his choice. It was the choice, and it was time to make it. Clamping down his heart for what was to come he didn't spend long mulling over it. What was to ponder really? His son would never forgive him for giving up. To him at least it would appear that way. It would toughen him, and in return Rick would be hated for all time. But Rick wasn't giving up on him, what money he could spare he would give to the child and his sister. If he survived long enough perhaps the boy could have something to build on.

Rick knew he had to harden himself for what was to come. So, he turned away from looking at his son and walked outside to greet the boys Mamaw. The mother of his wayward wife was a good woman even if her daughter wasn't. She had retired and had moved out of downtown into the countryside. His son would have cousins and family around him. And most of them were good people. It wasn't enough for Rick but it would just have to do.

Henderson, West Virginia – 34 Flemming Street

Mar 1st 2058

Camila had been patient, she had played along and done as she was asked. But it had been weeks and they were no closer to finding this "power" than they had been their first day here. Her mother and grandmother had to be apoplectic with her out of contact for weeks on end. It was time to get back to her mission, to do what she had come to do. But the very thought of that mission made her sick to her stomach.

It was early and Malcom and the boys were up on the mountain searching for more clues. Jessie was in town talking to the residents like always. It was time to make her escape, go someplace with cell coverage and make contact. As she opened the door to the minivan and got in, she saw Cyrus was sitting in the back. She slammed the steering wheel out of frustration and cursed. Cyrus didn't seem in the least upset.

"Morning, don't know why you are leaving. I know it's not what you really want child."

She looked up in the rearview mirror. The arrogance of this being unglued her. She was tired of being pulled about by the strings by people like Cyrus, or mother, or grandmother.

"What the fuck would you know about me?   Just because you snap in and out of places doesn't make you all seeing."

Looking into his eyes she didn't seem to be getting her message across.

"You don't know me, you have no idea what I am, or who I am!"

She pushed some of her hair out of her face and huffed.   But Cyrus still seemed unmoved.   He took a breath and then turned his head to look outside. The snow from winter was mostly gone now, leaving the town a semi-frozen muddy mess.

"I can read you child, just like I can read my children.   You forget you are a Grey. That makes you mine, I am the visitor for all Grey, even you."

Then his face seemed to shift and instead of softness, it seems to harden.

"I know all about your mission, and what you have been training for.   I am not blind child."

There was a pause and Camila looked up in the mirror.   He wasn't normal in anything, if he said he knew…

"You were six when it started.   The day you were told of your purpose.   I know all about your trip to Boston, and who you met.   I know what she asked of you, and what you agreed to be.   I have watched you replay that memory in your mind over and over.   I can see why you feel so trapped.   Those strings you feel pulling you child, they aren't from me."

Camila had to tell herself to breathe.   Only a select number knew the full truth of her mission.   This mission wasn't just an assignment it was a life calling.   Every second of every day since she was a little girl had been in preparation for this.   Nothing was more important, and nothing that got in the mission's way was allowed in her life.   Other friends, distractions, interests… nothing.   The only education she had received was tied to helping achieve this goal.

"Your mother crafted you for a purpose, for someone.   You have done well Camila; I will give you that.   You are exactly what he desires to a tee.   He can't help but love you.   He doesn't now, but he will, it's only a matter of time.   You fight like him, you have his interests, and you know him in ways no other woman can.   I know it wasn't easy for you to become this.   But you mastered it, he can't help but fall for you."

Camila's hands were shaking now; she had planned on many things. From others finding out about her purpose to other challenges. But never in her training had she planned a counter for an alien who could read everything in her like a book. How in hell could she defend against him?

"You don't need to child. I won't stand in your way; it's not my place to do that. My role isn't to rule over the clan, it's to arm its members with what they need to survive, and to thrive. If you want to carry out your mission, you won't hear a peep out of me."

Camila turned to look at him. His face revealed concern, and worry. She took a breath and wondered if it was even possible for such a thing to be true?

"You would just stand by while I marry him, build a life with him? You know what that means, what I will do after I own him? I will twist him, into what they want. It's the only thing that matters to them Cyrus…. the only thing."

Cyrus just shook his head yes, and she turned fully in the seat now. Astonished he would even say this, much less agree. She doubted his seriousness and his honesty. After a long pause she asked why.

"Because he will love you, ultimately what I want for him is happiness. In the end you will make him strong, fill a need that he has, and be a strong wife for him. He is going to need that in the century's to come. But child we both know the truth. You don't love him, and you never will. You are incapable of that, and before you commit yourself to this…. You should consider what life will be like for you."

She closed her eyes and lowered some in the seat. The harder she worked on mastering herself to be the perfect wife, the perfect partner, she despised him more and more. She had tried to not feel that way but she couldn't help it. As the years had gone on, it only got worse. And now that she was here, well it hadn't got any better.

"Think for a moment about the children you will give him. Think what will be asked of them, and of you. You are going to lie to them every day of every week. You will love and cherish his children, but you will still have no love for him. How long can you endure before you take some lover? How long before they are found, just like these women with Travis. All of them think they can make love to whomever they please. They are wrong, it's going to be found, your children will learn of it. They will look at you the same way Malcom looks at his parents, or how you look at yours."

He was putting voice to her worst nightmare. She had thought long and hard about what would be asked of her in the coming decades. Not just her time, and her bed, would be outside of her control, but even her children. They had to be lied to, misled. The very same betrayal she felt from her mother, was going to be repeated again. But this time it would be her children feeling betrayed by her. Cyrus didn't bring this to her attention; this he just took from her soul. The same fear that haunted her since she was old enough to feel it.

Camila felt the tears form and fall and she didn't prevent them like she did so often. To be the Camila her mother desired, it required all of her wants and her desires to be subordinate to them. Camila couldn't have a preference; it had to be his. Camila couldn't have an interest; it had to be his. Camila couldn't have any opinion or feeling that didn't match her intended target. The only way she could be something different, was in her heart. Because every other part of her life was selected for a man she had never met, at least until recently. Camila couldn't help but resent him. Her heart stubbornly refused to accept him and it was killing her soul. For the first time since she was a little girl she sobbed in front of another soul. In her spirit she was naked, and alone, and defeated. She had failed, this man knew, well everything! A part of Camila had wanted nothing else but it to fail. She sunk into the seat so far, she was nearly half way down. Hidden from Cyrus's view but not his words.

"Child you haven't had time to be anything other than this product you are selling. That isn't any way for a woman to be. I may not be human, but I have lived here long enough to know what you are doing isn't healthy child."

Her eyes closed and with her hands blocking them from view, she pondered his words. No, she had to agree this wasn't any way for a person to live. She wouldn't have wished this on anyone. But if she failed in this, what would mother think, what would grandmother think?

"There is another way child. I can cut the strings that bind you. I can make you human, or wipe the memories of everyone, so they forget you. Let you live your life as you want. Would that please you?"

Camila broken and alone, sat wallowing in her failure. Hearing that lifeline made her heart jump, but only for a moment. She pushed back up in the chair so she could see him in the rear-view mirror again. She only had to ponder his offer for a moment.

"I don't even know who I am, how in hell am I supposed to know what I want?"

Cyrus smiled at that and put a hand on her. He switched back to his natural form which didn't scare Camila now. He moved from the back until he nearly surrounded her. It was an odd feeling, warm and comforting like a blanket on a cold day. When he began to speak into her mind she was astonished at the being he really was. The men in her life were emotionless things that lived on stimulation. Inside they were dead things that only moved from one desire to the next. Food, sex, thrills, those men only lived on those. They were incomplete children who knew nothing of something higher. This wasn't Cyrus, he was deeper than any male she had ever met before.

"This clan means a great deal to me child. You may not be my grandchild but you still belong to me. Let me help you, I can show you a different way. Nothing would please me more than to help you. But if you still wish to carry out your mission I won't stop you. I won't tell the boy about this conversation or the truth of things. It would only hurt him if he knew. Either way child what I am saying is, I am here for you. Please give this a chance, give yourself a chance."

Her mission a failure, alone, defeated and at the end of her emotions Camila felt out to this being that wrapped around her. Could she trust him, should she trust him? She felt betrayed by her mother and her grandmother. They never seemed to care about her, only the mission and what they would get from that victory. Did they care, Camila seriously doubted they did. She had worked so hard, so diligently for this moment. Her way was always clear, if painful. In a way victory was in her grasp, but it meant nothing to her. That alone was what caused her to choose. Camila realized she had nothing to lose really.

"What do you want of me?"

A moment later she heard and pondered what the alien had said. He could have easily forced his will on her, but he hadn't. He could have manipulated her into it, but he didn't. She could feel his honestly in his statement, he would let her do as she planned. But if she did this, she would be abandoning her honor, betraying everything she had ever loved or known.

"You aren't betraying them. You are learning who Camila really is. Find out who she is before you sentence her to a life without love, and without truth. I promise you; this place will teach you whom you really are Camila.... If you let it."

Henderson, West Virginia – Doug's Diner

Mar 1st 2058

Camila had cleaned up the best she could. You could tell she had been crying but she didn't care. Most of the locals gave her a wide birth. In any case she had no need for human interaction. No one would expect her to be charming today, well at least almost nobody.

"Oh sweety, did Malcom say something to upset you?"

Camila smiled for the one person in this town she didn't mind talking to. Gale owned and operated the small diner that fed the whole town by the looks of it. Keeping herself trim in this town was a challenge with Gale's cooking. She had a delicious apple pie and made some of the best meals in miles. None of which were light on calories or carbs. But when she offered a slice of pie and a coffee Camila didn't say no.

"No, it's nothing Gale, I just am in mood is all. How did the bake sale go? Did they raise enough?"

Gale still looked concerned but she put a cheery look on her face as she described the sale and how much they had put aside for the local boy who got hurt a few months back. His family didn't have much and all the hospital visits to Logan were mounting up. Next as usual Gale checked up on Cyrus and Malcom. Camila answered honestly and without thinking.

"Where are the boys today, they still working on that old place up the road?"

Gale knew about the young boys that come up with them weeks before. They were going through an old trailer their dad had owned when he lived here. So far, they hadn't found anything of note. The locals just knew the boys were looking to clean it out to make some extra money. Gale listening to her seemed to be a bit concerned. So, Camila asked about it.

"Oh, it's nothing, just silly local superstition is all. You want another slice honey; it's on the house."

Before she could say no another slice appeared. With how she felt she gave in and took the slice. She looked up at the wall to the framed photo. Camila had ignored it for weeks until one day she had asked Gale about it. It was of a young Gale and her husband Doug. He was dead now, cancer two years before. Leaving Gale to go on without him alone. Camila loved to hear the stories though. Gale and her husband had been very loving from the sounds of it. Wanting to forget about vampires, missions, and deceit, Camila asked for another story.

"Oh, you have heard them all sweety, it's not like they are special or anything. Just two simple folks loving each other is all. I am sure you and Malcom have all kinds of great stories… you never share them, but I know you have them. With the way you look at him I know you love each other."

Camila smiled sweetly for her, even if she couldn't be more wrong.

"We do, but right now I just wanted to hear about Doug. He sounded like such a sweet man. How did you meet him."

Most women often relay how they met their love to others. Most of the time it's a sweet and fun way to reminisce. Even if the story isn't true, it didn't matter. It was about seeing someone you care about in the best light. Most of the stories she had been told over the years were like that, mostly lies but that didn't matter. It wasn't evil just a way to feel a bit closer to the person you were talking to. But something about Gale and her face when she asked, triggered Camila. Gale was worried and didn't like speaking about it. Very odd for Gale, and for most women no matter their relationship.

"Oh, we were young…. Did stupid things. Not much good in that story sweety. You want another coffee?"

When Gale got close enough Camila could see real worry now. She put out her hand and covered Gale's and asked to hear the story. There wasn't anyone else in the place at the moment so it wasn't like she had other customers to worry about. After an awkward delay, Gale cleared her throat and shook a bit as she spoke.

"Guess there is no harm. Not every story is sunny sweety, some stories are just plain bad…. And I have to say our meeting sure ranks in that. I…. well, I wasn't a good woman back then. I was stupid, I didn't have a lick of sense in my head. I run off from home when I was 16, did some things I ain't proud of to get by."

She tossed the towel she was carrying on the counter without thinking, causing part of it to cover the half-eaten pie. It was a nervous response to trauma. Camila patted her hand to encourage her and let her know it was ok. Gale was a sweetheart and the only real joyous thing she had found here. Gale turned back to the picture and pulled it off the wall.

"Doug, well back then he was a real mess. I met him in the Barn, that was a rough bar I liked to go to when I looked more like you, than like this."

Gale smiled for her and Camila smiled back. In a way Camila hadn't really noticed it before but at one time Gale had probably been very pretty. That was when she took a closer look at the picture. They were both young and different. In that moment Camila identified with Gale more than before. One day she would look like her, have lived like her. Unlike Gale she could revert and live far longer in years. But the inside…. That couldn't be reverted. Camila was already carrying a lot of baggage and Gale was showing her what another couple of decades would do for hers. Gale might not be a vampire, but she was a woman and Camila felt connected to her.

"Took years for both of us to get straight, we were so messed up when we were your age. But we did, Doug got hired at Lockheed and the kids weren't far behind. Looking after those young'uns makes you grow up in a hurry, let me tell you. By the time the kids were older we were a lot more than just husband and wife. He knew what I was going to say before I said it, and I knew that old bird just as good. Built up a lot of trust in all those years…. A lot of good years. He wasn't always like that, but the older he got, the more loving he was. I suppose time does that to men, some of them soften up right nice. Doug was like that, he had a big heart for critters, young'ens…. and me."

Camila loved those stories and the look Gale had at telling them. Gale was back there, with Doug and it showed a different side of her. Gale was always friendly but she came alive when she talked about Doug. There was something sweet and genuine about it, something Camila had never seen before. It wasn't how her people lived, and clearly it wasn't how these American Grey lived either.

"I can see you are struggling sweety, trust me I know how you feel. Malcom is a nice man but he seems a lot like my Doug, he is all focused on his job. They get that way when they are trying to provide, but they forget sometimes how to love us you know? That's why it's important we don't forget how to love them. They just need reminded sometimes."

Camila smiled for her friend but then noticed the picture a bit closer. She recognized that building in the background. It was a building in Medford. That made Camila happy, something else they could connect on.

"Hey Gale did you meet Doug in Medford?"

The moment she said the word, Gale leapt back from her hands and looked as if she had a knife pulled on her. Gale put a withered hand on her chest and began to breathe quickly. Gale mumbled something and ran to the back. Camila was so astonished she just sat there for a time in shock. Why on earth would Gale react that way to….

"You get on out of here… I don't want your kind in my place! Just get…. I didn't break my promise, you just tricked me is all! Go ON… GET!"

Gale came out with a huge chef knife from the kitchen. It was wobbling so because of how frightened Gale was. Camila wasn't worried in the slightest but she was highly curious. She loved her talks with Gale and had connected with her. The thought of hurting her was nowhere in her mind right now. Not to mention she had never seen Gale come unglued before.

"Gale honey I don't know what has you so worked up. I am not going to hurt you."

Gale stood there a bit longer trying to hold the knife still but failing to. It got so bad Gale gave up and put it on the counter. She landed hard into one of the stools and in a very soft broken voice spoke to Camila.

"I don't want no trouble, especially with vampires."

Camila smiled and took in a breath. A light bulb went off in her head and she wondered if she had just stumbled into that stupid secret of Cyrus.

"So, you know about us, ok then. Gale honey I don't know why you are so scared but the last thing I want to do is hurt you. We are friends. I just recognized the bakery in that photo is all. It was one of the first places I went to when I arrived in Medford. Why on earth are you so scared, I don't have the first reason to hurt you?"

Gale took a breath, and grabbed the knife again when Camila sat down a couple stools away. When Gale spoke again it was with a pitiful whiney voice. The last few words she nearly whispered.

"When I left that horrible place I promised I wouldn't talk. I haven't! I kept my promise, so did Doug."

It took a bit to get out of her but Gale and Doug had once been residents of Medford. Humans who had found themselves thralls of an Emerald vampire named Brooke. Gale now calmer told the story.

"We were thralls to her, couldn't do anything unless she wanted it. You're a slave, to whatever they want. If she wanted you to hate the thing you loved then you did. If she wanted you to do something horrible then you were happy to oblige. Most wicked thing I ever saw. It not natural child, I…I was never sure if Doug married me because he loved me or if because Brooke ordered it. Thank God we got clear of that place."

Camila asked quietly and with some small bit of sympathy if all that talk of love was just for show. Or was everything Doug and her had just part of them being thralls. Camila could see her chew on that for quite a while before she answered.

"No, I suppose it wasn't all her. We were married a long time after she freed us, and I haven't seen her since. Me and Doug had a lot of good years together, no child I suppose it wasn't her. But when we served her child, well I suppose you know all about that don't you? I told that thing I wouldn't talk, that I would keep her secret, and we did. Now here you are, well you can go back to that place and tell her I kept my word... so did Doug."

Camila saw the fear, the fierceness and liked every bit of her fire. What really amused Camila however was the way she described Brooke. Almost like she was some sort of slave master and her and Doug were innocents. Camila knew Brooke very well from her time in Medford. Not to mention all the research files on people she had read from her mother. Brooke was a sweetheart not that unlike Gale. She had a mess of kids and smothered all of them with love and cookies. Not to mention any of her patients in the hospital. Brooke was now the chief surgeon at the local hospital.

"Gale I am not an Emerald. I am a Grey, and Brooke isn't looking for you at least as far as I can tell. I don't think you have anything to fear. Especially not from me, besides who would I get pie from if I did?"

Gale smiled a bit and stopped brandishing the blade in front of her. It was still close but it wasn't in her hand now.

"I knew a few Grey back then, Ghosts in the night was what the others said. Warriors who fought in the war for the country. Lot of 'em never came home from what I remember. Lots of 'em are up in Woodlawn was what Brooke said."

Even though Camila wasn't from Medford she was still a Grey. And she had read the file on that too; nearly all of the male Grey had not survived the war. Almost the entire male population of Grey Medford had given their lives. Even separated by a generation, Camila could not help but mourn her fellow clanmates and their sacrifice. Camila shook her head as she replied.

"Yes, it's a shame, no other way to say it. A whole mess of my kind are up there. Honey, I promise I am not here for you. I am just low is all, I wanted to feel good again. You telling stories about Doug is the only comfort I have here."

Gale's head cocked to one side, clearly, she felt sorry for her friend but she quickly recovered. The woman in front of her was a vampire and Gale's experience with them wasn't a positive one.

"If you aren't here for me, then why are you here?"

Gale took in breath rapidly and started to speak quickly. It finally hit her that if Camila was a vampire, then the others were likely to be ones too. Before Gale could fly off the handle again Camila spoke quickly.

"Calm down, yes, they are, but again we aren't here for you sweety. We are looking for something."

Gale calmer now, asked what it was. Camila told her everything she knew, especially all she knew about Travis who had been here twenty years before. Gale however had only been in town for a decade. He had been long gone when she got here. However, Gale misunderstood what Camila meant, she thought Travis was missing since they were asking about him.

"I am sorry for your husband, has to be horrible not knowing his daddy. But if you are looking for him here honey you aren't going to find him. Lots of young men go missing up on this mountain, always has been that way. They walk up the hills and never walk back down. Lots of folks think they know why, but it's all nonsense. There aren't no banshees or witches who take'em, just a bunch of locals making up stupid stories."

"But Gale, it's not like there aren't strange things out there? I mean come on, you know about vampires. If it's not something like us, what would cause people to disappear?"

Gale looked down for a moment and then back with a soft look.

"The truth is life here isn't easy, and sometimes folks give up is all. He probably went up there and hurt himself, accident maybe, or on purpose. I knew a lot of boys who did something like that, mostly after filing themselves full of booze. War twists people, even your kind."

Camila remembered that Gale had talked about superstitions in town earlier. She had ignored them but perhaps she shouldn't have. But what did missing people have to do with this power Cyrus wanted to find? For now, Camila just focused on Gale.

"I am so sorry I scared you, truly Gale I am. I would have never said anything if I knew about your past. All I want to do is find what I can. But that has nothing to do with you, and I won't say a word about this to them when I get back."

Chapter 21: Disappointment

Henderson, West Virginia – Heart Reality

Mar 1st 2058

Malcom had been talking to Paula and getting to know her. At first it was strictly to gain some insight into the town and its people. But later it was more, as the weeks passed and Camila ignored him, he had noted Paula's interest. She didn't seem to mind he was supposed to be married, but did tease him a bit that he was playing with fire. Today they were just talking business, in this case the town and its history. The last couple of these visits she had made it clear she was wanting more than friendship.

"Mom loved growing up here, she told so many stories, I felt like I knew it before I ever got here."

The look on her face was electric. She somehow looked younger. She wasn't a vampire, otherwise her eyes would give it away. That was when he finally noticed how made up she was.

"I would think Henderson is too quiet a place for someone like you with all your interests? Don't you ever get bored with all this quiet?"

Paula was dressed in something very tight and not exactly office friendly. The fact he knew exactly what she normally wore compared to today said something to him. Clearly, he was paying more attention to Paula. He was looking too closely now, something she didn't call him out for. That knowing smirk on her face put one on his.

"Awhile back, you know I heard about this Travis you mentioned… he was your dad, right?"

On hearing his dad's name Malcom nearly fell out of the chair. His eyes opened larger and he pushed further in the seat closer to her as if doing so would unravel the mystery.

"Wait you do?"

That caught Malcom in surprise, they had talked about his dad on and off but she never said she knew anything. Then she put a thin hand on his leg and began to tease her way up to his groin before stopping.

"Oh, I know lots of things, you would be surprised at what you learn in this line of work."

She might be older but she was attractive. And Malcom was bored. Camila had made it clear she wasn't interested. That ship had apparently sailed. He was about to lean into a kiss when Jessie and the boys barreled into the office in a rush to get his attention.

"Malcom you wouldn't believe what we found! Dad had a HUGE stash hidden in that trailer! It has to be what Granddad was looking for!"

He saw the look of curiosity and amusement in Paula but knew their moment alone was truly over. He only got a quick goodbye before he was nearly dragged by the boys back to the trailer. The moment he got outside the cold air hit him like a hammer. He hated being on this mountain in winter. He hoped whatever they found would be it, so they could leave this place.

Once inside with the door closed Jessie went to a broken-down dresser, ripping off a side panel. The force she used caused a lot of dust to stir, blocking his vision for a moment. When it cleared and he stopped choaking on it, his eyes grew large.

"Holy shit! How much is in there? There has to be at least a hundred thousand dollars....at least."

Malcom hadn't seen that much physical money before. Folks hardly used real money anymore. Everything was electronic, tied to your phone or other devices.

"If I remember correctly, about 1.6 million."

Like always Cyrus had appeared out of nowhere. He was standing in what used to be the kitchen, or at least what was left of it. Everyone was getting used to it now, so no one jumped when he spoke.

"That's a great find; it's your father's stash. But that unfortunately isn't what we are looking for. For now, put that cover back on Jessie. We will have use for that later, especially after you find the power."

Malcom and everyone else let out a disappointed sound. Looking at Cyrus it was enough. They had been looking for 6 weeks and everyone was done.

He started to say something but Pops interrupted him motioning for them to step outside. A moment later and after they walked out of earshot, he began to speak with a tone Malcom hadn't heard before.

"I asked you to take charge Malcom, to be a leader. You haven't done it yet. And what you were going to say just now, how do you think that makes you look? You are letting them know you're ready to give up."

Malcom was taken aback by his sharp tone; it was said quickly and with force. Pops was always easy going and soft. He asked without thinking why he would say that.

"Because you haven't done as I asked, you aren't leading. The only thing on your mind is bedding Paula."

"Now wait a moment pops, that isn't fair. Paula is a grown ass woman. And she is coming on to me! What in hell do you care if I take her to bed? You didn't seem to mind when I was bonking Camila?"

Another thought entered Malcom's mind before he let Pops speak.

"And don't act like that wasn't your plan. That device, or jewel wasn't there by accident. You wanted us to screw. I am sorry if I didn't fall in love with her like the Aqua do. Look I tried but she cut me off. She won't even talk to me pops. For that matter she is Meridian, she probably just wants to steal something anyway."

It was quiet for a moment and when Pops didn't respond Malcom felt more unsure of himself. The look on his face was harder somehow, meaner.

"I don't have time to hold your hand and explain everything to you. I thought you Grey were tough; I thought you were able to deal with a simple task. Malcom, I have given you six weeks to figure out what is staring you in the face. You could have solved this in an afternoon."

"Pops come on, give me a break! I am not a detective, Grey are warriors. Give me a blade or a gun and show me a target and I am your man. But if you want me to find this thing I need more, like a lot more."

Cyrus fished something from his pocket and looked down for a moment before he responded.

"You have all you need Malcom. Why you can't you open your mind to this…"

Cyrus sighed allowing his face to show a deep frown. He put his hands back in his pockets still holding whatever he had taken from them.

"I didn't make the grey, but your mine now. I thought you were different; I thought the Grey were more than just killers. Am I wrong…. Isn't there more you want, more to your life?"

He felt his pops probe him, not just with the eyes but more. He was fully in human form but Cyrus could do things even in that form. Like read him from the inside out.

"Yeah, Pops sure I do. I want…. folks to respect me, like they do with dad. I want to earn it too. Look, I know we kill and I am ok with that. I don't think of myself as a killer though, well…we do what we have to do. Pops I am sorry if I upset you, but I am just frustrated, we all are. We want to go home; can't you just give me a hint?"

Cyrus took him by the arm and led Malcom back to the car they had driven up in. When Cyrus took his other hand from his pocket it revealed the keys.

"You want a physical challenge then so be it. I can give you what you want son, but you won't like it. I can promise you that. Whatever you do, you have to face it on your own. That is what you want, to earn respect…. Isn't it?"

Malcom saw the look on his pops face. It was direct and searching. He responded like he did in the service or to his instructors in the Agoge. Curt, rapid fire responses with a tough masculine exterior. Pops just smirked.

"I am going to be gone a few days. It's up to you to find this power, and to lead the others. Mark me son, this place is not as it seems. You will need to be ready to respond when the time comes. And most important of all, I am not going to save you child. I am done holding your hand."

"Pops I am ready; I will make sure the others are too. I won't fail you… you will see."

The smirk didn't leave him but his response caused Malcom to question his confidence.

"I am sure you think you are."

Medford, Texas – Medford General Hospital

Mar 2nd 2058

Rick took another long breath and let it out. All morning long he had been here getting tested. Hopefully it would be the last time he had to come in like this. It wasn't because the folks here were a pain to deal with, it was just because he hated what today meant. And he hated being poked and prodded. He knew he was ready; he didn't need the doc to confirm that.

"Any pain during that last run you did for us, any issues?"

Rick smirked; at his age he shouldn't be able to run 5 miles without pain. Especially with what had been done to his back and knees. But Brooke and her son had managed to fix all of that over the last few weeks. Now he felt nearly how he had felt when he was 17.

"Nah Doc, it was all good. I have to say you Emeralds are something else, thanks for fixing me up."

Brooke smiled big at that, she was a cutie and if she was single Rick would have been working to bed her. But besides being a vampire, she was probably 200 years old or something. She looked 25, but she could be 2500 years old for all her body showed.

"Sally, would you step in here for a moment?"

Rick saw that Brooke was finishing up, tossing the gloves she had on and putting away what she had used in the exam. A young woman entered, not as pretty as Brooke but around the same physical age. Rick knew her, during the physical therapy portion of his treatment Sally had supervised it a couple of times. Unlike Brooke who was always full of smiles and encouragement, Sally was kind of a bitch.

"Sally when you did his work up for phase 3 did you notice this? His right bicep is nearly 15% smaller than his left?"

Sally put down the chart she had on him and looked closely at his right side then back at the chart. She tightened her mouth and sucked in her lips just a touch. A clear sign she was pissed.

"No mom, I noticed it in my exam but I didn't put it in his chart."

Rick asked if it was a problem but both women ignored him. Brooke looked irritated and bore in her.

"We have talked about this before. You have to double and triple check your work. Rick was scheduled to join his clan today, and now we have to delay that while we schedule another round of adjustments. You know how humans are, they get nervous before the change. Now he is going to have to wait longer. That's not fair to him young lady."

Rick tried to tell them it was ok, as far as Rick could tell his arm was fine. He was far healthier now than he was just a few months ago.

"Hey not to interrupt but isn't this just a waste anyway. Once I revert everything changes… right?"

Mother and daughter were at odds and forgetting he was even here. From the way Sally was acting Rick would bet she wasn't any older than she looked. She wasn't anywhere near as adult in her reactions. The moment her mother gave her the rebuke she opened her mouth and narrowed her eyes in anger. The kind of thing someone who hasn't found themselves yet does when they get corrected. Sally started to raise her voice but her mother stopped her with a raised finger and a firm look. Quieted but not quelled Sally seemed to burn in resentment as Brooke finally turned to acknowledge Rick again.

"Rick I am sorry, but I am going to advise Travis you delay taking your signet today. Sally, I want you fixing this now, and I will be back in an hour to see the work. It better be perfect young lady."

The moment she left Sally quietly mocked her mother and scrunched her mouth repeating the words her mother used. Rick just laughed, which reminded Sally he was here. She looked confused for a moment then caught herself. Without another word Sally began to stare intently at his arm. She was doing what all those Emerald did when they were using their vision.

"How long have you been doing this kind of work?"

Sally didn't answer right away, looking at him for a split second before returning to her task.

"Since I became an Emerald, plenty long enough to know what I am doing. Yes, I didn't write it down but it's not like you can't use your arm or anything."

Rick felt the pain in his arm and knew she was changing him. Once things began to die down pain wise, he asked how she could do that.

"Never you mind that, we just do. Now… are you satisfied?"

Rick saw the attitude and didn't respond. She started to huff and leave but he stopped her.

"You really hate the work don't you. Why not do something else?"

Sally gave him a nasty look and quickly left. Rick tested his arm and shook his head. These emeralds were a strange lot. Then he heard a familiar voice talk to Brooke outside the curtain. A moment later it jerked open and the kid doc from the Agoge came in.

'Hey Rick, you all clear, Travis is waiting on you."

Brooke moved in and held up things saying he needed more time that his arm had just been worked on.

"Come on doc, so what one arm is weaker than the other. Am I really going to die from it if I become a Grey today?"

Brooke didn't pay him any attention at first quickly looking at the work her daughter had done.

"Perhaps if you were anyone other than a Grey. From what they put my son through I wouldn't be surprised if they push you out of a moving helicopter just to see if you can survive it."

Rick's arm involuntarily flinched, he could feel warmth and knew this was Brooke doing so fine tuning on his arm. It was far gentler than what Sally or Calvin could do.

"Nah mom that isn't until tomorrow, tonight he has to step in front of charging horse and catch it."

Brooke shook her head but gave a small smile. Rick tried to make it clear he was ready, and then asked if his arm was ok.

"Yes, I suppose you can, other than this Rick you're in good shape and your back and knees are 100%. But don't think you can just shred them and I will be here to put them back together again. Try to take it easy tonight, especially that arm, ok?"

Henderson, West Virginia – Henderson Consignment

Mar 2nd 2058

Jessie was working on a meal for everyone. Sighing she wondered why this assignment was dragging on this long. There wasn't anything exciting, unless you can call cooking and cleaning interesting. The boys were over at the trailer and Malcom was off sniffing up that blonde realtor's skirts again. Not that it bothered Jessie, anything to keep him away from Camila.

"Hey is Malcom upstairs?"

Jessie smiled for the skank and lied saying she didn't know. As big as a place as this was it should keep Camila busy for an hour or more. Instead of taking the bait however she stopped and returned back to the kitchen where Jessie was slaving away.

"Have any of the people you talked to said anything about boys and men disappearing?"

Jessie wasn't a huge fan of talking to the locals so she had done as little of that as possible, but she had talked to a cute guy and he had said something about newcomers disappearing suddenly.

"Nope nothing. If you think it's important tell Cyrus when he gets back."

Jessie was busy and wasn't even bothering to look up but she could feel the stare. When she did, she found Camila was not pleased.

"I don't know what your problem is, but I would appreciate it if you could be just a bit more reasonable. I just want to figure this stupid thing out so we can go home. I know you hate it here just as much as I do."

Jessie couldn't argue with that, even though Cyrus was sustaining them she still longed to feed. And she worried about her thrall. He promised that their thralls would be ok while they were gone but Jessie wanted to marry her thrall one day. She was worried about his mental state having no direction for six weeks. Not to mention she missed him. Seeing Camila wasn't leaving until she fessed up, she decided to share.

"Fine…. Bart told me about it the other day. He didn't say it was only men though. He claimed it was visitors that they just disappeared right after they arrive. Is that enough can I get back to this?"

Camila huffed and started to leave. Jessie went back to watching what she was doing and was already trying to forget about here when Camila said something from the staircase.

"By the way Bart is telling everyone in town about how easy you are. You might want to put a stop to that before the rest of his friends see if they can get a ride."

Jessie shot her head up and saw the smug bitch's smile. It wasn't any of her business. Jessie didn't respond, she couldn't come up with a proper insult fast enough.

Chapter 22: Ships in the Night

Medford, Texas – Woods outside of town

Mar 2nd 2058

Rick was running at fast as he had as a boy, but he was still using the skills taught to him by his teachers in recon. At first maintaining silence discipline was nearly impossible but he quickly found he could run and keep it up. He was bounding through the woods as quiet as a mouse. He could run faster still, as a new vampire he had seen Travis and Jacob tear ass through the tree line. But he couldn't afford that. He was hunting them now. Tracking them as they were tracking him.

The trick was to get to them first, and in a position they couldn't see. As a Marine using NVG's the night wasn't something to fear. But as a vampire the night meant nothing, his eyes could see everything. But they were a beacon to other vampires. It was literally shining a flashlight in the darkness.

"Hi Rick… your dead…. again."

Rick stopped on a dime. Jacob was standing against a huge pine and revealed his eyes and his position. That was when Rick realized they could hide their glow when they wanted to.

"How in hell do you do that, that's cheating you didn't teach me that!"

A hand fell down on his back as his friend laughing came around to his front.

"Serves you right for all the crap you pulled on the confidence course with me. I promise I will show you all about that but we have a lot of miles to cover before day break. The next exercise is for all of us to run for Orville and take up sniper positions on top of the county courthouse. We are going to be armed for real on this one, so don't get seen otherwise a bunch of frightened cops are going to take a shot at you."

Rick had been running and training without pause since lunch time when his friend had put that orb in his hands. Yet he knew at least for now he had a lot left in the tank. Rick had been in that courthouse to sign papers. It was one story structure that had once been a laundromat. Orville wasn't exactly a huge town.

"How in hell are we going to be on the roof of that building without being seen?"

Jacob laughed and disappeared in front of him. Something that surprised Rick but it shouldn't have. These vampires could do… amazing things.

"It's our nature Rick, I know you feel it even now. A desire to hide, to blend in, it's a hunter's instinct. It's part of our call as Grey men Rick. Try it yourself, feel that desire inside you to be unseen give in to it."

It took nearly five minutes before Rick could cloak himself. The moment he did it felt like he was a new man. As a soldier your fighting instinct was something you could always tap. But this was more animal, and it surprised Rick how much he liked giving into that feeling.

"Now that you are cloaked it's going to be awhile before you will uncloak again. The first time one of us does this, our bodies fight uncloaking. You should be fine for the little test we have. We are going to play counter sniper and the mission is to locate Jacob before he can get dialed in. I will be your spotter."

Rick saw the older style bolt action rifle that Jacob had left behind before leaving. Apparently, this one was for him. He was concerned; did Travis expect him to shoot at Jacob?

"No, it's just a test, no blanks or live rounds tonight. And we don't want to scare anyone. The point is to stay hidden; this is a fine game so long as no humans see us. But no training is effective without some risk, something to lose if we fail. That is why we do this, to raise the stakes but in as safe as way possible. Once we have Jacob in your scope then the game is over and we can all feast."

At the sound of food Rick nearly salivated, all this activity he suddenly got eager feet. It wasn't like him; he was generally an experienced old man who didn't act like an eager child anymore. Travis explained a moment later when it was obvious that Rick was under a new influence.

"It's our call pushing you, Rick. The best way to describe it is that we are wolves. We desire to hunt and to test ourselves, and the skill of our prey. Don't try to fight it, you can't. But don't let it push you to make stupid mistakes either. You don't have super powers. Your skills and powers are limited; don't let it get to your head. Now come on we will have to run at our top speed just to get into position before daybreak. I don't intend to let Jacob beat us; he will never let me forget it if he does."

Rick was breathing heavy now and it concerned him. One feeling he felt now, was not new. A desire to hunt, a desire to kill. He had felt similar things before but there were private things he couldn't share with anyone who hadn't, well at least done the kinds of things he and Travis had done. Travis took a step closer to him and lowered his voice.

"I know its primal and it feels good. But the first time you use that well…. you already know what happens. It's just like being a human Rick. This life is going to leave you with things you don't want to remember. Things you can't process easy, and at times you will hunger to be a part of it again. Even when it's the last thing on earth you want to see."

Rick looked at his friend and shook his head. It was overwhelming, but he voiced what was in his head right now. He was satisfied his friend wasn't shocked or repulsed by it.

"Your body is telling you it's time to feed, and not the kind of food you are used to. Part of the reason why I am running you so hard is that I have a thrall lined up for you in Orville. I need you hungry so you will enthrall them. That desire you feel right now is your body telling you about your need. Don't worry it will pass, master it so it doesn't master you. Keep that lion in check and be the master of it Rick. Know it will be fed soon, and take comfort in that…. ok?"

Rick took a long breath and swallowed a drink from the canteen he was carrying.

"Roger that, I just didn't figure being a wolf was this…."

Rick didn't want to say desirable; he liked being this again. Something he had put away and finally after decades mastered. In a moment he was again a hunter and a killer for lack of a better word. Just like when he was a Marine training for war he wanted to be used, to be utilized. To test his ability and to see his skill mastered. That meant taking life, and just like before he desired it. It was both a comfort and something unsettling. He couldn't explain it, even to Travis but somehow, he could see in his friend the same understanding.

"You are one of us Rick, just like before you aren't alone. You have brothers who will stand beside you and die beside you. Our lives are yours, just as yours is ours. Jacob and his team are your brothers now. You will hunt in their pack and you will feel all the things we both felt long ago. Trust in your instincts and follow your training. I promise you once this training is over, you will understand."

Henderson, West Virginia – Henderson Consignment

Mar 2nd 2058

Malcom was trying to wrap his head around what was going on. Paula was coy about giving details about dad. She claimed it was secret and that she would only tell him if he met her on the mountain. She made it sound like it was just an excuse to have sex, something that sounded good to Malcom. Or at least it did, but something about the way pops had looked at him made him question the wisdom of hooking up with Paula. Clearly, he wanted him to be with Camila, but why? He hadn't explained or even admitted the truth. But that necklace being in his room wasn't an accident. He knew for a fact it wasn't there when he selected the room. Pops wanted them together, but why he hadn't a clue.

As Malcom was deep in thought he walked into his room to get a shower and consider Paula's offer. On entering he discovered Camila sitting on the bed.

"Can we talk, I need to tell you something."

"Sure, so…. we are talking now?"

Malcom had said it with more edge than he wanted. She frowned for a moment but she let it slide.

"I told you I needed time; Malcom this isn't easy for me. This isn't what I thought…. well, you…. Malcom, I care about you."

Malcom saw something that struck him the moment he saw it. She looked vulnerable, it reminded him of how she looked before when he was viewing the real Camila. But Grey women did nothing but play games.

"That's nice, but you are going to have to forgive me. I have a hard time believing that. You being Grey and all… you women are all alike. You wouldn't know honestly if it slapped you in the face."

He strolled in shutting the door and loomed large over her. Hoping she would just show her cards and leave. Malcom didn't believe for a moment a Grey woman could love another Grey man without first controlling every last ounce of him. He was tired of the strings and wanted to cut every last one of them, not add more. She closed her eyes for a moment but didn't respond. When she opened them, they were filled with emotion. Her voice timbre changed and he heard real weakness. Something Grey… man or woman never did.

"Yes, I am a liar, ok. Yes, I deceive, is that what you want me to say? I wanted to use you, I wanted to see if I was ready…. ready to be what I was made to be. But this is your fault, Malcom. You…oh…. you…. I can't think straight when I am around you. You peel me back to me… it pisses me off ok!"

Malcom saw a lone tear go down her face when she raised her voice. This was a damn fine performance; Camila was a better actor than he had given her credit for.

"Just tell me what you really are doing here Camila. You aren't here for me, or to love me. You sure as shit aren't here to better relations with Medford. Just tell me what the fuck it is you want, honestly, I might even help you do it. I am so sick and tired of all this Grey bullshit, hell I might do it for you. God knows I am ready to just…"

He let his voice trail off not revealing to her just how ready he was to give up his birthright. Malcom was done; he had even begun in the last few weeks to consider asking pops to cure him. Let him lead a life outside of Medford. But that was weakness, and duty dies slowly when its dear to you. She smiled for a moment and then looked closer at him with a questioning look.

"You don't hate being a Grey, you love it. Malcom… look I know you, there isn't a man in our clan I respect more. You actually believe in what you want! You aren't like the others; trust me I know."

"You don't believe in what you want?"

She took a breath and just shook her head no in response.

"Why are you here Camila, the real reason."

The look in her eyes changed and both now had tears overflowing them, threating to burst beyond her eyes.

"I…am here to replace your mother. I was meant to come to Medford and become Queen. That is what my duty is, to undermine and unseat all those who love him. Then I could steer this clan towards what the others want, once I own your father that is."

Malcom heard it and laughed, as lovely as Camila was his father was a lot smarter than that. He had his hands full as it was. Seeing the disbelief however she continued.

"It's true…. I know him, Malcom. I fight like him, I know his secrets, his desires. I have crafted myself to be his only, trust me he wants me, Malcom. I saw the look he gave me."

The laughing stopped when she said the line about fighting. She did fight just like him, it was why they were so well matched. Malcom had been Travis's apprentice, and copied his style. It might not sound like much to a human, but to a Grey to fight like someone was to feel like someone.

"Ever since I was a little girl, I have been studding him. Learning his history, what pleases him, what doesn't. I believe what he believes, what matters to him… matters to me. It's all I know Malcom, my whole life its… all about your father."

Malcom tried to comprehend this, at first, he just had laughed. But now he felt so many emotions he couldn't process them. She was quiet now, just looking at him. If she was meant to seduce his father, then why try to seduce him?

"What was I, practice or something?"

Camila closed her eyes and shook her head yes. He didn't really know how he felt about her until just then. For the first time in his life, his own tears began to form. He wasn't aware of them until he felt them fall quickly across this face.

"I am sorry Malcom…. Truly I am. I do care…."

"STOP…. just stop Camila. I don't want to hear it."

Malcom closed his own eyes and wanted to flee, go somewhere, and hit something. She had never wanted him; he was just an accident. No not an accident, she was like all the other Grey. He was just a means to an end.

"What about my mother, what were you going to do with her…with me? When you got what you wanted, what of us…kill us, discard us? Fucking women and your strings… it's all you do, pull us and dangle us around to get what you want."

"Malcom, I didn't want this, it wasn't my choice.   It's my duty…I…. I hate the fucking strings as much as you do.   Don't you think I hate them too?   Do you really think I desire to love your father?   I CANT Malcom!   I tried… it's my duty, but I can't! because…."

Malcom looked at the broken thing before him and grew angry. It was just another act, something she was doing for some reason he couldn't fathom.

"You know what I think.   I think you enjoy it, controlling us, owning us.   You are just like Susan, and Dolly and…mom.   You don't care about us, love us… we are just toys.   Well, I am tired of being played with.   You want dad, be my guest, take him.   You can stand in line behind Dolly and the rest of them.   Hope you enjoy it."

He slammed the door behind him, barely hearing the plea from Camila for him to come back.   He stopped in the hallway when he heard her sob.   He had never heard a Grey woman sob before.   He didn't think it was possible even.   A part of him wanted to believe her, wanted to go back…comfort her. But the moment that impulse hit, so did the memory of her words.   He burnt any feeling for her he had out of himself and found another room to go to, leaving her behind.

Henderson, West Virginia – Camila's room

Mar 2nd 2058

It was late and she was about to turn in.   She had done as Cyrus had asked.   To be honest with Malcom about her mission.   It was his only ask, but it felt like he has asked for the moon.   Camila had been slow to discover her feelings for Malcom. It had started small, just respect really. But for Grey respect was far more than it was for others.   Respect formed the core of Grey relationships.   Far more than any human could possibly fathom.

Why can't he understand?   Can't he see that he isn't the one in strings?   What choices do I fracking have?

She started to correct herself at her stupidity.   Why have feelings for him, he couldn't possibly understand her?   She should have kept her mouth shut. Now…. well the mission was dead before, after this, it really was dead.

"He understands you just fine, but he needs your patience too."

She laughed a small thing at hearing Cyrus's voice. Never far were the puppet masters she thought.

"I am not your master; I am your visitor. I don't rule over you child, I want to be your grandfather...like I am for the others."

She looked over at the mist that floated near her. She started to ask him about his saying he was leaving. But like most things, the puppet masters often lied. Instead, she asked why he had her tell Malcom the truth.

"Because he deserved to know. Child he is connected to you, he loves you. He doesn't realize it yet, but he does. That is why he got so upset at you when you were honest. It hurt him a great deal. He had seen you as someone different, not the sexy confident shell you project.... But the weak one, the real one. He cares about the real woman inside you, but he doesn't know if he can trust you. And he has his own strings, ones he is desperate to cut now. Thanks to you..."

She looked at the mist with a questioning look. Then she better understood, or at least thought she did.

"You want him to leave the clan? Why....."

It was quiet for a long bit as the mist changed color and seemed to settle into a whiteish version of grey.

"No child, I want him to grow, to learn. The Grey have lived in such a way for too long. I want something different, something better for my Grey. I think Malcom can help me create a new.... better path. But he needs to see in you, what I see."

Camila laughed wondering what on earth Cyrus saw in her. Figuring what he saw was her ability to twist others. It was what mother most admired about her.

"There is a grace inside of you child. But it's been locked up, hidden by the duty you slave for. The two of you are the same child.... can you not see it?"

She did, but she didn't want to believe it. She had dismissed it for many reasons. Not least of all that she had trained to be his fathers, not Malcom's.

"What about his father? You said you wouldn't interfere, that he would love me. Aren't you interfering now?"

She heard a warm and hearty laugh from him and it felt so comforting. He was around her again in her mind and speaking to her like he did before.

Through all of this at least she had gotten to meet him. Cyrus was a decent…being at the very least. There was something very comforting about him, and she was beginning to treasure that feeling.

"Ok so I am interfering a little…. Child is it so wrong of me? He is my grandson, and I know his heart and soul. I can feel it, just as I feel your own. I may be alien to your world, but I know of love. I see the two halves and how even now, they are coming together. If the two of you would just be patient and open your eyes to it…. The two of you would become something beautiful. I know it like I know anything child. You just have to have eyes and see."

Camila was emotional, the idea that she could…. No. She looked at the mist and took a breath. All of this was just a distraction, these emotions…. Were just that.

"Cyrus I…"

"You don't have to say it child I see you closing the doors of your understanding. Everyone has to walk their own path. I know you feel you are walking someone else's… and you are. But you can choose another."

Camila wasn't impressed, he just wanted her to walk his path. How was that any different?

"Leave me alone."

The moment she thought it the mist disappeared and she closed her eyes forcing her emotions back into their box. She might have ruined her duty, or she might not have. It was time to get back to it. Ruined or no, she had a duty. It might hurt; it might be horrible but it was hers. That she understood, that she could live with. But this pain… this she couldn't.

Orville, Texas – Best Western

Mar 3rd 2058

The exercise was over and the three of them were tired and worn out. They had eaten here at the hotel's horrible restaurant. But the meal didn't at all sate what Rick wanted. Jacob sitting across from him and Travis was still sore about the outcome.

"I give it to you old guys, you got me. But a millisecond more and I would have had you."

"Bullshit, more like 10 minutes slow, son."

Rick smiled at that; he had Jacob in his scope before Jacob even had his rifle up. It helped that Travis was his spotter, it would have taken him a lot longer to see Jacob in that spot he had picked. As father and son bantered with each other Rick shook his head. The bright Grey light that he could see was comforting to him. It was because he was one of them now. But mentally it was just weird. It felt right and good but it set him and his fellows apart from everyone else. Rick wasn't human anymore, but he still thought like one. But none of this, the eyes, the victory, the food, or the banter really mattered right now. All that he could think about was this hunger inside him. He didn't know how to take a thrall or what he had to do, but whatever it was he was more than fricking ready. When the banter slowed down Rick interrupted.

"Come on man, I am dying here. When do I get what you talked about before…when do I get fed?"

The moment he said it he regretted his choice of words. While correct it opened him up to teasing.

"Damn you ate a whole steak and eggs what more do you want Rick?"

Jacob said it while chewing on bacon and then turned to his father. Travis right on cue also cut into him.

"I told him to choose the pancakes, way better than whatever imitation steak that was he gulped down."

Rick shot a quick stare to the kid and then back to Travis. Thankfully they didn't make him wait any longer. Travis just smirked for a moment and then reached into his pocket to retrieve something.

"Room 301, your thrall is inside waiting on you. She is expecting a special visitor, take it easy with her, ok?"

Rick suddenly felt all of this was too real. He was going up to a room with a complete stranger? How, just what did he have to do to enthrall her? He started to ask a thousand questions. Who was she, what did she think was going to happen? For that matter, exactly how did you enthrall someone? Instead, he asked the obvious.

"Am I going to hurt her when I do this? Is it possible to kill her?"

"No, she will be fine Rick. Go on."

Rick moved even if his judgement told him he was putting himself at grave risk. As he walked and then climbed the steps to the 3rd floor, he asked himself what he would say to this person when she opened the door. He came up with a few stupid ideas of what to say, hating all of them. When he knocked on 301, he took a breath trying desperately to hold down his desires. His body needed fed, and that more than anything, was what had driven him to this spot. When the door opened the astonished woman didn't waste time in hearing a word he was going to say.

"RICK! What in hell are you doing here? I should have known that was you! Why can't you just leave me alone? Haven't you got it through your head, were done!"

It was his wife, and she was dressed in some negligee and all prettied up waiting on someone. When she slapped him, it pulled him out of the fog he was in. He caught the second slap and drove her inside. After closing the door, he pushed her further allowing some of his anger to drive him. But before he could say a word he felt something different, and his vision became cloudy. He heard a buzzing sound that grew so loud he thought it would deafen him. Then the wave of pleasure hit him and he heard his wife gasp. After years of marriage and a heart that had once been all about her, it only took that gasp to make him focus only on her.

Forgetting the anger, forgetting the shock of seeing her here he asked her if she was ok. She didn't speak, her mouth was open and her face was slack. He had to hold her up lest she fall into the floor. When her eyes opened, they did so with laziness. Once fully open Rick saw the shape in them denouncing that she belonged to him in a different way now. He had enthralled her, and didn't even really remember doing so. It just sort of happened.

"Rick what in hell did you do?"

Rick had her in his arms, she was limp and a tiny bit fearful. He spoke calmly and slowly to explain, guiding her to the bed so she could be supported without him holding her. Their discussion would go on for more than an hour. When he asked her questions, she had to answer them. As a thrall her will was bent. Not fully gone, as he was to find out. His first round of questions was to learn how and why she was here. It had to be Yelina's doing. His new "mother" didn't much like his ex and made that clear.

His wife told the tale, not that it pleased him much. She had been lured here by the opportunity to make a lot of money. Three days before she had accepted the offer from a rich man she thought. Tickets to Vegas at first, all paid for a party there, just for her. Then more tickets to Texas, and to here to meet her new sugar daddy. Rick was disgusted by her, and her actions. Next, he asked if this was the first time she had done something like this. His ex-wife had apparently an expensive lifestyle that she preferred. She had been whoring around on him the whole time he was married to her.

The more questions he asked the more upset she became. Scared at first then angry when she realized it was a new ability in Rick that prevented her lying to him. As her vampire she answered every question truthfully and honestly. She resented it bitterly, being a thrall apparently didn't make her docile.

"Do you really think you are just going to have me in your home being your little housewife? You are so pathetic Rick, I will never be that little perfect thing. I…"

"Shut up, just close your mouth."

When Rick told her to shut up, she did, much to her shock and horror. He shook his head remembering some of what Yelina had taught him over the last couple days about what thralls were like, and how to deal with them.

"I know it's a shitty deal, and you don't like it. Frankly I don't give a shit. I thought I was going to have some pretty white girl who looked at me with awe. Guess both of us get disappointed?"

His wife glared back at him, her eyes narrow and her mouth thin and pulled in. She was huffing like a caged animal ready to strike. Yet she was held back, his control over her was tentative barely holding back the tiger. When she spoke next it caused him to shake his head at her ability to not feel an ounce of shame.

"Is this how you treat me, after all I have done for you?"

"Oh yeah, all you have done, you are something else you know that? You lost any respect from me that right when you whored yourself out and left me with our son."

Rick felt any regrets disappear realizing again just who his wife was. He needed a thrall, and right now she would do nicely.

"You may not be a housewife but you are going to feed me woman. I don't really care if you like it or not. But it won't be all bad, I will take care of you, make sure you have what you need."

Rick wrote his address on a piece of paper and tossed some cash from his wallet.

"Get cleaned up and take a cab or rent a car I don't care, but be at that house and have dinner ready for me when I get home."

Rick heard the curses and the foul temper thrown his way but didn't stay long to absorb it. He had better things to do, and a new life to start.

Chapter 23: Truth and Consequences

Medford, Texas – Cassia's home

Mar 3rd 2058

It was nearly time to leave, something Travis wasn't fully ready for yet. He had kids missing, well sort of missing. No matter what he and Jay had done they couldn't get Cyrus to show up. Mom wasn't any help; she was a shell of her former self. What had happened between them no one would say, not even his wives. Whatever had gone on while he was in France had seen the removal of his mother from the Agora. He had said his goodbyes and tried his best to be a good son, but she was a mess.

"It's going to be ok, if I get any word, I will task Jacob and his team."

Travis smiled for his wife, even if she didn't return it. He put feeling into his voice. He was leaving and he didn't like going like this.

"I know you will, but please look after mom, I don't like leaving her like this but I have to."

Yelina shook her head yes and looked away. They hadn't touched since he had taken Dolly. Nor had they talked about what was going on. Now wasn't the time either, as he was going to be with Dolly for weeks when he arrived in Europe.

"I know I made a lot of mistakes, and things aren't…. well, they aren't right between us."

Yelina looked up at him with a sad look. He hated this, their relationship was in trouble, he needed to stop everything and focus, but he couldn't. He didn't have time to take it slow; he was going to be on a plane in a short bit.

"Yelina, do you still want to be together? I…. know I haven't been great as a husband lately… that's putting it mildly. But ever since I got back from France you seem really distant. I feel like…well I feel like you don't love me anymore."

Yelina turned her head looking at him. It was cold in a way. Something he wasn't used to seeing from her. Of all the relationships in his short vampiric life, Yelina had always been the most loyal, the deepest relationship he had. But that had died somewhere in the last couple years and Travis wondered why.

"Honestly Travis I don't know what I feel anymore. You should go; you don't want to keep Dolly waiting."

He could hear the bitterness in her voice. That was when he understood that she knew. Of course she did, they were Grey, and such things couldn't stay a secret for long. When you love someone, you begin to see things others don't. Little changes in your expression, and what they mean. In that moment both knew what the other was thinking. Or so Travis thought anyway. When Yelina spoke next it shook him to his core.

"You aren't the only one who cheated, I had another for a time."

Travis's mouth fell open and he was crushed by that news. Yet he had no right to be, he had failed with Dolly. The only encouraging thing he saw was that Yelina wasn't emotionless, she was losing her composure and fighting tears. That meant she cared, about him possibly, more likely their marriage. It was very quiet between them for a moment while Travis considered his next words carefully.

"Yelina, I don't want us to end like this."

At hearing that she shook her head and the mask she was clinging to slipped a touch. Her eyes began to water and she struggled to look him in the eye.

So… she still loves me.

Still but there was a deep fissure between them? Travis took a long breath and continued.

"I haven't stopped loving you, I…. don't understand what happened between us though. I know what I did was wrong, I didn't go up there to make love to her. I just needed to clear the air. I never stopped loving her and I let that get the best of me."

"Yet you have been with her many times. That wasn't the only one Travis."

On hearing that he took a step back. Yes, he had made love to her, but only once. On thinking that he felt guilty, one time, or a thousand times it didn't matter. He had broken his word.

"Yelina, I didn't touch her until the day before she left. I know that isn't much of…"

"You didn't make love to her last year when I was in New York? Or when the two of you went to that client meeting in Florida?"

Travis saw the confused look on her face and was honest when he said no.

"The first time we shared anything was in the link in front of you. I went to see her to make it clear we can't be together, and that was when I…well you know."

Travis listened to the quick words that passed from her lips. When he discovered why she thought this, he felt another knife in his heart. His daughter Janet had told Yelina he had never stopped being intimate with Dolly. That he had been going behind her back to make love to her for years.

"Travis look, I need time to figure out what comes next. I love you but you aren't the only one who is confused. Maybe we should separate, I don't know. I know this, I am not happy, and frankly neither are you."

Travis looked at her and shook his head in agreement. He wasn't happy, not with this arrangement and not with the fact she had taken another. He wanted to ask who it was so he could rip out their throat. But then she would have the same justification to deal with Dolly. Something that caused the anger in him to calm back to a simmering fire.

"I am lonely Travis; I feel like the only thing you have time for is the clan. You never want to be with me, even when you are here you aren't. Look, I am not blaming just you, I screwed up. I took another I…. broke my word to you."

Yelina had to choke the last words out. Hearing that also cooled his fire just a touch more.

"When I went to New York I got drunk and I let someone touch me. It was stupid and it…. didn't please me or make me happy. What I wanted was you, I still think I do… but I can't live like this sharing you with Susan and now Dolly… again. I deserve to be your only."

Travis's eyes shut on that, so it had finally come to this. He knew it would, it was only a matter of time. Even he had longed for the day when he could live in peace. The trouble was he still loved them all, and choosing was simply impossible for him.

"I know, you do. But I can't…. hurt them for you."

With that she went back inside the house with his mother and closed the door. Travis got back into the car like a zombie. In all his adult years as a vampire he had the three of them beside him. They were the mothers to his children, and he loved them deeply. A part of him was upset feeling somewhat justified in making love to Dolly. Like Yelina, he was lonely, he felt isolated and alone. And the constant pressures from the clan was becoming too much.

Twenty minutes later he found himself pulled up to Art and Nancy's house. He hadn't thought to come here, the vehicle had just managed to find its own way. He was in the car sitting in the drive way so long he got noticed. A small knock on the window snapped him out of his deep thoughts.

"Hey I thought you Grey liked to creep out on us Aqua from the shadows? Now you are just going to sit in our driveway and stare?"

The unfamiliar voice caught Travis's attention. He looked and saw a face he hadn't seen in years. He was out of his car and embracing him as fast as he could, astonished at who had greeted him.

"Holy shit! When did you get back in town Gerold?"

"Today, actually I am just passing through. On my way to a dig in Spain. Dude, you look like a space cadet, something wrong?"

Travis laughed and shook the hand of Nancy and Art's son. Travis hadn't seen him in years. Not since he went up north to go to college. Gerold was always a quiet one, but Travis had always liked him. As a young boy Gerold wanted to know everything about the Grey. Travis had semi-adopted the boy. Nancy had encouraged it hoping it would bring Gerold out of his shell.

"Sorry got a lot on my mind, actually I am heading out to Europe later today myself. It's good to see you kid, your mom has been missing you like crazy, has she seen you yet?"

Gerold smacked him on the arm and laughed. Travis saw a side of him he hadn't seen before. Gerold looked like has on top of the world. He asked about it wondering what was going on with him.

"Trav, I found someone, I am engaged to be married man."

Travis struggled to hear about this woman he described. It felt strange to hear about one person's joy just starting as his was coming to an end.

"This Hope sounds like a lovely person; how did she handle learning you are a vampire?"

On that his joyous expression died, and Travis chuckled. The boy hadn't changed as much as it seemed. He was still reluctant and private.

"Kid you can't keep something like that from someone. If you love her you need to tell her."

"I know Trav, it's just hard you know? I don't want to lose her, hey you going inside to talk to mom? I was just heading out but I want to visit with you…"

"No man, I was going to ask her about something but it can wait. I need to get on the road myself."

A few more niceties were exchanged between them and then an idea hit Travis.

"Hey you said you are going to Spain; you talk to the Tourmalines yet and get a contact over there?"

The boy nodded that he had already. The Tourmalines were a clan based in Europe that folks in Medford registered with before they went to Europe. While they were over there, they would be watched. This gave Travis an opportunity to send a message, where Gerold was going was exactly where that nebulous group was said to have folks. At least according to what Dolly had found out so far.

"Hey when you get to Europe and talk to your contact, would you send a message for me?"

"Sure, anything you want, but if you are going to Europe why can't you?"

Travis had to be careful here, he was going to Europe but he didn't want to tell the boy where. He was going illegally and not telling the Tourmalines. Where he was going, they weren't in charge anyway.

"I have my reasons, but if you could tell your contact that the King of the Grey wants to meet someone from the Associates. That would be a help."

Gerold shook his head yes and then they said their goodbyes. Travis hoped he could talk to these people and put an end to this vendetta that had somehow grown up against Gerold's people. As a Grey, and Jay's brother, he wanted to help if he could.

Hinton, West Virginia – Travelodge room 130

Mar 3rd 2058

The phone rang several times before the tired female voice greeted him.

"Hey Susan this is Cyrus. I don't have a ton of time to talk but I wanted to let you know everything is fine. We will be back soon, take care!"

Cyrus hit end on the call before the shocked Susan could say a word. What she thought didn't really matter, he had done what he needed to do. That would be just enough for Susan and the others to track him. With that accomplished Cyrus looked at what was in front of him today. Right on cue a tall young man, muscular and confident walked up to him.

"Sir you dropped this in the lobby."

Cyrus smiled for the young man and took ahold of the wallet he had dropped within sight of him.

"That's very kind of you, what's your name son?"

"Walker sir, have a good day!"

Cyrus smiled and allowed yet more of his precious power slip through the wallet into the boy. He was another human; one he had his eye on. He clearly felt something from the change in his expression as Cyrus allowed the boys future to flow into him. Without another word Cyrus entered his room and closed it. The boy continued on from the sounds of his footfalls. Cyrus knew it was only a matter of time. This one would have a different path now. A new creation, one needed for the near future. Changing the boy was draining, and he longed to sleep, longed to return to his form. Longed to rest one last time.

But there was still much to do before he could rest, so much to do that he wasn't sure he could do it all. But he must... his Grey needed him just a bit more.

Texas – Somewhere near the border with Arkansas

Mar 3rd 2058

Travis had his mind on many things, but not on what he should. As he pondered his mistakes, Travis looked out the window of the small plane he was traveling in. The Admiral was sitting across from him speaking. Instead of listening to him, he was thinking of Yelina. Wishing he could turn the plane around and go fix things.

"Travis did you hear me? This is important."

Travis looked up at the man, he looked annoyed that Travis had allowed his mind to wonder. Instead of responding he just nodded.

"You have to destabilize the situation enough to move the needle. But its Greece, the Islamic groups are ready to go to war with the state on the crackdown. You have to tread carefully Travis, you and your people."

Travis had this briefing before but it didn't hurt to hear it again, especially with his mind focused on Yelina. Sighing he sadly put her away. He couldn't save his marriage, at least not today. He just had to hope he could later.

"What about the European Union, will they support this guy?"

The Admiral sat back uncomfortably in the chair and looked closely at him.

"Right now, no. You have to find a way to elevate him in the international eye. And as I said before whatever you do has to appear organic. If anyone catches a whiff that you or the agency is involved, well it's over. You can't kill your way to victory in this Travis. You need to outthink both the Islamist's and any other challengers. You can't crush any of them, at least not right away."

Travis reviewed both what the Admiral had told him and what his own sources had told him. Travis did not trust this man or his agency. But the intel he had received supported what he said.

"We will be ready Admiral; I already have by best people in place."

Chapter 24: Cry Havoc, and Let Slip the Dogs of War

Medford, Texas – Cassia's home

Mar 3rd 2058

The last six weeks had been difficult to say the least. She had gotten over the shock. Not for a second did she ever expect to hear Cyrus speak to her like that, or to have her place in this clan removed. But six weeks without a word, without a peep from Cyrus was too much. She knew she had to be patient, Cyrus was deliberate and didn't move on a dime. But for Cassia she hated the wait.

Her attention was shaken by her cell that went off. Since her downfall no one called. She had made many enemies over the decades and now that her power was gone, so had the attention and respect. The number was one she had been dreading. It was a burner number but one she had memorized. Yelina was working on the dishes in the other room. Cassia quickly moved further out of earshot. This took her into her own private study. Taking a breath, she answered the still ringing phone.

"What are you trying to pull Cassia? We had a deal and we lived up to our end of the bargain."

Cassia walked over to the image on the mantle. Her beloved sons were all standing together smiling for the camera. Everything she had done, was for one of those. She stared a moment at Travis's unmoving image and began to become somber. She was slow in her speech, her fears over him were like an anchor dragging down her own intellect.

"I take it you haven't heard from Camila either. It's not me Ana, Cyrus took her and some of my grandchildren on some sort of mission. I haven't heard from them yet."

Cassia was assaulted with verbose assaults on her word. She couldn't blame Camila's mother; a lot was riding on her for the Meridians. Eventually the conversation circled to the only thing that really mattered to Ana. Cassia didn't bother to worry about anything but this.

"I gave you my own daughter, my own daughter Cassia! She is exactly what you ordered. The perfect wife for your son! Do you think I am stupid, do you really think you can play with us? I want the orb now Cassia. You have my daughter, give us the orb!"

Cassia looked at the image again and realized she couldn't delay any longer. Closing her eyes and wishing her husband could just appear now, begging him to in her mind. Still, he did not.

"Fine, you can have it. Where do you want to meet?"

Paris, France – Château de Malmaison

Mar 4th 2058

"Travis has left Medford my lady."

Rose was looking at the text message from her daughter as her assistant entered the room with the news.

"Is he doing what we expected him to do?"

The man only smiled in reply. Travis was stupid, so easily swayed, so easily directed. Still not everything was going to her desires. Rose took in a breath, as usual there were complications. Camila had disappeared. Cassia apparently didn't even know her own husband. She had sworn Cyrus wouldn't interfere, that it went against his code. Well on some level he had, and Camila was completely off the board. No matter, she was only meant to be a distraction.

"My lady what shall I tell your daughter? She is livid and feels you have betrayed her."

Rose paid little attention to this, Ana was high strung and easily ignored. Rose had gamed this out already, and had her suspicion confirmed a moment later. Ana had already called Cassia asking for the orb directly. She looked at her assistant, he was ill at ease waiting on her words.

"It was stupid of Ana to call her. Someone will notice and begin to put things together. Tell Ana nothing…. she no longer matters anyway. Ana has done her part."

Rose heard the man leave and she made her way to the window. She would miss this place, of all her homes over the years this one was one of the most precious. But the game she was playing had bigger stakes than just a chateau. She could build another, especially if she was successful. Rose looked at a different phone, one laying on the desk nearby. It was time, Travis was where she wanted him as was the Medford and Meridian Grey. She picked up the phone and began to speak in Turkish. Her words were short and clipped. But they achieved her intended result. With that done she took one last look at her home before she fled. She would never return, no matter… she would be closer to Sparta now. Closer to her real home…

Medford, Texas – Yelina's home

Mar 4th 2058

Rick was tired he and Jacob had been training hard with the rest of the team. He was truly one of them now and he felt it keenly. A part of him had found comfort in the life, especially the deep bonds forming between him and the others. They weren't brothers as Travis had said they would be. That would take time, likely time in combat.

As it was, both him and Jacob had been summoned to Yelina's house. His adoptive mothers, a title Rick didn't like but had to accept. As for Jacob he could get used to the boy. He was too serious but other than that he was a good kid. As they approached the door, he saw that Yelina was standing outside waiting for them with an irritated Susan. He shot a look over at Jacob whose eyebrows went up in surprise. Yelina looked like she was dead serious, a sentiment confirmed a moment later.

"We have a mission for your team Jacob. Your brother has been found; we want you to get out there and bring them home… understand?"

Jacob mouth formed an entertained shape and declined to let loose a peep. Rick decided to answer for both of them.

"Not really, there is only one helo here, we can't take the whole team. Besides aren't they with the big guy?"

Susan looked angry at that and stepped forward to confront Rick. But before she could, Yelina put a hand on her. Susan didn't reply but the snarl she gave her was clear. When Yelina spoke, she did so with quiet focus. And the face communicated her emotions rather too well.

"I thought I made it clear Rick; you are my son now. I give you orders and you follow them. Did you question your orders when you were a Marine?"

Rick just smiled thinking of what to say. He wasn't in the military, and he wasn't a fool.

"Yeah, I suppose not. But if I didn't know what was going on I didn't take a risk I didn't believe in either. How about you tell me what is going on so we don't get a nasty surprise…. Or is this little op a circle jerk?"

Susan shouted something in anger catching Rick by surprise. He had seen the Grey women get serious before, but not in a panic. He saw that panic now and looked at Yelina.

"We are worried about our children Rick. Cyrus took them weeks ago and he hasn't told us what he is doing. Susan's son…he is just a kid, she……well we, are worried for him. Take a helo, and anyone you need and go get them. It's not combat, but we want you there as fast as you can get there…. ok?"

Henderson, West Virginia – Malcom's room

Mar 4th 2058

Malcom had steered clear of Camila. She was up to something; of that no one was blind to. Most thought it was to cause trouble, or perhaps steal the orb. Grandmother had taken that into her custody so that wasn't possible. But the more Malcom thought about it, the more he understood Camila was serious about dad. Why did that bother him? Mom and the others could take care of themselves, besides dad wasn't going to….

"MALCOM!"

The urgency in Jessie's voice pulled him out of his obsessive thinking.

"I can't find Jonathan and Clint; do you know where they are?"

Malcom took a second to pull his brain out of the circle it was in with Camila. It took a moment, which caused Jessie to push even harder. She was in a panic which confused him.

"Look no I don't, what's the big deal it's not like they can get into trouble here. They probably just went back to the trailer to look for more stuff from dad."

Jessie gritted her teeth and yanked hard on his arm pulling him towards the door and up to a window that looked out on the ground below. It was covered in freshly fallen snow, and it was coming down hard.

"That's why you idiot, there is a huge fricking storm coming in. And if you would get your head out of the clouds for a second you would have known that. They aren't in the trailer; I just came from there. Camila hasn't seen them either, no one has for hours!"

Another female voice rose up from the first floor, concerned and upset from the tone. A second or two later he saw Camila at a run stop short of the place where they were standing.

"Malcom its bad, there are things in the streets. Please tell me we have weapons."

"Things? What things?"

Henderson, West Virginia – Blair Mountain

Mar 4th 2058

"Paula are you sure it's safe being all the way out here?"

Paula smiled for Clint; he was the most cautious of the two brothers. He would be the one she would have to be most careful of. As old and skilled a huntress as she was, even the young could be dangerous. Especially children sired by Travis, they weren't vampires like their father, but they were still something to be wary of. Paula remembered well Travis and his skills. If they were even a fraction of their father, then tonight should prove interesting. Truly a once in a lifetime opportunity to test themselves.

"Don't worry silly, I promise it will be worth your time. And you have me to keep you safe, don't you? This is my home; I know it better than anyone."

She could see the look of doubt creep onto Clint's face. Jonathan however would follow his brothers lead. He was afraid, she could smell it and its scent was delicious. Soon she would feast on that, allowing her instinct the control that it sought. Paula smiled for both boys, but it wasn't for the reasons they believed. Paula was a huntress, bred and created just to deal with vampires. Their existence was nothing like that of human or vampire. Their purpose was razor sharp in its intensity. Paula had prepared for a day like today. Her daughters were close now, eager and excited for the hunt. So many of them, all newly created and trained. Each with new gifts, unseen by the vampires.

"You…said dad came up here…why…It's like. Really cold."

Paula turned her attention back to Jonathan and put a loving hand on him.

"Your father loved this mountain; this was where he wanted to spend all his days. He hunted here, trained here, and found a home. There is a special place your father went to, that has to be what your grandfather is searching for. If your father left something, he would have left it there."

Clint was still suspicious. His eyes said a great deal for a human. He would have to be delt with first, then his brother.

"But how did you know him, wouldn't have you been a little girl back then?"

Paula smiled remembering Travis, her mother and those times. They had been good years, a time for discovery. She missed those times, the innocence. But like all beings you have to grow up, and she had long since done so. It was a precious moment that nearly drove her to emotion. Normally to be reminded of them would cause her to become human like in her temperament. She might even cry… But not when prey was so close…. so…temptingly close.

"I was, me and my sister used to run through that store of yours every day. Travis would make carvings to sell… like this one. See, this was something your dad made for me."

Paula showed the boys the walking cane with the wolf's head. He had taken a long time carving it, and it was something Paula treasured. Nearly the only thing that she kept from that time.

"Holy crap that is so cool! Dad carved this?"

Clint was sufficiently impressed that it totally disarmed him. As Jonathan grew close to get a look Paula edged away from them. This was the place, and the time for the boys to discover that not all wolves look alike. Some are pretty and smile and tease. But they will kill you all the same. It was a pity she was going to violate these innocent ones, but that is what hunters do to prey. Besides…. it was fun.

Chapter 25: Horror

Appalachian Mountains, Tennessee – 19,000 Ft

Mar 4th 2058

Rick was strapped in along with the rest of the team. They only had one bird worthy of cross-country flight and it was 06. To say it was an old bird was an understatement. The fricking thing was nearly as old as Rick. One of the last Blackhawks to come off the assembly line in Connecticut. The helo was more a museum piece, than a working helicopter. Hopefully this bucket of bolts will stick together. Rick kept his mind off the boredom, and concerns over the helo, by going over the plan. He smiled remembering that it was his plan after all. Of those available tonight there wasn't anyone else with more experience. The majority of the team had been called south to deal with a contract that had gone bad. They had left only six members behind in case of an emergency. As it was these six guys were the only ones left in Medford to answer the call.

The plan was simple, the helo had travel pods attached so they only had to refuel once on the trip. That had been accomplished at a small field south of Nashville. They had enough fuel to get to Henderson but the helo wouldn't be able to loiter long. Perhaps a few minutes before it would have to divert to Logan airport. There wasn't a suitable landing spot so they would fast rope onto the target building's roof. Each of them had done that several times before. Only for Rick it had been several decades since his last leap out of hovering helo.

"Weather is getting bad over the target, whiteout conditions Rick.... I recommend we land in Logan and you can go on from there."

Rick got the message over the intercom tied into the ear protection he was wearing. Inside a helo it's as loud as sticking your head inside a running lawnmower engine. As team lead, he had the only intercom. The pilot was an experienced one, and if he was saying it was bad then he meant it. But Rick saw that look from the matrons, he better not come back without the kids. If something had gone wrong, Rick didn't want to delay.

"Negative, as long as you can IFR your way into the target then we will go."

Rick was using pilot lingo, if he was able to fly on instruments only, rather than visual or VFR. It could be done, flying in a whiteout condition. But it was dangerous and there were limits. There was a long pause, and when the pilot responded he could hear the irritation.

"Roger that, IFR to target and deploy. Be advised we will not be able to stay. I can't keep this piece of junk stable in those kinds of winds."

Rick acknowledged that and looked out the window to see how bad it was getting. It didn't look like anything to worry about, but that could just be here. There was a tap on his leg from Jacob who sat next to him. None of the others had headsets and didn't hear the conversation. But they knew there was one. He couldn't communicate to them without hand signals. Rick just gave them all a thumbs up sign, letting them know the op was still on. Each man nodded and then turned their attention back to their gear or looking out the side windows.

Rick could see the anticipation and the concern. Helos had a bad habit of crashing. When they did it wasn't uncommon for no one to walk away. Rick's last operation as a Marine had ended that way, with only him walking away. The rest of the team unable to speak, tried to act calm. Jacob was worried for his siblings, had to be. Tony, Jake and Dalton were experienced and didn't have skin in this. Other than they were fellow Grey, these kids weren't family. The only person happy to be here was Calvin the emerald doc. He didn't get to go on missions. The funny thing was for a guy who had never served he had done more fast ropes than Rick. The strange kid really liked the life. Some did, at least the one Rick had in the military. This Grey one…. It wasn't quite the same.

Rick went over the process of fast rope. They would first open the doors and get hit with that wind and cold. They would extend the small boom with the ropes and then allow the weighted ends to fall out hitting the roof below. Then Rick would signal one from each side to dismount. In a stable helo it wasn't hard, just jump out the door, catch the rope and slide down, easy. The only trouble was in high winds or enemy fire, helos tended to be anything but stable. Rick had witnessed accidents before. Kids who had jumped out and had the helo move as they did. Those kids never found the rope that had been right in front of them a second before. Most of them well… they didn't fare well with the ground when they met it.

"Rick we are about two and a half out from target. We are on VFR at the moment but we will be in IFR in an hour or so. If it gets any worse than what

Wilmington is reporting, then I am diverting. I am not losing my license over a babysitting op... clear?"

Rick responded in the affirmative and sat back to get as comfortable as he could. It was hard with all the equipment they carried. On his back was a small combat ruck with some essentials. A helmet with "NODS", or night vision. Rick laughed at that one, he didn't really need night vision as a vampire but it helped with peripheral vision and at long distance. Especially the thermal sight he had attached to them. On his leg was strapped a sidearm and a short-barreled rifle slung upside down on his back. The muzzle had to face down when they rode in helos. If it went off shooting the floor was ok, the engine that was inches above their heads, not so much. Each man had the same equipment. Except for Jacob who had a large backpack radio and Calvin who had medical supplies.

The last passengers on this helo were two smallish crates that sat between the men in the center of the well. One contained an autonomous rover dog. It was a scout and was operated by Jacob, one of his many talents. The other crate had gear, and surgical supplies in case of a mass casualty. It was all most likely for nothing; they would probably land and find the kids eating a meal in front of a warm fire. It wasn't like that place was full of PLAN soldiers out to kill them. Even if it was, those kids were vampires.

PLAN...shit, where is my head right now?

Rick smiled looking out the window. For a moment, just a moment he had been living a different life. For a second the war was real, if in a small tangential way. He hadn't seen a Chinese soldier in 20 years. That war was over, and tonight's biggest danger was in surviving the trip. Not what was waiting on them. Yet old habits die hard, and Rick couldn't help but find himself planning on how he would handle a hostile LZ.

Henderson, West Virginia

Mar 4th 2058

Camila had seen the beginning of hell unleashed. It was as if demons had risen from the cracks of the earth to slay the town folk. There wasn't time to gather much, winter coats, a weapon or two. If Gale was right then the boys were up on the mountain right now, if they were still alive that is. Just then Jessie and Malcom arrived behind her at the front door. The sounds of screams, and the sickening sounds of the dying were all around. One older man was lying not far from them in the snow, his abdomen split open from side to side. His insides were spilled out into the snow, with the diming light it wasn't bright red, just dark and spreading slowly. The man wasn't the only body in the street.

"God what is going on, what did this a bear?"

Camila had caught sight of what it was but she didn't dare describe it to the others. They would think her mad if she did. Instead without talking about it first, she motioned them to follow her. Jessie was reluctant to follow but a second later Malcom and her were behind her as they tucked low and moved towards the café where Gale worked. All three were cloaked now but they couldn't rely solely on that with all this going on around them. Whatever "it" was there was more than one of them. Jessie started to ask a question and Camila balled her hand into a fist and gave her a stern look. They needed to be silent, cloaking did nothing if they were chatting in the middle of all this….

When Camila turned back around, she saw a young girl standing in front of Gale. The girl was that Fraser girl who Camila had seen in the Café many times. She was standing skin close to Gale and the look on Gale's face was….

"Oh my god!"

The girl had Gale off her feet, pinned against the door of the café. Gale's eyes were hollow and her mouth was open with a bit of blood coming out. Then she saw how Gale was being pinned. The girl removed her right hand from inside Gale. Instead of short fingers the girl had long sharp points. No sooner had she removed them when she plunged them back into Gale's chest. The small sound that escaped Gale's mouth showed that she was either dead already or close to it.

"What the fuck is that?"

Jessie's question was out loud and carried far on the cold air. The girl while still holding Gale against the wall, turned her face towards them. But it wasn't the face of a girl… or a human. Her eyes were two or three times the size of a humans. The eyes were all black and when she opened her mouth it was filled with sharp teeth that were oversized and extended past her lips. They flexed and moved as she made a growling sound towards them. Dropping Gale, she moved with one motion towards them. Gale's body steaming in the cold air fell off the long points of her left hand. She was incredibly strong as it appeared she was handing all Gale's body weight with ease.

No one moved, all where entranced with the sight before them. Vampires were apex predators they feared nothing, but other vampires. At least until today, what Camila saw caused her heart to nearly beat out of her chest. Terror wasn't something she had ever felt before, not as a vampire anyway. The thing that came towards them flung up its claws to strike her and like a fool she stood there motionless. Was this what it felt like for humans when they stalked them?

The sound of gunfire was so loud that Camila dropped to the ground as if she was flattened by a stone. A millisecond later she looked up to see that Malcom had unloaded the mag in his small automatic into the beast's chest. It smiled for a moment and then seemed to backpedal and fall. No one moved less it get up again. Camila looked over to Gale and saw her still open eyes begin to be covered in the quickly falling snow. She was clearly dead, the look of horror on her face. One that matched Camila's own right now.

Their pause ended when more sounds erupted around them. More sounds of insides being opened to the snow. Sounds of death and fear, and hovering above all, the cold. Malcom turned slowly towards Camila and Jessie. Camila was about to taunt Jessie about her shaking but then noticed that she was too. In a low whisper Malcom with eyes that bugged out of their sockets spoke.

"If the boys are out in this? How in God's name do we find them?"

Camila remembered what Gale had said and looked at Malcom with all the fear and worry she had. In that moment she took comfort in the strength there. He was terrified too, but he was also angry. Seeing that stopped Camila's shaking and gave her enough courage to speak.

"Gale said men disappear all the time, that they go up to the mountain and are never seen again. If these…. things are the cause, then that is where they went."

Malcom looked around for a moment and looked at Jessie who said nothing. Then he turned back to Camila and sighed.

"That mountain is fricking huge, there are paths going everywhere! Did she say anything else…like which path?"

The sounds of the dying seemed to ebb but the ever present cold seemed to needle them with unrelenting intensity. It had to have dropped 20 degrees in the last hour. It was getting darker, and there was nowhere to run.

"That was the only mag I have, sure as shit this is what Pops was looking for. Any ideas what we do next?"

"We fight that is what, let's go back and get more ammo. That store has to have more somewhere."

Camila liked hearing Jessie's enthusiasm but then they heard the girl Malcom had shot, begin to move. Jessie screamed in fear seeing that this thing was still alive. Malcom took charge and led them back to the store where a quick search was performed. The more they searched the more panic filled their actions. All the frantic searching produced nothing. Then the inevitable occurred, the sounds of scratching on the glass caught their attention. A moment later it shattered and in came not one of those things but multiple. Camila was closest so she picked up the heaviest thing she could find at hand which was a cast iron skillet. Using her reflexes and speed she dodged the things first swing for her midsection. Using all her strength she landed the oven side of the skillet down on its head. A second after it crumped, Camila wound up her arm gathering as much force as she could bear and hit it again. Its head landed with a thud so loud Camila wondered if it damaged the floor.

To Camila's right another beast went down as it was impaled by some metal rod Jessie was wielding like a sword. Still both beings got up showing angry eyes and teeth that seemed to pivot as its mouth moved. Camila was the first to speak. Thankfully Malcom wasn't panicked yet.

"Why doesn't these things just DIE!"

More sounds of more creatures could be heard outside. Camila felt her bladder release and was only surprised it had taken this long.

"Staying here isn't going to work, let's go out the back!"

The three Grey vampires ran out the back door and into the woods behind the store. Where they were running, and in what direction none of them knew. But putting their effort into their legs felt good right now.

Henderson, West Virginia – Blair Mountain

Mar 4th 2058

Clint had been looking at the amazing wolf head for only a moment when he looked up to say something to their guide. It was getting dark and colder. But Paula wasn't there, he called out but in the growing darkness it was quiet. Then he heard a noise behind him.

"Clint…. its. a wolf."

Clint turned wondering why Jonanthan said that, of course it was. He always knew dad was amazing with wood but he didn't know he could carve something like this! But when he turned his brother was looking at a place just out of his eyesight. Adjusting for the darkness and the brush he saw movement. Time slowed, Clint's breathing stopped and he froze as he saw the wolf come closer. It almost seemed peaceful and friendly until Clint made a sound. Then the wolf snarled at him showing its teeth. With the danger came Clint's training and senses, all of which took over. His senses became alive and the hairs on his arms and neck stood on end. His hearing became acute and he just made out additional movement behind him. From the same direction Paula had been standing, soft ominous sounds emanated. He slowly turned in that direction but instead of finding Paula, he saw two more wolves. Each were focused right on him.

Clint knew in a moment they were in real danger. Paula was gone, they were high on this mountain and no one was nearby. Jonanthan drew the small blade he always carried. Clint only had the cane. The wolf that had come out first was also the first one to strike. It leapt for Jonanthan, Clint using all his strength was lucky and landed the wolf head of the cane right on the wolfs head as it came close. The cane broke the moment it made contact and it stopped his attack. Enough time for both brothers to go back-to-back. A defensive posture both had been taught in the Agoge.

Clint was scared and now he was unarmed. But that little blade wasn't going to do Jonanthan any favors either. The only thought that entered Clint's mind just then was how fast his brother was breathing. Clint took comfort in the fact he was calmer in the face of things. A moment later he said without thinking the motto of the Agoge.

"Life is Duty, and Duty is life."

It sounded hollow even to Clint and Jonanthan didn't respond in words. But his breathing slowed, that caused Clint to smile. He had helped his brother, done his duty. As the two of them used shouts and swipes of their hands to keep the wolves at bay the pack circled around them. When the moment came it came without warning. A wolf got in Clint's blind spot and pulled him down off his feet by pulling on his exposed right arm. The teeth dug in and the pain caused him to shout as he fell. Feeling Clint separate from his back, his brother quickly fell on the wolf using his knife. Plunging it deep into the animal.

The others in the pack only delayed a moment before each found soft flesh and unprotected limbs. The screams of pain and defeat were loud, and they carried down the mountain for miles.

Henderson, West Virginia – Base of Blair Mountain

Mar 5th 2058

The night had long since taken hold. Malcom wasn't sure if it was midnight or later. None of them had a watch or a phone. The snow was getting thick and you couldn't see much in front of you. The sounds of death and the dying in town had long since faded as the three of them made their way on the path. Dedicated to following it not so much to find the boys, as to escape the town. But then clear sounds from up ahead of them on the path brought them to a stop. There were screams and sounds of animals in a fight. This sound, clearly that of Clint and Jonanthan put fire into Malcom's belly.

"STOP, MALCOM WE CANT MOVE THAT FAST!"

Malcom turned in anger at Jessie who was trailing behind him and Camila. He ordered Camila to stay with her as he ran ahead. Without waiting on a response, he shot ahead running as fast as his legs and vampiric power would carry him. It felt good to send raw power into his legs and to have purpose to his rage. He was responsible, and he had allowed himself to grow unprepared and lax…. Again. And now his brothers might be paying the price. He had to get there; he had to stop the things from hurting them.

A few minutes later he finally arrived at a clearing where a fight had just occurred. There was blood everywhere. So much of it that Malcom's heart sank. There were clear drag marks and tufts of fur where what Malcom suspected was wolves had attacked them. Their clothing was in tatters, covered in fresh blood. Anyone who had tracked prey before would see the futility of searching further. What he would find would not be hurt young men. What he would find would be only the chunks of what the wolves didn't desire to eat.

Five minutes later both girls arrived and Jessie began to gasp at the sight. Malcom looked at Camila and they shared a look. She knew as well as he did that they were gone. The distant sound of howls only served to highlight his failure.

"Come one it sounds like they are further up the trail, we need to get there before…"

"Jessie they're gone…. There isn't anything left to save."

Jessie's mouth flung open and she was speechless. She pointed to the direction of the howls and then looked back at the pools of blood. Growing angry and defiant she took a step towards Malcom.

"Coward… If you won't do something then I will!"

Jessie bound on a flat run before Malcom could say another word. Tired, broken at what he had just seen he was slow to chase after her. Camila was not able to keep up and fell behind, but a minute later Malcom found the trail Jessie had created….it simply disappeared.

"Where did she go…. Malcom she was just ahead by a second? Why are her tracks gone?"

Malcom turned to the newly arrived Camila and shook his head. The cold crept into every pore, every corner of his body now. It was well below freezing and somehow it seemed darker. As if the snow was blocking the very stars in the sky. The moon was absent and only the lights from the vampiric eyes cast any visibility now.

"It's so dark we might have just run past her. Let's… circle back a bit and see if she veered off somewhere."

Camila cold now and looking lost and worried whispered something to Malcom that he almost didn't hear.

"We are going to die up here, aren't we?"

Malcom looked at her and realized just then that she was probably right. On this mountain they were the prey. The boys were already dead; he was damn sure of that. If Jessie was missing, she might be soon.

"I don't know but I am not going to just stand around waiting on it. I am going to find Jessie; I need to know you have my back?"

Camila shook her head yes and they went back down the mountain a bit. They would circle around where her tracks ended for another two hours looking for any sign of her, but there was none.

Henderson, West Virginia – Center of Town

Mar 5th 2058 (12:06 AM)

The pilot had been cursing the moment they went into hover. The winds were really up, and the visibility was next to nothing. When Rick opened the doors and allowed the weighted ropes to drop. He had to just hope they hit something solid. He could neither see the building below them, or hear the ends hit the roof. Without orders and to Rick's irritation the men began to go down the ropes. Everyone was eager to get of this flying deathtrap and on to solid ground. No one was willing to wait for his command.

Once all were gone, he waited another 30 seconds before he kicked off the crates and slid down the rope himself. He nearly missed the rope but managed to wrap around it like always. Sliding down the thing into the snow. He found solid ground come out of nowhere a second before he hit it. Feeling that roof under his feet was about the best thing he had felt in 6 hours. A moment later the ropes were cut loose from the helo and it powered away, trying its best to get to altitude to make it back to Logan. With its departure Rick and his team looked at where they had landed. They were on the roof of a 3-story building, that was about all they knew. None of the town's lights were working and it was dead quiet.

Rick did a quick headcount and found everyone had gotten there safe without injury. Jacob was already working on the rappel lines; they would use them to get to the surface quickly. From the looks of it this building didn't have direct roof access. A few shaky moves later and Rick was on the ground with his team with their weapons out. The wisdom of this was quickly discovered when they found the first bodies. Semi-covered in snow and frozen pools of dark liquid surrounding. Everyone's rifles were now up and the safeties were off. Now they were looking for orders, this wasn't a babysitting ride, it was combat.

"Cloak and stay in formation, let's move to the police station. Best place in town to hunker down. Move."

The six of them in formation began to move as quietly as they could down the street. Once in the street they broke into two columns with one man on point on either side of the street and one man covering their rear. As they moved, they found body after body littering the street. None of them were the kids. Rick allowed himself a curse internally, with this much death it wasn't likely the kids were safe and sound. Something really fucking bad had gone down, and they had just dropped right into the middle of it.

"Fuck, fuck, fuck…."

Rick kept whispering it to himself until he realized he was. A bit embarrassed at his lack of discipline he scolded himself internally. He wasn't ready mentally for combat, not so soon. But he had to be, clear as shit he was in the middle of it now. A fisted hand shot into the air in front of Rick and both columns on either side of the street stopped. A sound…. Low and growling? An animal perhaps? Then the eyes opened in the darkness and Rick saw the most terrifying image of his life before him. Death itself was looking at him and it looked hungry. Rick didn't have to give the order to fire, it wasn't necessary. Every man knew the score, and looking at what was coming for them. They weren't ready… not by a long shot.

Henderson, West Virginia – Blair Mountain

Mar 5th 2058

Jessie had run as hard as she could to find the wolves. But she had run so fast and so far that she had lost track of… well everything. She finally stopped in a clearing to get her bearings. The cold was oppressive and the jacket she had tossed on wasn't cutting it. It wasn't the warm one she had purchased in Huntington weeks before, but the stupid one Camila had purchased. She was shivering, worried for the boys and now freighted for herself.

She thought she heard a sound to her front, but it was so light that she assumed she was dreaming it.

"Just what I need, now my mind is playing tricks on me. Why didn't I just tell Cyrus no… I would be home and WARM right now!"

It felt good to let her words out into the darkness. Allow an avenue for her fear to travel. The void around her was dark and ominous. She imagined all kinds of dangers, wolves, bears, those things in town. She never wanted to see one of those things again. Then she heard the sound again, light and airy. She called out to Malcom and then to Camila. Still the night was silent. Then eyes appeared in the void in front of her. The moment they did, her heart came to a crashing halt.

The void moved and it entered the light cast by her vampiric eyes. It was a panther….an honest to God panther.

"Where if fuck did you come from? Panthers aren't…. from here…. oh, please tell me you are just my imagination?"

The panther looked at Jessie with that stare. She had seen it often enough in other predators. She was the prey now, and it saw her as such. With that her grey fighting spirit was triggered and she stopped being afraid. Jessie had a long knife in a sheath on her back. She slid her thin arm around her back while looking the animal right in the eye. Predator to predator, who was stronger? Jessie almost laughed just then, it felt good. To test herself against this beast. She would either win or die. But she would see if her skills were as good as they say. The panther made its move before the tips of her fingers found the handle of the blade. And with that…. The dance had begun.

Henderson, West Virginia – Blair Mountain

Mar 5th 2058

It had been a long time since they had fled up the mountain, and it felt like an eternity since Jessie had run off ahead. There was no sign at all of her, and the snow was just about complete in wiping out any further chance of seeing tracks. They had stopped to listen, hoping to hear Jessie call for them.

"We will find her Malcom, we will."

Malcom turned to her and saw something that surprised him. It was her, not the confident Camila, not the sexy Camila. The real woman, the one he only got to see glimpses of. He hadn't been feeling emotional, he was focused. But seeing that face he couldn't help but think of his mother, and of Susan and Dolly. What would he tell them if he had nothing to bring home but himself?

"God what have I done"

A hand shot to his and Camila grew skin close as she spoke softly to him.

"Your duty Malcom, what you always do. We both have fought tonight for our lives, and we aren't done. If we get out of here, we will tell them the truth. Everyone fought hard for their lives."

Malcom felt the coldness. Not just in the temperature but in his own evaluation of his efforts. When Pops had said he was leaving and warned him, he had clearly meant it. Malcom in his arrogance didn't believe Pops would put them in danger. He started to say what he thought of his decisions tonight when Camila stopped him.

"We aren't done, so shut it with that crap."

He saw the fear in her eyes and realized he wasn't done being a leader. She needed his confidence, needed to see he had a plan on getting them out of here. Seeing that need he shook his head and put a smile on his face he didn't feel.

"Let's circle back to the east. I think there is a…"

The sounds of a woman screaming, and then it to be cut off quickly bounded from high up the trail. Camila looked crushed; another had fallen. Malcom looked back at her and asked a question.

"You ready?"

A nod and the two of them were running at full speed in the deepening snow towards the sound. Hoping they would find Jessie alive and well, but knowing they wouldn't. In that sound had what Malcom would have described as one of pain and distress. And something more, the sounds of death.

Henderson, West Virginia – Henderson
Consignment

Mar 5th 2058

"Rick he's dead… sorry."

Rick sighed and quickly put the loss out of his mind. His six-man team had only gotten up the street a little way when these screaming banshees bounded towards them. The man in front of Rick had been impaled and killed right in front of him. Most of the team was still out in the street growing cold. Only Rick, Calvin and Tony were still alive. Jacob had died within seconds. He didn't have time to mourn or even process it.

The banshees had made two fresh attempts to enter the store and four of them had held them off. But the last time Jake had taken a huge slash to his legs. Calvin had done all he could to stop the bleeding, but it was just too much for him to deal with. The radio was still on Jacob's body outside and was simply unreachable. There was no Calvary coming to help them, that was their role.

"Conserve your ammo, aimed shots only. Make each of them count ok guys?"

Nods from everyone and looks too. Each of them knew they were not going to survive this. Thankfully they didn't get any more time to think about it. The banshees made a fresh attempt that had to be answered. Rick swallowed and laser focused his mind on surviving the next five minutes rather than the next five hours.

Henderson, West Virginia – Williams Overlook

Mar 5ᵗʰ 2058

It was daybreak and still they had not found Jessie. Malcom had given up hope when they came to a clearing with an amazing overview of the valley below. The town, and even Logan in the far distance was in sight. It was beautiful and it would have taken Malcom's breath in how stunning it was, if he had any feeling left in his body. They needed to get warm, vampire or no they could still freeze to death.

With the sun now far higher in the sky they had a fire finally going. Malcom had found a lighter in the jacket he had taken in his rush to leave. It didn't fit him well but it was better than nothing. As soon as they got the fire going both huddled as close as they could to it and each other to raise their core temperature.

"I failed Camila…I got my sister and my brothers killed up here."

Camila shivering was skin close to him. She wanted to say something but it was just too cold. He could tell however that she didn't blame him. It was a comfort, but not much of one.

"You failed yes…. But not in killing them. Just leading them."

Malcom looked up and on the other side of the fire was Paula. But she wasn't alone. Dozens and dozens of those creatures stood around her and all of them were inching closer. They were predators seeking their final prey. Malcom knew they didn't have the strength to fight one of them, much less the hundred or so that seemed to be gathering. Malcom had probably the strangest thought enter his mind. He was going to die, and while he felt guilt over his lost charges. What he really couldn't get out of his mind right at this second, was the fact he hadn't gotten a chance with Camila. A real one….

"I am sorry Camila, sorry……Sorry I spoke so harshly to you."

It sounded so limp so incomplete but Malcom had no words for how he felt. He couldn't understand his feelings, or his desires right now. Other than he wished desperately to be anywhere other than here. Camila looked at him and slid off the jacket she had on and tried to look Paula in the eye. He smirked at her small act of bravery and matched it.

"Isn't that so cute…. She wishes to meet death as a warrior. Well child me and my daughters have no quarrel with you. Only the children of Travis. You can go…."

Malcom didn't have to see Camila's face to know she wasn't going to believe that.

"Its true girl, our issues are with this half-trained thing behind you. Him and his brothers and sisters, they have much to answer for. You… I don't know you. You are from far away are you not… Go on, go back home vampire."

It hit Malcom just then that Paula knew what they were. She must have always known.

"It was you…. your what grandfather wanted us to find. How did you know about my dad… what are you?"

Paula ignored Malcom and moved close to Camila. Malcom tried to move but found himself bound by the sharp claws of the things behind him. As they scratched at his flesh he had to try to hold back his pain, but once they pierced his flesh he shouted. A second or two later they had him firmly under their control. With his vision returned he saw that in that time Camila had also been taken, although the girls holding her were not cutting at her. A fresh cry of pain from Malcom as one pincer cut deep caused Camila to shout out for him.

She was worried, fearful but not for herself, but for him. They shared a look and it was one he hoped would convey what he felt. He wanted her to go, they couldn't fight. But perhaps she could get home, tell father how they had fought. Then he could…. What get revenge? That seemed hollow to Malcom. He would be dead, as would the others. What would that change other than more death?   He mustered what little strength he had and used his weakening voice for Camila's benefit.

"Go on Camila…. Its ok, me and Paula are just going to have a little talk.   Tell mom… I tried, ok?"

Paula in human form and finding all of this entertaining, found his latest speech not so much.

"Oh, how lovely…. Go my love I will love you forever…. What a load of shit that is.   She is here to fuck your father you idiot!   She is going to go home, murder your mother and then spread her legs wide for Travis.   What do you think Camila, how long before Travis forgets these children like he always does… hum?   How long before you replace his babies with your own?"

A moment later Camila was dragged off down the mountain by some of her creatures.   Malcom seeing his death approach just took some solace that at least one thing he cared about wouldn't die tonight.

Chapter 26: Lessons Learned

Henderson, West Virginia – Blair Mountain

Mar 5th 2058

Camila tried to resist but the claws cut into her each time she pushed. Defeated and alone she allowed herself to be carried further and further away from where Malcom was being held. A few minutes later she heard him scream, and the distinctive sound of his flesh being ripped open. She screamed as loud as she could to drown out the death of someone…. She loved.

When the path looped around a large boulder it took a dip down. Camila had remembered how hard it was to climb up it as weak as they were. Instead of thinking about Malcom, or Jessie, or the boys, she allowed her mind to wonder on anything but. Growing up in Meridia, the feeling of sun on her bare body. The taste of her favorite drink. She tried to live in that thought but could not ignore her flesh, as it was handled so poorly. Then without warning the beings carrying her stopped. When Camila opened her eyes, she saw a familiar face looking at her.

"So… what is it you have learned child."

It was Cyrus in his human form. Camila looked up tired and bloody and without strength to hold up her own form. She didn't reply she was beyond simple things like words. She just looked at him knowing he had never stopped pulling the strings. All of this was his doing, all the death, the pain the suffering. It was all him.

"Yes, child I am pulling the strings. It's my clan, and I need to know what kind of vampires I have. You have proven yourself young lady. Far more than Malcom, or Jessie, or the boys could. If you want my son as yours, then I will bless that union. You are strong, defiant, and will make the perfect Queen for him. If that is what you want."

Camila felt a wind hit her, small but steady. It did nothing to loosen the bonds of the creatures that held her. But unlike during the night, this wind was warm and it gently raised her body temperature to something above freezing.

In a moment she was well enough that she could process his words, and respond with her voice. Tired and used up as that voice might be.

"I don't love Travis…. I don't want him Cyrus, I never did. What I wanted was Malcom…. I…"

She had wanted to say she loved him, but that was not truthful. She had only hurt him, that wasn't love. Perhaps if she had told him what she really was from the start, then at least they wouldn't all have come here. He was lost for nothing…. for absolutely nothing.

"How could you allow him to die? He was your grandson; they were all yours Cyrus? Are you that cold that you would kill them to make a fucking point?"

The warm wind that had gently warmed her had done enough to bring back her own fire… if just for a word or two. Cyrus however looked unmoved.

"All Grey have the same calling, to serve their duty. You are all warriors are you not? Is this not a death worth having? Did they not fall in battle, did they not die honorably? Isn't that all there is to be Grey?"

She wanted to scream no that it wasn't. But Cyrus wasn't wrong in what the Grey was taught. Even Malcom with his parents had taught much the same things to him. Malcom's duty was everything to him. All that man wanted was to be respected, to see in the eyes of his peers, simple respect. Was that so much to ask? Apparently so, and to Camila it was a huge fucking waste.

"He deserved more Cyrus…. they all did."

On saying that Cyrus smiled broadly and approached her. He took ahold of her removing the claws from her sides. Camila closed her eyes, defeated and broken. Ready to lay down and join Malcom. She felt life itself ebbing from her bones and wondered if she might not join him after all?

"No child I have need of you. I am surprised it took this long for one of you to grasp this. But you Camila… you finally found what I was looking for."

Camila opened her eyes and saw that both the young women who were beasts before were back to young women. They were both kneeling with their heads down towards Cyrus. Then she felt her body renew, Cyrus was healing her and warming her bones back to what they were.

"A warrior can only fight with all their skills when there is something worth dying for. Duty itself is not enough; glory is just snow that melts in the light of day. And respect, as dear as it might be, it's just vapor that rises and is gone child.

But family…. That is what sustains us, lifts us child. Without family, without a home child, no warrior can be complete. You are right, Malcom and the others deserve more. Much more Camila, so much more! Duty without love, is empty, something you well know. That is what I wanted you and Malcom to discover. And you did. It took you a lot longer than I thought…. But you did."

Camila felt strong enough to stand without Cyrus holding her up. She tested her legs and they barely held. Enough for her to take a breath and center her emotions. Still, she could not wrap her head around what he meant, and why so many had to be sacrificed to learn it. Just when did she learn such a thing?

"There is more to life than duty. You began to learn this when you weighed my words about your future. You know you want and desire children one day. And the thought of betraying them like your mother has betrayed you…. it crushed you. But it was your duty, everything you have been taught said you had to follow it. But you choose a different path…. why Camila?"

Camila was confused she hadn't done anything different since that conversation other than to admit to Malcom that…

"That you care about him, that your mission is not for him. And you tried to tell him that wasn't what you wanted. That you wanted him instead. But he wasn't ready to hear it. Camila that wasn't your duty, but you did it anyway. Because you saw a higher duty, one to family. You love him and you refused to betray him. You made your choice and it was for something higher than duty."

Camila stood there shaking, unsure of herself and of everything. There was some truth in this, she thought to herself. Telling Malcom the truth went against her duty. But she had done it because ultimately, she wanted more. She wanted Malcom to love her, and be what Travis could not be for her. A partner, a warrior, a lover…. a mate. But he was gone…. sacrificed to prove a point.

"They are not sacrificed Camila, these huntresses can play with your mind, dull your senses. Even make you see what isn't there. Malcom isn't dead, nor are the others. Your friends, even the town is safe. They are shaken like you, but they live. Now granddaughter what shall we do with you? I can do many things; what would you have me do for you? Set you free…. I could take the memory of you from all who know you? The strings as you often say would be cut for all time. Would that please you?"

Camila was not any better for being told it was all a dream. She still felt the wounds, and the injuries she had suffered were very real. A part of her struggled to believe his words but she knew he was more than capable of this.

He had already proven that. Cyrus encouraged her again to make her decision on what she wanted. She wanted many things, things she didn't hesitate to list now.

"I want Malcom to be safe… all of them to be safe. And I want him to be free Cyrus. Give him the respect he deserves. Make him the fricking king for all I care. If that is what will please him… give him that."

Cyrus looked at her like a father looks at a young child asking for toys.

"What about you, what do you desire child. You only need to ask."

Camila felt oddly quiet in her spirit just then. Her whole life she had felt pulled, pushed, cajoled into a direction. A path that at times even she had desired and worked for. But now, she felt free. As if that mission, Travis, her mother, her grandmother no longer mattered. But that still didn't tell her what she wanted. She didn't know this Camila, this woman with choices.

"I want to know who Camila is…. that is what I want."

Henderson, West Virginia – Williams Overlook

Mar 5th 2058

Malcom heard voices, unknown, foreign. He was so tired, so done that he simply lay there doing nothing. All the fight was out of him, now would come sleep. He thought he was near death, his vision was dark wasn't that what death was? Yet he felt the warmth of a fire close to him and it felt…. Good. A comfort in a moment when he….

"Are you going to just lay there all day? Seriously?"

Jessie's voice caused his eyes to fly open in a flash and he was disoriented when he did. He was flat on his back looking at the sky.

"About time, you know how long I have been holding this form so you can see this. You have to check this out brother…."

He turned to his left where he heard Jessie's voice. But it wasn't his sister he saw before him. It was massive black panther looking at him with fangs and big eyes…. focused directly at him. At once his own eyes bugged out, the beast was only inches away.

"Oh my God that was so worth it! I wish you could see the look on your face now bro. What do you think, do I look good as a cat?"

Seeing the panther move its mouth and have her voice made Malcom wonder if perhaps he had entered some sort of Vampire Valhalla where they were to roam the mountain as animalistic predators.

"So, guys what do you think Malcom will turn into?   I think a turtle, slow ponderous and stupid."

Malcom heard the boys laugh and he looked and saw two wolves looking at each other. When he said their names both wolves approached. It was Clint who spoke directly to him, much to his shock.

"Yep, it's me, I wasn't scared for a moment Malcom, I knew Pops wouldn't allow anything bad to happen."

"Bullshit you pissed yourself when that first one bit you. I saw it!"

Jessie laughed and laid down on all fours putting her long chin on her paws.

"Each of us fought and lost to these animals. Then we woke up as them, Grandfather was there and explained that it's a gift. I have to admit it was easier to wait on your slow ass with all this fur. Hell of a lot warmer like this than when I am a biped."

A twisted thought entered Malcom's mind to pet that giant cat next to him but he resisted. The more he let the cold air hit him and the sights of these…animals he realized he was not dreaming.

"So, your animals now…. forever?"

All of them laughed with the wolves now sitting with tongues hanging out of their snouts.

"No stupid we can control it and go back and forth when we need to…. Watch"

The massive panther morphed from the huge furred predator back into his little sister. She proudly stood up now back to her old form, but with one major thing missing. Something Malcom wasn't about to let slip.

"So, you can change back…. but the clothes don't come with?"

Both wolves began to laugh hysterically and Jessie realized she was standing naked on a cold ridgeline. She Immediately began to shiver and without warning morphed back into the panther to have dignity. The laugher suddenly ceased and the wolves began to growl. Even Jessie moved into an aggressive stance and took a step past Malcom back towards the path. Something was coming, and they clearly could hear it, even if Malcom couldn't. Jessie explained a moment later.

"Pops is coming, but he isn't alone… those things are with him."

Malcom tried to stand but he was injured. He had slash marks all over his body and deep puncture wounds that were still open. When he moved one of them re-opened and blood poured out of the gap in his arm. Seeing this all three of his siblings moved in front of him to protect Malcom. Something he was thankful for, he couldn't move.

"Its all-right children, Paula and her little ones are not here to hurt you."

A moment later both Paula and Pops came into view. The beasts were still making signs they were not pleased until Cyrus spoke for a second time.

"Children, they will not harm you, again they are not here to do that. The trial is over; it's time to go home. Paula and her children will let you pass. Jessie, take the boys down the mountain. There is a team from home waiting on you. Just don't let them see you as animals ok. That is a secret just for the three of you ok….?"

Jessie turned her panther head towards Malcom, clearly asking him in a way if he wanted her to stay. Malcom took a breath at the absurdity of things and decided to let them go.

"It's ok Jessie, take the boys back down. Try not to bite anyone on the way there, ok?"

As Jessie and the boys passed Paula, they gave her a dirty look and growled a bit. Malcom liked that, but wondered what on earth had just happened. And of course, where in hell was Camila. Instead of asking everything at once Malcom tried to push himself up into a sitting position. Something he mostly failed at until two powerful "daughters" of Paula yanked him up hard and onto a nearby rock. It was tall enough that it propped him up. He didn't have to hold up his torso, which was good because he couldn't.

"Pops… please tell me this wasn't some sort of game, because if it was…"

"If it wasn't boy then you would be dead, as would Jessie, the boys, and your brother Jacob and his team. Not to mention the entire human population of the town. I have to admit Malcom, when you fail… you really fail."

He wasn't joking and he wasn't happy with him, that much was clear. Malcom took a breath feeling all the injuries and his body tell him he was bleeding out.

"Seems awful real right now Pops, is everyone ok?"

Paula looked at Pops and then nodded. She took a step back but didn't leave the clearing. Much to his relief Pops began to put his hands on him and heal his wounds.

"Eventually they will be, the towns folk won't remember but the huntresses are going to remember. They had their way don't you think? You didn't provide much of a fight."

Paula made some sort of comment that Malcom didn't listen to. Whatever she said, she was not impressed with him.

"Son you were in command, and you got everyone killed. Now tell me what did you do wrong. What was your first mistake?"

Malcom felt a bit better now that his lifeblood wasn't leaking everywhere. Still, it hurt like a son of a bitch. He was tired and he didn't have time for self-reflection with things like this. Pops saw that easily enough and knelt down so he was eye level with him.

"You should have taken your party out of here son. You never should have stayed, not even an hour after I left. I told you there was danger, and you were not prepared for it, nor were you equipped for it. You had humans in your care, your brothers. They had no business on a battlefield, or up on a mountain alone in the dark. You should have taken everyone back to Logan and then back home."

Malcom thought about that for a second, that thought had not once entered his mind, and the reason was simple.

"That wasn't our duty Pops, we are Grey, we follow our orders. You gave us a task and we fullfed it. We found the monsters and we fought them. That was our duty, not running away from it! What would happen to me as our leader if I ran away from battle?"

Cyrus just shook his head in disappointment at his answer. He saw something along those same lines from Paula just without any positive emotions.

"Son your duty is to preserve the life of those that follow you first and foremost. The mission…your elders can say it is all that matters but it isn't. Those were your brothers Malcom; they aren't even vampires yet. You should have preserved their lives."

Malcom thought about it more and saw the moral in it, but it didn't match the creed of the Grey.

"To hell with orders, creeds, or any of that shit! Malcom they are your brothers; they mean more to you…or should mean more to you than anything. If you can't sacrifice your career, your life, for the lives of your team, then you don't deserve to be a leader. That is the highest order any leader must follow. To put the needs of his subordinates above his own. You should have left son; it's not that different than the mistake that got you fired in Meridia. You didn't put the needs of your people ahead of your own. You were dreaming about glory and how you would get promoted. You didn't take the time to see your subordinate who was betraying you. It was there boy… you should have seen it."

That smacked Malcom so hard in the face he didn't respond.

Even Pops thinks I am not worthy. Holy shit….

"That isn't true, I do think you are worthy. That is why I am out here teaching you. Malcom you are a brave soul, you have grace and strength in you, and I know you can be so much. But you lack the wisdom you need to be a leader. You listen and follow but here son…. You haven't learned here yet."

Cyrus pointed to his heart and it did nothing to clear his understanding. All he knew was he had failed, nearly gotten everyone killed in this test or whatever it was. Then he again noticed there was no Camila, and Pops hadn't mentioned her. So, he asked about her…. That caused Cyrus to sigh heavily and stand.

"She's gone son. You need to let her go."

Malcom looked at him and he had a sad look about him. Was she dead he wondered?

"I thought you said everyone would be ok… where is she?"

"The Camila you knew is dead. What she is or who she is now I can't say. I promised I would let her choose that on her own this time. Without my interference, so I can't tell you she is ok. Wherever she is son, you need to let her go."

Malcom felt suddenly very empty. On this climb into the mountain there had been a very small comfort. He hadn't thought about it at the time, yet his spirit knew. He was standing beside someone he respected, someone worthy. He would have gladly done much for her. It was an honor to know someone and serve with one like her. Even if they fought, even if she wanted his father. She was his equal, there was something there but Malcom couldn't put it in words or really put his arms around it all.

"I don't want to Pops, just let me talk to her please. I…"

Cyrus turned and looked at Paula who scoffed at his emotion. Something Malcom hadn't realized he had in his voice when he said it.

"This is what father left us for? Him?"

Cyrus looked at Paula with a small angry look. Malcom was astonished when he saw Paula nearly wilt in shame from it. Malcom started to put two and two together.

"What does she mean Pops when she said father? What is she talking about?"

Cyrus looked at Paula and then back at him, this time with a small smile.

"Son you weren't here to conquer these people. Paula is your sister. Your father adopted her when she was a child, raised her until she was an adult."

At saying this Paula kicked some rock that was near her foot and looked down on Malcom.

"Until you came here, father loved us…cared for us. Then you and your mother came and he left. He had young vampires to raise, little ones who needed his guidance… his love. Well, I needed that love! My sister needed that love…. It wasn't just you and your others…. He had a home here Malcom… he was happy here. You took him from us… from all of us."

Malcom watched as Paula departed as did the others who followed her. Some looked concerned for their mother, others looked at him with disgust. When the sounds of their moving was at an end Cyrus continued.

"Paula is bitter about losing Travis to you. She looked up to him, treasured everything he taught her. Ripping him away from them….was one of the hardest things I have ever done. But it was necessary Malcom. You needed him then, as did your siblings. It was time for him to go home and be the King he was made to be. To be the father he should have been. Had I done a better job as his…. perhaps…."

Cyrus trailed off in a place not here, and not a place that held him or Paula.

"Pops what's wrong, I… don't understand"

Cyrus had this lost look about him and he sat down next to him with his back to him. He put a hand on his for a second but didn't say much. The starts to words that never got completed. In all his interactions, he had never seen Cyrus so unable to speak.

"Your father grew up without me. His mother raised him and Jay without my help. I thought it was important then, best for their future and all. The man I selected was a good one, and he cared for the boys… the best he could. But it wasn't me Malcom…I wasn't there for him. Travis will never forgive me for that, not now…. not in a million years. In his heart I am not his father. I didn't want that for him, having you and your siblings despise him… for not being there. He had raised Paula and her sister by then; it was time for him to love and raise you son."

Malcom had seen hints of this, but only hints. Dad never respected Cyrus, never loved him openly. They didn't speak about it; it wasn't the Grey way. But now he knew, but it still didn't explain… well all of this.

"Malcom don't you see…. The point is at the end of the day, at the end of your battles…. It has to be FOR something. Respect and honor well they don't cut it son. I am not a Grey and I don't pretend to be. But with my kind it's not that different. We want to know EVERYTHING, any knowledge we want it, Malcom. But at the end of the day, what the hell is it worth knowing something…. If it isn't FOR something. You son, you are why Travis fights so hard. Why he lives as a vampire when he doesn't want to be. Why he fights to be King when all he wanted was to lie down and rest on this mountain. He does it for you son."

Malcom knew his father was a good man, and he had no doubt about his Pops either. But the duty had strings, and those strings had no love. As much as his father had given up for him, he still didn't live up to the standard he professed. What did any of this mean? More importantly what did it mean to him?

"You want your family to forgive you, give you another chance. That is understandable… but your family needs it too. Your father didn't make love to Dolly because he is weak. He made love to her because he loves her … for better or worse he does. Until your father can sort out his heart, he will continue to fall short… for everyone. He has a hard choice son, one I don't envy… nor should you."

Malcom scoffed at that but then he thought better. What if he loved someone like that, and he had to choose between them. Could he, Malcom thought he could. Thought he would never get caught in such a stupid trap, yet he had been in this one.

"What I wanted you to get son, is that duty and honor and your call…. It has to take a backseat to the ones you love. Even if it means others look down on you. Even if you hurt others sometimes. I hurt your father once, when I made that choice, I did it because I wanted to save him. I would make that choice again, and again, and again…every day. But it cost me dearly Malcom…. Sometimes that is what it's like being a leader. You pay a cost few see. You can be like your father if you want…. Maybe even be King one day. You have that in you, the strength, the knowledge…. Just not the wisdom…. Not yet."

Cyrus got up and moved towards the trail. Malcom was still so deep in thought to what he had said he didn't react. He was almost out of sight when he called out.

"Hey what about me…. I am not exactly able to run down this mountain you know?"

Cyrus laughed and then looked around the trees that surrounded the area. There was an eagle flying and circling the area.

"You will be fine…. Take your time son."

Without another word or consideration for his health, he was gone. Malcom shook his head and sat there. He wasn't about to get up soon. It was day now and he could see so far and now…. now it took his breath. It was a lovely place, a wild and dangerous place. But the sight was to die for. You could see for miles and the snow covering everything was like something from a movie. Yet he had so many regrets…. oh, so many….

The eagle was soaring in the wind rising the in currents and seemingly hovering one moment and moving at great speed the next. What that must feel like, to soar with the wind. Not a care in the world, no duty, no requirements. It had to be a short life living in such a place. But what a life it must be. He wondered what it was after. Probably a small thing it wanted for its meal. Then it got close soaring up to his altitude even going so far as to fly right over him and past.

"Wow that was… cool!"

Malcom shook his head, that was as close to an eagle as he had been.

"Thank you… Glad you are impressed."

The naked form of Camila came out from behind him and sat down next to him. His mouth fell open and the smile that hit his face was instant.

"So, everyone gets to be something cool but me huh… I like your choice…it suits you."

Camila smiled a toothy grin and shook her head in agreement.

"Malcom its…nothing like you can imagine. You have to try it, I dived down like a thousand feet in a second… it's incredible! Come on, try with me."

Malcom laughed at her enthusiasm; glad she had found something to be this happy about. But he was still just a vampire, just a man. As far as he knew that gift was for those who had earned it, he was after all the man who had failed.

"I wish I could… I am so happy for you Camila, but what about dad? What about your mission…. Your duty."

Her smile never left but she was looking at him with a searching look now.

"I am free Malcom, don't you see. I don't have to follow that anymore. I can be me; I don't have to be her anymore."

Malcom smiled and put a hand on her face which didn't last long. His body still weak could not hold it in place without a lot of pain.

"Being with your dad is never what I wanted…never. Malcom, I found something… something amazing but its worthless if I don't have someone to share it with. Someone special…. Someone I love."

Malcom sat there wondering what had happened to Camila. This wasn't that woman; this was a different one.

"How do you know I am what you need, and not dad?"

She helped him to his feet and kissed him which he didn't resist in the slightest.

"Because I am not her anymore, I don't exactly know who I am yet… but I want to find out…. With you."

Henderson, West Virginia – Center of town

Mar 5th 2058

Cyrus had his brood gathered, all now back in their vampire form. The two boys along with their new wolf ability had been granted vampirism by Cyrus. They would now enter the Grey world officially having passed his test here in Henderson. Rick and the team were confused and understandably concerned.

"Look Cyrus not to push things but what about those creatures, were they real or not?"

Cyrus watched out of the corner of his eye as Paula walked into the Heart Reality office.

"Oh, they are all very real, and any vampire who crosses the line should fear seeing them again. Keep that in mind for the future, ok?"

Rick started to ask something but looked more confused than before. Probably because like all other vampires they didn't know what line it was that was crossed. Cyrus didn't do anything to elevate his confusion, but did smile when he asked about Camila and Malcom, and if they were coming or not. Cyrus looked up high up on the mountain to a pair of eagles that were soaring, diving and in generally having a ball. He smiled for Malcom; his boy had figured it out after all. He was afraid he wouldn't.

"Not today, Rick, maybe one day… but not today. Now if you excuse me, I need to go say goodbye to someone."

Rick was about to ask what that meant but Cyrus didn't give him the chance. He followed Paula into the office she was hiding in. Inside he found her emotional and in a chair with her legs crossed, hoping no one saw she was crying.

"You know he loves you, he hasn't forgotten. He hasn't forgotten any of them. He still loves your mother's memory as he does all those he has lost."

Paula shifted uncomfortably in her chair reaching for a tissue from her desk. She started to say something but paused thinking better of it.

"I know he does; I just miss him. Mom never got to say goodbye like... well like the others did. I hated so much you taking him.... Mom wasn't the same.... I wasn't the same."

"Those kids needed him.... just like you did. He taught you so much in such a short time. He taught you to see good in people, not just duty. I love that about my son; he has a giving heart. Always helping, always trying to help. But.... he needs you now Paula... now more than ever."

Paula looked up with tears now unhidden on her face. Her pain over losing her father was clear for anyone to see. But so was her love. She had agreed to help Cyrus in this, not because she had love for his children. If anything, she saw them as the root of her pain. But for Travis, she would do anything. Her face was now alert and her mind ready, so Cyrus begun.

"Your father is the rightful king... a good king. One me and his mother have made for just this time. But others... they are plotting to take it from him. To hurt him and his family. Paula, I need you and your daughters; I need you to hunt them and put an end to this."

Paula's face moved a twitch and it was deathly quiet in the room. The tears stopped, and her composure shifted in a way that would frighten any who watched.

"Who are they.... and how far can I go with them?"

Cyrus knew what that meant. She was asking what limits were being put on her and her people.

"None... kill them all."

Continue the journey with the vampire clans of Medford with the next upcoming novel. The release date is to be announced. Check out www.authorshawnmcdonie.com for information and links to find out more about Medford's Vampire Clans.

Made in the USA
Columbia, SC
09 September 2025